FLORIDA HEAT WAVE

FLORIDA HEAT WAVE

INTRODUCTION BY
MICHAEL LISTER

TYRUS
BOOKS

APR 2011

Published by
TYRUS BOOKS
1213 N. Sherman Ave. #306
Madison, WI 53704
www.tyrusbooks.com

Library of Congress Cataloging-In-Publication Data has been applied for.

12 11 10   1 2 3 4 5 6 7 8 9 10

978-1-935562-17-7 hardcover
978-1-935562-16-0 paperback

For

Ben LeRoy, Alison Janssen, and Jim Pascoe

Without whom this book—

and so many wonderful things in the world—

wouldn't exist.

ACKNOWLEDGMENTS

MANY, MANY THANKS TO

BEN AND ALISON for all you do
to bring beautiful books into the world.

JIM PASCOE for life-changing advice, making this book possible—
and designing a kickass cover.

ALL THE WONDERFUL CONTRIBUTORS.

MARK RAYMOND FALK, friend, brother, fellow committee member.
Alter ipse amicus

THE UNIVERSE for making me a Floridian.

FLORIDA for being so incredibly whacky and so surreally sublime.

ALL THOSE WHO CAME BEFORE.

The entire TYRUS TEAM, especially Rebecca Crowley.

PAM, AMY, ALISON, LYNN, AND BETTE
for care over and investment in my wordplay.

CONTENTS

INTRODUCTION

BY MICHAEL LISTER

Florida.

A place like no other.

In many ways a microcosm of the country in reverse (the north part of the state resembling the south part of the country; the south part of the state resembling the north part of the country), Florida is disorienting and deadly, dangling dubiously as if it might slide into the Gulf of Mexico or Atlantic Ocean.

A place of water—surrounded by, dotted with, flowing through.

A place of movement—like the ocean's tides. Migration. Sway. Cyclical. Rhythmic.

A place of crackers and snowbirds, shotgun houses and Art Deco—an environment of great risk and great reward.

Some people say Florida has no sense of place. They are wrong—or, at least, inaccurate. Florida has a sense of places—a plurality of exoticas.

It's both my natural and spiritual home, and I love it like only a native can, but there's a dark side to the sunshine state.

It's a place of intense heat—like hell, only hotter.

Oppressive.

Stifling.

Crazy-making.

The suffocating heat makes you do desperate things—it seeps in through your pores and sucks the life right out of you. Like the bloody smear of a swatted mosquito on sweat-soaked skin, violence erupts suddenly, but the damage it does lingers long after.

According to the biblical book of Ecclesiastes, evil happens everywhere under the sun. This is nowhere truer than the sunshine state. From the rural highways of the panhandle to the mean streets of Miami, evil deeds are done everywhere—and everything here takes place under the sun. But don't let the sunshine fool you. There's plenty of darkness lurking in the shade of our spreading oaks and swaying palms, down our dirt roads and on our interstates, inside our mobile homes and behind our fortressed mansions, beach condos, and retirement centers, and back in our mangroves and river swamps—a real bleakness beneath the natural beauty.

Florida is a beautiful place where ugly things happen—both to its environment and inhabitants.

Florida is a place where people come to die.

It hangs beneath the continent like a handgun holstered for quick draw—more a state of mind than one drawn on maps.

If Florida is a handgun pointed at Cuba, then the part I write about is its trigger, a reactionary place where just the right squeeze can be explosive. The peninsula proper is the barrel, a pawnshop special blued finished bearing traces of rust and corrosion beneath the oily polish of theme parks and retirement villages. The weapon ends where the state, the continent, and the world does, in Miami—a town perched precariously, like Florida itself, between worlds, between countries, between what was and what will be, old Florida all but vanished, new Florida emerging.

Florida's geographical diversity is only matched by its diverse populace. And those who write about it—as this anthology will so convincingly demonstrate. This diversity lends itself to a rich, varied crime fiction tradition. From the pine-tree lined rural highways of North Florida through the tourist traps of Central Florida to the tropical, international environs of SOBE, Florida crime writers continually offer up stories of sun-faded noir, orange pulp served freshly squeezed.

Those of us living in and writing about the hottest, wackiest, kitschiest state today follow in the footsteps of Charles Willeford and John D. MacDonald. We are their heirs, the recipients of a rich heritage of good writing, a responsibility to keep the sacred fire from going out, to honor them and the state we all find so endlessly interesting.

I'm very proud of this collection, and it gives me great pleasure to present it to you. I'm extremely grateful to all the contributors for their fantastic Florida stories, and to everyone at Tyrus Books, especially Ben LeRoy and Alison Janssen for their usual stellar work.

So, here it is—*Florida Heat Wave,* a sun-drenched, sweat-soaked collection of crime stories set in the peninsula pistol state by Florida's foremost crime writers. Pour yourself a big glass of 100% pure Florida orange juice (and a couple of ounces of vodka) and enjoy!

LOW-BUDGET MONSTER FLICK

BY MARY ANNA EVANS

In my own defense, I'll say that the job sounded good when I took it. Who wouldn't jump at the chance to get paid to spend a month in Florida doing wardrobe and makeup for the most voluptuous starlet on the silver screen, Carlotta Verona? Particularly when the wardrobe in question consists entirely of skimpy bathing suits and torn blouses … thin, wet, torn blouses.

It was hardly a year after Hiroshima. In those days, my nightmares still inhabited the sweltering damp hellholes of the South Pacific, and those nightmares were heavily punctuated with gunfire and haunted by death. I was picturing a few healing weeks on a broad sandy beach, surrounded by bathing beauties. (Did I mention that I was to be paid for this?)

Benny Schulz neglected to mention that I'd be working in a sweltering damp swamp that looked a helluva lot like the South Pacific, if I crossed my eyes and squinted. Benny Schulz was your typical lying, cheating, stealing Hollywood assistant producer, but he was my friend. How could he have known that he was sending me to yet another steamy jungle where the nights were haunted by death?

Benny hired me for this gig because I could build a face for any monster a movie mogul could imagine. Warts, scars, scales, open oozing wounds— Benny called me whenever a director needed a glamorous movie star to be ugly. I enjoyed doing warts and scales. Scars and open oozing wounds? Not so much. They put me too much in mind of the things I saw on Guadalcanal.

So imagine how I felt when I arrived in that godforsaken swamp and saw that this movie monster didn't need my magic at all. I was so upset that I bullied the director into letting me make a long-distance call, just so I could yell at Benny.

"Dammit, they're making a movie about a rubber fish! Or lizard or turtle or … shit, Benny. I don't know what it is. It's just an ugly-looking monster with a zipper up its back. The director's gonna put an actor in this rubber suit and throw him in the water, and that's that. Instant monster."

"So what's the problem?"

"Benny. It's an allover suit … not a square inch of actor showing. Know what that means?"

"It means we can put somebody cheap in there, 'cause nobody ain't gonna see who it is?"

Cheap was good in Benny's world.

"Benny, it means there's nothing for the makeup guy to do. Meaning there's nothing for *me* to do here but spread pancake makeup on Carlotta Verona's pretty face."

"'Zat mean you get to touch her with your bare hands? 'Cause maybe you can tell her she needs a beauty mark on her chest." Benny's constant lecherous leer had seeped into his voice and was oozing out of the receiver. I had a sudden urge to go wash my ear.

"You're wasting money, Benny. I don't come cheap. You coulda hired anybody to smear lipstick around. It's not hard to make Carlotta look good."

Benny's snort communicated the pain of an assistant producer watching dollars fly out the door. "Too late now. I already paid to get you over there. I could bring you home and fly somebody cheap to Florida, but it'd cost more than I'd save." This had to be true, because Benny didn't make errors when dollar signs were involved. When Benny thought about money, you could hear the percussive thunk of an adding machine lever being pulled. "You're just gonna have to stay there and find excuses to rub your hands on Carlotta. And her stunt double, who may actually have bigger tits, if such a thing is possible."

"Does the rest of her look like Carlotta?"

"Yeah, only more so. And since Debbie ain't famous, she ain't got a rich old ugly boyfriend like Vince Carmichael chasing her around. A chump like you might have a chance with her. I think you're gonna like this job. Feel free to thank me."

I mumbled, "Thanks," and hung up, but I didn't mean it.

I looked out at an endless array of cypress trees dripping Spanish moss. They shaded an untamed river fed by Glitter Spring, a watery abyss that belched out about a trillion gallons of diamond-clear water every day. I've still never seen anything like that water. It was clear as air. You could shoot a movie through it, which is precisely why we were there.

The landscape here hadn't changed since the dinosaurs walked. I could have written a blockbuster script about those dinosaurs. People would've been tossing their popcorn sky-high in happy horror. I knew I could do it, just like all those other people in Hollywood who were damn sure they could be actors or directors or … yeah … screenwriters. It just about killed me that Benny would only hire me for making monster makeup and smearing lipstick.

There were monsters out there in Glitter Spring, but they weren't movie monsters in rubber suits. They were cold-blooded, muscle-bound killing machines covered in scaly black skin and armed with fearsome teeth. Once, after we'd finished shooting, I asked the boat captain to take me close to those natural monsters, thinking I might get makeup ideas for my next horror movie. I learned that thirty seconds spent staring into the passionless eyes of an alligator felt like thirty seconds too long.

This California boy didn't feel safe in that primeval wasteland where pterodactyls would have felt right at home. I didn't feel like thanking Benny for sending me there. Not one little bit.

• • •

"Can I get in the water, Johnny? Please? It's awful hot."

Nobody but Carlotta called John Plonsky "Johnny." He'd been making low-budget monster flicks since Dracula was a boy, and he'd earned the respect of everyone in Hollywood except a few brainless starlets like this one.

Carlotta reached down into the water. Gathering a few drops in her cupped hand, she tried to dribble them across her front. I was too quick for her. I grabbed her wrist just in time to keep her from spoiling the pristine white bathing suit sheathing her perfect form. Every one of those drops would show on camera. In the time it took them to dry, Carlotta would start to sweat, and sweat stains are obvious on film.

The whole crew would be drawing their salaries while I escorted Carlotta to the hotel for a new suit and while I stood outside her dressing room, urging her to hurry. If Benny had foreseen this problem, there'd have been a clause in her contract requiring her to let me into the dressing room. I'm sure I could have poured her ample form into yet another tiny suit in a time-efficient manner.

Fortunately, I had brought way more bathing suits than I should have needed for this gig. (I'd worked with Carlotta before.) Otherwise, I'd have spent my days handwashing little scraps of white fabric, then waving them frantically in the muggy air till they dried.

She'd pulled this stunt once that day, already. John needed to shoot the sequence before she messed herself up again, and everybody knew it. I could see it on their faces as I hovered within arm's reach, ready to stop her before she splashed river water on herself yet again.

We were all as hot as Carlotta. Hotter, actually, because we were wearing more clothes. If I let her mess up another bathing suit ... well, one of these people just might shoot her.

"She can't work under these conditions, John," Carlotta's manager Bradley barked, adjusting his Panama hat to shade his face better. Her boyfriend Vince, who was bankrolling the film, adjusted his own Panama hat, which was bigger, more finely woven, and obviously more expensive.

John gestured at his uncooperative star, but spoke to the men in her life. "I just need her to sit still long enough for Louise to snatch her off the boat. Then she can go fan herself in her dressing room. Debbie can do the rest of the scene."

Louise and Debbie sat on the dock, chatting pleasantly about whatever it is that interests twenty-year-old girls. They were as blonde as Carlotta (whose real name was probably as plain as "Louise" or "Debbie") and they were as shapely. Debbie, in particular, looked just like her. This was her job.

When Debbie was struggling underwater in the monster's clutches, wet and half-dressed, moviegoers needed to believe they were watching Carlotta in mortal distress. Fortunately, Debbie was a very good actress. She could make you believe just about anything. In fact, she'd spent the last three weeks making me believe she was in love with me.

Louise, on the other hand, didn't look like Carlotta, nor any other woman of my acquaintance. She was heavily muscled and six feet tall, but perfectly proportioned for her size. The other two girls made men want to hug them and squeeze them and stroke them and romance them. Louise made you want to worship her for the goddess that she was.

And what was Louise's job on this movie set?

She was the monster.

When I told Benny that the monster needed no makeup artist, because the actor inside its rubber suit was completely invisible, I wasn't lying. Louise was a local girl who'd learned to swim in this fast-moving river. She could plunge to the bottom of the mammoth spring, swimming against the rushing water with powerful kicks and strokes. And she looked like a river nymph all the while, with her golden hair streaming behind her and her golden-skinned body slipping through the water like a shimmering fish.

Louise was a hundred percent suited to be the monster star of this movie, and she worked cheap. The crew for this movie was a hundred percent male, except for Carlotta and Debbie, and we approved John's decision to hire Louise a hundred percent. Actually, we thought he was a goddamn genius.

• • •

Lester Bond, owner of Glitter Spring and of the lodge perched on its rim, was a frustrated man. He'd bought the property with visions of a tourist attraction like Silver Springs. Hordes of paying customers, a fleet of glass-bottomed boats, hamburger stands, gator wrestling shows—if there was a Florida-tested method of separating Northerners from their money, Lester had hoped to build it on the shores of Glitter Spring.

Unfortunately, Lester wasn't a genius. He'd neglected to check the highway system funneling tourists into Florida's peninsula. Glitter Spring was just too far from a major tourist route, too far from an airport, too far from a decent-sized town. It was just too far from everything. When God made this jaw-dropping miracle of nature, He wasn't thinking like a grasping, avaricious human being, so He'd failed to put His miracle in a convenient spot. Lester Bond had stopped going to church, because he was really angry at the Almighty about this oversight.

Because of its inconvenient location, Glitter Spring sat out in the woods looking beautiful, all by its lonesome, like an old maid in a small town where all the good men were taken. If the spring's crystalline waters hadn't been tailor-made for underwater filming, Lester would have been bankrupt long before I met him. Only the likes of Tarzan and Esther Williams had brought in enough money to keep Lester's dream alive.

Evenings in the lobby of Lester's hotel weren't anything to write home about, especially when your home was Tinseltown. After dinner, we'd watch the dailies, and then Lester would turn up the lights. Air conditioning was a distant dream in 1940s Florida, so the lobby was gaspingly hot, even after dark. Still, we were young and we couldn't conceive of going to bed early, so we cranked up the electric fans and played cards or charades or board games. Sometimes, we just drank.

Lester played piano. It would have been nice if someone had sung, but Carlotta wasn't the kind of star with talents beyond looking good on camera. And she wasn't the kind of star who tolerated anyone else in the limelight. So if Louise or Debbie or anyone else possessed any hidden musical talent, they never showed it.

On that last peaceful evening, we were playing cards. Bridge tables were scattered around the lobby, and we'd been playing long enough that everybody'd had a turn at being dummy … which meant that everybody had spent time away from the other players' watchful eyes. Those who preferred drinking to cardplaying had wandered constantly to the bar and back, making their movements even more impossible to track. I believe that Carlotta and Louise went missing while the dailies were being screened, but there's no way to know for sure.

It says something about my devotion to the game of bridge that I had to look around for my girlfriend when I learned that Carlotta was gone. Or maybe it says something about my devotion to my girlfriend. But our three weeks of passion had left me under the *impression* that I loved Debbie. Anyway, Debbie was across the room chatting with John about how she could act *and* do stunts, in case he needed somebody like that for his next picture. It's fortunate for me that *she* didn't disappear that evening, or I'd have been left with the guilt and embarrassment of knowing my girlfriend went missing right under my own nose. Vince wasn't so lucky.

I'll give Vince credit for being a better boyfriend than me. He'd been passed out on the sofa for hours, but he'd gone looking for his lady love immediately upon regaining consciousness. When he couldn't find Carlotta in the hotel, he knew something was wrong. That city-bred woman would never have ventured out into the swamp alone.

Louise hadn't yet found a boyfriend among the crew, astonishing as it may sound. The sheer size of her scared the heck out of most guys. I myself was taller than Louise by a good three inches, but she still scared me now and again. We'd been looking for Carlotta for an hour before anybody noticed that Louise was gone, too. I wasn't sure how worried to be about big, strong, competent Louise, until I remembered the size of the alligators living on the far side of Glitter Spring. They could have swallowed that strapping girl alive.

"What could have happened?" Vince asked, his voice tinged by the kind of visceral, physical fear that didn't often bother people in Hollywood. "They were here and now they're just ... not."

Everyone's eyes strayed to the black, leathery body of Ol' Jack, the enormous one-eyed alligator that Lester had paid somebody to shoot and stuff and mount. Ol' Jack dominated the spacious lobby, and his glass eyes glittered as if he knew how good humans tasted. In an instant, we ceased to be a convivial crowd of cardplaying drunks. In that instant, we began to be afraid.

When sudden death reaches out its monster hand, confusion descends. On that moonless night, both darkness and confusion were utterly complete.

• • •

As I've said, Lester's resort was a million miles from nowhere, which explained its stunning commercial success. This meant there was no light beyond the bright windows of the hotel and the glittering stars overhead.

Lester was accustomed to this kind of darkness. We Hollywood folk were not. He flung open his utility closet and handed out lanterns and flashlights. The swamp was alight as we crisscrossed the countryside, calling out for Carlotta and Louise. If there was any clue to their whereabouts, it was invisible in the dark and we trampled it.

At every turn, my lantern reflected off the glowing green eyes of alligators lurking under palmettos or floating in still waters. The light seemed to keep them at bay. I wondered if Carlotta had brought a lantern with her. I would never have ventured into that wilderness without one, not even on the promise of a screenwriting contract.

Eventually, we found Louise. I found her, actually. She was perched high in a deerhunting stand, clutching a burned-out flashlight. She was weeping and she wouldn't tell me why, but that magnificent Amazon body was unharmed.

Amazon or not, Louise was heartsore. I escorted her along the riverbank, with a gentlemanly arm around her waist. This did not endear me to Debbie.

When she saw us coming, she slipped a ladylike hand into the crook of my other arm and clamped down hard on the soft flesh of my inner elbow. The two of us escorted Louise the rest of the way back.

Everyone was relieved to see Louise safe, but she was the only beautiful woman found in the swamps around Glitter Spring that evening. We all lay awake that night, wondering what had become of the biggest movie star for miles around.

• • •

At sunrise, Carlotta was still missing. The sheriff and his deputies were puttering around as if they knew what they were doing. John, on the other hand, was stumped.

"Do I keep filming? Or do I shut the movie down and send people home?" he asked me.

He'd asked those questions all night long, seeking guidance from the bigwigs in Hollywood. He got helpful answers like, "*No!!!* Don't keep filming! You can't keep spending money on a film that's lost its star," and, "Of course you gotta keep filming!! Do you know how much it's *costing* us to keep that crew in Florida??"

John was an artist, even on a low budget. He'd had all night to develop a plan. "I've gotta presume Carlotta's out in the swamp pouting and she'll be back any minute, ready for her close-up. But if I'm wrong, I think I can save the movie. We shot the last of her close-ups yesterday. Debbie was going to do most of the remaining scenes, anyway. I might have to finesse a few shots … you know … put a hat on Debbie or shoot her from behind, but it should work."

"Debbie's gonna want a raise," I said, because I was her boyfriend and I felt like I should look out for her.

"She's already asked for it. Got it, too," said John. It seemed that Debbie didn't need her boyfriend all that much. Fortunately, I've always liked self-sufficient women.

At John's instruction, we boarded the boat that took us out to the calm lagoon where much of the movie had already been filmed. The empty monster suit lay on the deck where the crew always left it. This had seemed like a strange way to treat an expensive prop until I stopped to think: Who, in the middle of the Florida swamp, was going to take it? And what could possibly hurt the thing? It was made of rubber.

We were silent and businesslike. We could probably have made the movie even more cheaply if we'd always been so focused on the movie. It felt far better to work than to wonder what happened to Carlotta.

John planned to film some scenes with Louise in the monster suit, hauling a kicking-and-screaming Debbie deep into the lagoon. It was a good plan, until Louise started to get dressed. She was carefully unzipping the monster suit, ready to crawl in and be an actress, when she suddenly went off-script.

Flinging her arms over her face and screaming, it took Louise three long-legged strides to run the length of the boat and throw herself into the lagoon. There may have been alligators in that still water, but Louise was always more comfortable with nature's monsters than she was with the human kind.

The rest of us hovered around the half-open monster suit. We all knew what was in there, but I was the wardrobe guy. This put me in charge of the suit, so I was the one who had to finish unzipping the thing.

The fully open zipper exposed Carlotta's bare back. A couple of bruises marred her creamy white flesh, but they were nothing compared to the wound on her head. Her glorious blonde curls, matted with blood and muddy sand, spilled out of the opening.

The cameraman had been a seasoned newspaper photographer long before he got into pictures. Without even pausing to think, he swung the movie camera around and pointed it at Carlotta's body and the crowd hovering over it.

Nobody said anything. Since I was closest to the corpse, I felt some responsibility to respond to the ugliness at my feet. I had nothing to say except, "Somebody find the sheriff."

John, being a director, knew exactly what to say and do. He made eye contact with the cameraman and said simply, "Cut and wrap."

• • •

Later in my career, I worked on the set of *The Andy Griffith Show*. If only Andy had been the sheriff who investigated Carlotta's murder ...

We could have used his homestyle, Southern-bred wisdom. Instead, we got a tobacco-chewing, Yankee-hating heap of ignorance named Sheriff Meany. (Really. That was his name.) He paced importantly across the hotel lobby, exuding all the warmth and charm of Ol' Jack the stuffed alligator. We suspects loitered, waiting to be questioned. I saw in seconds that Sheriff Meany would not be solving Carlotta's murder and that he might arrest someone ... anyone ... to get this job over and done with.

Since I had ambitions of someday scripting a courtroom drama, I felt compelled to solve this crime myself. I also object strenuously to the prosecution of innocent people, particularly when I'm one of the innocents under scrutiny. So I took a clear-eyed look at the facts.

Carlotta's murderer was almost certainly a part of the movie crew or the hotel staff. Someone would have heard a car or boat motor if an outsider had slipped in. It was possible that someone had come in on foot or rowed upstream for more than a mile against the significant current of the Glitter River, but my money said the killer had been in the hotel that evening.

That presumption still left several dozen possibilities, but few of those had anything to gain from Carlotta's death. Quite a few had something to lose. I decided that my investigation would revolve around people who were personally affected by Carlotta. They could be affected for good or ill, but my deciding question was this: Who *cared* about what happened to Carlotta? Because people rarely die at the hands of people who just don't care.

Her manager Bradley cared. Whether he cared about Carlotta herself was open to question. Perhaps he was distraught that his primary source of income was now dead and stuffed into a rubber monster suit. The witless sheriff had finally called a doctor to sedate the weeping man, who now lay sprawled on a couch, one arm flung across his face.

I didn't like to admit it, but my girl Debbie cared. She'd bitterly resented Carlotta's conceited airs. I couldn't tell you how many times she'd told me, "I can do everything she does and more. I could carry this picture. And I'm a professional. You wouldn't catch me whining about the heat or forgetting my lines. I just need a chance to show John what I can do."

Well, now Debbie had her chance. Fortunately, she was too dainty to stuff a hundred-and-twenty pounds of dead weight into a monster suit … but Louise wasn't. And Louise was huddled in a chair with her head under a blanket, trying to hide the fact that she hadn't stopped weeping since she was found alone in the swamp.

That distress was probably going to send Louise to jail by lunchtime, because Sheriff Meany seemed to see her tears as proof of guilt. And Louise's refusal to say why she'd been alone in a deer stand at midnight wasn't helping.

I myself had my eye on Vince, Carlotta's so-called boyfriend. Displaying the reptilian heart of your average Hollywood citizen, he'd spent the morning on the phone, checking to see whether the movie was insured for the murder of its star. Once his insurance coverage was confirmed, he looked relaxed and almost happy.

John, to his credit, had shed his own reptilian armor the instant Carlotta's body was found. While there was a reasonable chance she was alive, he'd continued his cold-blooded efforts to get his movie made and to get it made within budget. Once she was unquestionably dead, he'd reverted to being a human being. There had been a tenderness in his tolerance for Carlotta's silliness that made me believe he cared for her. I was also convinced by the pain in his eyes. Don't forget that I made my living designing faces. I read them better than most people.

John glanced in my direction and I shifted my eyes away. Bradley fell into my field of vision, which worked well for me. Unconscious on the couch, he was hardly likely to yell at me for staring at him.

Bradley shifted in his sleep and his arm fell away from his face. The makeup artist in me was so startled that I quit sneaking glances and frankly stared. The whole right side of his face was pink and puffy. Yeah, he'd had his arm resting on his face for awhile, but not *that* long. And his arm would not have made the five separate welts extending from his cheek to his hairline.

I spend a lot of my days repairing famous faces that have gotten themselves slapped. I recognized the pattern on Vince's face. Trust me.

Men don't ordinarily go around slapping other men, and I knew only one woman for miles around capable of inflicting that kind of damage with one strike. I was pretty sure I knew who had made Louise cry. The question was why.

• • •

I was relieved to see that Louise had quit weeping. Tears aren't any more tragic on a pretty face than on a homely one, but I'm a man, after all. I would have wrestled a gator for Louise's entertainment, just to keep the tears off that lovely face.

Sheriff Meany was not pleased to see me escort his prime suspect out of the lobby, but he let us leave. The man had deputies guarding the exits, the parking lot, and the dock. Louise and I weren't going anywhere.

Ignoring 1940s propriety, I hustled Louise into her room and closed the door.

I patted her on the hand, then got straight to the point. "I know who you were with last night, and I don't think you killed Carlotta. I just have one question: Why did you slap Bradley silly?"

She looked at the palm of her hand as if it still stung. "Why do women usually slap men?"

"Because they get fresh?"

She laughed. "Oh, Bradley's been trying to get fresh for weeks. I kinda like it, or I never would've agreed to meet him last night. No, I slapped him because of the lipstick on his collar. Some woman wiped her face on Bradley so well that I could see the smear in the dark, with just my flashlight."

Lipstick? I was a makeup artist. Now the woman was talking my language.

"What color lipstick? I guess it wasn't your color, or you wouldn't have slapped him."

"Brownish-red," she said in a mildly revolted tone of voice. I understood her revulsion. That color would have been ghastly against her blonde hair and golden complexion … which meant that it didn't belong to Louise or Carlotta, either. If I'd smeared that color on the lips of any of the three blonde sirens making this movie, John would have confiscated my makeup bag and sent me back to Hollywood.

Was Bradley's lover on the hotel staff? Hardly. The cook was on the wrong side of seventy. I'd wager that the austere housekeeper's pale skin had never made the acquaintance of any cosmetic beyond bar soap. And both waitresses were dark-skinned brunettes who favored cherry-red lips, because cheap, loud makeup attracts big-tipping men. Very few women could get away with lipstick the color of dried blood.

Dried blood …

What had Louise really seen on Bradley's collar?

• • •

Sheriff Meany didn't like Bradley's looks, so it wasn't hard to convince him to ask the publicist to produce his shirt. Bradley had progressed quickly from his first response, "I can't find it," to his final response, "You'll have to talk to my lawyer about that."

Sheriff Meany wasn't completely stupid. He knew that a man who was unable to find a just-worn shirt in a small hotel room was a man who was hiding something. Looking at me with an expression approaching respect, he asked, "You got any more bright ideas?"

"Have you found the murder weapon?"

"From the looks of the wound and the mud around it, I'm thinking the killer used a rock. Unless he was an idiot, he killed her with it, then dropped it in the river. The whole river bed's limestone. The murder weapon won't look any different from any other rock, not after the river's washed the blood off."

"Could you look for the spot where the killer *got* the rock?"

The sheriff opened his mouth to call me an idiot, then closed it. Because if you thought about it, there were only a few places that made any sense at all. There were some good-sized rocks used for landscaping around the hotel grounds, and there were plenty of rocks along the riverside. That was about it. Why would anybody walk into the vermin-infested swamp and away from the river and its perfectly good rocks?

It didn't take long for Meany's deputies to find a damp hole in the river-bank. The muddy sand at the bottom was the same pale color as the mud on poor Carlotta's head. I was feeling very proud of my deductive prowess, until Meany mentioned another clue that I quite frankly never saw coming.

Love is indeed blind, because it never occurred to me that the footprint in the muddy sand next to that damp hole would be dainty and feminine. It just never crossed my mind that this print would perfectly match my sweet Debbie's shapely foot.

∙ ∙ ∙

When you spoon-fed Sheriff Meany a seamless sequence of clues, then led him patiently to their correct solution, he could be made to see the truth. Debbie and Bradley had been carrying on the kind of affair often seen in Hollywood. He was losing his hold on the client who served as his gravy train. She was pretty and ambitious as hell. Together, they'd planned to seize Hollywood attention and keep it.

With Carlotta dead, Vince's insurers would have made certain the picture got made. By killing Carlotta as soon as her close-ups were filmed, Debbie was set to walk right into the starring role for the remainder of filming. John already liked her work. The odds were good that he'd start to see her as leading lady material, and a star would be born. Or so Debbie and her ambitious new manager hoped.

Bradley had been sleeping with Carlotta for years. It had been his price for taking her as a client in the first place. During our weeks in Florida, he'd taken Debbie on as a new client … and extracted the same price. The two of them must have been blessed with rare vigor, since their trysts had taken place after he left Carlotta's bed and she left mine.

At first, I thought that Bradley had been trying to add Louise to his stable of client/lovers. Taking on a woman as physically daunting as Louise on a night when he'd already visited Carlotta and Debbie would have been … impressive … so I was crediting Bradley with stupendous vigor until I saw the subtlety of what he'd done.

He'd seduced Louise and taken her into the swamp by boat for their rendezvous. Carlotta was already dead by this time, because her blood on his collar had gotten him slapped. This fight with Louise had made it that much easier to do what he'd always intended … leave her in the deer stand with a burned-out flashlight and no safe way to get back to the hotel. No Florida girl would go wading alone through gator territory in the dark. When she was eventually found, not far from the murder site, she'd be an obvious suspect for Carlotta's murder. She'd have been presumed to be as murderously jealous of Carlotta as Debbie was, and she was a lot more physically capable of murder.

And how did the two conspirators actually commit the crime? The sheriff eventually found a faint smear of blood proving that the murder happened on the boat. I presume that Bradley used his stupendously vigorous charms to lure Carlotta into a passionate embrace and that Debbie sneaked up behind her and whammed a muddy rock onto her head. A bit of blood must have gotten onto Bradley's collar, and probably a whole lot of gore got onto Debbie. We found one of the little teeny bathing suits I bought her, bloodstained and wrapped in Bradley's shirt, buried under a cypress tree downstream from the hotel.

When faced with that bundle of clothing, Bradley told us everything, hoping for mercy since he didn't do the actual killing. Debbie never said a word. She didn't need to speak. I knew the truth when I saw the dailies.

It was not a good day for shooting a picture. We only got thirty seconds of film … but that half-minute tells a hell of a story. It begins with a blur as the quick-witted cameraman whipped around and caught the wordless horror on Louise's face as she ran from the monster suit and its hideous contents. Proving that he was an artist with a lens, he pulled back just a bit and focused on our faces as the rest of us took a long dark look into the abyss.

I can still see the scene he captured. It is etched on my retinas, my eyes, my heart. This moment, which will never shine down at an audience from a silver screen, is the moment when our low-budget monster flick reached the level of true art.

John's face is a study in heartbreak.

Vince stares down at the bloody nothingness that had been his lover. He communicates no feeling. He just looks like he wants to be sick.

Debbie and Bradley aren't looking at Carlotta at all, because they've already seen the monstrosity hiding in that pitiful rubber suit. They're looking into each other's faces. I've looked at that still shot a million times, and I still can't tell whether their eyes are communicating love or fear or loathing. I've come to think that murderers aren't capable of love or fear, not really. Every emotion for them is some form of loathing.

And where did my gaze turn in that stomach-churning instant? My eyes aren't focused on Carlotta or her killers. They're not focused on anything in range of the camera. I'm looking past the cameraman, down the boat's long deck where Louise just fled from the sight of death. I'm looking for the only woman I have ever loved.

*   *   *

I did get my dream career as a screenwriter, though I can't say it was completely on my own merits. It never hurts to be the spouse of a bankable star. Though Louise never displaced Esther Williams as queen of the movie mermaids, she was always bankable. And she was always lovable. When she turned those wide blue eyes on the camera, her sweet nature showed through, and movie audiences loved her almost as much as I did.

Her acting coaches drummed the rural Florida accent out of her, but she can still turn it back on for me. She knows how much I like to hear her say, "Ah love yew, darlin'."

And I answer her, in my flat Tinseltown tones, saying, "I love you too, darling. And I always have … ever since I first saw you wearing that stupid rubber monster suit."

OVEREXPOSURE

BY JAMES W. HALL

Johnny Fellows discovered the naked woman standing on a precipice when he was eight years old. She filled an entire page in the photography magazine, a perfectly focused black and white shot artful in its simplicity. Voluptuous nude woman poised on a stony perch.

Johnny found her in the basement among a stack of his father's photo magazines. Photography was his father's hobby, a laborious and chemically messy activity in those days of 1955, requiring a cramped darkroom, trays of dizzy smelling liquids, a clothesline where the drying prints hung, and long hours working alone in the red-lit darkness.

In the back room of the local barbershop, Johnny had seen bare-breasted women in *Playboy Magazine* but their crotches were air-brushed clean. On the walls of the gas station where his father, Arnold, took his car to be serviced, pin-up pictures of sexy babes were plastered everywhere, their crotches hidden behind feather dusters or conveniently placed objects. And he'd seen a few generic girlie magazines passed around at school. But none of the breasts Johnny had seen, or the sumptuous hips or graceful legs compared to the brazen nude in his father's photo magazine.

The woman on the rock was tall with loose, luxurious black hair that fell down her back. Her arms were poised slightly away from her wide hips as if she meant to take a swan dive into some unseen canyon. Her breasts were full and round, her nipples as dark and taut as fresh raisins. A tangled thatch of pubic hair formed a mysterious shadow a few inches below her navel.

He studied that bush for hours when his father was away on his business trips and his mother was upstairs relentlessly cleaning the house.

His parents didn't question Johnny's long absences in the basement for they believed he was engaged in a constructive hobby. In one corner of the basement he had cordoned off a workshop area where he fashioned model cars from kits. He specialized in Ford hotrods, the '32, the '40, which he modified with his X-acto knife and soldering iron. Johnny chopped and channeled their molded bodies and customized their interiors with corduroy and other fabrics that he glued to the bucket seats to replicate rolled and pleated upholstery. Then he delicately placed screws that allowed the seats to swivel outward. His creations had even won trophies at local contests.

It was the first pubic hair of Johnny's life. Lush and snarled like a nest that some strangely beautiful creature had woven and left behind in the branches of a tree. Hiding inside that mat of hair was some unimaginable bliss that weakened Johnny's knees, flushed his cheeks, and tensed his breath.

While he listened to his mother's tread on the floor above, he held the photo up to the light, cocked it at different angles, even used a magnifying glass. Still he could not penetrate the dark wooly triangle.

Months earlier while exploring his father's stash of magazines, Johnny had first discovered the photograph. The page was dog-eared, a small fold in the corner as if something in the photo had caught his father's attention. Arnold Fellows was a plain and colorless businessman who neither cursed nor boozed nor sinned in any way that Johnny had ever noted. He wore dreary suits and seemed more pale and quiet than the other fathers. So Johnny was certain he'd marked the page only because the photographer had employed some arcane technique that his father was trying to master.

Johnny, however, was struck dumb by the eroticism of the image and returned to it again and again, lured from his glue and spray paint and his modified antique Fords. Drawn to the cabinet where he knew she was standing on her rock, everything exposed. Her dark hair, her deep navel, her swollen hips, her faultless breasts.

She became for him, during those hours when he stared at her, the guiding image of his adult life, his anima, his secret touchstone for sexual thrill. The woman on the rock in black and white with the shadow of her perfect body flattened on the cliffside to her left. The incalculably deep cavern that opened before her was beyond the frame of the photograph. But he knew it was there. She had that look on her face. The expression of someone teetering on the edge of an abyss.

He called her Myra. He didn't know why he chose that name. To his youthful ear it sounded vaguely exotic. When he considered Myra later, and the role she would play in his adult life, he could never sort the chicken from the egg. Had his fascination with the photograph of Myra, the long hours he'd spent gazing at her, implanted that image of a dark goddess in his psyche? Or was that image preexistent in his sexual genome, and Myra simply became the first and clearest manifestation of what was already lurking within him?

After graduating from college, Johnny married a thin blonde, whose body type and complexion was similar to his mother's. He loved Candace in a clear-cut, uncomplicated way. He found her familiar and easy. Like Johnny, she worked in the public schools. Candace taught math to the brightest high school kids, while Johnny was a guidance counselor in a nearby junior high, which meant he spent most of his day dealing with children who were failing in every imaginable way.

Candace and Johnny had half a dozen friends they met for dinner now and then. On school nights in the evenings while she graded quizzes, Johnny watched TV and nursed a single glass of wine. He read an occasional novel, whatever was popular at the moment. It was not a challenging life. Nor was it tumultuous. None of the prickly rancor he'd witnessed between Candace's parents, none of the strained indifference he'd observed between his own.

They had a child, a son named Jason who resembled his mother, thin and tall and blond. Though he was a bit of a loner, Jason never acted out, and seemed a happy child. He did well in his studies, won a scholarship to a state university and found a job teaching math in a junior college in Georgia. Once a month they talked on the phone, and visited on the holidays. He had a girlfriend and it looked serious. The Fellows genes were going to pass on.

Over three decades Johnny and Candace fell into a satisfying routine in the bedroom. Saturday was their sex day. Her orgasms were reliable and definite and afterwards they smiled at each other the rest of the afternoon. They rarely argued. They made decent money, had solid benefits. Politically they were nearly in full agreement and the areas where they disagreed caused them to have a few spirited debates, though nothing acrimonious. Before he married Candace, Johnny had slept with five college girls. Since their vows, Johnny was absolutely faithful to her and he was certain she was to him. By all the customary measurements, their marriage was nearly perfect.

However, the woman on the rock who he'd last seen when he was eight, never left him for long. It was as if Myra was lodged in an essential vein restricting the normal flow to his libido. She was always there, poised to dive. Daring in her nakedness. Dark-skinned in his memory, perhaps tanned from the sun, perhaps from some ancestral strain. She might have been from gypsy stock or Mediterranean. Sometimes when he was walking through crowds at the mall, he saw fleeting fragments of Myra. Her dark hair kicking up across the shoulders of her blouse. Her strong nose. Her hourglass body with black sand tickling through it continuously.

At times when he and Candace were making love, Johnny had closed his eyes and Myra appeared before him unbidden, her wide, welcoming hips, her ravenous appetites. Lusty and primitive, a mystery he'd never solved.

At fifty-eight Johnny retired. Together he and Candace decided she should keep working to retain their health insurance and because she claimed she still enjoyed the students.

Johnny decided he would try to write a book, a collection of anecdotes he'd been filing away for years. Some funny, some sad, some tragic. An insider's guide to the silliness and outrages of public education. Candace rooted him on.

At home alone for the first time in his adult life, Johnny fell into a routine. For an hour or two in the morning, he piddled with his manuscript, wrote a few sentences, maybe even a paragraph or two, then he reread his efforts, saw nothing but flaws, wound up deleting every word he had written, and drifted to the Internet.

Without ever consciously deciding to do so, he began to search out porn. He wasn't horny. Even after thirty years, Candace never failed to arouse him, and he seemed to have the same effect on her. Theirs was, by any textbook definition, a sound and healthy marriage.

Yet, there he was, utterly unfettered for the first time since childhood, and Johnny Fellows found himself surfing madly through the most obscene websites imaginable. He explored every fetish he'd heard of and many new to him. Lesbians with strap-ons, golden showers, women having sex with horses and other barnyard creatures, men with other men, women drenched with the sperm of a dozen men in leather masks. Men with silicone breasts, dressed as slutty women, showing off fully-functioning cocks. Old women screwing teenage boys. Teenage girls giving head to granddads, women dressed as nuns pleasuring themselves with gigantic, multi-headed dildos. It was all just a click away. He took the free tours, never subscribed, never used his credit card number. He just browsed and browsed and browsed.

After weeks of that, well into his first free semester in over fifty years, he began to circle in on what he'd come to consider his own domain. He found he liked to look at hirsute women, Earth Mamas, Hippie Goddesses, Hairy Honeys. Johnny was drawn instinctively to women with mounds of pubic hair like Myra's.

Finding images of such women was more tricky than he might have expected. While Johnny hadn't been paying attention, apparently the fashion of sexual display had altered, and women began to coif their pubic patches, trimming them to narrow strips, or manicured valentines, or most frequently, to shave their mons pubis bare.

Johnny assumed the style grew out of one of the modern age's last taboos. The forbidden allure of prepubescence. Fully sexualized women simulating innocent girls.

As the raunchy pictures filled his computer screen, Johnny felt no urge to masturbate. Instead, what he experienced was a persistent and cavernous yearning. While his eyes roamed the bodies of anonymous women, he suffered a vast ache in his soul. An absence that yawned within him as large and unknowable as that bottomless canyon that opened below Myra's bare feet.

In early October he realized one morning that he'd been obsessing over surrogates for Myra, and that's when he decided to hunt for her.

It seemed to John Fellows that the Internet had absorbed most of the tangible world and nearly everything that once existed in three dimensions was floating in cyberspace, if only one had the skill and resolve to search it out.

Within a single day he located a site that trafficked in old issues of *Modern Photography*, the magazine she'd appeared in. Many of the pages within the magazine were reproduced and viewable online, but to his irritation, he could not locate Myra's picture among them. Unsure of the exact date of the magazine he had spent so many hours absorbed in, Johnny ordered every issue from 1954 and 1955. Furthermore, he paid an outrageous sum to have all twenty-four of them delivered the next day.

That night in a fever of expectancy he sat on the couch and pretended to be alive. Candace was watching their favorite sitcom and giggling along with the laugh track. Johnny held himself still, feeling the fracture lines branching through him as though he might crack apart right there and spill out a grim confession to his sweet blond wife, reveal that he had sinned against her, that he had betrayed her, that indeed, their whole romantic life together had been one long sham. For half a century he had been furtively in love with a woman named Myra. A ghostly being who haunted his reveries, whose perfumed breath whispered into his dreaming mind, and even now in his deep middle age, this seductive mistress had more than once materialized in his sleep to harden his cock, make him grind against the mattress until he released a flood of nocturnal emissions into the secret flesh behind Myra's nest of hair.

"Is something wrong?"

He made himself breathe. He made himself look at her.

"No," Johnny said. "Why do you ask?"

"You're so quiet."

"I am?"

"Yes," she said. "Very quiet."

"It must be the writing," he said.

"Not going well?"

"It's harder than I imagined. I'm just preoccupied."

"When are you going to show me something?"

The commercials ceased and the sitcom resumed. Johnny steered his eyes to the set and chuckled at the first comedic moment.

"Soon," he said. "When I'm comfortable with it."

"You can show me anything," she said. "No matter how raw it is. I'll go easy on you."

Johnny swallowed. He produced a smile for Candace, his devoted wife, his friend, his lover. He presented it to her and she seemed to buy it.

As the sitcom moved through its unvarying formula, Johnny's blood turned slowly to sludge, until he could bear it no longer.

"I'm a fraud," he announced.

By then Candace was into the show, and missed the pathos in his voice.

"Oh, stop. You're just learning to play a new instrument in the band. Writing can't be easy. Give yourself some time."

She laughed at something one of the actors said.

Johnny sat silently, feeling the fractures branch out from an immense cavity in his chest, sending shoots of anguish and dread squirming into every extremity.

At noon when the FedEx man arrived, Johnny didn't answer the bell. So disgusted with his disloyalty to Candace, he wanted this transaction to be devoid of human contact. He waited at the edge of the curtains to make sure the man would leave the parcel as Johnny had stipulated on the note he taped to the mailbox.

After the truck was gone, Johnny went to the door, ducked outside into the dazzling noonday sun, and scooped up the package. His hands were clumsy and damp. His heart was losing traction.

He shut the door and stood sightlessly in the living room. That flare of sunshine had stunned him. Johnny held the box with one hand and with the other he knuckled the blinding ache from his eyes just as he'd done so many times as a child after another of his father's flashbulb portraits.

When his vision finally cleared, he carried the package to his study and set it on his desk. He stared at it numbly. He opened a drawer, removed a knife, thumbed open a blade. He drew a straight line down the seam of the strapping tape with the clarity of purpose a cardiac surgeon might employ on his first stroke.

He spread the flaps and released into the air the tart mildewed scent of the antique pages. He lifted the magazines one by one from the box and lay them on the carpet at his feet, making a cartwheel around himself. Johnny had imagined it would take hours to sort through all those issues before he located the photograph. When he'd viewed the covers on the computer screen, none struck him as familiar. But apparently the image had lingered in some subliminal stratum of memory, for seeing them lying before him, Johnny knew instantly which was the magical issue.

On the cover was a black and white photo of a muted desert landscape at sunset, with a single tumbleweed kicking across the dunes.

He collected the others from the rug, and stacked them back in the box. He set the box on a top shelf in the study closet and shut the door. He carried the magazine to his desk and sat down before his computer. The cursor was blinking at the top left corner of a blank page. Its patient beat mocking his own churning heart.

As if by some charmed decree, the magazine fell open at his touch to her photograph. In a swoon of shame and delight, he felt it all flood back. He saw the long-ago basement. He saw his father's darkroom, the workbench, the pans of woozy fluids. Johnny watched himself draw the magazine from the pile, leaving the stack askew so he could reinsert it in the same place when he was done. He flashed through the hours he'd spent with Myra. Every delicious fantasy he'd entertained. He heard the echo of his mother's step as she did her housework, the scent of model car glue in the air, the helpless longing that consumed him as he pried behind her pubic hair to see what wonders the world had in store for him.

She was more beautiful than he remembered. With a subtle thrust of her chin and upward tilt to her face, she seemed both defiant and full of wanton pride. Yet there was an undertone of disquiet in her eyes, as if her nerve was being tested by the cliff's staggering height.

Her eyes were large and dark and her eyebrows heavy. There was a trail of hair leading up from her bush to her navel. A fine dusting of hair on her thighs. And the hair on her forearms coiled as dense and dark as Johnny's own. Myra was unshaven. Primitive. A natural woman.

The photographer was identified as Ernest L. James.

Johnny swiveled to his keyboard and did a search on Ernest James. For the first half hour he learned little, then he hit a Web site that featured the photographer's work, among other landscape artists. Johnny clicked through dozens of his photos. No nudes. But a great many rocks and granite walls and stark cliffs and boulders.

So that was it. The woman on that mountainside was not the object at all. She was there, Johnny saw, simply to highlight Ernest L. James's true fascination: Geology. The earth. Formations created from great forces clashing one against the other, thrusting upward, dramatic outcroppings, peaks and pikes and crests and summits. The scar tissue of creation.

Myra was simply a counterpoint. An umbrella in the drink.

For most of the afternoon he stared at her photograph on the shiny page and feasted on a thousand guilty memories. The cursor blinked. The house was silent. What had once inflamed his eight-year-old mind still set his heart ablaze. The man he was today and the boy he'd been were absolutely equivalent. In every important way, he knew not a single thing more than he had in that basement. It was all still mystery. What was hidden behind Myra's profusion of pubes remained hidden and enthralling. Johnny was eight, Johnny was fifty-eight. The woman on the rock had not moved a muscle, nor had he.

It was nearly four o'clock when Johnny woke from his trance and thought to page to the end of the magazine and search the directory.

In fine print, he found the model's name.

Lila Calderon.

As his heart lurched and swayed, he heard Candace unlock the front door and step inside their home.

"You need to let me read some of it," Candace said to him at dinner. They were watching *Wheel of Fortune* while they ate the pork fried rice and spring rolls she'd picked up on her way home.

"I will. I will."

"You're getting gloomy, John."

"Gloomy?"

"Depressed. Sad, inward."

"I am?"

"Yes," Candace said. "I know you. You're disheartened."

"I'm okay. I'm good. I'm adjusting to being alone all day. That's all it is. Knocking around the empty house. I miss you."

"You're not writing at all, are you?"

One of the contestants had selected a vowel. The letter A. They always chose the letter A. A for alchemy. A for adultery. A for addiction. A for asshole.

"There was this girl when I was young."

"A girl?"

"Yeah, when I was a kid. Eight years old."

Candace tried without success to smile.

"You never told me about a girl when you were eight."

"She was older. Like mid-twenties."

"Johnny! What are you talking about?"

"I had a crush on this older woman."

"Like a neighbor?"

"Yeah, sort of. Anyway, I'm trying to write about her. Her name was Myra."

"Myra?"

Hearing Candace speak the name shocked him. He couldn't believe he'd blurted out his secret. He floated out of himself and looked down at this moment with incredulity. Would this neutralize his fixation? Opening the sore, letting the festering juices leak out, would this cure him? Was he even sick? He didn't feel sick. Desperate, perhaps. Intense, yes. But not sick.

"So you're trying to write about your first crush."

"I guess you could call it that."

"That's sweet. That's good, Johnny."

"You're not jealous?"

"Should I be?"

Johnny smiled his way past the question.

"I meant to write about my job. About school. But I sat down in front of that damn computer, and this was what came out."

"Let me read it, Johnny. It sounds great."

"Not yet. Oh, I do want you to read it, of course. I want your reaction. But it's still awkward and full of mistakes. Give me a while. A few more days."

Somebody had won a red Mustang convertible for solving the *Wheel of Fortune* puzzle. Johnny and Candace watched the woman run down to sit behind the steering wheel. She had long black hair like a Spanish priestess. Thick rich black hair. At the sight of it, Johnny's heart began to thrash so recklessly he had to stand and slip from the room lest Candace hear its throb.

The next morning as soon as she'd pulled from the driveway, Johnny began to insert Lila's name into online people-finder sites. An entire industry was thriving on reconnecting those who'd become lost to one another.

Each Web site had a teaser page. Type in the name, the database went to work while showing an animated spinning wheel. A few seconds later a list materialized.

Every Lila Calderon in America. Their age, their city. Possible relatives.

There were four Lila's in the US.

Only one was in the right age bracket. Lila Calderon, age 75, Santa Monica, California. For a mere twenty dollars, Johnny would be provided her exact address, her phone number. For twice that he could access any public records that included her name. Property, DMV, deadbeat parent lists, divorce, marriage, assets search, criminal history, and more.

Johnny typed in his credit card info and two minutes later he was looking at a map of Santa Monica with Lila Calderon's house marked with a red arrow. Her phone number. Two possible relatives. Lillian Sanchez, age fifty. Marianella Anderson, age twenty-five.

Johnny worked the math. He'd been eight. If the Lila standing naked on the mountainside was twenty-five when the photo was taken, she would be seventy-five today. Lila of Santa Monica.

Johnny stared at the possible relatives. Lillian Sanchez of Manhattan, age fifty. A name like Lillian might be simply a coincidence. Then again, could Lillian be Lila Calderon's daughter? Which would mean, of course, in the hasty arithmetic he was doing in his head, that Johnny's Lila would have given birth to Lillian sometime in the twelve months following the photo.

He looked again at her stance on the promontory. He tried to read that proud face, tried to interpret its deeper resonance. Had she been pregnant? Had she known? Had she suspected? Was she delighted by the life growing within her? Was she full of foreboding? Was the photograph a celebration of her secret or was it her swan song?

He looked at the telephone beside him on the desk. It was nine in Johnny's Miami, only six in Santa Monica. Was she up? Did she sleep late?

A woman answered on the first ring. A simple Hello.

His writing study became a whirl of color and shapes. He felt seasick and disconnected from the moment, as if his consciousness had not yet caught up with the impulsive acts his body was committing.

"Hello?" she said again.

Lila's tone was quiet and serene. The voice might have belonged to a woman twenty years younger. Not a smoker, not a woman who had screamed herself hoarse at men or other calamities. At peace. A drowsy contentment as if she had no fears and no enemies and no regrets.

"Is someone there?"

"Is this Lila? Lila Calderon?"

"That is my name, yes."

Johnny hung up.

He sat back in his chair and tried to breathe. He watched the cursor blink. Five minutes might have passed, or it might have been an hour. So lost in the smog of his imagining, so bewildered by his own mad pursuit.

The phone rang. The caller ID said Santa Monica, California.

His hand snaked out, trembling, and he watched himself lift the receiver and bring it to his ear. He could not manage to speak a word.

"You just called me," Lila said. "Do you need something?"

There was no ill will in her voice. A simple curiosity. But then again, to have made such a call to a stranger at six in the morning, there had to be strong currents steering her. Something more compelling than curiosity.

"My name is Johnny."

"Johnny Fellows, yes, I know."

She had him on her caller ID just as he had her on his.

"Yes, Johnny Fellows."

"And why is it that you called me?"

Something awkward in that phrasing. An accent? Was she Spanish? Her voice had an aristocratic flair. Not quite haughty, but bold. The same pride he'd seen in her jut of jaw.

"Were you a model?" Johnny said. "A photographer's model?"

"Long ago, yes, I was."

"I searched you out," Johnny said.

"I suspected this was true." Her voice was dreamy and knowing.

"It's crazy, I understand that. But I fell in love with your photograph. 1955, *Modern Photography*, Ernest L. James."

She was quiet but he could hear her puttering. The whisking of sheets? Were they silk? Or perhaps she was she slipping into her robe? No, it wouldn't be a robe, but a kimono. The kimono would be black as her hair was black with the same deep luster. Dragons were embroidered on its back. Their red eyes, their long curved claws.

"Arnold, your father, is he well?"

"Arnold?"

Johnny felt a skewer slide deep into his bowels.

"Your father, Johnny. How is he? Does he know you're calling me?"

"You know my father?"

The walls of his study were bleeding light. His dizzy eyes, his spiraling gut. The woman on the phone, Lila Calderon, she'd spoken his father's name with a familiarity that was unmistakable. And Johnny saw again the bent corner of the magazine page. That dog-ear.

"He died," Johnny said. "Two years ago. Cancer."

"I see," she said with a faraway tranquility as if she might have suspected this. "I'm sorry for your loss, Johnny. I'm deeply sorry."

Johnny lost it. He began to jabber into the phone, demanding to be told how she knew his dad, but getting no response, then pleading with her to reveal what the nature of the relationship had been, bullying, beseeching, his words rushed out messily for minutes, then he halted.

"Are you there?"

She was not.

She had gone away, left the line to hum with miles of emptiness.

He could picture her in Santa Monica. She had set the phone back in its cradle, walked to her bathroom, stood before the deep tub, let her kimono fall to the tile, ran the water warm, dusted it with herbal soap, let the faucet flow until the water reached the brim, then slipped beneath the foam to linger away the California morning, to sip green tea, to recall the ancient smoky nights, the long lather of love with a man who no longer existed.

Candace was flummoxed.

"You're going to California?"

"Just for a day or two."

"What's going on, Johnny? You're in some kind of trouble, aren't you?"

"No, no, it's not any kind of trouble."

"What then?"

"The woman," he said. "Myra."

Candace said nothing, but she wasn't pleased by this turn.

Johnny felt the air dying in his lungs. A vice closing against his sternum.

"I need to go," he said.

"Why, for godsakes?"

"To see her, to speak with her. For my book."

"For your book?"

The television was running. It was always running. The cable news, the blather of the world. Their dinner plates were on their laps. Chicken with rice and mushrooms. He'd taken a bite and felt it turn to lead in his gut. And then he'd set off on this exercise in insanity.

"The woman I had a crush on. I spoke with her. I tracked her down and called her on the phone. And somehow it came out that my dad and her, my dad and her had some kind of affair, or relationship, or something, I don't know. She hung up."

"Where have you gone, Johnny?"

"What?"

"Where have you gone off to? What's happened to you?"

"Nothing's happened. I was writing the story and this came up and I started thinking about Myra and trying to imagine her, where she was today, and I don't know, I just reached for the phone."

"You called a woman in California. A stranger from fifty years ago."

"I'm nuts."

"I'd say so. I'd call that a little nuts."

"I want to interview her."

"You're not a reporter, Johnny. You're a retired guidance counselor who's been spending long hours alone in your room. You've cut yourself off from the world and it's made you spooky and off-balance."

"Spooky?"

She peered at him with a touch of dread as if his body might be disintegrating before her.

"Yes," Candace said. "I'll stand by that. Spooky."

He left Candace a note. He told her that he loved her. But he had to do this. He felt compelled. She'd hate him. She'd never forgive him. She might not be here when he got back. But Johnny Fellows had jumped from the ledge where he'd stood for decades alongside Myra and he was falling weightless through the immeasurable air—nowhere to go but down.

Lila's house was hot pink. Vivid and glowing beside her neighbors' whites and beiges. Gaudy bougainvillea cascaded over her front porch, and the blooms of an ancient jacaranda sent a flurry of blue snow across her patio. The bungalow was old Spanish with a view down an alley to the Pacific, a block away.

Johnny parked his rental car at the curb, switched off the engine and sat for a while trying to remember who he was.

He was, he had come to understand, his father's son, the drab and spiritless man Johnny had never even tried to get to know. He was in involuntary lockstep with him, following the breadcrumbs to a holy grail programmed into his blood. He was on a quest to confront the woman who'd stoked his inner fires and stoked his father's as well. The woman who had undermined his marriage in ways both subtle and profound.

Is that why he was here, to save his life with Candace? To dispel Myra's spell? To break the hold her nakedness had on him? To set himself free?

Or had he come with some dim yearning to seduce her? To charm her to her bed and draw aside her clothes and view the body, that thick nest of hair that had obsessed him so, to curl his fingers through its snarls, to take a fistful of it, to bury his face in its coils, its musk, to draw into his lungs the atoms of her hidden realm? Was he still an undeveloped eight years old? Was he still trapped in the basement, in the darkroom, still dizzy and insane from inhaling the glue, and the pans of harsh chemicals?

A woman was tapping on his window.

She stood in the street. Her hair was short and graying, but he recognized her eyebrows, still thick and dark, her cheekbones, her bold chin, her wide-set eyes. The flaunting, aristocratic look.

He rolled the window down.

"Johnny?"

"Yes."

She wore jeans and a loose white shirt with green vines embroidered across her heavy breasts. On the vines were small red buds, hundreds of them, tight, unopened buds.

She held out a padded mail envelope. No label, the flap sealed.

"This is for you."

Johnny took it from her and lay it in his lap.

"It's everything we did," she said. "Arnold and I. It's all there. That's the sum total of everything that happened."

"I want to talk to you."

She shook her head and her smile was grave and final.

"Just for a few minutes," Johnny said. "Talk with me, please."

"Go home to Candace. Work harder."

"Candace? How do you know Candace?"

She looked off toward the beach.

Candace had called her. Found her on the Caller ID, spoken to Lila.

"What did you tell my wife? What did you say?"

"It's all in there. Everything I could possibly tell you is in the envelope. That's all there is, all that happened between your father and me. Now go."

Johnny sat at the gate, waiting for the red-eye flight back home. The envelope lay in his lap unopened. He watched the people in the lounge area. He listened to the announcements. He watched the passengers flow around him with the slow ungainly silkiness of underwater performers.

He made it home by nine AM. Her car was gone. Candace might be at school. She might have gone home to stay with her parents.

Johnny walked inside. He checked her closet. He checked the kitchen and the luggage cabinet. She was at school. He closed his eyes and drew the first breath he'd managed since he'd left Santa Monica. He wiped his eyes dry.

He carried the padded mailer to his study and set it on the desk beside his computer, and jiggled the mouse to wake the machine from its slumber. He watched the cursor blink. Watched it blink on the empty page of his empty manuscript.

He tore open the mailer and reached into it and drew out another envelope. Printed on that envelope was the name of the photography store in

Miami where fifty years before his father purchased fluids and film and an occasional camera or lenses.

Inside the second envelope were dozens of photos of Lila Calderon.

In each she was naked. Some were taken in natural sunlight, outside in patios or screened-in backyards, some were taken indoors against a variety of prosaic backdrops.

She had displayed her body for Arnold Fellows, shown him everything she'd shown Ernest L. James. But as Johnny dealt the photos one by one from the pack in his hand, setting each on the desk beside him, it was clear the woman in these pictures was not the erotic goddess Johnny had worshipped for half a century.

The upward tilt of her jaw came across as crass and petty. Her eyes were guarded, ambiguous or vague. Whatever instructions Arnold had given her had not coaxed from her the defiant authority Johnny had witnessed in the magazine photo. Each of her poses seemed posed. Her arms awkward at her side. Her hands as gawky as broken chunks of brick. Even the lush hair between her legs that thrilled Johnny to his molten core, seemed blurry, indistinct, amateurishly out of focus or overexposed.

There were three sets of photos. One group was taken while Lila was still in her twenties. In the other two she was at least a decade older. But in that interval Arnold Fellows had made little progress in mastering his craft. Whatever artistic techniques he had acquired over the years were insufficient. His passion could not offset his incompetence.

He'd taken dozens of girlie shots and paid whatever fee was arranged, and flown home to bring Lila's image alive in that basement darkroom. Arnold had to have known his failure. He could not have been so cloddish as to deceive himself into believing he had done justice to his model. Because of his own artistic limitations or deficiencies within his character, he had turned

Lila Calderon into a vulgar slut.

Johnny stacked the photos and slid them back in the envelope and replaced it inside the mailer. He went to his desk and pulled out the issue of *Modern Photography* and turned to Myra's photo on the cliffside. He stared at her body, at the sleekness of her skin against the jagged planes of rock. He studied her glossy black hair, which lifted infinitesimally on a breeze that seemed to swell up from some place within the earth's unfathomable depths. Her dark eyes looked out and penetrated the lens, looked into the photographer's eye and beyond him, beyond his shrouded head, off into some distant era that had not yet arrived, into the far-off room where Johnny Fellows sat, his heart finding a new measure, slowing for the first time in a long while to something like a natural pace.

"Well, look who came home."

Johnny stood in the foyer, waiting, as Candace opened the front door. Through the doorway a slash of golden light was projected across the floor, its dagger tip touching Johnny's feet.

"Yes, I'm home," he said. "If you'll have me."

She set her purse on the table by the door. She took her time with her school books and her papers. She shut the door and bolted it. She was slim and blond and her hips hardly swelled at all. Beautiful in her own way.

She turned to him and in her eyes was something more solid and more certain than he'd detected there before. For five decades Johnny had failed to see her clearly, failed to capture her carnality in the thousand snapshots he took of her every day. He'd blurred her beauty, cheapened her essence with his own insufficient craft.

"You need to tell me everything."

"Yes."

"Absolutely everything."

"I will."

"If you skip anything, I'll know it. I will, I'll know, Johnny. No matter how hard it is to tell me, you have to do it. If you're going to save this, you have to say it all, down to the smallest detail."

"I'm ready."

"So do it right now. Look me in the eye and tell me everything."

He could feel the truth rising into his throat. Not scared of it. No longer alone in the basement with the secret woman, her unbearable perfection.

"I've been away, Candace. I've been off somewhere for a long time."

She nodded. Yes, she knew. Maybe she'd always known.

"So that's the first thing," he said. "I'm here, I'm finally here. And now I want to get this right. You and me. I'm going to give it everything I have."

"Well, that's a start," she said. "That's at least a start."

REVENGE OF THE EMERGING MARKET

BY JAMES O. BORN

He's just another New Yorker, not the damn Queen of England," Dale said, shaking his head at his partner's frantic effort to bring out a shine on the brass banister that separated the five stairs up to the landing.

"Dale, haven't you learned anything through our association? All New Yorkers *think* they're royalty. What he sees is what he'll think of us. If we look rich he'll think we're rich." Randy Hubbard directed his attention to a smudge on the bay window that looked across the Intracoastal then out over the Atlantic Ocean. He smiled thinking that the exorbitant rent he'd paid the stuck-up Philadelphia-based landlord was worth it. For Fort Lauderdale it probably wasn't even that bad. It didn't matter, he'd move out after two months and declare bankruptcy. No one would collect a dime. Not the landlord, not the investors, not even the Goddamn phone company. This would be sweet, just like the last time. Then, next time, maybe he could do it for real. If there was enough money in it.

Dale followed along like a shadow as Randy shined and polished every surface in the office. It made him nervous the way Dale was sticking closer than he normally did, and sometimes the squat little man could be a close talker.

Dale finally said, "How much you gonna ask for?"

Randy turned, his eyes scanning for something to step around and put some distance between him and his chubby little business partner. He wondered if Dale would be worth the trouble without his securities license. Randy finally said, "We'll get five, six hundred K today then hit him for another six hundred on the real estate end."

"You really think he'll go for both?"

Randy was back polishing the window. "You think he'll be satisfied with just one fortune when we offer him two? I'm tellin' you Dale, this fish is easy. It's that tall Mick from Boston who's coming in on Friday that'll be a challenge. We'll have a few drinks with lunch, that'll soften him up. If it weren't for the liquor, them Irish would rule the business world. They're a fierce bunch." He backed away from the window to survey his efforts. It looked like a clear force field from a *Star Wars* movie. Randy could even see a person on the deck of an open fishermen not far offshore from the public beach.

He bumped into his partner. "Goddamn, Dale, why are you underfoot today? Give me some space."

"Sorry," mumbled the shorter man as he opened the gap between them but kept pace as Randy hustled through the quiet office. Their first business venture had been a bust-out computer parts firm. Randy had opened the company and convinced a dumbass construction worker with some cash from pot sales to invest eight grand in the start-up. He even told the idiot that he could be president of the company. They got paid to set up a patsy in case anything went wrong. What a great country. Dale lined up credit using a shaky Dunn and Bradstreet report that showed the construction guy as a former

Xerox executive. The dipshit couldn't even spell Xerox. They used the credit lines to order computers and parts from every company that accepted their bullshit, which was basically everyone. Then they undercut the competition on bids to other corporations as well as the military. Since they didn't intend to pay for the parts it was all profit anyway. And good profit. Once the bills for the parts came due they simply shut down their grungy little office in the cheap part of Ft. Lauderdale west of I-95, and said they had failed in the computer business. No harm, no foul. Just a bunch of debts that the corporation owed. They didn't intend to resurrect that little company. And the president still laid drywall up in Palm Beach County. Beautiful.

Randy knew some of the parts suppliers were pissed and had made noise about going to the cops, but there was nothing they could do to him. Dale had worried about his Series 63 securities license but in the end no one cared. It was the price of doing business in a place as wild as South Florida.

This endeavor they had now was bigger, bolder, and potentially a lot more profitable. They'd used the profit from the last scam to finance this one. They had moved past small, anonymous offices and mail drops. Now they had the look of a respectable business. And Randy had learned that looks were more important that anything around here.

They had five separate rooms in their corporate empire. The entry, the main room, the trading pit, which was really four desks with phones, and the two offices, which each man claimed. Randy's was on the Intracoastal side with a view as spectacular as the main room's of the Seventeenth Street Causeway to the south. They had seen the Goodyear Blimp rise from its hangar to the north in Pompano Beach twice in the six days they had rented the space. Randy wished they could stay here. This was the kind of place that oozed respectability and was so far removed from his normal existence that he sometimes forgot how to act. Like telling Dale he'd "whip his ass" if he didn't line up dependable people for the trading pit. He had to watch that shit. He also realized that, based on the rent and the deposit, the landlord knew they weren't on the level and planned on getting his money up front. He'd claim ignorance if anyone ever came by to ask about the company that stayed for less than two months. A lot of people did business that way around here. As long as you showed the cash up front you could claim you were going to be a tenant for the next fifty years and no one would blink. That was why the east coast of Florida from Miami to Boca Raton was the fraud capitol of the western world. Randy was just happy to be part of it.

The two men strolled through the office as Randy leveled picture frames of Florida wildlife. He smiled at the irony that Northeasterners couldn't resist Florida real estate when they were shown photos of the animals that were being displaced by the new residents. The best photos hung in the trading pit, where Randy intended to casually stop and chat with their investors while the phones rang off the hook. He'd paid the guy who fixed the gas pump on his Chevy thirty bucks to call the four phones on a rotating basis between two and two thirty.

The photo Randy adjusted now was of a Florida panther. If he used that term now all anyone thought of was an underachieving hockey team, but Randy remembered seeing one as a kid when they went camping in Martin County. Even something as plain as an armadillo, which were plentiful a few years ago, were never seen now. But there was no cash in little smelly animals and the fucking New Yorkers were going to move here anyway, so Randy didn't see any problem making a few bucks on the whole trend. Besides, if he made enough money now maybe a few of these bastards wouldn't be able to afford to move down. Looking at it from that perspective he figured he was doing his civic duty as a Floridian.

He turned to Dale. "You got the sample all set up?"

"It'll work like a charm."

"If this asshole wants to look at the fountain, he won't figure it out?"

"Not a chance. Looks like a water nozzle. The bag will be good and hard. With the phones in the background he'll feel the excitement."

"Should we move the fountain into the pit?"

Dale scratched his second and third chins then looked out the window toward the Atlantic. "No, no I like the phones as a more distant but constant sound from the other room."

Randy nodded his head in agreement. These investors had hired a private, independent lab to check out the viability of their product. It had cost Randy ten percent of the potential profit but a scientist from the lab had certified the product. Now all the investor wanted was to see it in action.

Finally they were ready. He looked at his knock-off Cartier watch. One fifty-five. If this guy Golden was a real businessman he'd be here any minute. He looked over at Dale and noticed a line of sweat trickling down the side of his face, pasting his stringy hair to his skin. "Jesus, Dale, what's with you?" He reached over and wiped at the perspiration with his bare hand.

"Sorry, guess I'm a little nervous is all."

"Get into the washroom and clean up. This whole deal is based on perception and the perception that you're a sweaty little pig won't help."

Without a word Dale scurried off to the restroom. Randy called after him. "Don't forget to turn on the accent a little when he gets here. He'll feel more secure thinking we're rednecks."

Dale nodded as he disappeared into the small but plush restroom.

As the bathroom door closed, the front door opened and a man in his late fifties with the look of a gambler who liked to eat and drink stood in the doorway like he had to be escorted in. Fucking New Yorkers.

Randy smiled and stepped toward the man who was an inch taller than him and a foot wider. "Mr. Golden, please come on in." Randy offered his hand. He could see Golden's eyes take in the office and the view.

Golden had a grip like a man used to working slot machines. "You guys spend a lot on office space."

Randy was taken aback and considered several responses. "Some of our clients expect a certain feel to the place."

"Thirty-two years in the garment industry and I learned to spend money on my house not my office."

"That's exactly why we're hoping you'll be interested in our business plan."

The big man in a casual peach-colored shirt looked over the entry room with its vista and the photographs of animals his grandchildren would never get to see and said, "This is pretty quiet for a place of business."

Randy let his eyes dart to his "almost Cartier" and see it was still two minutes to two. Before he could say anything he heard the first phone ring in the trading pit, two rooms away. Then the next phone and the next. Randy let out a quick nervous laugh and looked up at his fish that suddenly didn't seem so fish-like.

Randy said, "Here, let me show you around." He took a few steps toward the main room when Dale popped out of the bathroom, adjusting his shirt like it was stuck on that matte of chest hair that often got him confused for an otter at the beach.

"Mr. Golden, this here is my associate, Dale Timmons." He looked at his partner and was disappointed to see that not only had he failed to stop his serious perspiration, he now looked disheveled like he had just gotten out of bed. He wanted to project a slight backwoods impression to this man who had made a fortune selling truck loads of fabric and leather, but Dale had taken it a step too far. What had gotten into this tubby little turd?

Dale stuck out his hand and said, "Pleased to finally meet you, sir."

Golden looked apprehensive to take the smaller man's porcine hand. Dale's thin comb-over still splayed out in several directions as he smiled and pumped their investor's hand like a politician.

Randy led them through the entire office, savoring the look of the three young men and one woman answering their endlessly ringing phones. Two desks sat empty to give the impression of a larger staff.

They paused at the door to Randy's office. He wanted the older man to get a glimpse of the view he commanded and of his shelf of business books. Now, after seeing him in person, Randy wondered if this throwback businessman had any idea who Jack Welsh was or if he had ever seen any of these titles. He had impressed Randy as a guy who'd been successful through hard work and breaking balls. That's why southerners had such a hard time in the cut-throat corporate climate.

"Shall we talk in here?"

Golden immediately shook his head. "You said I could see a demo." He stopped mid-thought and gave Dale a look that said, "Back out of my space," then continued. "You led me to believe there was a demo here. We don't have to go out in this godforsaken humidity to see it, do we?"

"No sir," said Randy, inching his way back toward the fountain and bumping Dale back physically so he had a few feet to himself. "Right this way." He turned to his partner and said, "Dale, get a couple of the bags to show Mr. Golden."

Golden watched the tubby partner hustle into the smaller office then said, "If it weren't for Verge Labs certifying this shit I'd never believe it."

Randy knew he had him. "This works and besides, the big money is in the real estate. Either way we're profitable. Very profitable. If it'll make you feel better you can just ignore our 'bag of land' product and still get involved in the condo sales. Or you can do both. No pressure here." He smiled at his large fish as he listened to the phones and knew the old man heard them too. No, no pressure here. Not unless you want to miss a chance to make a fortune.

Golden said, "I'd like to see the demo before I decide."

As if on cue, and it actually was on cue, Dale came back with two burlap bags a little bigger than a shoebox each. They weighed about twelve pounds apiece.

Randy smiled as he took a bag and hefted it in his right hand. "Here you go." He handed it to Golden, who also felt its weight. Then Randy added, "Feels like gold to me."

Golden held the bag upright and tugged at the banded cord that held it shut. The opening loosened and he peered inside.

Randy said, "Go ahead, you can touch it. That's the beauty of it: the ingredients are all natural. That's what'll keep the tree huggers quiet."

Golden reached in and pulled out a handful of the bag's contents then worked it through his thick fingers like sand at the beach. Finally he said, "This shit will work?"

Randy nodded. He knew this fish was hooked. Now he could land him easy. The mixture of sawdust, shaved plastic, light cement and actual beach sand looked perfect.

He and some of his "redneck" buddies had talked up the idea of a way to claim some of the Everglades once the right mix was in the Florida legislature. Randy didn't know of a better group than they had right now. These money hungry morons were in the news every day for one ethical lapse or another. Reasonable growth control was lower on their list of concerns than pregnant pigs. Literally. They had passed a law to protect pregnant pigs but the land use policy of the state was a shambles. Developers controlled every thing and no one seemed to care except the dwindling number of Florida natives. Randy saw himself as a defender of the frontier. He saw no reason why a defender couldn't get rich. Shit, he'd be a hero in a lot of people's books.

The actual vote of the legislature wasn't important. Just the perception of what they would do. At least to make the plan sound plausible. Shit, if offshore drilling and giant bio-research facilities were okay, then a few thirty-story condos in a swamp wouldn't raise any questions. Besides, he just had to sell the idea, not implement it.

Golden said, "Let me see what happens when this concoction expands. You said that water activates it."

"That's correct." Randy smiled, using the one his first boss taught him. The smile that made his eyes twinkle. "We can use this little fountain." He led the older man over to a basin, which had a small stream of water that projected over three coral-like rocks. Randy made a show out of setting the bag in the water and soaking it well then shoved the nozzle of the spray insulation can into the front of the bag. Golden never stepped closer than a few feet. For once he wasn't upset Dale was crowding them so bad. The little doofus made it hard for the man to come too close.

Randy used one finger to press the hidden can of insulation and felt the foam start to inflate into the bag. It became rigid in less than three seconds. If it worked right, the sand and sawdust mixture would be stuck to the outside of the foam in the front of the bag and look like it just expanded. It just had to look good this one time. The investment was for large-scale production. By the time this old fart figured out there was a problem, they'd be in bankruptcy and apologizing that things didn't work out.

He faced Golden and smiled. Playing with the bag he said, "Takes a minute but it firms right up." He handed the bag to Golden who squeezed it and then, with out asking permission, opened it to examine the inside.

Randy smiled, thinking it couldn't have gone more perfectly.

Dale squeezed in next to them, radiating a body odor that went with that fountain of perspiration he'd been leaking all morning.

Golden looked hard at Dale until he took a step back. Then he turned to Randy without any expression, the bag still in his hand.

Randy's heart started to pump faster and, for the first time, realized he was dealing with a man who had been in different businesses for the past forty years. A man used to scams and angles. He was the type of man who had developed Florida in the first place, displacing species and causing housing to soar so locals had to move. Randy felt certain their plan had been discovered.

Then Golden smiled.

Was it a smile of appreciation or a predator who had caught his prey?

The older man's face softened and he said, "The lab says this will hold as a foundation. What about condos?"

"We need more testing. That's what this round of capitol will finance."

"How many investors so far?"

"We intend to raise ten million. We'll base the investment on a percentage of the capitol." Randy studied the man's face. He was hard to read but he didn't seem wary. Maybe this was working out. Maybe he was about to reel in the big fish.

After another thirty seconds of studying the bag and considering things, Golden turned his attention to the six-foot-tall posters of the artist's rendition of "The Preserve."

The older man turned his large frame to study the layout.

Randy said, "Each tower is self sufficient with a pool and amenties. They are all named after a native Florida plant or animal. The Panther is the first one. The Key Deer and Alligator will go up next, followed by the Sawgrass, the Manatee, and the Palmetto."

Golden nodded and said, "I like that. Sounds like a fitting tribute. Will interest older people in Connecticut and Massachusetts too."

"We intend to advertise in the *New York Times*, *Boston Globe* and *Hartford Currant* to start." He was pleased he was able to pluck those names right out of the air with no notice. He was born for this kind of work.

Golden asked, "How many units total?"

Randy smiled. He had him. He stepped over to the glossy poster showing six stylish condos rising on the edge of the vast Everglades. Palm trees scattered around the pools at the base of each tower and deer feeding near the closest tower. Randy said, "Six towers with twenty eight floors and two penthouses. " He pretended to do some rough calculations in his head and then said, "Five hundred and sixty units with twelve premiums that take an entire floor."

"What will those go for?"

"Two million apiece to start."

Golden nodded and then stepped to the bay window to stare out at the Atlantic. Randy gave him some space and remained at the poster display. Dale looked torn about whom to crowd. He stayed at the posters.

Randy winked at his partner. He had to admit he was a little nervous too. This businessman from New York, the center of all smart people according to them, seemed to have taken his bait and he had a lot of room to negotiate. He could throw in a condo since they'd never even be built. He almost chuckled when he thought how he often heard New Yorkers refer to South Florida like it was a foreign country. They called it an "emerging market." Did they not expect that some of the indigenous people of this emerging market wouldn't be smart enough to attract capitol on such a far-fetched scheme? One thing Randy knew for sure was that if you offered to make someone rich, or at least richer, greed clouded judgment, experience, and ethics. He'd seen it over and over.

Now Gerald Golden of Manhattan turned and listened to the phones still ringing off the hook. He smiled and said, "Would I be the first investor?"

This was a hard question. Say he was and he might get worried about why no one was risking money yet. Say he wasn't and he might not like being behind the curve. Randy risked the more conservative approach. "We already have several major investors but there is room for several more."

Golden nodded and said, "I'm in."

Randy let out his breath and stepped across the room to shake hands. Dale trailed like he was on a tether.

Golden said, "Let me do some juggling and move some cash, then I'll have a million transferred into your business account after we sign the contract."

"I have a standard contract if you'd like to see it."

"My lawyer has to look it over."

Randy froze. A fucking lawyer. He might see a chance to make points and gouge Golden at the same time by doing some independent research and recommending against the investment. Randy tried to think of something. Some high-pressure tactic to move it along when Golden offered, "He just looks at the contract—he has no sense for business. Should only take a day or two. By Friday we can be partners."

Randy considered this as he smiled, hiding his fear. Then he noticed that all at once the phones stopped ringing. He checked his watch absently. Two thirty. Shit, he should've sprung an extra thirty bucks to make the calls keep coming. His mind started to race as he considered what Golden had said, how close to a deal they were, the phone issue, and fucking Dale breathing on his neck. Fuck!

He took a breath, cleared his head, elbowed Dale and said, "No problem, Mr. Golden, whatever you want. We have others coming in during the week so we're in good shape." It was a ground ball. Just something for the old guy to think about. If he didn't act, someone might beat him to this easy money.

Golden nodded and said, "Good, we'll get this show on the road." He turned toward the door.

Randy followed, then stepped ahead to help him ease outside. He needed a few minutes to recharge and gather his wits. These types of sales were hard. Cars were easy. At least you had a product. This was harder when the product was just dreams of wealth.

They paused at the door and shook hands with Dale right between them. They both looked at the chubby, sweaty, smelly stockbroker.

Randy turned the knob and opened the door, saying, "This was a real pleasure, Mr. Golden." Then he froze as he saw three men in casual clothes standing directly in front of the door in the hallway.

Randy said, "Can I help you?"

The tallest one in the front calmly held out his hand and let his wallet fall open to reveal a badge and Ft. Lauderdale police identification. "Randy Hubbard?"

Randy felt his face flush. "Yeah."

"I'm Tom Lester, Fort Lauderdale PD. These gentlemen are with the Defense Investigative Service. We need to talk."

"About?"

"About Computer Parts International."

Randy swallowed, thinking about his bust-out that had financed his lifestyle and this venture. "What about it?"

"Were you the original owner?"

"The president was . . ."

The man stepped inside. "Cut the shit. We know who's who and what you're doing here."

Randy was afraid to look at Golden. He knew this deal was done.

"Look, you have no evidence on this or any other company. Now I'm gonna ask you to get your ass out of here so I can go back to work. Unless you have something that might convince me I should talk to you."

The Lauderdale cop smiled.

That unnerved Randy but he stayed tough.

The cop reached across Randy to Dale who was shaking at the encounter. The cop grabbed a handful of Dale's shirt and yanked it up, revealing an electronic device, wire, and a tiny microphone taped onto his chest. Patches of his thick hair had been crudely shaved away.

Randy thought he might vomit.

Golden said, "I got no part of this," and started to walk away.

The Lauderdale cop said, "There's a man from the SEC interested in speaking with you, Mr. Golden. We'll escort you down to the little office he's waiting in." The cop turned his attention back to Randy. "You have thirty seconds to decide if you're on the bus or under it."

Randy looked at Dale who shrugged, fighting back tears and saying, "They were going to take my Series 63 license."

Randy looked back at the cop, who was now smiling broadly, and said, "You don't understand, I'm trying to save the state."

The cop nodded. "So am I."

A TAMPA MAN

BY ALICE JACKSON

Police Detective Dan Hawkins imagined the bulging veins in Captain Johnny Casano's neck comprised a roadmap. The blueish outline headed southwest from the older man's fleshy earlobes, then made a sharp turn due south before disappearing beneath the loosened knot of his necktie. Hawkins visualized the lines ending at his ribcage, somewhere south of Key West. The image helped Hawkins ignore his brother-in-law's rant about the professional risk he had assumed in finagling a spot for him inside the detective division. Hawkins considered telling Casano he could have gotten the promotion on his own, but if he kept quiet, chances were good Casano would run out of steam or pass out from a lack of blood flow to the brain. Hawkins didn't want to engage him in debate. He just wanted him to shut up.

The black ceiling fan failed to cool the heat of a Florida fall pouring through the open window. Briefly, the wail of a siren from the parking lot two stories below the Tampa Police Department's Fourteenth Precinct blotted out Casano's rant.

The big man yanked off his plaid sports coat and threw it across his cluttered desk before he stooped in front of Hawkins's face and yelled, "You're small potatoes in this department, but the chief's heard that Bobby Kennedy may be sending his G-Men to snoop around. It's all speculatin', of course, but something like what you did could cause a lot of problems! Do you understand what I'm tellin' you here, Jughead?"

Hawkins waited a few seconds, pretending to ponder Casano's question. "I would think if the attorney general were bustin' up anything in Tampa, it would be Santos Trafficante's network."

Casano ran his hands through his greasy flat-top and wiped the Vitalis onto his trousers. "You don't understand anything, do you, boy?" he muttered.

What Hawkins understood more than anything else was the fact that he loved his wife Jeanette. Loved her enough to exchange the Florida Keys where he had grown up and the deputy sheriff's job he had adored for the life of a big city cop he hated. Loved her enough to take constant shit from this idiot.

Loved her enough to hide information about Trafficante, the reputed mob boss of Florida, from Casano.

Casano dropped into the chair next to Hawkins. "Tampa ain't Key West, ya know? Down there, you have small-town law and order. Sure, where I learned to police in Jersey we did things the same small-town way you fellows did down in Key West. But, hey, up in New York City that wouldn't have shook it. New York was the big city where they did big-city law. Now, I ain't meaning to imply that Tampa is New York, ya know, but in comparison to itty bitty Key West, it could be. Big cities do things that could result in a whole different interpretation of the facts. Are you following me here?"

Hawkins clenched his teeth. "Johnny, if I'd known Mort Goldstein was your source I'd never have gone to his place without telling ya. I told you that. I told you several times."

Casano sighed, whipped out a white hankerchief to wipe the sweat from his face, then carefully refolded it. "Danny Boy, Mort told you, didn't he?

When you and that big galoot buddy of yours from Key West waltzed in? Before the guns blazed? He mentioned my name, didn't he?"

"No, he didn't. There wasn't time. It all happened so fast, Johnny. We didn't have no conversation with Mort, ya know. He pulled a gun on us the minute we walked through the door. If we hadn't shot 'em, he would've killed one or both of us. I told ya it was self-defense for me and Tom. Either shoot him or get killed, pure and simple. Ain't nothing small town 'bout that."

Casano's nostrils flared like he was about to rev up for more ranting and raving, but instead, he folded his arms, closed his eyes and leaned his head back against the wall, looking for all the world like he was napping. Several minutes passed before he leaned forward and slapped his hands. "This may not be as bad as I had previously anticipated. If Mort didn't say nothing about me or the fact that he was my snitch, then it all may just be so much water under the bridge."

Surprised by Casano's change of mood, Hawkins waited for the other shoe to drop.

Casano rubbed his callused hands together. "In fact, Danny Boy, this may have actually created an opportunity for me and for you."

Hawkins relaxed. He might make it out of this jam okay, depending on what Casano had in mind.

"Now, I don't want you to think I'm condoning the fact that you and your friend out there in the hall blew away a gold-plated snitch of the Tampa PD without so much as a howdy do, but this thing may not be as bad as I first thought." He pulled a piece of paper from his pocket and squinted at some notes in his handwriting. "You know I got a little action on the side?"

Hawkins shrugged. "I've heard some talk. You and some other captains have a detective agency, or some such. I've heard it mentioned, but I don't ask no questions 'cause it ain't none of my business."

"Yeah, keep it quiet. Chief understands because he knows a police salary don't go far. One day when you and Jeanette have a houseful of kids, you'll be needing extra money too." Johnny picked up a paperclip from the clutter atop his desk, bent it open and cleaned his fingernails. "In fact, one day when you get to be my age, you'll be needing more money and something else that's about as important."

"I'm sorry, Johnny, I don't follow you ..." Hawkins began.

Casano chuckled as he dug deeper at his nails. "A man has needs, Danny." He stopped digging to wave a finger towards his crotch. "The little woman gets older, and the guy down there needs more attention."

Hawkins felt the blood rising in his face as he stood. "I love Jeanette. If you and Viv are having problems, maybe ..."

Casano threw back his head to cackle. "We ain't got no problems, Danny. It's a fact of life that if—and with you this could be a big if—you get to be my age, you keep problems out of your marriage by taking your problems someplace else." He shook his head in exasperation as he handed the piece of paper to Hawkins. "That's my girl's name and telephone number. She's a dancer at Golden Palms. She's got a girlfriend, another dancer, whose boyfriend is threatening her. See what you can do 'bout helping her."

Hawkins looked at the paper and wondered if Betsy Snow was a real name. What kind of woman would voluntarily run around with the hulking Casano? People cheated on their wives, but Judith's sister, Viv, was a great woman. Something about this didn't smell right.

"I really don't need any extra money ..."

Casano slammed a hand down on his desk. "Who said a damned thing about extra dough? You're doing this, boy, because you're in a jam. You shot someone you shoulda let live, even if he was gonna blast your ass first! You owe me! You either do this for me, or you're gonna have to go home and tell

Jeanette you're reassigned to walkin' a beat on the streets in Ybor City!"

Jeanette had been so proud when he'd made detective, Hawkins knew there was no way he could lose his shield. The fat ape had him either way, so he might as well do the job and get it over with. "All I've gotta do is meet with the girl and see if I can help her out? That's it?"

Casano leaned back in his chair, flashing a shit-eating grin. "Well, there is one more little thing you oughta know 'bout. The guy who's threatening her. It's Julio Marchese. Ever heard of 'im?"

"The same Julio Marchese who's a city councilman?"

Casano pulled a cigarette from his coat pocket and dangled it from his lips as he flicked a lighter with one hand. "One and the same. I knew you were a bright boy, Danny. Now, git outta here!"

Outside in the hallway, Hawkins motioned for his partner, Nick Goenflo, to follow him to the break room.

"How'd it go? We still got jobs?"

Hawkins closed the break room door behind them. "We got jobs. I've just gotta do a little favor for the Fat Man."

Goenflo made a wiping motion across his forehead to indicate his relief. "Mama and the babies can still eat! You should be relieved. Why you lookin' so glum?"

"It all sounds strange," Hawkins said.

"Strange, huh? Well, not having a job would be stranger. You gonna do the favor for Fat Man or not?"

Hawkins poured a cup of coffee for Nick, then one for himself. "Yeah, I guess. What other choice do I have?"

Nick reached for the noon edition of the *Tampa Tribune* left on a nearby table. "Look at this headline, man, Kennedy is coming to Tampa!"

"Bobby Kennedy?" Hawkins thought back to what Casano had said.

"Hell, no! The president, man! President Kennedy is coming to Tampa, and there's gonna be a motorcade. Wonder if Jackie's coming with him? Remember how we joked back in Key West that she was the biggest reason to vote for JFK? Let's take the girls and go see 'em."

"Sure," Hawkins replied, "but first, I gotta go see a stripper at Golden Palms and handle that favor."

• • •

Casano's stripper squeeze had been right. The woman seated across from him was one of the prettiest Hawkins had ever seen. Her brunette hair was pulled up into a beehive beneath an equally dark scarf, and both matched her dark eyes. Her only flaws were the black and blue bruises that ringed one eye and skipped across her cheeks, confirming that her boyfriend had carried out his threats.

A rumba tune from the jukebox competed with the Spanish chatter that filled the eatery. Smoke from cigarettes and cigars mingled with the spicy odor of sausage and peppers as they sizzled on the grill. Outside, street vendors hawked Cuban sandwiches, fresh flowers, and fruit stacked atop colorful carts lining the main avenue. Lunchtime in Ybor City, the biggest Cuban community outside Havana, meant at least a two-hour break.

Judith Wright had insisted on meeting Hawkins here. For decades, Ybor City had attracted cigar makers from South America and the Caribbean to fuel the dying art of cigar rolling. The Cuban revolution daily added to the Tampa population, gradually turning South Florida into a bilingual city. Since he'd arrived ten minutes earlier, she hadn't spoken a word, and he wondered if maybe her English was limited. He checked his watch. In fifteen minutes his new Chevy sedan would be fair game for the meter maid. It was time for answers.

"Exactly what can I do to help you?" he asked.

"How long have you worked with the Tampa police, Detective Hawkins?" Her eyes flitted from diner to diner. She pulled a cigarette from her purse and followed it with a lighter.

"Three years, ma'am. Before that, I worked Key West."

Her eyes rested on him as she dragged at the cigarette, setting its tip aglow. "Do you really know Tampa, Detective? I mean, do you know the players?"

Hawkins was tired. He was doing this only to make Casano happy. He really didn't want the third degree from this dame. He looked at his watch. "I don't have much time, Judith. Why don't we just stop beating around the bush and get on with what you need?"

She nodded towards a booth in the back where a swarthy man with greasy gray hair sat staring at them as if hypnotized. "Tell me if you know that man, Detective Hawkins."

Hawkins leaned out of the booth to get a better look before turning back to Judith, who had a broad smile plastered across her face. "No, I don't, and I really don't see what this has to do …"

Judith stubbed out her cigarette, gathered her purse and stood.

Hawkins grabbed her wrist. "Hey, you were the one who wanted to meet with someone! What's going on here?"

Judith yanked her hand from his grasp. "The problem, Detective Hawkins, is you clearly don't see what's going on."

She threw back her shoulders and walked to the booth where the man sat. The two appeared to exchange pleasantries before Judith slipped into the seat across from him, and he pulled out a package of smokes to offer her one.

Confused and irritated, Hawkins ripped several bills from his pocket and threw them on the table. He'd done his favor for Casano, and no doubt Fat Man was laughing right now over a wild goose chase with a crazy dame.

• • •

The pink princess phone's shrill ring woke Jeanette first. She mumbled a few words as she switched on a lamp, then punched him with the receiver. "It's for you. A woman. She's crying," she muttered.

Hawkins sat up in a hurry and grabbed the phone. Racking sobs greeted him. "Who is this?" Hawkins demanded.

The sobs slowed to sniffles. "It's me. Judith. I'm sorry, but I need to talk. Can we meet?"

Hawkins looked at the clock. It was almost 3 a.m. "Talk or play riddles again?"

Judith's sobbing increased.

Jeanette glared at him, then rolled her eyes before turning her back and moving to the far side of the bed.

"Look, it's late. My wife is angry. She gets upset when women call me in the middle of the night. Cut the games." Hawkins wanted Jeanette to know this woman wasn't a friend.

"I couldn't talk to you at the diner. That man you didn't know, he's part of my problem. He's following me. He's a very dangerous man. I had to lie to him. I told him I was meeting you because you were from New Orleans. I told him you were my sister's foster father."

"Do you even have a sister, Judith?"

The sniffles started again. "Yes, I do! She lives in New Orleans, too. That's why I'm here, working at Golden Palms. The money I make keeps her in a convent boarding school. She's a good kid. She won't end up like me." The sobs returned.

Hawkins glanced at his wife. Jeanette was cooling off, but she wasn't going to like his going out to meet a crying woman one bit. Just another reason to curse his fat ass brother-in-law.

"You know the coffee joint near the bridge to Davis Island?"

"The Hot Pot?"

"That's the one. Meet me there in twenty minutes." Hawkins stood. "You've got fifteen minutes to tell me what's wrong."

Hawkins handed the phone back to a stony-faced Jeanette. "Hon, I gotta go, okay?"

Jeanette remained silent and still as Hawkins dressed and closed the bedroom door softly as he left.

• • •

Davis Island was one of Tampa's wealthiest neighborhoods, a place where only really old money settled. The Hot Pot on Breland Avenue was where the island's servants stopped to eat before and after work. It was one of the few Tampa eateries not connected to Trafficante's network.

Judith sat in a worn booth in the back. Hawkins dropped onto the cracked and taped plastic seat opposite her, took off his snap-brim hat and set it aside.

Judith's face was even more bruised than when he'd last seen her. Hawkins looked at his watch. "Talk, Judith. Time's running out."

She nervously stirred her coffee. "I need someone I can trust. I asked Betsy to help me, and she talked to her boyfriend. I guess he's the one who sent you."

Hawkins sighed. This was going to take a long time. "I'm here. Talk."

She looked around the restaurant. They were alone, except for a young punk in a leather jacket who was more interested in combing his hair in the reflection of the front window than what they were discussing.

"That man you saw in the restaurant, the one you didn't know?"

Hawkins nodded.

"He works for Santos Trafficante. You know him?"

Hawkins looked into the bruised eyes. "Judith, every cop in Tampa knows Trafficante. What's this about?"

"Do you know Julio Marchese?"

"Your boyfriend?"

A smile began on her lips, then died. She looked up at him. "Girls like me don't have boyfriends, Detective Hawkins."

Hawkins shrugged. "Whatever. I take it Marchese laid the beating on you."

Tears filled her eyes, and she dabbed at them with a tissue. "The councilman and I had a disagreement. That's why I needed someone to talk to. Marchese knows about something that's gonna happen. Something bad. Next week. I hoped that maybe if I told the right person, they could stop it. If Marchese finds out I'm talking, he'll kill me. He'll kill anybody who knows me."

"Are you going to tell me what this thing is, Judith? I'm waiting."

The waitress returned to refill Judith's coffee and ask Hawkins if he wanted a cup. Judith turned her face to the joint's window, hiding her tears.

As the waitress left, she grabbed another tissue from her purse before the tears flowed again. She looked around for anyone who might overhear her, then whispered, "They're gonna kill the president. He's coming to Tampa next week. Trafficante is gonna have him shot!"

• • •

Hawkins leaned against the bridge's railing and flicked his half-smoked cigarette into the murky waters of Tampa Bay. Daylight was still a good hour away, and fog hung low along the walkway.

"Johnny Casano pay you enough money to toss away your smokes like that?" The voice belonged to a trench-coated man, his dark collar buttoned up to ward off the chill. His expensive fedora cast a shadow across his face, but Hawkins didn't need to see his features. He knew this man.

"Pays me more than you do," Hawkins replied, reaching into his coat for another smoke. He offered one to the man, who refused it.

"So they think they're going to kill Kennedy," the man whispered.

Hawkins pushed his snap-brim back on his forehead. Twenty-four hours had passed since Judith had laid everything out to him. "What did Washington say?"

"You should lay low. Pick up what information you can. Washington is handling everything else."

"Will the president cancel his trip?"

"Hard to say. But you don't need to worry about that. The big question now is whether or not things are too hot to keep you on the inside. You can walk away right now," the man said.

As Hawkins turned to leave, the man laid a hand on his arm. "You sorry you ever signed on with us? You could have stayed down in the Keys."

Hawkins hesitated, thinking about Jeanette and how little she knew about his work. Worse yet, what it would do to them if Casano was involved. "I'll finish what I came here to do. I'm a cop," he told the man before walking off into the fog.

• • •

A week later, every available law enforcement officer in the Tampa area was pulled in for added security for the Kennedy visit. Before daybreak, Hawkins and Casano had set up a surveillance post inside the storage area atop a five-story warehouse that overlooked downtown Tampa. Casano had tried repeatedly to get rid of Hawkins. First, Fat Boy had ordered coffee, then it was doughnuts. The last excuse had been an urgent need to phone the chief's office. Hawkins expected Casano to demand a urinal next. The motorcade was due soon.

The dark warehouse reeked of dust and decay from hundreds of boxes filled with outdated records for the City of Tampa. The smoke from one of Casano's cigars mixed with the smell from the greasy breakfast he'd fetched from the corner grocery hours ago.

Hawkins resented his assignment, especially since it paired him with his slimy brother-in-law and kept him away from the action. Every muscle in his body was tense. He wanted to be out on the street where he could do some good. Where he might have a chance to help the FBI save President Kennedy. Worse yet, he still couldn't figure out why the FBI had permitted Kennedy to come to Tampa when they knew Santos Trafficante had concocted a plan to kill him—especially since the FBI hadn't shut Trafficante's intentions down. Still, Kennedy was the president, and while he liked to stare down every adversary, it was plain crazy to bait 'em like this.

In the street below, office workers jostled with school children and housewives on the sidewalks. Several members of the John Birch Society carried posters pleading for Kennedy's impeachment. A small group of Negroes stood far behind the crowd, carefully avoiding the whites as they sought space along the curb.

Casano, sweating profusely, mopped his face with his ever-present handkerchief and looked at the growing crowd.

"There woulda been more people if Jackie hadda come with him," Casano declared. He used old Army binoculars to survey the street north and south. The muffled sound of snare drums wafted up through the huge open window. "They can't be far away."

Casano turned from the window to face Hawkins squarely. "You and I gotta have a talk here."

Hawkins stepped beside Casano where he could get a good view of the president out the window. "So, talk," Hawkins replied.

The snick of a revolver froze Hawkins.

"Don't move and put both ya hands behind your back," Casano instructed. He backed several steps away and kicked some old boxes aside. Out of the corner of his eye, Hawkins saw him pick up a walkie-talkie. Casano keyed it and began to talk.

"Unit Two. This is Three. You copy?"

A raspy voice answered over static. "Yeah, we got him in our sights. If he moves, he's gonna be dead … just like Kennedy."

Casano sat the walkie-talkie down so he could wipe the rivlets of sweat from his fat jowls. "You hear that, bright boy? Don't move a muscle. We've got a rifleman trained right at ya."

Hawkins's eyes scanned the buildings across the street. He saw no one. "What're you up to, Johnny?"

Casano shifted his revolver to his left hand, then kicked boxes aside to pull something out into the open.

"Turn around," Casano ordered.

Hawkins turned slowly, his eyes opening wide at the sight of a rifle, its scope glinting in the noonday sun that shone through the bare windows.

"What in the hell are you doing?" Hawkins demanded.

"I'm not doing anything. You are," Casano said. Using his foot, he shoved the rifle across the floor, keeping the revolver trained on Hawkin's head.

"You're gonna pick up that rifle very slowly. No funny business, ya hear? There's a guy in a window of the building across the street with you in his gunsights. You make a wrong move, and your head's gonna explode like a watermelon," Casano said.

On the street below, the band began playing "Hail to the Chief," and Hawkins estimated the motorcade was about a block away. "I still don't understand what you want me to do."

A sick grin spread across Casano's jowls. "Why, Danny Boy, you're gonna make Santos Trafficante very happy. You're gonna kill his biggest enemy. You're gonna make a name for yourself today. You're gonna kill Kennedy."

"Like hell I am! Are you crazy? I knew you were dirty. I didn't know you were stupid too!" Hawkins hissed.

"Stupid? That would be you, Danny Boy. You think you can waltz into my department and snitch on me? It don't matter none if you're my brother-in-law. You're gonna do this for Mr. Santos. Then, I'm gonna take care of you. Also for Mr. Santos."

Anger rose like bile in Hawkins's throat. "What makes you think I'm gonna be stupid enough to do this?"

"You love Jeanette, don't ya?"

Instinctively, Hawkins tensed, preparing to jump Casano, but the sound of the gun's hammer froze him.

Casano picked up the walkie-talkie. "You got that package all wrapped up for me?"

Static proceeded the answer. "The blonde package? Yeah, we got it right here."

Casano's lips barely moved as he replied. "Make the package talk so my boy can hear it."

"Dan, help me …" was all that followed, but it was enough for Hawkins to recognize the woman's voice. He stepped towards Casano.

"Move another inch, and both you and your lovely wife will die," Casano warned. "Do what I'm tellin' ya, and Jeanette lives. You're gonna die either way, but mess it up, and you both die!"

"You stupid bastard. Life would have been easier if ya'd been honest," Hawkins whispered.

Casano chuckled. "Why, so I could get a low-budget retirement, then drop dead with a heart attack? I like Mr. Santos's retirement plan better."

The music ceased, signaling the drumsmen to return to the muffled beats. The cheers from the crowd told Hawkins the president would be passing beneath the open window within seconds.

"Pick up the rifle now, or I blow your head off and my friend does the same to Jeanette!" Casano shouted above the roar pouring through the window.

Suddenly, Hawkins dropped and rolled, his right hand connecting with the rifle in a blur. The first shot's crack was drowned out by the screams and music from the street. The second shot was muffled, plowing into tissue and bone.

Casano fell face up on the wooden floor, the blood from the fatal bullet wound to his brain mixing with his sweat.

Hawkins moved to the window just in time to see the back of Kennedy's Lincoln, its bullet-proof top removed, moving south. The young president continued to wave to the crowd even as the car's driver picked up speed.

"Unit Three, you there?" came frantically from Casano's walkie-talkie. "Johnny, what happened? Come in!"

• • •

"You did good work, Dan, but we just can't help you on this one." The man in the trenchcoat clung to the shadows.

They stood at the same railing where they had met earlier. The man smiled, trying to ease the distaste of the message he was delivering. "I know you hoped this would get you a job with us, but the director says you aren't ready yet. He swears if you do this last job for us, then you get what you want."

Hawkins stared at the Sunshine Bridge that stretched across Tampa Bay. "My wife left me. You know that? Said she couldn't live with the man who killed her brother-in-law, even if he was trash. Plus, she couldn't understand why I wouldn't do what Casano wanted if I really believed they'd kill her."

"I wondered about that myself, Danny."

Hawkins sighed. "I woulda known my own wife's voice no matter what. She ain't got a New Orleans accent." Hawkins turned to look at the man's face. "Has Judith turned up anywhere yet?"

"Nothing yet, but we'll keep looking," he said. "Look, Danny, you caught a bad break on this one. You know the Bureau can't let it out that someone came that close to killing the president of the United States. Besides, do you know how hard it was to convince the chief to go along on the accidental shooting story on Casano? Hell, he wanted to charge you with manslaughter!"

"Yeah, the chief's a real straight shooter, ain't he?" Hawkins prepared to leave. "What do you want me to do now? What's the next carrot ya gonna dangle in front of my nose?"

"The director wants you in Dallas," the man replied, pulling out a paper. "I don't know what's going on, but you arrive on November 21. It's all hush-hush. But, Danny, Mr. Hoover himself insisted on nobody but you for this job. You gotta take it."

IFFY

BY JOHN DUFRESNE

You already know the *what* pretty much. Now I'm going to tell you the true *why* and *how* of what I've done. It's a compound of things that led to it. I murdered those seven or eight beautiful children. They had their whole brilliant lives ahead of them, and I mowed them down in cold blood. Everything that happened happened on a whim, and that's what I liked about it. Wrong place, wrong time for the children. Right place, right time for me, you could say. It's all a matter of your point of view as to how you see a thing. I had no hope, you understand. I had no future, no family, no job, and no friends. (I know people, but I don't hang.) My pockets were empty; my heart was hollow. I had nothing to give. The only thing I have in this life now is to take. And that's what I did. I took. It's not fair that I did, but life isn't fair, and that's a lesson we all learned today. When a man loses everything, he is free to do anything.

The killings today got started back in '04 when my wife Patti left me and took the kids to her parents' home over in Lakeland. And just like that I lost my babies and my in-laws, who treated me like a son, and who I cared about more than I ever cared about her, to be honest with you. I married her out of necessity. It didn't take Patti long to get the divorce and the new life and the kids and the house and the car and the everything else, and I got the bills and the loneliness. And then when I found myself alone in a dingy studio apartment above Bartow Dry Cleaners, I went shopping and bought a big-ass flat-screen TV and a recliner and a dog, and I bought them all with bad checks. And it didn't take the sheriff's department long to find me. I lost my job at the phosphate mine after the arrest. I wasn't paying child support. Fitzy, the little pit bull, wouldn't stop crapping and pissing on the rug, so I borrowed my uncle Ray's shitbox and drove Fitzy out to a sinkhole by Combee Settlement and dropped him in. No, I didn't. I sure thought about it, but I had cooled off by the time I reached the pit, and so I just set him loose over by Gibsonia. He chased the car for a half mile, I bet, before he tuckered out. When I got the court summons, I left Polk County and lost myself here in Broward. I sold the *Sun-Sentinel* at Sheridan and Federal, got a weekly room at the Dixiewood Motel. And I entered into what I think of as my Golden Age.

Before I could prosper, however, I had to become someone the cops were not looking for. That happened when, one sunny morning, I found a black leather wallet behind a bus-stop bench on Dania Beach Boulevard. Inside was a driver's license, a social security card, and a laminated funeral card with a cut rose on the front and the deceased's name, Alice Rose Engdahl, on the back with a poem that began "Do not stand at my grave and weep" and ended with "I am not there, I did not die." The guy was about my height, weight, and age—close enough, anyway, for government work. I was able to distress the driver's license photo sufficiently so I could present myself at the DMV and get myself a replacement with my own mug shot, and that's the day I became Elvis Engdahl.

I went by my benefactor's house on Halloween and watched him greet and treat the neighborhood children. I never got to see his actual face because he was made up as Dracula and his wife as an angel. I loitered across the street trying to be as inconspicuous as the little gray sedan in Dracula's driveway, but when you're alone, you stand out. He spotted me. The Engdahls had hung an inflatable zombie, which wasn't scaring anybody, from the scrawny black olive tree in their front yard and played spooky music from a boom box on their porch. Elvis Engdahl had a modest house, an angel of a wife, and a sweetness toward the children that I envied.

When Dracula straightened up, looked over at me again, and held my gaze, I thought it best to move along. I never took a thing from Elvis Engdahl except his name and his address. Sometimes in the middle of the night when I was wide awake in bed and staring at the ceiling, I'd imagine myself in the Engdahls' house, sitting on the sofa, sipping a beer, watching the TV with Angel, and maybe she falls asleep on my lap during the Marlins game, and I get a call on my cell phone, and it's one of my buddies from work who wants to know if I'd like to go airboating on Sunday. It's all pretty pathetic, I suppose, the fantasy, but if you have no life, you have to imagine one. Otherwise you can't sleep.

And so I became a new man with this heartbreaking new history—orphan, widow, drifter, something the ladies might find appealing—and a brand new confident attitude. Call me El. Or Double-E. Or Mr. Engdahl, if you must. When the late-night clerk at the Hess station on Federal was shot in the throat and killed during a robbery, I applied for his job. The old me would not have seized that opportunity. There weren't a lot of eager beavers lined up to apply for the vacancy. I was hired on the spot. I bought a refurbished Smith & Wesson Chief's Special and a pre-owned Kel-Tec Sub 2000 with my first paycheck at the Knife and Gun Show in Lauderdale. I was not about to become late-night victim number two. I carried the Special to work and slipped it onto the shelf below the register. "Yes, sir," I'd say. "Please don't shoot! Let me get that money out of the register for you pronto." And I'd pull out the .45 and blast the motherfucker between the eyes. On slow nights I'd make a pistol of my hand and rehearse the scene in slow motion over and over again, try to imagine every possible scenario. The way I see it, if you fail to plan, you plan to fail.

Friday was my night off. I'd stop into work, pick up my check from Stavros, cash it across the street at Pay-Day Loans, then go to Los Incas de Oro for dinner. I'd have anticucho de pollo, papas fritas, and a Cusqueña. I'd wind up on a barstool at the Wayside Inn. Friday is Naughty Night at the Wayside, meaning these models in nighties parade around serving guys crackers and cheese. The lie is that you'll be so impressed you'll buy the silky merchandise for your old lady. The truth is that guys like to look at gals in their underwear, and the place is packed. One of the models one night caught my eye. She had shoulder-length licorice black hair that she wore in bangs, Egyptian eyes, and bone white skin. I called her Cleopatra; her real name was Justine, but she went by Tina. She told me I should buy her the negligee she was wearing, and I did. And I bought her two vodka tonics. We hit it off like they do in the movies. We put on the juke box and slow-danced to a song by one of those bruised divas who's so devoted to her abusive boyfriend. Later we stopped by Discount Liquors for a bottle of ginger brandy and walked to her place—the Mr. Lucky Motel by the Circle. In the morning she told me that she believed God had sent me to rescue her.

We walked to the Coral Rose Café for breakfast. We held hands the whole way like we were teenagers or senior citizens. And we couldn't stop talking about ourselves. Of course, everything I told her was made up—the parents, Di and Eddie, killed in a tragic automobile accident when I was seventeen, the military service, the combat medal, the stillborn child, the darling wife who died of cancer, my own struggle with grief and depression. I was learning about Elvis Engdahl at the same time Tina was, and I admired what I heard about me. I felt taller all of a sudden, and wiser. I stopped using the f-word so much. Tina told me that she'd grown up on Long Island with an alcoholic father, an obsessive-compulsive mother, a brother who's now a registered sex offender, and an older sister who married a CPA, sold her soul for a summer house on Nantucket. Everyone in her family was a disappointment to everyone else. Tina, herself, dropped out of Siena College to follow her boyfriend to Florida. The less said about that parasite the better, she told me.

We ate like wolves, and we couldn't take our eyes off each other. She poured ketchup on her scrambled eggs, sprinkled salt on her grapefruit, and dripped Tabasco on her grits. She ate her toast with a knife and fork. I had seconds on the corned beef hash. She told me that modeling negligees was her hobby. She actually made her living as a prostitute. I told her those days were over now, and she squeezed my hand. She smiled, bit her lip, and wiped away a tear. We stopped by the Hess so I could show her off to Stavros and to Dawn, the morning clerk, who had had her chances with me. Later Tina and I went house-hunting and found a one-bedroom duplex on Harding Street. We moved in. New curtains, new welcome mat, a set of dishes, and a set of towels. We bought a microwave and started staying in on Friday nights. We'd watch a movie, split a six-pack, and eat Lean Cuisines, just like any happily married couple. We read newspapers and talked about where we'd like to be in five years. Me, I said I'd like to be working on a boat in the Bahamas. Anywhere but here, she said.

I opened a checking account at the Wachovia bank because I thought you said the name like "Watch over ya," like the bank was a guardian angel, but it turns out you pronounce it like "Walk over ya," like the bank's your ex-wife's attorney. Anyway, the account was my little secret. When I had enough money saved, I planned to surprise Tina with a decent car. With a car we could go places. I worked extra shifts whenever I could, and when I wasn't working, I was with Tina. On Saturdays we took a cab to the Winn-Dixie to do our food shopping for the week. On Sundays we took a bus to the beach or to the track.

Tina's little secret was she hadn't stopped turning tricks. For a while I pretended I didn't know what was going on. I ignored the evidence she hadn't the wit or the will to conceal—the foil condom wrappers in the waste basket, the twenty-dollar bills on the nightstand, the unfamiliar body odor on the sheets. When I finally said something, Tina told me she was bored sitting around all day. I told her to walk to the park, why don't you, or get a hobby. Learn how to cook, for chrissakes. Well, that set her off. She tossed an ashtray at the TV and broke the screen. She started packing her suitcase. I apologized, rocked her in my arms and scratched her back. She cried, hugged me, and said how she needed to feel useful, needed to pull her own weight, needed to contribute to the household. She agreed to look for honorable work, and it wasn't long before she landed a waitressing job at IHOP. I switched to days so we could be together at night, and everything was once again hunky-dory.

We spent many of our evenings at the Lamp Post Lounge. The Post didn't attract the dirtbags who hung out at the Wayside. We had our favorite table by the window; Bobby G., the bartender, knew just how we liked our drinks. Our home away from home. One night, the owner, Herbie Dyson, who I'd never seen before, came in and walked to our table and said to Tina,

"What did I tell you about bringing your business in here?" I was thinking I'm going to have to smash my cocktail glass into his face, but Tina held my arm and said, "This isn't business, Dyson. Elvis here is my fiancé."

Honest to God, you could have knocked me over with a feather. Tina had said the word, and I became the item—the fiancé. Suddenly, I was a man with a future and not just a parade of todays. Like they say in the Bible, the word was made flesh. I was so happy or dizzy or something that I bought the house a round. I kissed Tina, and I realized when she blushed that her words had cast a spell on her, too. Bobby G. told Herbie we were cool. Herbie looked at us and said, "I don't want to see any funny business in here."

Tina's waitress pal at the IHOP, Lourdes, told Tina the Hard Rock was hiring experienced waitresses, and Tina wanted to apply. I said, "What's wrong with IHOP, Tina? She said, These Canadian snowbirds don't tip. She said she could triple her income at the casino. But you'd be back on nights, I said. We'll never see each other. She said, Quadruple it, even. I'm trying to improve myself, Elvis." And that's when I got this roller-coaster feeling in my stomach. I saw myself left behind selling smokes to jerkoffs from the homeless shelter while she's serving cocktails to high-rollers at the poker tables. Well, she got the job. I figured to make the best of it, and I suggested we pool our money now that we're engaged. She thought she'd open her own account, thanks. I was worried. I'd seen love turn to shit overnight before. My friend Trini's wife left him for a woman. He said he should have known something was up when he came home from work one night and saw a newspaper article taped to the fridge with the headline "All Sex is Rape."

Me, I didn't get any warning. Or maybe I missed the signs. I was working eighty to ninety hours a week. Tina told me one morning that she'd met someone. And then she turned and walked out our door. Left everything she owned. Nothing I do is ever enough. When I almost reach a pinnacle at something, it's taken away. Always taken away. I know if I achieve a certain something, it will be snatched from me. So why bother? And that's about the time my toothache started, the toothache I've had for fifteen months. I found out later from Lourdes that Tina moved to Jamaica with her boyfriend Neville. She's never coming back. Never ever, she told Lourdes.

The woman I assaulted yesterday, Dorie Hansen, I met a while back at the Hess. She'd been a regular customer, lived in the neighborhood. She liked her salty snacks and Diet Pepsis. I'd always talk with her about this and that, joke around. I gained her trust, you could say. When we met, I was still with Tina, so Dorie, I suppose, didn't see me as any kind of romantic nuisance like the street vermin she was used to dealing with, who only got the one thing on their simple minds because they know that no matter how quick and indifferent the sex is, it's still the best thing that's going to happen to them all day. Then after Tina split, Dorie felt kind of bad for me. She'd listen to me whine and never say "Get over it" or "It is what it is" or "It's all good" or any of that bullshit.

And when Tina left, I have to tell you, my life went south in a New York minute. At first I didn't know what to do with myself. There's only so much time you can spend at the gun range, only so much time staring at the TV. By then I'd saved three grand, and I figured I'd take a long weekend, buy a ticket to the Bahamas, and enjoy myself. Even Dorie thought it was a good idea—be sweet to yourself, she said; you deserve it. So I went to the bank, filled out the withdrawal slip, and gave it to this little teller with a laughable emo haircut. He told me he was sorry but there was no money in my account. I said, Thatcher, there must be some mistake. Then I spoke with the bank manager, who pulled up the account records, and sure enough, the cash was gone.

She said, "When your wife closed out your joint account, we apparently asked her if you would be wanting to close out your personal account as well."

"My wife?" I asked Ms. Condon if I could take a look at her computer screen. There it was, the bad news in black and white and the copies of the two driver's licenses, Elvis's and Angel's. Only Angel's name was Marta.

"And it looks like you came in on Friday, and you closed it." Ms. Condon looked at the driver's license and then at me and then back at the license.

That son of a bitch Engdahl, the fucking thief, was trying to beat me out of $3000. I didn't see that I had any choice here. He certainly wasn't going to give me, some Joe Schmo he didn't know from Adam, the money in his account. So I set his house on fire. I didn't need to burn it down; I needed to flush him out while I stood across the street with my Chief's Special. When he ran out the door in his boxer shorts, I'd shoot the bastard, and I'd let Angel live so she could think about what a calamitous series of events she set in motion with her greedy behavior. I filled a five-gallon gas can at the Hess, rolled up a blanket from home, and walked to Engdahl's house. This was before dawn. I doused the blanket, draped it over the propane grill by the back door, threw the match, and scooted across the street. I sat at the curb between a Chevrolet and a pickup. When the propane tank ignited, it must have blown out the back of the house. The ground shook. Flames leaped over the roof. Lights came on next door. The front door flew open, and I raised my pistol, and then these two kids run out, followed by the parents, and they're all Chinese! Engdahl didn't live there anymore. The joke was on me.

After that I was on edge a lot of the time and swabbing my throbbing tooth every twenty minutes with Orajel. I found out that if I kept a cheek full of bourbon on the tooth, it worked just as well, so I hid a fifth of Fighting Cock behind the counter at work. Then one night I caught this homeless half-wit stealing an Almond Joy, and I pulled out the Special and put it in his face. He cried like a baby. I didn't want cops involved, for obvious reasons, so I let the derelict go. But he squealed to Stavros. I denied everything, of course, but there it all was on the surveillance video. I lost my job. Since then I've been living in a financial prison. I was back to selling the *Sun-Sentinel* on street corners. I had no future, just like those children I killed today have no future, only that was something they didn't know and didn't have to be tormented by.

I want you to know that I'm not a monster. I'm just like you. And I'm not crazy. People might say I don't know what I'm doing, but I don't shit myself. I don't piss my pants, do I? I know what I'm doing. And something has to be done so something like this doesn't happen again, where someone can't arrive at a point where they might be capable of slaughter. This should not happen. You should put me up against a wall and shoot me. You really should.

Then I ran into Dorie at Los Incos de Oro. She was eating veal hearts and yuca. She was like my only friend in the world. She said she'd heard about the unfortunate business at the Hess. I said, "No good deed goes unpunished."

Dorie likes taking walks, so I started going along. We'd walk to the beach, stroll the Broadwalk and stare at all the overweight French-Canadians in their bikinis and Speedos. I began to imagine the two of us together. Dorie isn't much to look at, but she's sweet and genuine, and that counts for something. Then I began to imagine us having sex. I hadn't been with a woman in a while. I pictured her naked and hot, glazed and delicious. I figured I had to get her alone, away from the crowds and into the mood. Get a little lubrication in her maybe. I bought some peppermint schnapps. Then I suggested we take an evening stroll, maybe by the Dania Beach pier where it's quiet, and we can talk. When she agreed, I figured she'd done the addition and knew what was up.

So we're on our backs in the sand by the lifeguard shack, staring up at the stars, and I was thinking *Can I do this?*, and Dorie said she didn't understand how anyone could see a bull or a crab or anything else up there in all that confusion. I touched her arm. She said, "What are you doing? I turned on my side and slid my arm across her waist. She said, What do you think you're doing? I put my hand on her shoulder and my leg over her legs. Elvis, she said, don't!" I moved my hand over her stomach and down there to Yeehaw Junction, and she slapped me. I guess I went into a kind of shock. I was on top of her, but it didn't feel good like I wanted it to. Dorie fought back, and I was impressed with her spirit. I like a woman who fights back, who thinks she's got something valuable to protect. It angers me when they don't put up a fight. That just proves they're whores. I only slapped her once. It wasn't *violent* violent. I saw the horror on her face, though, and it . . . it just broke me. So anyway, I couldn't keep it up, so to speak. Her will won out. No release, no penetration. I realized that this would have gone better with a perfect stranger. I cared about Dorie, and that was the wrench in the works.

After the incident, after I apologized, I took a drink of schnapps, and we talked, and I thought things weren't that bad—she wasn't hysterical or anything, but I was guilty as hell, and I said, "You got a right if you feel you need to, to, you know, call the cops or whatever, because I remembered the three or four minutes of horror she went through. I told her to think of a punishment for me—anything, I said, and I'll do it. I'll be your slave if you want. You want someone hurt, I'll hurt them. You can hit me in the head with a tire iron. I thought she might smile at that idea, but she was trembling and crying and nodding her head and reassuring me that she'd be okay, but she sounded iffy. Any kind of punishment system you devise, I told her, I'll go through with it." I mean she did endure those few minutes of hell because of me. I left her there because she wanted to be alone. To collect herself. I was hoping she wouldn't call the cops, but apparently she did because when I got to the corner of Harding and Twentieth, I saw the flashing lights of the police cruisers parked in front of my house. I don't blame Dorie for what would happen next.

I waited until I saw the cops leave. And then I waited some more. I crept through a few backyards and scaled a couple of fences and snuck into my place through the back door. I grabbed my backpack and sleeping bag. I was in and out in under a minute. This is what I mean about being prepared. I had my firearms, a box of ammo, a flashlight, waterproof matches, and a first-aid kit in the backpack. I knew the house of cards was crumbling down, and I needed to sit somewhere calmly and think. I went to Arby's and got a coffee. I couldn't eat anything what with the constant toothaching.

After what I did to Dorie, I knew I'd be labeled a sex offender, and that would scotch things with my kids if I ever got the desire to see them again, which I figured was a good possibility. I knew when the cops picked me up, I wouldn't be Elvis Engdahl anymore. I'd just be me, derelict dad, fugitive from justice, check bouncer, assault-and-batterer. I felt like a loser, and I was tired. I walked to the beach and fixed myself a little camping area in a thicket of sea grapes. There's feral cats in there, possums, raccoons, and at least a half-dozen people from what I could tell. There's like a whole little community living out of sight right under everyone's nose. Time was running out for me. What future did I have? I just didn't have a future. And I suddenly knew I'd never be leaving this beach, and that knowledge was a great relief. And then I understood what I had to do.

I thought at first about mowing down as many people as I could. I'd wait till noon or so when the beach crowded up with spring breakers, climb the lifeguard shack, dispatch the lifeguard, and then turn the Sub 2000 loose on the swimmers and sunbathers. Then I'd wait for the cops to show up and start picking them off one by one until I ran out of bullets, and then the cops would take me out. I wasn't going to kill myself. Suicide is spineless. My fantasy was beginning to look like a bad mall movie where all the wild but appealing teenagers get slaughtered by the psychopath. I got a better idea.

I set up on the edge of the sea grapes. I couldn't be seen, but I had a clear view of about twenty yards of beach. I lay on my stomach with my weapon at the ready. Whoever entered my line of sight would be punished. Simple as that. It would be completely random. I would not choose—God would, or Fate would. I'm nearsighted, but I'm a crack shot. I might have had a career in paintball, but Patti convinced me I sucked at it, and I was pussy enough in those days to believe her, and that's another reason why I hate that twat. Pardon my French. I waited. The sun came up. I heard laughter and then voices— a man and a woman—approaching, and then silence. I may have fallen asleep. Before I knew it, the shadows of the coconut palms had shortened.

And then out of nowhere come these eight kids. I pegged them for highschool age. Four lanky boys, all wearing wrap-around shades, and four adorable girls with cute little figures in these scanty bikinis. They didn't look like anyone I'd ever met in my life. These young people today, they aren't like us. They're like some beautiful alien life-form. The boys tossed a football to one another while the girls arranged blankets, beach bags, and towels. Would you believe it?—I had to pee. I wondered if I should give them time to spray on the sunscreen and settle in. That way I could see how they coupled up. I sized up the boys. I was a tad concerned about the hero factor. Sometimes you'll run into some Mighty Mouse who wants to save the day. I guessed that the tallest of the boys, the boy with the barbwire tattoo around his bicep and zinc oxide on his nose might like to think of himself as a super hero, so he was going down first. I stuffed in my earplugs. I had the Special by my right elbow. I aimed the Sub at the boy's chest and fired. His knees buckled, and he dropped. One girl screamed and yelled his name. "Eric," I think she said. I shot her. The others all dove to the sand and rolled themselves into balls with their hands over their heads. Six little pillbugs. I started spraying prey. Pop! Pop! Pop! I have to say it was like shooting fish in a barrel. One of the boys got up and ran. I shot him and then fired at the only person still moving, the girl in the teal bikini, who was crying now and crawling toward the water and reaching out like the ocean was going to save her. Her body twitched for a few seconds, and then it didn't.

This was not done for pleasure. Pleasure was not a part of this operation.

By the way, I think you'll find that the boy who ran, he was faking his death, playing possum. People do that. It's a common enough behavior in these massacres, if you study them. It's not so much a cowardly response as a shrewd tactic. Play dead and hope for the best. If the boy survived, so be it. I say more power to him.

And then I heard sirens and realized that someone on the beach, someone I couldn't see, had called the cops on a cell phone. I considered reloading both weapons, stepping out of the sea grapes and opening fire, but then that would not have been arbitrary like I wanted it. So I stood up and drained the swollen lizard. I heard the police helicopter. I raised my arms, stooped under the sea grapes, and walked out onto the beach. I knelt and then lay face down in the sand and locked my hands behind my head.

If you tell me eight people died today, then I'll take your word for it. Guilty as charged. I want to be punished. I want to pay the price. I deserve to die. But I won't apologize because I'm not sorry. I won't lie. I honestly wish I felt sorrow, but I don't. I feel nothing, just a big empty. If I told those eight grieving families, those sixteen devastated parents, that I was sorry, would it help them in any way? No, it would not. Would it be like spitting in their faces? I think it would. Words don't mean anything. Words are noise. They are cheap and pointless when it comes to this kind of atrocity. Words will not deliver solace. Words will not bring those children back. Words will not turn back the clock.

I've heard folks say that it was a miracle, an act of God, that more people weren't killed on the beach today. But that's insane. There was no divine intervention; there was me, like I told you, me laying down my carbine and surrendering. This ain't about God. This is about me. I did it. I took what wasn't mine to take. And I don't regret that I did. I regret plenty of things. I regret going all the way back to kindergarten. I regret my old man left us. I regret I married Patti. I regret my meanness to Dorie. But that's all water under the bridge. I don't live in the past.

PERSONAL EXPERIENCE

BY CAROLINA GARCIA-AGUILERA

Miami Beach, July 2010

"Listen, Arlene, there's a hell of a lot of money riding on your getting this right. I'm not going to let you screw it up." Susanna was in her office in New York, and I was in my apartment on South Beach.

"Susanna, please calm down." As my literary agent, her fate and mine were intertwined. There was a lot of money involved—that, and both our reputations.

I could easily picture Susanna in her cluttered office, holding a cigarette in one hand, and a Diet Pepsi in the other, pacing around the room. I had never seen her eat anything—to her, cigarettes and diet sodas seemed to satisfy all food group requirements.

Susanna was not about to calm down. "If I have to come down there myself and babysit you until you deliver the kind of manuscript that Tom Albion is expecting, I swear I'll do it." Susanna inhaled sharply, then, a few seconds later, exhaled.

"Your career is finished, Arlene—in the toilet—if you don't fucking fix this manuscript. You'll go back to writing bodice rippers, and dressing up like

Little Miss Bo Peep at Romance Writers conferences—you won't even be as-signed a panel—you'll just be part of 'gen pop,' sitting in the audience silently criticizing the panelists; your career will tank so fast that being described as a mid-list writer will seem like you're on the upswing." There was no stopping Susanna when she was on a roll. "No more 'Mary Mahoney'—you'll be pub-lished under some pathetic pseudonym."

Susanna kept calling me by my real name—Arlene Frumkes—something she only did when she was truly upset with me. I was in deep shit, and we both knew it.

I sat back in my chair and looked out at the Atlantic Ocean in the dis-tance. Even though it was close to noon, I was still in the workout clothes I had worn for my two-hour session of "sweaty yoga" on the beach below. Su-sanna was relentless when she wanted something, normally a wonderful trait for a literary agent, but one that could be very trying if one was on the re-ceiving end as I was just then.

Everything Susanna was saying was true, so there was no point in trying to defend myself. Even though the book hadn't yet been in the best shape, I had e-mailed her the latest draft of the manuscript that I'd been working on for the past six months. Susanna had wasted no time in making it crystal clear that it just wasn't good enough shape for her to pass it on to Tom Albion, my editor at the Edgar Press. I'd already received (and spent) close to two hun-dred and twenty-five thousand dollars—the first payment under the contract. No wonder she was screaming at me.

The image of Susanna in her office kept getting clearer and clearer. Dressed all in black (the uniform for literary agents in New York), surrounded by piles of manuscripts and books, Susanna would be sitting in the broken down dark brown leather chair that she had owned for thirty years. There would be a half dozen opened cans of warm Diet Pepsi as well as packs of cigarettes within arm's reach. The one window in her office would be partially cracked open to allow the smell from the Marlboro Lights that she chainsmoked to escape—she had dismantled the fire alarm in her office years before.

Susanna, who was quite tiny—I don't think she even hit five feet, or weighed a hundred pounds—liked to wear loose, baggy clothes that made her seem even more elfin. Susanna was rather unfriendly looking, with beady black eyes that missed nothing, a thin slash of a mouth, and sharp, birdlike features. She wore her hair cropped close, less than one inch in length, and had lately taken to dyeing it an unfortunate shade of red. I wasn't sure how old she was, but I had heard her describe in vivid detail what she had been doing when President Kennedy was shot, so she clearly was deep into AARP territory.

"You don't have to come down here, I promise I'll get you a manuscript you can send on to Tom." If the stress of having her down here didn't kill me, the second hand smoke from her Marlboro Lights surely would.

"Look, Arlene, I know you can do it—actually, the book is pretty good—I like the scenes with Miranda—how you introduce her—but, the actual murder scenes that you describe—well, frankly, those chapters are shit—they read as if you just went on the internet and researched how to shoot someone and then carve them up." Ouch! That had been exactly how I'd done the research.

"I'll rework the murder scenes—I know what I need to do." I lied.

"I hope so—because if not, Tom won't accept the book, and, of course, you won't get paid. They'll probably sue you to get back what they already paid you, too. Money I know you already spent," Susanna reminded me, rather unnecessarily. "Word in publishing circles gets around fast—I don't have to tell you what that'll do to your reputation when people find out that

Tom Albion rejected the first book of a multimillion dollar three-book contract." Susanna took a drag of her Marlboro Light. "You'll go back to writing
the kind of shlock you were writing before I found you."

Susanna, to her credit, seldom brought up the subject of what my life had
been like before she entered it, but it was clear that had it not been for her, I
would still be Arlene Frumkes, with a life in shambles, and no prospects to
change it.

"I'm so grateful to you, really I am." I hurried to assure her.

I had started my writing career pretty much by accident. After graduating from college, I had gone on to get my Master's degree in elementary education and had accepted a job as a teacher here, in Miami, at an inner city
school. Although I enjoyed working there and the benefits were great (hell, I
could have even been able to have my great-grandmother's teeth fixed on the
dental plan), the salary for teaching second grade was miserable. Slowly but
steadily, I had been incurring more and more debt, but, not having any other
options, I had stayed there, at the school.

Then, while on a break at the faculty lounge, I had come across an an-
nouncement inviting teachers to enter a short story writing contest. I had
never really thought about becoming a writer before, but the five thousand
dollar prize the first place winner would get was just too tempting. I wrote up
a story about my dog Daisy, a mutt that I had saved from a certain death at
the pound, and how, dying of cancer, she had taught me about the important
things in life, sort of a canine version of *Tuesdays with Morrie*. (I had made up
the dog.) Three months later, on the very same afternoon the check cleared,
I quit my job, and turned to writing full time.

I found out that the easiest way to break into publishing was by writing
romance novels, so I had started off by writing the cheesiest novels ever—

bodice rippers that featured damsels in distress, heroines who, after serious set-backs—physical, and/or emotional (two were penniless orphans; one was blind; one was in a wheelchair; one was gay but wanted to lead a straight life; one was bipolar, and off her meds; one, an adoptee, had fallen in love with her birth brother, etc.)—managed to triumph.

The covers (mass market paperbacks, unsurprisingly) of my eight books said it all, featuring photos of drawings of the naked, golden haired hero-ines—all lusty, busty, and slightly dusty—with that "just-been-fucked-within-one-inch-of-my-life" look in their impossibly crystalline blue eyes. In three of them, the hero was standing off in the corner, staring at the heroine with a sexual predator look in his eyes; on another three, the heroine was riding (side saddle, of course) an excited stallion who was standing on his back legs; in the last two, the heroine was lying in bed, naked, naturally, with the sheets art-fully arranged around her voluptuous body.

I was never going to get rich writing those kinds of books, as in total, I had earned less than a hundred thousand dollars in ten years. My lack of in-come—plus four marriages to shiftless, no good, chronically unemployed and unemployable men—ensured that I would never be able to support myself in the style to which I aspired.

Susanna had come into my life at exactly the right time. My career was in the toilet and my credit cards (the ones that had not been canceled) were maxed out. I had just handed in the last book of a two-book contract, and my editor had just told me the house was not interested in offering me another. I wasn't even a lower mid-list writer—I was more like upper lower list—not exactly the kind of author whose books made it into the Sunday *New York Times* Book Review section.

I wasn't doing much better on the personal front: I had just served husband number four with divorce papers—the rat had forged my signature on some credit card applications and had taken out cash advances for thousands of dollars.

During that particularly bleak time, I had been living in a studio apartment over the garage of an estate of a very wealthy German developer in Miami Beach. My landlord had, in exchange for me performing a few menial tasks around the estate, given me a break on the rent—otherwise I would have been on the street.

Susanna had called me completely out of the blue one day, and, after identifying herself as a literary agent, stated that she had been following my career and thought I was not writing in the correct genre. She said that the way I laid out the stories and developed characters had convinced her I would make an excellent mystery writer. However, it was my attention to detail—critical in a mystery writer—that had convinced her I would be successful in that field. She ended by telling me she'd like to meet me, and asked me to come to New York, to her office.

Never having been represented by a literary agent, I immediately accepted her invitation. That same afternoon, I sold the most valuable of my wedding rings—gold, thank God, was over a thousand dollars an ounce—and bought a ticket to New York on Jet Blue for the next day.

At her office, Susanna again told me that she thought I had enormous potential as a mystery writer, but that in order for that potential to be realized, I had to put myself in her hands. I would not only have to reinvent myself both professionally and personally: I would have to work my butt off, but that if I did as she said, I would soon be a "literary star." I promised her that I would never let her down.

When Susanna had told me I would be "working my butt off" she wasn't just referring to my writing, but also to my physical appearance. In order for a writer to be successful, they had to develop a "writers' persona" and be physically attractive, telegenic, charming, and interview friendly. She would put me through the kind of training that the Marine recruits underwent at Parris Island.

To show how serious she was, Susanna had even fronted me ten thousand dollars. Now, just when I was on the verge of breaking out, I had delivered a sub par manuscript. The promise I had made to her in her office, that I would never disappoint her, sounded hollow. I had to fix the manuscript, unless I wanted to go back to being Arlene Frumkes, the failure, living on a financial edge.

"Susanna, I told you that I would not let you down, and I stand by that promise." I spoke in a firm tone of voice. "I will deliver the kind of manuscript you expect."

"You'd better, Arlene." Susanna said ominously. "I'll call every day to check in on you. If I don't like what I'm hearing, I'm flying down to Miami and staying with you. I've worked too fucking hard for the past thirty years to have it all go down the tubes because you can't write a decent death scene!" Susanna spat out the words. "I'm giving you ten days to turn in a manuscript that I can pass on to Tom."

"You'll have it in ten days—probably even less." I hoped my voice sounded more confident than I felt. "I can do this. Trust me."

"And may I remind you again that you have to give the money back to Edgar Books if Tom turns the manuscript down." Susanna was relentless.

I had already thought of that, of course. How could I not have? "Susanna, I meant it when I promised you you'd have an acceptable manuscript, and I will."

"I'll call you tomorrow." Susanna announced before hanging up.

I got up, and headed to the terrace. As I looked out over the brilliant blue waters of the Atlantic Ocean, I knew that I was in real danger of losing my beloved apartment—the one I had given the down payment with the money from the advance of the book. I thought about the long, difficult journey I had taken to get to where I was.

I pictured the brutal hours of long workout sessions with Faustus, the former Marine drill sergeant, that would end with me collapsed in the gym, soaking wet with sweat, gasping for air. As much as I hated the time with him, there was no arguing with the results—in just three months I had dropped thirty pounds, and four dress sizes. I'd never thought of myself as overweight, but Susanna kept reminding me that the camera would add at least ten pounds, so I just did as I was told and continued to starve myself.

Even though I was just thirty-seven years old, Susanna insisted I have Botox injections to eliminate the tiny lines under my eyes—in the age of HDTV it was impossible to hide any flaws. My skin was exfoliated so often that I feared I would look like a Brazilian rain forest that had been stripped bare; my hair was cut, styled and colored; I even had Lasik surgery so I could do away with my glasses. Susanna had insisted that I give away all my clothes, and advanced me money for a new wardrobe. I felt as if I'd been on an episode of *What Not To Wear*. In six months, I was reborn as Mary Mahoney.

Susanna and I had decided that the quickest and most effective way for me to break into the very crowded mystery field—South Florida was teeming with mystery writers—was to write gritty, police procedurals type books, hardcore novels. I intended to make Dennis Lehane, George Pelecanos, James Ellroy, et al seem as if they were writing young adult mysteries.

After much thought, I came up with the character of Miranda Maples— a private investigator-cum-forensic-scientist investigator. Miranda would be cast in the role of the classic private eye—a disillusioned loner who lived by her own moral code, shunning normal convention. All that, however, did not preclude her from being a knockout: tall, blond, busty, brainy and leggy, who dressed in killer designer outfits. In her role as a private investigator, Miranda would look into the circumstances under which victims had been murdered, while in her role as a forensic investigator, she would analyze the physical evidence at a crime scene to recreate how, exactly, it had been that the victim had met his or her fate. Miranda's dual occupations gave her plenty of opportunities to get involved in a world filled with blood and gore. No case, no details, would be considered too gruesome or chilling for Miranda Maples. After all, this was the world of *C.S.I.,* and readers would expect details. I read periodicals, publications and journals that had to do with forensic investigations. I came across an interesting tidbit: Sherlock Holmes was considered to be a forensic investigator.

To this day I still don't really know how she did it, but Susanna somehow managed to talk Tom Albion, the editor-in-chief of Edgar Books, into offering me a three-book contract, for a series featuring Miranda Maples. Not just that, but the contract was worth the staggering, unheard of sum of one and a half million dollars; as my literary agent, Susanna's fee was fifteen percent of that—a tidy sum.

Susanna had flown me up to New York to meet with Tom. I was to bring the first ten chapters of the first book, plus detailed synopses for the next two. The original plan had been for me to meet Tom at his office in the morning, but, somehow, the ten o'clock meeting had segued into lunch. (Was it my new wardrobe? The Botox? The veneers? The body Faustus had carved out for me?) By the time I left, Tom had read the first ten chapters of the first book as well as the synopses of the other two—I had ended up with a three-book contract worth millions. It had all been quite unorthodox—books were not purchased that way. Susanna's plan had worked.

The first book involved Miranda investigating a shooting. Writing the book was easy enough—my skills had been honed by producing all those romance novels—but it had been the scenes where the actual murder took place that were challenging. If readers were going to believe Miranda as a private investigator as well as a forensic science investigator, those were the scenes that had to be the best. I must have written and rewritten those scenes dozens of times, but instead of improving, they worsened.

I had exhausted all my options as to doing any more research: I had *In Cold Blood* practically memorized and could even quote verbatim from certain passages; had watched hours upon hours of movies that dealt with the subject; downloaded documentaries about killings (Discovery Channel, A&E, and the Learning Channel were invaluable); had ridden along with police officers to crime scenes, etc.

Not even stopping to shower and change out of my sweaty clothes, I sat in front of the computer and began typing. Three hours later, having made no progress, I walked over to the liquor cabinet in the corner of the living room, and poured myself a stiff drink of Jack Daniels—then another. I did not stop until I had drunk four glasses—neat, no ice. The liquor hit me hard, and almost immediately the room started spinning around. I carefully made my way to the sofa, and lay down.

Less than a minute later, I threw up on myself, but I was so drunk that I couldn't move. I must have lain there for a good hour, with vomit all over me—bile mixed in with Jack Daniels—a horrible stench, one I thought I would never have to smell again. Slowly, painfully, I forced myself to get up from the sofa and gingerly made my way into the bathroom where I stripped off my clothes and threw them into the trashcan. There was no way I was ever going to wear them again.

I turned on the shower, ran the water as hot as I could stand it, and stood under it for a good five minutes. For once in my life, I was going to take my late mother's advice. "Arlene, in life, if you want something done right, you have to do it yourself."

Susanna wanted me to write a realistic murder scene? Well, I was going to do just that. I, who was so law abiding that I'd never even left my car in a 'handicap parking' zone, was going to commit a murder, the only way to be sure to accurately describe it.

Could I really do it? Kill someone in cold blood—for money? I had no illusions about the reason why. There was no way I could return to living hand to mouth over a garage apartment; I could kiss my apartment good-bye; there would be no more Botox, highlights, three hundred dollar hair-cuts; weekly manicures and pedicures; veneers, etc. I would watch as my face and body returned to its pre-Mary Mahoney appearance.

I may have been desperate, but I wasn't stupid or foolhardy. I had to be very careful not to get caught, but with meticulous planning, I was confident I could do it. The difficult decision made, I felt a calm come over me, and I was able to sleep the night through for the first time in weeks.

The next morning I went for an early morning run on the beach followed by a swim in the ocean. It wasn't even eight o'clock when I sat down at the computer. I broke down the plan into three separate but equally important components. First, I had to find a victim, someone whose disappearance would not arouse suspicions; second, I had to find a place where I could kill the victim in exactly the same way the murderer did in the book without being detected; and third, I had to find a place to dispose of the body without being seen. Each of those would present a challenge, to be sure, but nothing that I couldn't handle with careful preparation.

I began by logging on to the official Web site for the Everglades National Park, a place I had visited on several occasions. The park was truly enormous, comprised of over one and a half million acres—one hundred and twenty miles long; fifty miles wide—by anyone's calculations, a vast, lush wetland area offering many places in which to dispose of a body. I read about the many species of animals that lived there—American crocodiles, bobcats, panthers, wild boars, vultures, etc.—most, if not all, that would doubtless be happy to be offered a tasty meal. The park was open twenty-four hours a day—good for me—but it was constantly patrolled by officers from the National Park Service—not so good.

After finishing the research on the Everglades, I next turned to finding a place where I could commit the murder in privacy—a place close to the entrance to the park. I sure as hell did not want to be driving around unfamiliar roads with a body in the trunk of the car and concluded that entering the park from the south would be best, at Florida City.

Florida City was a known dropping off point for drugs—principally marijuana—being flown into the state on small planes prior to being distributed around the country. The marijuana came in large bales, so I assumed that the drug dealers would need a secure, private location to divide up the shipments—just as I did. I Googled information about Florida City, and found that there were what seemed an unusually high number of storage units—all offering privacy and security—around the entrance to the park. Perfect. I wrote down the telephone numbers and addresses of a couple of them.

As far as finding the victim, well, that would have to wait.

After a late lunch—low fat tuna salad and water—I gathered the supplies I would need for my research: a small Igloo cooler filled with several bottles of water; two cans of mosquito repellant; a pair of top of the line binoculars, and, of course, maps of the area. I got into my Land Rover (I owed two months on it, so it was dangerously close to being repossessed) and set off for Florida City.

The sun was just beginning to set when I arrived at the entrance to the Everglades National Park. I stopped at the small wooden building, paid the entry fee, and entered the preserve. I drove around for a while, before turning off at the Royal Palm section of the park, a freshwater slough that, at first glance, seemed to suit my needs just about perfectly. The specific area that I was interested in could not be easily seen from the paved road; additionally, there was a medium sized pond nearby—murky, algae filled water that, with any luck, was teeming with hungry crocodiles and crabs; and, just in case those did not do the job, there were vultures perched on the bare branches of the tall trees in the distance, an area referred to as a cypress dome. After marking the exact place on the map on my lap, I turned the car around, and got back on the main road.

Once outside the park I went looking for the storage units. The first one was located on an unpaved side street, behind a six-foot-tall concrete wall topped with concertina wire. As I drove by it, I was able to count ten rows of room-sized steel units, the doors all secured with large steel locks. I parked the car just behind a large eucalyptus tree, a spot that allowed me to observe the entrance to the units, but still remain unnoticed. For the next three hours I sat in the car, watching the gate to see how much activity came in and out, but no one entered or exited the enclosed facility during that time. This place was so perfect that I did not bother checking out the second one.

I had left the most difficult—and disagreeable—task for last: finding the victim. Having decided earlier that a homeless person would come as close as possible to the "ideal" victim, I planned on driving to the two shelters I had read about on Google, but, fortunately, I did not have to do that as, on my way there, I had passed a food store in front of which were eight or ten men lounging about, drinking from cans in paper bags, and smoking cigarettes. I pulled into the parking lot adjacent to the store, where I could have an unobstructed view of them without being noticed. From their demeanor—chain-smoking and drinking steadily—and unkempt appearance I felt I could safely assume they were homeless drifters.

I studied each and every one of them, trying to assess which one would best serve my needs. Although I was small of stature, thanks to Faustus's brutal workouts, I was very physically fit. Still, I did not think I could carry a person much larger than myself, especially as dead weight was much heavier than live. After calculating their weights, I decided that the youngish looking man with longish blond hair cut into a mullet, who was wearing cut-off overalls, would be the most easily manageable. Having made my pick, I headed back to South Beach.

I would have liked to have had more time to refine my plan, but I did not have that luxury. Susanna was now threatening to come down to Miami four days from now. That, and the fact that I kept getting messages from the management company of my building demanding payment of the fees—this morning I had received a registered letter.

The next morning, using a disposable cell phone and giving a false name, I phoned the number listed for the storage unit in Florida City, and informed the manager I was interested in renting one of their larger units for a year. I told him would be wiring the money from a Western Union office and that I would call him in a few hours to make sure the transaction was complete, at which time he could give me the unit number. I would be supplying my own lock. The manager must have been used to having customers rent units that way, because he did not ask a single question—he just gave me the wiring instructions to the bank.

To be sure the conditions were the same, for the next three days I drove to Florida City at the exact same time I planned to commit the murder and ran through the plan. Sure enough, nothing ever changed: the entrance to the Everglades National Park was always open; there was no activity at or around the storage unit; and the same group of men loitered outside the food store. On the second day, I went to a Home Depot about one hour south of Miami, and, using cash, bought the items I needed. At a uniform store in West Miami, I purchased protective clothing. In Florida City, I went inside the storage unit I had rented, and checked it out. The space was perfect. I set the items I had purchased at the Home Depot for the following night in one of the corners, and left.

I must not have been as cool, calm, and collected as I had thought I was because I had the weird sensation that I was being followed. The feeling was so strong that I kept checking in the rearview mirror, but I could not spot anyone. Besides, who would be watching me? I hoped my nerves were not getting the better of me.

That last night, I could not manage to get more than a few minutes of rest at a time. Could I really murder someone in cold blood just to be able to correctly describe a scene in a book? Finally, just as dawn was breaking, I managed to sleep for two hours without interruption. After a morning swim and run on the beach I sat down in front of the computer in a last ditch effort to write a plausible scene, but as before, that eluded me. The day crawled by.

At three o'clock, I began to make my final preparations. Thankfully, the nervousness of the night before was gone, and I was able to go about my activities in a methodical way. My concentration was broken only once, when

Susanna telephoned. I thought it strange she called me in the middle of the afternoon, especially as we had spoken just a few hours before. I reassured her that the rewrite was coming along very well.

I went downstairs to the garage of the building, got into the Land Rover, and drove off. My first stop in Florida City was at my unit in the storage facility. There, I began to quickly and methodically change my appearance. After braiding my long blond hair, I tucked it under a baseball cap; next, I put on a blue jean jacket three sizes too big that I had bought at Sears two days before; and, then I inserted a pair of lifts inside my sneakers, which instantly added several inches to my height. Using the mirror, I drew on some heavy dark eyebrows over my normally thin, light ones.

Eyewitness accounts of a crime were notoriously unreliable, so I had decided that it would be prudent to accentuate several easily identifiable characteristics that would throw off any kind of accurate description of myself. Outside the unit, I smeared some mud on the license plate of the Land Rover to obscure several of the numbers. I simply could not be too careful.

I parked the car across the street from the entrance of the food store, and for the next couple of hours, watched as the motley crew assembled. By now, I was familiar with their routine: first they pooled their money and bought a pack of cigarettes; next, one by one, they filed into the store and purchased bottles of beer—they favored Pabst Blue Ribbon—which they would take outside to drink. The first beer never lasted too long, for each man would drink a second and a third in quick succession. Every so often, each of the men would walk the half a block or so to a clump of bushes, out of sight of the street, to pee.

After an hour, my victim would be on his fifth beer and need to relieve himself. His friends would continue hitting the drinks hard but my fellow, a lightweight, would slow down after that, and chain-smoke cigarettes. That night was no different. I watched as he went to the side of the building to relieve himself, then waited until he had finished before approaching. I was pleased to see that he was weaving slightly, and his pale blue eyes were unfocused. Good.

"Hey, my name is Nora." I greeted him in a friendly way. "I'm a photographer." I pointed to the camera I was holding. "I was wondering if I could take some pictures of you. You have wonderful cheekbones, anyone tell you that?"

"Cheekbones?" The man put his hands to his face, and rubbed it. Then he opened his eyes a bit wider, and asked suspiciously, "Pictures? What kind of pictures?" The man started swaying a bit, and he reached out to the wall next to where he was standing to steady himself. "I don't do that naked stuff. Or anything with kids."

The fact that my victim was so quick to ask questions about naked pictures with children immediately made me wonder if he'd had experience with those. "Oh, no. Not those kinds of pictures." I hurried to reassure him. "These are formal pictures—you'd be totally dressed. And no children are involved. I'd pay you, of course, for your time." I showed him a hundred dollar bill. "It would just be for a couple of hours—my studio is just a few blocks away. You'd be back with your friends in less than two hours."

"Oh, okay. Two hours, huh? You sure that's all it would take?" Anyone listening to him would think he had an agenda full of appointments. "And you'll give me the hundred?" I showed him the money again. "I guess so."

"Good." I took him by the arm. "My car's right here. Come on."

The victim got into the front seat of the Land Rover, and immediately closed his eyes. He must have been drunker than I had thought. I walked around the car to the driver's side and reached under the seat for the bag I had placed there back at the storage unit. "Here—this beer will help you relax for the shoot." I shoved the can of beer into which I had dissolved a Roofie—the drug known as the "date rape drug"—earlier.

The word "beer" must have had magic connotations for the victim, for he immediately opened his eyes, and held out his hand for the can. "Gee, thanks."

I watched as he drank half the contents without stopping. It would take between fifteen and twenty minutes for the drug to take effect—so I could not waste any time. I drove to the storage facility. The young man had almost passed out by the time we got to my unit.

I took the time to look him over. This man had once been someone's baby, probably wanted and loved. I was tempted to go through his pockets to see if he had any identification on him, but I stopped myself. The last thing I wanted or needed was to put a name to him, to humanize him. Well, he would not have died in vain—he was going to give up his life for another—mine. A selfless act.

"Here, here we are at my studio. Time to get out of the car." I didn't want to have to carry him unless it was absolutely necessary.

"Huh?" The man looked around confused. "We're here? Where is here?"

"At my studio, for the photos, remember?" I needed for him to be sufficiently awake to follow my orders, but not too awake to figure out what I was doing. "Come on, let's go inside."

The young man somehow managed to coordinate his body enough to get his legs to hold him up, but once inside the unit, right by the door, he collapsed into a heap, out cold. I poked him a few times, the last ones hard, but he did not move.

"Shit." I whispered. In my book, the victim was laying on his side, spread out flat, and he was all crumpled up. It would not do.

I put on the one-piece plastic jumpsuit, goggles, and gloves that would protect me from any blood splatter, and dragged the victim to the middle of the unit, just over the drain in the floor. I could have shot him where he lay, but as I was going to have to move him later on to dismember him, there was no point in having to move him twice. I laid him out exactly the same way my victim was in the book, and, without giving myself time to think about what I was doing—or to back out—I assumed the pose the murderer in my book had. To muffle any sounds, I first held a small white cotton pillow over the muzzle of a gun I had stolen years earlier from my second husband. Then, after taking a deep breath, I shot him in the side of the head.

Just as in my book, the young man did not die immediately. Good. I'd gotten that right. I calmly stood up, and went to get my laptop, then began describing the scene in minute detail: the sound of the shot, the size of the hole the bullet had made as it entered his head; the twitches of the victim as the life flowed out of him; the blood seeping slowly out of the wound; the way his skin changed colors; then, finally, the death rattle. It was all I had expected, and much more.

I was amazed at how composed I had been through the experience, but that could quickly change. I checked to make sure I was completely covered up—the last thing I needed was to get the victim's blood on me—he could have had some illness.

I began my next gruesome task. Images of the bathroom scene in the movie Scarface in my mind, I proceeded to dismember the victim's body, cutting him up using the chain saw I had bought at Sears. The victim had barely any muscle and his bones were quite soft—so cutting him up was not as labor intensive as I had feared. I waited until most of the blood had drained from his body—to lighten the load as much as possible—before placing the cut-up parts of the body into the heavy construction bags, and tied the tops off with rope. By the time I finished, I was sweating profusely.

I made sure no one was lurking outside before placing the five bags in the back of the Land Rover and covering them up with a couple of blankets I had purchased for that purpose. After that, I returned to the unit and re-moved any items I had brought with me. Once the place was completely emptied out, I washed the whole area with water from a garden hose that I had connected to the spigot outside. Holding my nose to avoid inhaling the pungent odor, I splashed the contents of three bottles of bleach around to get rid of any smell of blood that might be lingering. I put the protective cloth-ing I had been wearing—jumpsuit, gloves, and protective glasses—in a small bag, and stuffed them under the passenger seat. I locked the unit, and left.

I drove slowly to the entrance of the Everglades, and handed the sleepy guard the ten-dollar fee. Just in case any of the rangers might be patrolling, looking out for visitors at such a late hour—by then it was close to one o'clock in the morning—I drove about aimlessly for the next fifteen minutes. Only when sure that I was not being observed did I head for the place I had picked out earlier. I stopped the car at the edge of the pond, and, with the motor still running, dragged the bags out quickly, taking care to loosen the ropes so the animals could get at the body easier. I needn't have worried, for no sooner had I gotten back into the car than I could hear the water in the pond being sloshed around, then saw some shapes moving around silently in the darkness. It was beyond creepy.

I passed through the entrance—happily, the guard was dozing so he did not see me leave—and drove for the next hour until I reached the outskirts of Miami. There, I stopped at a gas station, and parked outside the view of the surveillance cameras mounted on the roof of the convenience store. I went into the ladies' room at the side of the building, took off the clothes I was wearing, and put on different ones. Even at that late hour, there were several cars in the parking lot, so I had to wait until I was sure I was not being watched before heading back to the Land Rover. Once in the car, I added the clothes I had just taken off to the ones I had placed a few hours earlier under the front seat. Then I drove back to Miami Beach.

In the parking garage of my building, I carefully cleaned off the mud from the license plate of the car, and went upstairs. Once in my apartment, I poured myself a stiff Jack Daniels, then, after drinking it, another. I then sat down at my computer, and using the detailed notes I had taken at the unit, completely rewrote the death scene in the book. The sun was coming up when I e-mailed Susanna the new version.

No sooner had I pressed the Send button than the enormity of what I had done hit me, and I put my head down on the desk and just sobbed. Had I really just killed a man in cold blood? I, who had not been to church in twenty years, began praying: "Please, dear God, make it all have been a dream." I couldn't get the vision of the victim's sightless eyes, as he stared off into the distance, out of my mind. The events of a few hours ago kept playing over and over again in my head, as terrifying as one of Wes Craven's goriest, scariest, most horrific movies—only what had just happened was not make believe and would not be over in two hours.

I went down to the beach for a swim and a run then made an enormous breakfast. After turning off the phones, I took a Xanax and went to bed. Thankfully, the Xanax did the job, and I slept until late the following afternoon.

When I awoke, I saw that Susanna had left me several messages—voice-mail; text; e-mails—congratulating me on the new pages, and informing me she had been so pleased by them that she had already inserted them into the manuscript.

I had been about to respond to her last e-mail when my phone rang. It was Susanna. "Mary, I've been trying to reach you for two days! Where the hell have you been?"

Susanna called me Mary. I was back to being in her good graces. "Oh, sorry Susanna—I've been working so hard that, after e-mailing it to you, I feel asleep."

"I sent the manuscript on to Tom—he just texted me telling me he was really liking it." Susanna took a deep drag of her cigarette. "Keep your fingers crossed—I'll call you as soon as I hear anything concrete back from him." Another drag and she asked. "How did you do you it, Mary? The new pages are so authentic, they read so real. What kind of breakthrough did you have? I'm curious."

I thought for a moment. "I just delved more deeply into my research, is all. Just approached the scene differently."

"Whatever you did, it worked." Susanna was euphoric. "I'll be in touch."

After hanging up with Susanna, I opened the front door to my apartment and picked up the two *Miami Herald*s—the day before and today's—and turned to the local section to see if there had been any kind of write-ups about a missing young man from Florida City. Nothing. I looked over the pages again to be sure I hadn't missed anything. Still nothing. I was safe! I promised God that if he let me get away with killing the young man, I would never, ever do anything like that again.

Two days later, Susanna called to give me the great news that not only had Tom loved the manuscript, he was moving up the publishing date, something that was quite rare in publishing, a business that made a snail's pace seem as if it were breaking speed records. However, the best part was that he was approving the release of the second set of funds due me upon the acceptance of the manuscript. Life was good. Still, I could not forget Florida City.

The novel, which received glowing reviews, was an instant success. Tom, sensing the potential of the new series, had ordered a huge first printing of the book, a number that assured it a spot on the secondary of the *New York Times'* Bestseller List. My telegenic looks apparently helped sales, as I was booked on just about every television show available. The buzz was such that there was even talk of a television series.

I found it a bit alarming that every reviewer commented on how realistic the murder scene was depicted. Tom, wanting to strike while the iron was hot, requested that I finish the next book in the series in six months, so he could publish it a year after the hardback, releasing it simultaneously with the paperback of the first one.

Every so often I would check the newspapers to see if there was any mention of a missing homeless man—surely the victim had a family that would miss him; or, his fellow drinking buddies—but from what I could tell, nothing had been reported. In time, I began to relax, believing I had actually gotten away with it. My relief was overwhelming.

I sat down to write the next book of the series with my confidence at an all time high. However, much to my dismay, exactly the same thing happened. I simply could not get the death scene to work. It was déjà vu all over again. Somehow I must have known that I might have to reenact again what I'd had to do for the first book, for I had not only kept the items I'd needed to kill the first victim—garbage bags; electric saw; plastic jump suit, etc.—but I had also prepaid a year's rent on the unit. And so, with the deadline looming, and Susanna's calls getting more frantic, I broke my promise to God that I would never, ever, do that again, I found myself driving down to Florida City again.

It was quite eerie being back there. As I drove down the main street, heading towards my first stop, I was relieved to see that outwardly, nothing in the town had changed during the past nine months.

First, I went to the park, and drove to the place where I had disposed of the body. I was feeling very nervous as I looked over where I had parked the Land Rover before, next to the pond, but, thankfully, there, too, everything seemed to be exactly the same. The only difference I could see was that the water level was slightly higher. It was reassuring that the vultures were still perched high up on the branches of the leafless trees. Were they any fatter? I couldn't tell.

Next, I drove to the storage unit, and again, everything seemed to be the way it had been months ago. I headed to my last stop, the food store, to see if the conditions there were also unchanged. There was a group of men loitering around, but these weren't the same ones as before. Good. The men were more transient than I had thought, which lessened the chances that they would report another one of their own missing. The homeless men, not surprisingly, did not want to call attention to themselves so it was unlikely they would bring in the police to investigate.

Even though I was probably operating out of an excess of caution, just as I had done before, I drove down twice more to Florida City to make sure conditions were the same as on previous days. On the third day, on my trip to the food store, I picked out my victim—a slight, Hispanic looking male. Then, on the fourth day, after he had left the group to go and pee on the side of the building, I made my move, and invited him into my car. A beer spiked with a Roofie, followed by a quick trip to the storage unit, a few turns of the hunting knife purchased for just this occasion, and I had the information necessary to describe the death scene perfectly.

Just as before, the reviews had been outstanding—I had even scored a starred review in *Publishers Weekly* and a surprisingly positive one from *Kirkus* (known for nasty, negative reviews)—pleasing Susanna greatly, and prompting Tom to push up the publishing date yet again.

As before, there was no mention of the crime in any of the papers. Could committing murder be this easy, or, was I just clever in my planning and plotting? Or, could it be that I had chosen the perfect kind of victim, someone who was so under the radar that he would not be missed? Whatever the reason, I was becoming increasingly emboldened by my acts. And, so, even though I found it repugnant to have to do it again, I returned to Florida City for book three, but I wasn't as emotionally detached as before.

When it came time to hand in book three, thankfully the last of the books under the contract, I found that I did not want to have to kill anyone anymore. I'm not sure if that came from my having developed a conscience, or it was the fear that what I was doing could not continue to be undetected and statistically the odds of my getting caught kept increasing. Or, could it be that maybe I was becoming too dependent on committing murder to be unable to describe a death scene without doing it? Or, it could have been that God was going to punish me for what I had done: killed three people, as well as broken my promises to Him.

I may have murdered three men in cold blood already, but in my eyes, I was no female serial killer. I sure as hell was not Aileen Wuornos, the Florida prostitute who had murdered seven men in one year, whose story had been brilliantly portrayed by Charlize Theron in the film *Monster* (I had seen it at least half a dozen times). I had done what I'd had to do for the sake of my novels and not because I had issues with men, or because I enjoyed killing. In my eyes, it had been a matter of self-defense—nothing less than the matter of my survival.

The Miranda Maples series may have been a huge success, but even if Tom were to have offered me another multiple book contract, I was going to turn him down (I hadn't told Susanna of my decision yet). I was absolutely certain that I did not want to keep the series going. I was done with writing death scenes and all that that those entailed. I didn't want to go back to writing romances, but there were other ideas I could come up with that that did not include describing death scenes in gruesome detail.

Not exactly surprisingly given the success of the series, Tom offered me another three-book deal, for double the money. I told Susanna that I wanted to move on, do something else, but she would not hear of it. I was unmoved by her entreaties, but her powers of persuasion—and my need for more money to support my increasingly lavish lifestyle (at that time I was supporting a few boy toys, young guys that I liked having around for my pleasure, but that were quite expensive)—were such that in the end, I gave in but only for two books. I held firm about that.

Sadly, the same happened—just as I feared it might. In the fourth book, I still could not get the death scene right—this time it was death by arsenic poisoning. I had written up a description that was marginally acceptable, but I could not risk having Susanna reject it. And now, time was running out. Susanna was back to calling, texting and/or e-mailing me several times a day, reminding me that the manuscript was overdue, and that Tom was on her case asking for it. Unfortunately, because of some very bad financial decisions I continued to make, I had no choice: back to Florida City I would go.

Even as I was planning my fourth kill, I knew that statistically, the odds of my getting caught were increasing. Three deaths—and now, a fourth. I was still being very careful, always meticulous, but eventually I was probably going to screw up.

As before, the fourth book was a huge success—this one a finalist for an Edgar for best hardcover—the mystery field's highest award. I swore I would not kill again. I was determined to write the fifth—and last—book of the contract on my own. And then, no more contracts. Not for all the money in the world- it just wasn't worth it.

I should have known that I couldn't do it. Try as I might, I could not get the fifth book to come out right. This time, it was death by strangulation. At that point, I was just tired—I wanted to be finished with it all. I was willing to sell the apartment; break the lease on the timeshare in Aspen; even give up the pretty boys. If I were to live frugally, I wouldn't have to worry about writing for a while. All I had to do was to finish the fifth book. Then I would be home free. It sounded so easy, but I couldn't do it.

Exactly one week before the "drop dead" deadline for me to turn in the finished manuscript, the phone rang—Susanna. "What the fuck, Arlene? Where's the fucking manuscript? You've already had one extension—Tom's not going to give you another."

"I'm almost done, Susanna." I tried to soothe the agent. "It's given me a bit of trouble, but I'm getting a handle on it. You'll have it soon."

"Well, you'd better be almost done. Remember, you don't get paid until you hand it in—and, if you don't get paid, neither do I. I know you need the money bad. I know you didn't want to sign the contract for the other two books, but, you did—and now, you have to deliver." Susanna took a deep drag of her cigarette. "I'll give you until tomorrow afternoon or I'm coming down to babysit you." Another drag followed by a drink of Diet Pepsi. "I want to make sure you're sitting at the computer, working, and not going to the beach and fucking all those pretty boys you have on your payroll."

"There's no need for you to come down here." I thought about what Susanna had just said. How did she know about the boys? I kept those a secret from everyone. Had she been spying on me? "I'll get the manuscript to you, I promise."

"Well, you'd better work day and night to get it in, otherwise you'll be in big trouble with Tom. You may have made lots of money for him, but, Arlene, you signed a contract—a legally binding document," Susanna pointed out unnecessarily. "I'm not supposed to tell you this, but I will so you know how much is at stake: he's going to offer you a three-book contract after you hand this one in—for a shit load of money."

My heart sank. "Another contract?" I blurted out. "For three books? Featuring Miranda Maples?"

"No, Arlene, featuring Nancy Drew." Susanna snapped back. "Of course featuring Miranda Maples!"

"I don't know, Susanna. I'm tired of Miranda. I want to start something new—a different series, maybe, or a stand-alone book." I ventured.

"What are you, crazy?" Susanna screamed at me. "Miranda is a gold mine for you—and me! You want to give her up? Never! I'll never let you do that! Never! You live the way you do because of me—you'd still be fat, ugly, wrinkled with buck teeth and fucking losers, living in a hellhole if it wasn't for me. I made you! And, I helped you create Miranda! I got you the deals with Tom, and now you want to walk away from it? What kind of an idiot are you?" The venom spewing out of Susanna's mouth was formidable. "You will finish this book, and you will sign the contract for the next three."

"Stop shouting at me, Susanna. I'm not deaf, I can hear you perfectly well." I spoke calmly. "I'll finish this book and I'll do it on time. I'll honor this contract, but I won't sign another one. And you can't force me to. I'm sorry if that means you'll drop me as a client. I'll always be more grateful for what you've done for me that I can ever express to you, but my decision is final."

There was silence on the line before Susanna spoke again. "Sorry to tell you this, but your decision is not the final one. I'm e-mailing Tom now telling him to get the contract ready for the next three books—that you're so happy to write them."

"Did you not hear me? I told you I'm not going to commit to writing another three books—I'm done with Miranda Maples. I'll finish this book, and then I'm done. I'm not going to change my mind." I was determined that I was not going to let her browbeat me.

"Are you in front of your computer, Mary dear?" Susanna asked, speaking in a sweet voice.

"Yes, I am, why?"

"I just sent you an e-mail—there are four parts to it." Susanna informed me. "I'll wait until you open it."

I clicked on the new e-mail. Slowly, several images showed up on the screen, images of me. Shocked, I quickly scanned the photos: me at the entrance to the Everglades National Park; me at the edge of the pond; me outside the storage unit; me sitting in the Land Rover, first, outside the food store, then with the first victim sitting in the car; then, me loading the black plastic bags into the back of the car, and returning to the park. The last ones were of me in the gas station, entering and exiting the ladies' room. The next four sets of photos were almost exactly the same, except for the victims.

I was paralyzed, my eyes fixated on the screen. "I don't understand." That was all I could manage to utter.

"I'm happy to enlighten you, Mary." Susanna took a couple of drags of her cigarette. "When you couldn't hand in an acceptable manuscript for the first book, I thought you weren't doing it because you were fooling around—going out with your boy toys and partying at night, so I decided to contract a private investigator for a few days to take pictures of you screwing around, pictures I would show you to shame you into working." Susanna took a sip of her Diet Pepsi. "Well, imagine my surprise when my investigator told me that for four days in a row you had driven down to Florida City, and had poked around different places there: the Everglades National Park; a place where storage units are rented; then, sitting in the dark for hours in front of a convenience store! In between trips to Florida City, you went shopping at Sears, several Home Depots, a uniform store. Curious places for you to shop, don't you think? On the fourth night, you invited a young man to join you in your car, you drove him to the storage unit, then a couple of hours later, you come out, dragging five black, plastic construction-type bags, and head into the park! It was just too interesting, don't you think? And, then, on the fifth day, you sent me the new chapters with the rewritten murder scenes perfectly—and realistically—depicted?"

So, my sense that someone was watching me had not been wrong after all. "You had me followed?" I still could not believe what I was hearing.

"Oh, yes, and I did it again for the next three books—I waited until the last few days, just before the deadline, when I knew you were getting frustrated. I knew what you were going to have to do, Mary. I just waited, and, voila! Off you went, to Florida City, your new favorite hangout!" Susanna was clearly delighted by what she was telling me. "It cost me a pretty penny in investigative fees, but that's not all. The private eye I hired, well, he's written a book, and part of my deal with him is that I'll represent him, and get his book published. He's assured me that he won't say anything about your nighttime activities as long as I get him a book deal—and, I will. It's a good book."

I thought about what she had just said. "So, I guess I have no choice except to finish this last book, and sign the contract for the next three?" I asked unnecessarily. "You're blackmailing me into continuing to write the Miranda Maples series?"

"Blackmail is such an ugly word with bad connotations, but, essentially, that's right, Mary." Susanna spoke in a chirpy voice. "Look at it in a positive light. You get to stay in your apartment, and continue with the lifestyle you love. There are lots of boy toys out there that the kind of money you are making will buy. You've got a foolproof system going—you've minimized any chance you would get caught. Really, the way you planned the murders is perfectly brilliant. You could keep this going indefinitely—unless you slip up, of course. But I don't think you will, Mary."

"Or if you turn me in. Nothing lasts forever." I hung up the phone.

Less than five minutes later, I began conducting new research, and did not get up from in front of my computer until I had the information I was seeking: names and addresses for storage units in or around Manhattan. There were plenty of hardware stores around, so I wasn't worried about where I was going to purchase the items to carry out my plan. As far as a large body of water where to dump a body, well, Manhattan was an island, so there was plenty of water to choose from. I was scheduled to fly up to New York in three weeks for a couple of interviews, so I would have time to investigate further.

The next day, I drove down to Florida City to find my last victim. It would be the last time I would be going down there.

TRAPPED

BY JOHN BOND

I'm heads up at the final table of the big one in the World Series of Poker at the Rio, against one of the top guns—Negreanu or Ivey or Doyle Brunson. Some part of my brain knows I'm snoozing in my unmarked Crown Vic, parked in the shade of a spreading banyan at Rio Vista apartments near the Miami River, languishing between deep sleep and wakefulness. But it feels real. My subconscious decides my opponent's Chris Ferguson—the smartest guy in poker. Jesus they call him, with his flowing locks and beard. In Johnny Cash black with his Stetson and impenetrable shades like the eyes of some space alien, he reminds me more of *el Diablo*. He bets big, six times the blind. I peek down to two aces.

Engine running, AC blasting, routine chatter cackled from my Mobile Data Terminal—the twenty-first century's version of the old police radio. I rolled over on the bench seat, a crick in my neck, struggling to hold on to the dream. Should I raise back or smooth call with my aces, try to trap? Ferguson has no respect for my action. Why should he? Nobody does. What would McKool do? Trap, surely. But I'm afraid my aces will get snapped. Life's deck always deals me bitter cards. I decide to raise four times the pot. Either win it right there or maybe Ferguson will push and I'll become world champion.

A fist slamming on the window of my patrol car startled me into wakefulness.

"*Coño*," I muttered under my breath.

"Pablo! Wake the fuck up."

Eddie Figueroa, my desk sergeant. We'd gone to the academy together. I rolled down the window. The sweltering June humidity poured into the Crown Vic.

"Some upstanding citizen called in a complaint about a homeless guy living in his car," Eddie said. "Said it had been parked under this tree every day for a week."

I stammered, unsure what to say. I'd been catching a nap at the Rio Vista most afternoons for a lot longer than a week.

"Didn't you just get written up for a no-call no-show?"

I nodded my head. "Yeah, Eddie." And about twenty tardies clocking in.

"Sergeant Figueroa. Aren't those the same clothes you wore yesterday?"

"I guess so, Eddie. I mean Sarge." My baby-blue *guayabera* and tan chinos. I had gone straight from patrol to McKool's and back to work.

"I'm sending you home, Pablo. You, the lieutenant, and I are having a talk after seven AM roll call tomorrow."

"That's awful early, Sarge." I worked the eleven AM to seven PM shift, Wednesday through Sunday.

Eddie threw me an angry look. "And don't be fucking late."

"I got no more sick or personal time."

"Then you're suspended without pay for the rest of the day."

Coño. That would go in my personnel jacket. Not the best career move for a guy about to take the detective exam. "Sarge …"

"Go home, Pablito. Get some fucking sleep. My wife could pack in for a tour around the world in those bags under your eyes."

I drove to the little two-bedroom condo in Fontainebleau Park I share with my grandma. The Crown Vic's a take-home car, one of the perks of my job as unmarked patrolman, the step between beat cop and detective. My parents died in a car crash when I was nine and Abuelita is all the family I know. She came to Miami in the Pedro Pan airlift in '62. Seventy-five years old, she makes me breakfast every day—always *café con leche, pan tostado,* and *plantanos maduros.*

I slept like the dead for ten hours, then headed to McKool's. Down the Palmetto to the Dolphin and across the south side of the airport, less than fifteen minutes. I like the riverfront—it's the edge of my patrol district. I could make a good buck doing off-duty details arranged by the union, but McKool stakes me two bills of my first nickel in free chips when I come by his underground two-table poker game in a Miami River warehouse. The building sign says Miami Bridge Club; McKool even has a business license from the city. Running an underground game in Florida is a felony, but playing one a misdemeanor, not much worse than a parking ticket. Abuelita feels bad I work two jobs. I've never explained to her that McKool's is only sort of a job.

When I arrived McKool called me into one of his cluttered back rooms— queen-sized bed, couch, TV with Nintendo, folding card table with four metal chairs, little desk with a computer for people to play online while they wait for a seat, framed tourism posters of Vegas on the walls, walk-in closet off to the side.

McKool likes that I don't have baggage. No wife, no kids, no girlfriend— I can't afford dating and poker both. My deal is I stay until the game breaks. Some nights I bust out early, and spend my time playing Nintendo. McKool calls me Blue, even though I'm plainclothes, and says he'd rather have me than hire a security guard. He has Cartouche, from his days in the Rangers and Delta, but he likes having a cop in the game. Especially a cop who puts his paycheck in play.

"Tell the Pizzas to skip the next lap," McKool said to Cartouche. "I need to talk to them." Cartouche looks like a toffee-colored Mr. Clean but bigger, right down to the gold earring—and he never smiles. Doesn't talk much either, and what he does say is in an incomprehensible French-Canadian accent.

I bluff a lot, but people know it and tend to pay me off. McKool once told me good players design trap plays to use against players like me. Most people have a playing style—they call or raise or fold too much, bluff too much, try to run over the game too much, pay off too often or not enough, play too many or not enough hands. McKool says the trick is to encourage your opponents to make more of the kinds of mistakes they're going to make anyways. Trap them into being themselves. That's all too complicated for me—I play by feel. McKool says that's just an excuse for me to avoid the mental work necessary to beat the game. One reason I play by McKool's is he gives me poker tips—he says it's better for him if I don't go broke too fast.

Cartouche opened the door to the main room. Both tables were going strong, players eating and yakking and watching the NBA playoffs, chips clacking away. He beckoned to the Pizzas. McKool would never pull them out if it would jeopardize the five bucks a hand rake that pays his bills. McKool is all about the rake.

Joey the short one and Jimmy the skinny one followed Cartouche into the room. They'd showed up at McKool's for the first time on a Sunday. Bobby Two-Ways brought them by; he'd met them at the Italian-American Club's Saturday game, a wild and wooly twenty-five to fifty-dollar dealer's choice shootout. I'd played there once, lost two weeks' pay and never gone back. Their name wasn't Pizza, of course. They weren't even brothers, but McKool has a nickname for everybody and he called them the Pizzas.

"Yo, McKool, why you pull us out? The game's jamming," Jimmy said. Jimmy's dumb, but okay. Joey, though, he's a smart-ass. He always needles me in the game, tries to set me on tilt. You can tell he hates cops.

"Sit," McKool said.

Jimmy looked at Joey, as if for direction. Joey shrugged and sat on the couch. Jimmy took a seat next to him.

"You guys carrying?" McKool asked.

Jimmy looked to Joey again.

"Why would that matter?" Joey said.

McKool has a hard and fast no weapons rule. And no drugs. Bad beats at the poker table and weapons do not mix well together. Bad beats, weapons, and drugs are worse yet. I leave my service Smith & Wesson 4006 and my ankle piece in my cruiser when I play. I suspect Cartouche is armed; either way the guy is a human weapon. McKool explained it to the Pizzas. They weren't happy.

"In our line of work hardware is a necessity," Joey said.

"You'd probably be better off in my line of work. It pays the bills and then some with no hardware needed; easy living," McKool said with a smile. "Leave the heat in your car. Or check them with Cartouche. Or don't play."

No way would McKool bar these two fish—he builds his game around live ones. These two were doomed to go off for their last dollar. He was bluffing. Maybe. McKool's a hard read. When he moves on a pot, McKool stacks the chips. I don't know why it works for him but not me.

Jimmy looked at Joey. Joey hesitated, shrugged, then reached under his jacket and pulled out a Colt Diamondback and handed it to Cartouche. That's a fine gun, a smaller version of the legendary Python; they don't make them anymore. Cartouche reached in his pocket for a handkerchief then took the Colt. Joey nodded to Jimmy. Jimmy handed over two Glock G36s—the best semi-automatic handgun on the market in my opinion.

"That all of them?" McKool asked, looking hard at Joey.

Joey said to Jimmy, "The blade too."

From out of nowhere Jimmy produced a wicked-looking folding gravity knife. Cartouche entered the walk-in closet and closed the door behind him, then came out a moment later without the weps.

"Cartouche will return 'em when you cash out," McKool said. "We don't have to have this conversation again, right?"

After the paisans sat back in, McKool as usual sat me to the left of Florence, the ninety-ish trust fund widow from Aventura he calls Flapper. Shows up for dinner six nights a week, stays exactly nine hours, loses regularly and can afford to keep on losing forever—customers don't get much better than Flapper for a guy like McKool. Sometimes McKool sends Bobby Two-Ways or one of the dealers to give Flapper a ride, but usually she drives her big Caddy, which astounds me because she couldn't read a billboard with a magnifying glass, let alone see a stop sign or pedestrian. He puts me on one side of her and Bobby Two-Ways on the other because she always picks up her cards and holds them right in front of her face to see them. He knows Bobby and I won't take advantage by peeking.

A couple of hands in an eight came on the river making me trips. Flapper checked. I mentally counted her down—a little over two grand in front of her. I bet a nickel, trying to induce a call out of her.

She came over top on me. "All-in," Flapper said.

Feeling pot-committed and thinking I might have her, I called. Flapper showed the Jack-ten of spades—the eight that made my trips had made her straight, but she'd had me from the flop. She'd completely, totally, set me up to blow off all my chips. Even the blind-as-a-bat little old lady was setting trap plays on me.

I left the game just after sunup and drove to the MPD South District Headquarters in Little Havana and met Eddie right after the AM roll call. A woman was there as well—a suit. The LT introduced her as representative from Human Resources, there to witness my counseling. On television lieutenant's offices are spacious, with glass windows. In the real world, they are cubbyholes, barely bigger than a closet—the four of us scrunched into the tiny space. The HR lady asked me if I wanted my union rep present, but I waived my right. The LT ran through the litany of my absences, call-ins, no call-no shows, tardies over the past year. A long list. They asked me why I came in late or called in so often and I told them I had trouble sleeping, nothing more complicated than that. The HR lady suggested I see a doctor. They suspended me for three more days without pay, told me if my problem continued there would be more serious consequences, and had me sign a counseling statement.

• • •

I don't read poker books, but Bobby Two-Ways has a whole shelf full, and at his apartment in Surfside once I'd noticed a title that stuck with me—*Play Poker, Quit Work and Sleep Till Noon*. For the next three days I lived the life of a professional poker player. I ran good too, made more than my lost pay. My first day back at work I managed to punch in seven minutes and fifteen seconds late—technically I wasn't tardy until 11:07:30. I didn't get a tardy the first week, and started to feel I could balance my life as wannabe-detective with wannabe-poker pro.

The Sunday after my suspension I arrived at McKool's and handed Lefty Louie, one of the dealers, my three bills to buy in, but he shook his head. "Big meeting," Louie said, gesturing to one of the back rooms. "McKool wants you in there."

I tapped on the door and Cartouche opened it. The Pizzas leaned against the far wall, arms crossed. At the table with McKool sat a bald guy with waxed head, about five foot two and damn near as wide. His hands, big as cinder blocks and perfectly manicured, sat folded precisely in front of him. On each pinky he wore a chunky ring, not diamonds as I'd have expected, but some kind of old-looking stone. I took a spot on the wall by the door.

"Blue, this is Big Tiny," McKool said. "The Pizzas work for him. Tiny, Blue."

The fat man looked at me, then back to McKool. "Your cop."

McKool nodded. "Big Tiny wants to invest in my game. Says I need the muscle. I was telling him a little about my Army days. That I have Cartouche. And you. I'm okay with protection."

"It would be a mistake to underestimate our value," Big Tiny said in a high-pitched voice. "Big mistake. We got people. Our people got people. We'd take over your collections. Give you a spot to lay off your sports action. Make your life easier." He picked at an imaginary spot on a fingernail, then looked up and leaned forward toward McKool, said softly, "And safer."

McKool shook his head. "I appreciate your concern for my safety, but I don't think so. Thanks for the offer, though." He stood up, turned to the Pizzas leaning on the wall. "You boys want some chips?"

"Not tonight," Tiny answered for them. "I'm sure we'll be back."

They filed out through the door, me and Cartouche flanking it on either side.

Joey stopped two inches from me, got right in my face and softly patted my cheek. "Be seeing you soon," he said with a smile.

McKool gave me the eye and shook his head, so I let it pass.

I lost my first nickel in less than an hour. One five-way hand I flopped trip kings and Flapper caught runner-runner for an inside baby straight and pulled down a monster that should have been mine. I always seemed to start trying to claw back to even.

A little after two AM a loud whompf sound came from the riverside and everybody looked toward the door. McKool peeked out the peephole then gestured for Cartouche and me. "Lefty, Iron Mike, keep dealing."

McKool opened the door a crack and slipped through. Cartouche and I followed. At the far end of the parking lot along the waterfront, fire engulfed a cream colored Cadillac DTS sedan. The bright orange blaze cast flickering shadows and the flames reflected in the river's oily sheen.

"Big Tiny. He just had to pick Flapper's car," McKool said. He turned to me. "Radio it in. Tell them you were driving by and saw it, the situation's under control. Stall them." To Cartouche he said, "Have Mike and Lefty count them down and cash them out quick. Tell Two-Ways to take Flapper home."

"Jeez, McKool," I said. "I can't do that."

"Blue. That's why I have you. We have no time to screw around. Do it. Now."

I called in the fire, told them I was on the scene, nobody was hurt and there was no emergency, no rush. I talked as slowly as I could, and then transposed two numbers in the street address.

As the players filed out, McKool spoke briefly with each. When a thirty-foot MFD pumper pulled up twenty minutes later only McKool, Cartouche and I remained. McKool explained to the fire lieutenant that the bridge game had broken for the evening a few hours earlier, and one of the players—a little old lady—hadn't been feeling well and gotten a lift home, left her car behind. The fire had already died down and it took them less than five minutes to put it out. The Caddy was totally crisped. I'd get myself assigned to the case. Accidental fire caused by some kind of engine malfunction. Hopefully Big Tiny's crew had left no evidence of accelerants.

"I'll go to Flapper's with Two-Ways in the morning," McKool said. "He'll do the insurance paperwork with her." Bobby Two-Ways had been an insurance investigator before taking up poker for a living.

"We playing tomorrow?" I asked.

"Why wouldn't we?" McKool said.

· · ·

Monday and Tuesday are my weekend—I play after I take Abuelita to get her hair and nails done and for dinner at El Rincon or El Viajero. Even though it was my day off I stopped in at the station Monday morning to handle the paperwork on Flapper's car fire.

"Coming in on your day off. Nice," Eddie Figueroa said when he saw me.

"Just had to do a little paperwork," I said.

He looked at the file as I worked on it. "What were you doing down by the river at two o'clock in the fucking morning?"

I shrugged. "Like I told you, *amigo*, I got trouble sleeping."

"Anything special about this car fire? Gang bangers? Mob?"

I shook my head. "Some kind of engine problem. Civil matter. The old lady turned it over to her insurance company."

McKool gets his action going by playing gin in the afternoon with a few regulars, and then serving dinner. He's all about getting cards in the air and butts in chairs and keeping them as late as possible—and he's really good at it, building a stack of chips with players that he cashes as needed to get the action going and keep it going. I'm part of McKool's night crew, help keep his game going late. This Monday, though, McKool was worried about having enough starters to get the game off because of Sunday's car-fire incident, so he asked me to come early and stay. Monday is the night he has the most trouble getting and keeping the game going.

Lilith served dinner as always at six. Cards were in the air six-handed at six thirty—me and McKool, Bobby Two-Ways and Flapper and two gin players, Crazy Al and Luckbucket. Cartouche never played. By nine the game was eight-handed, the second table hadn't gotten going, and McKool was assuring everyone that there would be plenty of action. Big Tiny had smacked McKool where it hurt—in the red chips dropping into the collection box.

Lilith tapped me on the shoulder and handed me the cordless. "It's your grandma," she said. McKool discourages cellphones at the table, says they slow down the action, which means they slow down the rake. I had the game on speed dial at home.

"Abuelita?" I said into the phone. Lefty dealt me a Jack-nine suited, a fair hand but risky in early position. I'm inclined to get involved with anything that has play potential—usually I'd have called but I passed. I took the phone and stepped away from the table.

"*Mi hijo,* two of your friends are here to see you." Doo uff jore frenz are 'ere do zee joo—over fifty years in Miami and you'd have thought she stepped off the boat yesterday.

I have friends at work and the game, a couple of buddies from high school, but not many who even know where I live let alone who would just stop by. "*Por favor*, give one of them the phone, Abuelita."

Lefty put out a Queen-ten-eight, rainbow. I'd have flopped a straight.

"Blue. Your grandma's a real nice lady. Gave me and Jimmy home-made lemonade. Tasty. I'd be nervous leaving my grandma alone with no security or nothing. Miami can be a dangerous place, ya know?"

"What the hell are you doing at my house, Joey?"

"Me and Jimmy stopped by to chat. Should have known you'd be at McKool's. Any seats open?"

"No," I lied. "You need to leave my house right now, Joey. I mean right now."

"Hey, Blue," Lefty called over to me. "The action's on you."

"Fold me."

"We're leaving," Joey said. "Tell McKool maybe we'll stop by."

"Put my grandma on the phone."

"It's your blind, Blue," Lefty said.

I waved my hand, telling them to play over me.

"*Mi hijo?*"

"Abuelita, my friends are leaving. Wait five minutes, then call me back, okay?"

"*Si, pero por que?*"

"*No te preocupe*, Abuelita. Just *llameme* five minutes after they leave. *Entendido?*"

"*Si, mi hijo.*"

I grabbed McKool and pulled him away from the table, told him about the Pizzas' visit to my grandma.

"You gotta sit down, Blue, we can't leave the game short-handed," McKool said.

"I need to check on my grandma. You think she's okay?" All I could think of was Joey Pizza's leering face at Abuelita's kitchen table.

He rested his hand on my shoulder. "Blue, if they were going to hurt her they'd have hurt her—they're just messing with your head. I don't like it, and I'm sure you like it less—but I'm also sure she's okay."

I shook off his hand. "I need to go, man," I said.

"I need you here to keep the game going."

I started toward the door when Lilith brought me the phone. "Your grandma again," she said.

Abuelita started rattling about the nice young men who had just left and were their parents from Cuba and she had invited them to come to dinner with us next Monday, and they'd told her they'd talk to me about it.

It was my turn again to post the big blind, and McKool told Lefty to deal me in. He gently put his hand in my back and pushed me toward my seat. Convinced that Abuelita was indeed okay, I reluctantly sat down and took a hand, still listening to her chatter on in Spanglish over the phone. The game broke early and I rushed home.

McKool called me to come by around noon on Tuesday, said he needed my help with something. I knocked on the door and Cartouche let me in. McKool sat at the poker table poring over a thick file of papers. I sat next to him and he handed me twenty pages of computer printout.

"Look at this," he said.

I flipped through the thick report, glancing at the pages. The printout was all about one Tomaso Albinoni, aka Big Tiny, aged forty-four. A bad guy with a long history, he'd cut his teeth on the Brooklyn waterfront then come to Florida in the cocaine cowboy days of the late '80s. "*Coño*. This is intelligence, not law enforcement. DIA? NSA? Homeland Security?" I asked. "I'm LE and I would never be able to access this kind of material. How did you get your hands on this?"

"I've got people," McKool said. "And some of my people got people."
McKool's business and his life are built on people who owe him favors.

Big Tiny had his bejeweled fingers in, among other things, refugee smug-
gling, drugs, and of course gambling. The detail was incredible.

"Read the section on known associates," McKool said. "There. That
page."

Joseph Bodalato, from Queens, lots of petty crimes, served fourteen years
of a twenty-year sentence in Attica for second degree murder. Last known address on SW Sixteenth Street, down near Woodlawn Park Cemetery, where
Miami borders Coral Gables. "You and Cartouche pay Joey a visit," McKool
said. "He wanted to talk to you? Let's give him what he wants."

"I dunno, McKool," I said.

McKool smiled. "I need to make a little show of force."

Playing in McKool's game was one thing, doing his errands to pressure
mob boys another altogether. I wondered if perhaps he was setting me up, laying some kind of trap for me. "I don't think I should," I said. Was I being
paranoid?

McKool ignored my protestation. "He's there now; Lilith's staking out his
driveway. Take the Crown Vic."

"You know I can't do that."

"Take my Explorer then." McKool had shifted the question from whether
I would go at all to what car we were taking. He handed me a Mapquest to
Joey's house. "Go. Now. Just keep your mouth shut and follow Cartouche's
lead." He handed his keys to Cartouche.

We drove through the midday glare past the cemetery through neighborhoods of tightly packed CBS houses with orange barrel tile roofs amid

banyans and palms to Sixteenth Street. Much like my childhood neighborhood. As we turned the corner I saw Lilith parked in her Hyundai. Cartouche
pulled up in front of a house with jalousie windows and wrought-iron security bars much like all the others, except its yard was overgrown. We walked
through the gate in the chain link fence up a cracked walkway of concrete
slab, up three steps of brick. Cartouche rang the bell. No answer. He rang
again, held it long, an insistent *brinnggg*. Finally Joey came to the door, bleary-
eyed, barefoot and unshaven, wearing jeans and an open terry bathrobe. He
had a concave chest and a little pot belly.

He looked at Cartouche, then quickly tried to slam the door shut but
Cartouche jammed it with his foot. "'Allo, Pizza boy," Cartouche said in his
thick accent.

Joey shrugged and held the door open. He backed up into the living
room, which looked as if it had been picked up from a furniture showroom
and just dropped in place—sectional beige leather sofa, matching coffee and
end tables and entertainment unit with big flat-screen TV, generic oil land-
scapes hanging on the walls. A handful of empty Heineken bottles and a half-
empty bag of Cheetos sat on the coffee table. None of life's bric-a-brac that
said somebody lived here. An aluminum baseball bat rested against the wall
by the front door—if we hadn't woken Joey from a dead sleep he'd likely have
had it in hand when he answered the door.

"You wanted to talk to me?" I said.

"We got nothing to talk about," Joey said, backing into the room. "The
one who needs to talk is McKool—to Big Tiny."

I picked up the bat, poked Joey in the chest with it. "You like my
grandma's lemonade?"

"Put that down, Blue," Joey said as he backed up a few steps.

All I could think of was this sleazy piece of sewage in my grandma's kitchen, drinking her lemonade, oozing menace. "Miami's dangerous?" I poked him again, harder, pushing him against the wall. "My grandma's not safe?" I brought the bat up to his face, made as if to hit him. He flinched. I tapped his cheek with the bat. He brushed it away.

I brought the bat back as far as I could. Joey threw his arms up to protect his face. I swung away, but not where he expected—I brought it down with all of my strength on his left foot, smashing his toes. He screamed and before he could even move, I swung again, crushing his foot again. He fell to the floor.

Cartouche grabbed me by the collar and with one hand lifted me into the air. "We are not 'ere to kill 'eem," he said. He dropped me on the couch, then poked Joey with his toe.

Joey rolled onto his side, curled up in the fetal position, and moaned.

"'Ee will live," Cartouche said. He picked up Joey's phone, and handed it to him. "Tell zem to send an ambulance." He turned to me. "Come. Bring ze bat."

As we drove away Cartouche said, "We wair not s'pposed to do zat." Then he smiled a rare smile. "But I am 'appy zat you did."

•　•　•

Cartouche may have been happy I'd pounded on Joey Pizza, but McKool said I'd escalated things and we could expect some kind of retaliation. He did his houseman magic and got Tuesday's game going, filled with a wait list by eight. I didn't get to play, though—he had me on watch in the parking lot by the riverfront. Cartouche patrolled the street and driveway. McKool had given each of us little pen microphones that transmitted to an iPod-sized receiver with a Bluetooth earpiece he wore—we could tell him instantly if anything seemed awry.

I strolled up and down the concrete pier along the riverside at the end of McKool's parking lot, a little frustrated about not being in action, a little abashed about creating problems for McKool, more than a little angry at the Pizzas. You can't see many stars in Miami's halogen sky, but reflected city lights made their own starscape on the river's surface as it cut five miles through the heart of the city. A headless goat carcass floated past me on the rising tide. Piles of lobster pots and crab traps—rectangular wooden crates with a one-way door allowing crawling crustaceans easy entry, but preventing them from getting back out—lay scattered along the riverfront amid the repair yards, freighter terminals, and new construction high-rise condos going up. The night passed peaceably, but McKool didn't get his usual influx of latecomers, and the game broke a little after two.

McKool called me Wednesday morning. Lefty Louie had been mugged at his home after the game and Lilith wasn't answering her phone. He told me to call in sick, drop Abuelita someplace safe and come meet him at the warehouse. I told him I had no sick time left, but he said it was important and that he would have one of his players, Doc Rajah, write me a doctor's note. I called the station and left a message for Eddie, knowing there would be hell to pay later.

I took Abuelita to the home of Jorge Navarro near *Calle Ocho*. Jorge's little sister came over on Pedro Pan with Abuelita; he was one of the exile wannabe-commandoes who had spent most of the '60s training in the Everglades with weapons provided by the CIA for the invasion of Cuba that never came. Jorge undoubtedly had a cache of something under his floorboards, lethal if old, not unlike himself.

When I arrived at the river around eleven, McKool, Cartouche, and two guys stood in the parking lot poring over papers on the hood of a black Chevy Suburban with tinted windows. I recognized one of them—Long Jack Lawless, a friend from McKool's Army days who dropped by the game once in a while. About six foot four of bony angles, he had straight, silver-streaked chestnut brown hair that hung to the top of his shoulders. Long Jack always dressed the same—black tee, black jeans, black denim jacket, scuffed black Dingo boots, black-framed aviator shades. I didn't know the other guy, a thick, squat man in camo pants and olive green tee with olive lace-up boots. Long Jack nodded hello. The thick guy looked right through me. They both wore Bluetooth earpieces.

The four of them were examining a set of architectural plans and Google images of a wooded neighborhood. One of the properties, with a long gated driveway and a backyard of at least a couple acres, was highlighted in yellow. McKool pointed out the front and back entrance, ground floor windows, a pool cabana in the back. No dogs, he said, but two guards patrolling. It felt like some kind of wartime Special Ops briefing. I recognized the address printed on the corner from the sheaf of papers McKool had showed me the day before—Big Tiny's place. Nobody told me what was going on, but I suspected somebody would get hurt this morning.

"You carrying?" McKool asked.

"Service and drop piece," I said.

He walked around to the back of the Suburban, opened it up and handed me a pair of latex gloves. "Put these on. Lose your service piece." He reached under a black tarp and handed me a SIG P226, the semi-automatic handgun of choice for the Navy Seals, and two fifteen-round clips.

"What am I supposed to do with this?" I asked McKool.

"Hopefully nothing," McKool said "But better to have it and not need it than need it and not have it."

"I'm a cop."

"Exactly."

I shook my head "I'd do almost anything for you, man, but …"

"How'd you like to come to Vegas with me next month, during the World Series? I'll pay your expenses and entry into a satellite, give you a shot at the Big One."

Satellites are qualifying tourneys. McKool was offering me a shot at my dream. I pictured myself on ESPN in the final nine at the Rio, having bested thousands. Mountains of cash on the table, millions of dollars. Across from Jesus Ferguson.

These guys had come after Abuelita. Still, I didn't like it. Eddie Figueroa would like it less.

"Blue, I need you here. I'll owe you one." McKool collects favors. He doesn't owe almost anybody.

"Okay," I said.

McKool dug under the tarp again and pulled out two bolt-action M40 A3 rifles with five-round clips and sniper scopes and handed them with an extra clip each to Long Jack and his friend. "Got the plan?" he asked Long Jack. The A3 has an effective range of about fifteen hundred yards and is the standard sniper rifle of the US Marine Corps.

Long Jack grinned. "Like old times. Let's saddle up."

I shoved the SIG into my waistband under my shirt, put the extra clips in my pocket, and locked my Smith & Wesson in the glovebox of my car. Cartouche drove the Suburban southeast to Old Cutler Road, McKool riding shotgun, the rest of us in the back. Not far from the Deering Estate Cartouche turned south onto Old Cutler, the street completely canopied by live oaks and weeping figs and banyans. He took the first left and cruised towards Big Tiny's. A couple of houses away deep in the shade of thick, towering bushes he slowed almost to a stop. Long Jack and his friend hopped out, then disappeared instantly into the shadows.

Cartouche waited a moment then drove up the street to a wide scroll-worked gate flanked by an unmanned guardhouse. He pressed a button over a speakerbox, and a security camera hanging from the eave of the guardhouse whirred, swiveled and focused on the Chevy. The big gate squeaked and then rolled back. As we drove through, the gate rolled closed behind us. Cartouche drove up the long driveway through an unbroken green lawn leading to the house—a three-story white-roofed coral-pink British colonial with a wide portico and second-floor balcony and six massive classical-looking columns.

"Nice firing field," McKool said. "Good lines of sight. Too bad the back's not as clear." Three cars were parked near the front door. Cartouche did a three-point turn over the grass and pointed the truck in a straight line toward the gate. The three of us climbed out. "Blue. You need to keep your head," McKool said. "Keep your weapon in your pants. You're not in action unless you see Cartouche or me move. Got that?"

I nodded. "Got it."

"You lost your cool at Joey's. Do that today and people will die needlessly." He smiled. "Won't help you make detective, either."

"I got it, McKool," I said, a bit peevishly.

"Go knock on the door."

"Alone?" I asked.

"Yeah. Feeling things out. We want their attention on us—Long Jack needs time to get in position."

I knocked on the front door. It opened. Jimmy Pizza stood there with two stocky men, both wearing silver and black running suits, each holding a Mini Uzi with thirty-round clip.

"How's my friend Joey? Can he come out to play?"

"He'll come play with you when he gets out of the hospital," Jimmy said.

"McKool wants to see Big Tiny."

"So tell him to come in," Jimmy said.

"We getting in and out of here with no problem?"

"I'm going to kill you."

I smiled bravely. "Waste a cop at Big Tiny's front door? Very risky." I was ready to crap my pants right there on the doorstep.

"When Big Tiny lets me."

"Then when the time is right one of us is a favorite to die," I said. "I like my odds." He went to pat me down and I shook him off. "You're carrying. We're carrying. No traps, no surprises," I said.

"Wait," Jimmy said. He shut the door. He was back in just a moment. "Come."

I waved toward the Chevy; McKool and Cartouche joined me on the porch. We followed Jimmy down a white corridor the height of the house and roofed by an arched skylight leading from the grand foyer. Running Suit One and Running Suit Two trailed at close quarters. Off to one side of the hall was a salon, to the other a room with a baby grand. At the end of the corridor Jimmy threw open double blonde oak doors to a room bigger than my condo, with cathedral ceilings.

Two enormous Persian rugs covered the hardwood floor. In the center of the room stood a long wooden table with eight chairs lining each side and one at the head, one at the foot, a crystal chandelier hanging over its center. Soft late-morning light from the southern exposure flowed into the room through six double sets of French doors framed by luxurious drapes. On the east wall was a huge fireplace with a pile of animal hide rugs before it and a dozen pillows. Two antique Winchester shotguns hung above the mantelpiece. Floor-to-ceiling bookshelves lined the west wall. Here and there on the bookshelves stood some two dozen vases and statues and small marble sculptures that reeked of antiquity, each with its own tiny spotlight.

Big Tiny sat at the far end of the table, his meaty fists folded in front of him. "McKool," he said. "Nice of you to visit. A drink?"

Next to his chair stood Lilith, arms crossed, head bowed, hair atangle, shoulders hunched, hugging herself tight.

The French doors opened out to acres of sprawling lawns and bushes with little groves of trees, a pond far to the back and an Olympic pool with a cabana big enough to house two families of boat refugees. A pair of peacocks strutted on the pool deck.

"Thanks, but we don't plan on staying long," McKool said.

The Running Suits took position, one in the southeast corner of the room, one in the southwest, by the French doors. Jimmy Pizza stood to the right of the oak doors through which we'd come. I took position to the doors' left, Cartouche to my left. I felt I'd wandered into the estate of some pre-Castro Cuban plantation or casino boss.

"So," McKool said.

"So," Big Tiny said.

McKool walked over to Lilith and gave her a small kiss on the cheek, took her by the hand. She looked up into his face, and I could see that she had been crying. "How about I just take Lilith and we'll be on our way?"

"We have business to discuss."

McKool pulled a chair back from the table a few feet and held it for Lilith. "Sit here, Lil," he said. Then he settled into the chair catty-corner from Big Tiny.

"Twenty-five percent," Big Tiny said.

"The business isn't worth running if I give that up," McKool said. "I'd just as soon close the doors."

"Fine. I'll take the whole game. Give me the keys." Big Tiny held out his hand.

"I am the game. Running it's harder than it looks."

Big Tiny smiled. "Okay, then. I'll give you twenty-five percent to run it for me."

McKool shook his head. "I guess we have nothing to talk about." McKool stood up. "Come, Lilith." He walked over to Lilith's chair, and she stood. He took her by the hand and they started toward the double doors.

Jimmy stepped into the doorway, blocking it. McKool stopped a couple of yards away, then moved slowly towards Cartouche and me keeping himself between Jimmy and Lilith. The goons with the Uzis closed in a few steps from their corners and then held their ground. Nobody moved. McKool turned to look at Big Tiny.

Tiny shrugged and smiled. "Twenty-five percent," he said. "Be smart, McKool."

McKool sighed and shook his head. "Jack. Two," he said.

I heard the tinkle of glass breaking. Then again. Two panes of the French doors had been shot out. Just behind Running Suit Two a sand-colored statue on the bookcase exploded into bits. A bullet cracked into the oak door just inches from Jimmy Pizza's ear, sending splinters flying—one gouged Jimmy's cheek and blood trickled down. He started to reach into his jacket and I pulled my SIG, grabbed his right arm, twisted it up behind his back and shoved the handgun's barrel into his neck.

The Running Suits turned toward the yard and let loose randomly through the French doors, emptying their clips, shattering the glass. A peacock squawked. They each slammed in a second clip and let loose again, spraying the pool deck. Then a third clip. At 950 rounds per minute, 16 per second, barely 30 seconds had passed, mostly reloading time, since Long Jack's two shots had entered the room—the Running Suits had blown 180 rounds through the French doors and were out of ammo. One of the peacocks lay dead in a pool of blood on the deck; the other ran in circles, squawking. Smoke from the automatic weapons wisped at the end of the room, highlighted by yellow sunlight.

Cartouche's eyes followed the Running Suits—they had sprinted outside and were frantically casting about the backyard looking for McKool's gunmen. I sensed the tightness in Cartouche's body. McKool and Big Tiny never moved.

"Blue, what did I tell you? Let him go," McKool said.

I hesitated, then pushed Jimmy away from me into the center of the room. He whipped around to face me, his gravity knife suddenly in his hand.

"Jimmy! No!" Big Tiny barked.

Jimmy looked to Tiny then back to me. The dummy was actually making a move with a knife in a gunfight. I wasn't sure what he'd do and held my wep at the ready. Then he pocketed his blade and took a step back. But his angry eyes stayed with me.

"Put it away, Blue," McKool said.

I slipped the SIG back in my pants.

Big Tiny took a long look outside through the broken glass of the French doors. "I see," he said to McKool. "One shooter?"

"No."

"How many?"

"Enough."

"I had two guards out back."

"Nobody is dead."

"Yet, you mean."

McKool nodded. "Yes. Yet."

"We'd have a whole different problem if anybody died," Big Tiny said.

"That's why we're both still alive."

Tiny laughed, a high-pitched guffaw that shook his whole body. "Well, I certainly don't want to get blood on the carpets. Cost $85K each and are hell to clean."

"Definitely wouldn't want to get blood on the carpets," McKool said.

Tiny picked at his fingernail. "Make me an offer."

McKool walked over to Cartouche, who took Lilith by the hand and gently pushed her behind him. "I'll give you twenty grand for the antique Winchesters."

"They're worth fifty," Big Tiny said. "And not for sale."

"What they're worth matters?" McKool asked. "Some things aren't for sale?"

Big Tiny laughed. "I see."

McKool returned to the table. "You send me two players from start to finish every night. You guarantee their losses." He took his seat again. "You don't do any business with or bother my customers or employees without we discuss it first." He leaned back in his chair. "If I have problems with credit, your boys help with collections." He hesitated a long second. "If I lay off any of my sports action I'll give it to you, but I get the same price you give your own guys."

"That's it?" Tiny asked.

"That's it," McKool said.

"And for this I get?

"Ten percent of net. Plus your piece of the sports."

"I had in mind twenty-five percent of gross."

"I had in mind nothing."

"Fifteen percent of gross," Big Tiny said.

"I don't like percentage of gross deals—it's net that matters," McKool said.

"I don't like percentage of net—too easy to fudge expenses," Big Tiny replied.

McKool pondered a moment. "Ten percent of gross or twenty percent of net, whichever is higher. One of your boys can sit with me through counting down and doing my calculating at the end of each play. Settle up once a week, Monday night. Best offer." He stood up. "Last offer."

"You pay for my oak door, the statue and the windows. And a pair of peacocks—they're monogamous; one is useless," Big Tiny said.

"The door and statue, fine. Your boys blew out the windows and killed the bird."

Big Tiny stood, then walked over to the bookshelves and picked up a bit of broken statue, fondled it almost sadly. "This came from Baghdad. Hittite, four thousand years old. Got it cheap, though; Jersey guy at Port Elizabeth had a container from there. I'll order another and bill you."

McKool nodded his assent.

"That'll work," Big Tiny said. He spat on his hand, extended it to McKool.

McKool spat on his own hand and shook Tiny's. "Dinner at six. Cards in the air at six thirty. I'm counting on two of your boys being in chairs," he said. "Tonight."

"Done," Big Tiny said.

"And nobody carries in my house. Not ever." McKool walked to the door. Jimmy looked to Big Tiny. Tiny nodded and Jimmy stepped aside. I held the door for McKool. Cartouche and Lilith followed him out.

"We got unfinished business," Jimmy hissed to me.

"None of that, Jimmy. They're our partners now," Big Tiny said.

Jimmy glared at me and I smiled my sweetest smile. "You got a problem with me?" I said. "Come play. Let your chips talk."

We clambered into the Suburban and headed out toward Old Cutler. Long Jack and his friend slipped out of the shadows into which they'd disappeared, and we drove off down the wooded lane.

• • •

The Pizzas showed up for the game that evening at 6:07, Joey on crutches with an orthopedic boot on his left foot. When Lilith served dinner—meat lasagna with Caesar salad and warm, crusty Italian bread—they each tipped her ten bucks. She said thanks like she meant it. The game was going full swing by seven thirty, when McKool pulled me to talk outside.

"You helped a lot, Blue," McKool said as we walked along the pier in the summer twilight, the western sky pink and orange, lavender giving way to purple in the east. "Bobby said your report on Flapper's car fire made the insurance claim easy. Just an accident, no investigation. The car was leased. Clean paperwork; they just gave her another one. And your presence greatly reduced the potential for violence with Big Tiny. Nobody wants to kill a cop—it's too much trouble."

A pair of island-bound freighters guided by squat tugs heading east passed the skeleton of a high rise ascending just downriver from McKool's. "I didn't just do it for you," I said. "They messed with Abuelita."

"Not to mention Vegas," McKool said with a smile. "Whyever, you helped. If things had gone bad it could have messed up your career. Big time. I appreciate you standing with me."

"I still got work problems. I'm gonna catch hell for calling in. Try not to need me like that again. And I'm not sure what good we did. You gave up a percentage. Why didn't we walk out with Lilith after Long Jack fired into Big Tiny's?"

McKool picked up a flat rock and skipped it across the river's surface. He laughed. "Big Tiny lost," he said. "We won."

Suddenly I saw it. "You want to get your opponent to do what you want; you lead him into the mistakes he's most likely to make anyway." McKool had tried to teach me just that, how people create situations to induce action out of me. "When we talked to the Pizzas about carrying in the game you mentioned how much easier it was for you to make a living than them."

McKool nodded. "Bait. Joey's eyes lit right up—he was back with Big Tiny to lean on me two days later. It was a play."

In the distance I saw another freighter, inbound, city lights atwinkle behind it as darkness settled in. "It was your idea for him to move on you, not his. Why?"

"What it looks like—protection. You know how many gangs work South Florida. Besides your basic Italian families you got pro- and anti-Castro groups, God knows how many Columbian cartels, Rasta posses, Sandinistas and Somacistas, Puerto Ricans, Bloods and Crips from L.A., ex-IRA, Israelis, plus your everyday street bangers. It was only a matter of time before I had to fight somebody off." The westbound freighters cruised past us towards the river's end near the airport where most of the marine industries are. "You know what it would cost to keep on ready alert the kind of firepower Big Tiny can muster with a phone call? Now if somebody muscles me, it's his problem."

"Why Big Tiny?"

"Because the Pizzas gave me an entrée. And he's more or less reasonable, can be negotiated with. He's a businessman, a pro who knows violence is always expensive."

Big Tiny had walked like a fat, juicy crustacean right into McKool's lobster pot. "You trapped him."

"It's even better than that," McKool said. "The Pizzas fire up the game—now we get them every night. That's guaranteed shuffle-up and deal at six thirty sharp, plus an extra hour minimum late night—pure profit. They'll give action. More action, more players; more players, more hours; more hours, more rake. My collection issues should disappear; nobody wants to mess with these guys. And I get to lay off my sports action cheap when the book's out of balance—that alone nearly justifies the deal."

When they invite you to a poker game, it's not because they like you. McKool had held the door wide for Big Tiny.

We headed back inside. As we entered the room, Cartouche approached McKool. "Joey Pizza took another t'ousand," he whispered. "On ze book."

McKool smiled. "Big Tiny's good for it."

"Seat open," Dartboy Dave—the dealer covering for Lefty—called out.

"Go ahead," McKool said to me. "First nickel's on the house. Play good."

Dartboy rearranged the players so that the open seat was on Flapper's left. I got a rack of reds from Cartouche, sat down and posted the big blind.

I would play good, I promised myself. I had the World Series ahead of me. I looked at Jimmy Pizza three to my right—stuck and steaming and staring me down. He'd be firing, trying to run over me in pots. And I'd be ready to take his chips. Ready to lay a trap.

PAPER

BY JIM PASCOE

"Goddammit!" She stuck her finger in her mouth, sucking at the blood.

He looked up from the cold deli meat he was folding onto white bread. "What? Everything okay?"

"Yeah, just a paper cut."

He pulled a knife from the block. "Need to be more careful."

"Yeah, that's exactly what I need." She folded the paper again. Holding it between her thumb and middle finger (index finger and pinky extended), she slipped it into the envelope. "Don't want to behave recklessly around paper. Who knows what'll happen. Next time it—"

"Christ!" He slammed his fist on the thin Formica kitchen counter. "Don't, okay. Just fucking don't."

Her wet tongue touched the envelope flap and traced its edge. She never broke eye contact with her husband.

He dragged the knife across the bread, then wiped the blade with a paper towel and returned it to the block.

"Mail this for me." She pushed the envelope at him. Her red painted nails looked wet against the dull white of her skin.

He asked, "What is it?"

"Does it matter?"

"Fuck you. Gimme the letter." He grabbed it, pulling it toward him. He examined it carefully with a close, measured inspection.

"Jim, you can't open it."

"I'll seal it back up."

"I'm serious." Her words drifted past her lips with little seriousness and even less concern.

He held the envelope to the kitchen light, but all he could read was the address on the outside. "Who's this guy? Van Wagener? He a foreigner?"

"You don't know him," she said.

He glared at her. She returned his expression with silence.

"Deb, you …" He crumpled the flap of his lunch bag, strangling out all the air until his sandwich was closed tight in the brown paper. He put a rubber band around the whole thing. "You remember when I would do anything for you, anything you'd say? Do you?"

"Yeah."

"What happened?"

She considered making a snide comment about last December. But she knew he wasn't being literal. "You're going to be late."

"Then I'll get going."

• • •

He drove past the post office. The radio in his old Mustang didn't work. All he heard was his balding tires licking asphalt, occasionally hiccupping on the cracks in the highway.

The Port St. Joe sky swelled above him, the purple of early dawn bleeding through the egg clouds. He rubbed his eyes with the fleshy part of his thumb.

The envelope sat on the passenger seat.

What was she up to?

He sipped slowly at his 7-Eleven coffee, tasting more of the thin plastic lid than the sour black liquid. He hated milk and hated milk in his coffee. He remembered kissing Deb in the mornings—back when they still kissed—and hating the taste of sweetness her light coffee left on his tongue.

His eyes closed to the memory. He kept the car at a constant speed, kept his hands on the wheel. The car held the line on the straight, empty road. When he looked up, only the thin paper trees on both sides of him registered in his mind. A forest of fragile sticks, barely twenty feet tall, appeared everywhere he looked. Each tree looked thin enough for him to wrap a hand around, as if he could strangle the trunk. It reminded him of masturbation.

Ahead of him, not yet in sight, sat the paper mill, lying in wait as if work might suddenly spring on him, gator-like, snapping its jaws before returning to the dark waters of North Florida.

The address on the envelope read *Jacksonville*.

• • •

Aaron Inveigle had a smile like Humpty Dumpty, and Ream Robertson had a beard like a cloud, its curly black hair hovering on the taller mill worker's face. Jim sat opposite them at the laminate table. All three were drinking coffee in the break room before their shift.

The envelope was folded in half in Jim's pocket.

"I think my wife's cheating on me."

Inveigle spoke up, said, "You think or you know? Big difference between the two. Big difference, Jim."

"I don't have proof if that's what you mean." Jim crushed the empty 7-Eleven cup in his hand and tossed it into the trash.

Ream's words sounded like dirty oil leaking out of a broken engine. "Do you *need* proof to know?"

"I'd need proof to know for sure, wouldn't I?"

They both just looked at him.

Jim stood up. "Go to hell, guys."

Ream cleared his nose and spit the brown mucus into his coffee cup. "What are you going to *do* about it?"

"Why does he need to do anything, heh?" Inveigle turned to Jim. "You still getting laid?" His eyes went wide with slow recognition. "Aw you're *not* … well, yeah, okay okay. That shit's no good."

"If I wanted to get laid I could."

Inveigle blew air past his fat lips. "No doubt."

"She asked me to mail something, my wife." Jim kept the envelope in his pocket. "Some Joe I don't know."

"Well, you open it?"

"Nah. She asked me not to."

"Meeeow … ke-raack!" Inveigle laughed. "Ain't that right, Ream? Whip of the ol' pussy cat."

"I would kill him, the dude fucking your wife." Ream picked his nose, then rubbed his fingers together, crumbling the dry snot onto the floor. "I'd find him and I would kill him."

Jim tensed. "Like I said, I don't know anything for sure. You guys heard of a Van Wagener?"

"He a foreigner?" Inveigle asked.

"Let's say you *do* kill this dude and your whore of a wife—"

"Hey, fucker!" Jim ran to him, fists out.

"—You need an *escape* plan." Ream met him chest first, like a rooster. "You thought of that, Jim? Where you gonna fucking go?"

Through gritted teeth: "Nobody's killing nobody."

Ream kept talking. "I'm just saying. Shit like this messes up your mind all kinds of ways. Dark things cloud your fucking reason. I should know. I had an episode like that when I was in Jacksonville—"

"When the fuck were you in Jacksonville?"

Slowly: "Dark things cloud your reason."

The metal door to the break room opened with audible velocity. Behind it dopplered the low siren voice of the mill foreman.

"Ho! What am I payin' you nancys for? We don't make 'fuckin' around,' we make paper. You wanna work at a fuckin' around mill, move to Lauderdale and get VD. Now quit lookin' at me like you're learnin' something and get to fuckin' work."

The three workers weasled around the fat boss's girth. A ham hand collared Ream, holding him back. "You. Me. The office. We gotta talk. Let these jokers get back to earnin' a paycheck."

Jim could feel his neck still hot as he walked toward the heavy machinery. His temples hurt; his jaw sore from clenching his teeth. He looked over at Inveigle. "What was Ream getting at about Jacksonville?"

"The past is a maze, man. The future … shit, I don't know. Don't ask questions. That way you don't got to deal with the answers."

• • •

Of course he opened the letter.

He didn't even bother trying to slice it open carefully so that he could seal it back up. He just tore into the envelope, digging his finger under the flap, rending the paper into a white wound.

Overhead the exposed pipes dripped a mustard paste—corrosion from the mix of chemicals and extreme humidity. Turns out this Van Wagener was an old flame. A writer. A goddamned writer. It was fucking bullshit.

While his mind pinballed on the tilt table of fury, his fingers hit a sequence of buttons, switches, and levers he had memorized from rote. Jim operated the wet end of the Fourdrinier machine. He'd make a small adjustment, and pulp stock would flow into the machine headbox. Another knob would cause white water to splash out and dilute the mash. A turn of a wheel and the paste-like pulp would crawl onto the wire-mesh belt on its slow climb to becoming paper.

When he first met Deb he had told her that he did something else for a living—he hadn't wanted to admit working at the mill. Maybe it was the way she asked him, like it was a test to see if he was good enough for her. Had he been the kind to think fast, he would have asked what the hell *she* did that was so goddamn important. But all he could think about was how ridiculously white her skin was. So he lied about his job and listened to her talk about wanting to leave Florida someday.

One line in Van Wagener's letter drove Jim particularly bat shit. He wrote, "It wasn't my fault." Like hell it wasn't. Things don't just happen to people … there's this thing called responsibility. Maybe a pussy writer can let things just happen and then look down at the disaster with upraised hands and velvet-painting eyes. But you, sir, are the fucking instigator, the perpetrator, the cause, the man behind the wheel. It's your fucking fault all right.

That first night Jim had kept making shit up, trying to impress her. He had known she was smarter than him and that she knew exactly what he was doing. Bolstered by the evening's confidence, he'd blurted out, "Hey, how is your skin that white?"

She'd pulled at her shirt, stretching it down until she caught the edge of her bra and kept pulling, revealing the uninterrupted cream of her tit.

"No tan lines." It wasn't an answer, at least not to his question.

He wanted her to want him so badly. He couldn't think of another single thing to say.

In the end he didn't have to say anything. A forceful kiss and aggressive hands had provoked her to do things that had made him feel, in those moments, less than hollow.

He leaned hard against the Fourdrinier control panel. Too much water was spilling into the diluting chamber, threatening the mix. He felt dizzy. The blood rushed to his face; he started to lose sensation in his legs.

Van Wagener's letter began to crumple in his fist. He held it like a gas mask over his whole face. He breathed in and out.

Cheap copy paper smells like bleach. Even when you dirty it with ink and sweat from your palm, even if it lingers in a humid room with the cheap cigarette smoke of strangers, paper betrays no secrets; it still smells clean.

He thought about December.

• • •

"Open the fucking door!" Jim slammed his fist on the thin wood of the bathroom jamb.

"No. Not when you're like this."

"You want me to calm down, I'll calm down!" Jim paced in front of the door, pinching the bridge of his nose, trying to cut off the pain behind his eyes. "Come on!"

The door unlocked. She opened it and stepped past him.

"It's not what you think," she said.

He stood there fuming.

She went to her side of the bed and sat down on the edge of the mattress.

"He's just a friend," she said.

He recoiled his hand to hit her and she didn't fucking move. He spun away from her, bouncing on one foot. He left the room that way, hopping on the balls of his feet, wanting to stomp something out. He fell into the chair at his desk. He opened one of the desk drawers and slammed it back into the desk a couple times, needing to unload some of his aggression.

"Don't do that!" she screamed from the bedroom.

He yanked the drawer open as loud as he could to spite her. He stayed planted in the chair.

She spoke to him from the other room. "I don't want to leave Jacksonville. You drive me crazy when you act like this, like a little boy."

"Don't you fucking do that!" Jim let out a frustrated grunt. "You always do this, twist things around. I'm *mad* at you! Don't you turn this around. Fuck fuck fuck!"

"I'm not the one screaming," she screamed.

Everything went still. The desk drawer was still open. He began rooting around in the mess. Fingers filed past unpaid credit card statements. His knuckles bumped a loose deck of cards trying to stay together. Random electronic adapters floated to the surface. His hand dove in deeper until he felt the metal.

He pulled out a gun, an old .22 revolver.

He cracked open the cylinder slowly, quietly. He pressed the tiny bullets into the chambers. His hands shook like he was in cold storage.

A light went off in the bedroom. He looked up at the ceiling, at the light above him. He kept his eyes open until they started to water. His jaw sore from clenching his teeth.

He put the gun in his lap. "I love you."

He closed his green eyes.

• • •

"Goddammit!" Jim snapped out of the memory and into the reality of flashing lights on the Fourdrinier. His line was backed up and he expected Inveigle, who worked down at the dryer section, to give him hell. What he didn't expect was the painful shriek that came from Inveigle's small frame. It was the kind of sound that could hurt you.

Jim ran down the catwalk toward the other end of the machine. He knew that abandoning his station would mean problems in the line, but the pit of his stomach told him the problems were already here.

He had really only zoned out for a couple seconds—ten, twenty at the most—what could have happened in that short span? Certainly nothing that could be responsible for such a screaming.

A worker stumbled forward away from the loud, wet wailing. His knees nearly missed the metal grating of the walkway as he kept stumbling, trying to run without collapsing from nausea. The man couldn't hold it back. He buckled over and emptied his stomach.

"Hey, you okay?" Jim nudged him with the tip of his shoe. "What happened?"

"My god … fuck!" The man spit up thin bile that clung to his lower lip. "His face … his fucking face!"

Jim started to gag on the warm odor of the vomit, so he moved on toward the back. He jumped down a short ladder to the factory floor. Over near another control panel, a crowd was forming. Everyone looked down. Jim couldn't see Inveigle yet, but he could hear him. Hell, they could probably hear him in the next county.

Stocky workmen with tattooed shoulders flinched at the sound. Some of them teared up at what they saw. Jim pulled himself into the crowd, which, like the tide, tried to push him back. "Don't look for god's sake, don't."

Jim began to panic. Was this how it felt? He cried out Inveigle's name, but neither Inveigle nor anyone else answered.

Then the crowd seemed to part, slowly allowing Jim visual access to the accident scene. First he saw the large, looming drying rollers of the paper machine. Next to them were smaller cylinders called calendars, stacked tight together around the coater unit. These smaller rollers were used to compress the paper into a uniform thickness. But now the calendar stack was off axis, and it gave Jim a clear indication of what must have happened. If something knocked the rollers out of alignment, the super-heated starch used to coat the drying paper could have sprayed out toward the operator.

As he was processing this theory, he heard a few voices mention AKD. Jim's pulse went from a quick thrum to a deep, reverberating thumping. AKD was a type of chemical sizing agent used in the wet-end of production. Sometimes, as a cost-cutting measure, the mill would substitute fresh rosin from local sand pine trees. Sap.

Either way, Jim imagined that if, by some strange chance, while he wasn't paying attention at his board, some excess AKD seeped undiluted into the dry end of the Fourdrinier, then the hot starch spray would turn into highly alkaline glue. A thick, super-heated, highly corrosive adhesive. But really, he thought, what were the chances of that happening?

Then he saw Aaron Inveigle's face.

The man was curled sideways on the cement floor. His arms stretched out stiff behind him, locked at the elbows, and his hands shook at the ends like leaves on dead branches during a hurricane. His head rested uneasy in a shallow pool of discolored liquid.

Inveigle's forehead bubbled up with blisters. His eyelids had fused shut; his nose flattened. Where his fingers had stuck to his face were now torn holes exposing pink muscle. His mouth was a hole filled with teeth and lipless screams.

Jim clenched his fists, unable to turn away. He felt someone clamp down on his upper arm, drag him away from the crowd. It was Ream.

"I know what you did," Ream whispered into his ear.

"I didn't fucking do this."

"Don't worry. This shit isn't your fault. But that doesn't mean you didn't *do* anything. You *did* something."

Ream straightened his back and lolled his head side to side, looking for eavesdroppers. Everyone was preoccupied with other atrocities. He leaned in for another whisper: "Now's your chance." He shoved a package into Jim's hand. Jim grabbed the heavy object wrapped in a dirty, gray oilcloth.

With his other hand, Jim unfolded the cloth to reveal a medium-sized metal cogwheel. "What's this?"

"It's the missing piece of the machine."

"Don't bullshit me, Ream. What the fuck is going on?"

"I broke the machine. Took a piece out, so it's incomplete and don't work. Now it's you. You got to fix what's broken. Make it right."

"Jesus Christ!" Jim grabbed Ream by the lapels. "Did you see what just fucking happened? You're making jokes?"

"Didn't expect Inveigle to get hurt, but face the facts: someone always gets hurt."

Jim looked at his fists in front of him; they were no longer grabbing Ream. He stood a couple feet away and receded into the steam and distance.

Jim opened his fists. His hands, empty.

The next sound came from the foreman. "A'right, you nancys, clear out. Go home, go to a bar, go to a fish fry, I don't give a fuck. Just get the hell out."

Millworkers began to scatter like kitchen cockroaches when the light's turned on. Jim stood still, wondering why Inveigle had stopped screaming. It didn't seem fair. "What about Inveigle? Isn't anyone going to come and help? You want us to leave?"

The foreman's eyes look out into the thinning crowd, not connecting to anyone. "Ho! You people deaf *and* stupid? Make yourself scarce!"

The flow of Jim's coworkers was already carrying him out toward the exit. He had nowhere to go but home.

• • •

He turned the knob on his front door. Locked. Deb's pale red truck sat in the dirt driveway.

"Christ, Deb, what the fuck?" He slammed his fist on the thin wood of the jamb, as he reached for his keys.

He only had two keys on his ring. The silver one had FORD on it, and the gold one had SCHLAGE. He tried the gold one again. It fit, but it would not turn.

He threw the keys down and began to pace, pinching the bridge of his nose, trying to cut off the pain behind his eyes. "Come on!"

He heard the handle being worked from the inside. The door opened to show her face, her white skin glowing out of the darkness. Deb looked beautiful, more beautiful than he remembered her looking in a long while. She said, "Excuse me. Can I help you?"

"Accident at work. Bad. Now my keys and fuck, and why are we talking in the doorway?"

She had already begun to close the door on him.

"Hey!"

"I'm sorry I can't—"

"Deb, I'm in no fucking mood."

Her eyes twitched. She took a breath, leaning against the door, trying to keep it between them. She said, "I think you have the wrong person."

He pushed at the door hard, forcing her back into the house. He entered.

Jim looked at her face. "What are you trying to do?"

"Please … get out of my house."

"My house? This is *our* fucking house."

"I don't have much money … I'll give you the cash I have if you please—"

"This is because of *him*, isn't it? You don't want to talk about it and now I don't fucking exist?"

"I … I can scream. The neighbors are home …"

"Where's my shit?" He looked around. "It's gone. What did you do with it?"

He chased her down the hallway into the kitchen. He started opening cupboard doors. "Everything is gone. Even my lunch bags."

He pulled a knife from the block. She screamed.

He slammed the blade down on the Formica. He went over to the small table.

"Right here. It was right here."

She backed herself into a corner against the refrigerator. She was crying.

He pointed the knife at her. "Sit down. Sit down!"

The chair scraped across the floor. She sat down.

"It was right here. This morning. You were sitting there. I made my sandwich. You gave me that fucking letter."

He put the knife down, reached into his pocket. He felt the metal gasket that Ream had wrapped in the oilcloth. The letter was gone. He tried to remember exactly what happened. He knew he pulled it out, read it. Then that thing with Inveigle … did he set it down? Did he drop it? He had thought he put it back in his pocket, but he couldn't remember. It must be still there. At the mill.

He heard her short breaths, her sobbing, getting louder.

He leaned in toward her. "What did you say?"

She whimpered.

"Don't you fucking do that!" He let out a frustrated grunt. "You wrote a letter, *you* did. I'm gonna go get it and you'll see. You can fucking hide my shit and act like you're acting, but you … you just *wait*."

• • •

He drove back to the paper mill. The radio in his old Mustang didn't work. His balding tires licked asphalt, occasionally hiccupping on the cracks in the highway. The Port St. Joe sky swelled above him, but something was different.

He rubbed his eyes with the fleshy part of his thumb.

The sky called out a clear, pale blue. Not a cloud up in it.

Then he noticed the smell. Clean.

• • •

A chain-link fence surrounded the mill parking lot. He had to park on the street. He climbed the fence and crossed the empty lot to the large building.

He headed first to the break room. The coffee pot had boiled off, and a dark crud ringed its way down the glass carafe. He looked in the garbage. All that rested at the bottom of the plastic-lined barrel was a crushed 7-Eleven coffee cup. Jim knew that it didn't make sense for the letter to be *here*; he remembered waiting to open it at his station. It was out *there*. It had to be. Still, he wanted not to rush, take his time, retrace his every step in case he missed an important moment in the sequence that led him back here.

He walked onto the factory floor. The large Fourdrinier machine sat there, all three hundred feet of it. He laughed at the ridiculousness of it: he stood facing a machine that could spit out six hundred feet of paper per minute, and his goal was to find a single, crumpled, letter-sized piece of paper.

The area around his station appeared empty. He wiped his fingers across the control panel, eyes closed, feeling the knobs and switches like some kind of industrial Braille. No sign of the letter.

He looked at the head box, walked over to it, and lifted the lid to peer inside. No pulpy soup, no wet mash, just a dry empty metal bin. He turned to look over his shoulder, back toward the additive section where the ground wood was washed, bleached, and refined. Could the letter have traveled upstream, fighting its way back to its very origins? No. Jim started fearing the worst, that the paper was gone.

 A sound startled him. He couldn't place it, the mill was so large and open. It sounded like a rustling kinda sound. Like a leaf on a dead branch. Probably just an animal. Or was it a person? Had someone followed him? Had someone stayed behind from this morning?

He looked up at the foreman's office. Did the sound come from there? He stared at the darkness behind the office windows. Maybe the answers were hidden inside that room. He climbed the stairs, put his hand on the handle, and listened. Quiet. Opening the door he entered the dark.

Fumbling around for the light switch, his foot bumped into something. Lights on, he saw that he had kicked over a tall, thin trashcan. Paper had spilled across the floor. He shuffled his feet through it, making his way to the desk.

He sat down in the foreman's chair and immediately became angry. An image came to his mind, he and Deb kissing, the kind of kissing where you touch the back of each other's head. He pounded his fist on the desktop to chase away the memory.

He opened a drawer, rooted around just to see if something would come to him. But it was a bunch of nothing: financial documents, a deck of cards, spare fuses, and the like.

The documents gave him a thought. He went over to the black steel filing cabinet and started rifling through file folders. Employee records. The more he searched, the more frustrated he got. Something wasn't fucking right.

His paperwork—Ream's and Inveigle's too—gone. They must have been pulled aside after the accident. But why?

He looked at the waste paper that had spilled out of the trash when he'd knocked it over. How had he not seen it before? He dove to the ground and snatched it up.

In his hands, the envelope that Deb's letter had been in. It was further torn up and Van Wagener's name was missing, but Jim could still see the word "Jacksonville."

He looked around for the letter. No luck. He tore through the rubbish on the floor then dug in and emptied the entire can. He uncrumpled pages, pieced together sheets that had been torn. Nothing. However the envelope had made its way up here, the letter did not seem to have followed.

Jim threw the office door open and stepped out on the top stair. He hung his body over the rail and screamed down at the empty factory. "I know you're here! You can't fucking hide from me! You're just a piece of fucking paper!"

He jumped down the stairs, taking two or three at a time. He ran over to the dry end, where Inveigle had had his accident. He stood in front of the coater unit, looked up at the calendar stack that was out of alignment. He pushed one of the cylinders and it dipped down, almost like a bounce, revealing a space farther into the machine. Jim looked inside, and he could see the place with the part that was missing, the part that Ream had removed.

He still had the gasket in his pocket, so he pulled out the oilcloth. It felt heavier now. He pulled back the cloth corner by corner. The gasket was gone.

In his hands a gun, an old .22 revolver.

He held the gun at his side and walked the length of the Fourdrinier, back toward the wet end.

Something caught his eye, a flash of white. Looking into the jaws of the paper machine, he saw the letter.

He reached in with his left hand, extended his arm as far as it could go. The letter was far away. He pulled his arm back out and thought a moment. He knew he wouldn't be able to reach it that way.

He found a foothold on the machine and pulled himself up. Slowly and carefully he climbed into the guts of the machine. He inched his way farther inside, the space getting tighter and tighter. He pulled the gun closer to his body to try and fit better.

His knees shimmied his lower body into a ball creating a pressure that helped extend his left arm deeper and deeper. He could almost feel the edge of the paper.

The machine completely surrounded him. If the machine were running—if someone were to turn it on now—he wouldn't be able to get himself out fast enough. The gears and rollers and wires would cut him up, chew him into mash, turn him into paper.

A final push forward and he grabbed the letter. Pulling it toward him wasn't easy. He hadn't left himself much room. And as he brought back his arm, it got caught in another piece of the machine.

The mill felt warmer. Had someone done something to raise the temperature? Was someone in there with him? He angled his head so his could see the letter.

He examined it carefully with a close, measured inspection. He read it again. It seemed different. It was a confession, signed Jim Van Wagener. The name sounded familiar.

Another sound echoed through the mill. There was definitely someone here. He wanted to cry out, but he second-guessed himself. Maybe this person was looking for him. Screaming would only draw attention to his hiding spot. Still, it could be local kids, causing trouble. All they would have to do is flip a switch or two and start the machine.

His right hand, still holding the gun, started getting tingly, going to sleep. He adjusted his weight, pushed off against one of the cylinders, and the machine gave way.

He knew he would now be able to get himself out of this trap, out of the machine, out of the mill, out of Port St. Joe. But where to next? He had a feeling he was supposed to go to Jacksonville. But one way or another he felt that Jacksonville would come to him.

Somewhere in the distance, miles and miles away, sirens screamed toward him.

He knew it wasn't his fault, so he decided to do nothing but wait.

ESCAMBIA COUNTIES

BY RAVEN McMILLIAN

Zane, for the most part, had already made up his mind on what he was about to do, but he went through the motions of alternative reasoning for the sake of display. He opened the scuffed-up freezer door of his rental property refrigerator, looking towards the back corner behind a slab of venison, where a clear, plastic Gatorade bottle, the top half raggedly shorn off by a steak knife, sat filled with ice, an unblemished credit card trapped in the middle, hunched slightly sideways, sixteen numbers across the face still shining with an unused silver finish. Zane had $500 on that card; that was all they'd give him on it when he applied. He had been hoping for a few thousand more, to bankroll a jaunt to Atlanta, for no real reason other than to pretend he was still moving in a better direction in life, to spend a long weekend in a new place full of strange faces and stranger possibilities, where you roll the dice again and you might finally get lucky. When they only approved $500, Zane, in a rare flash of responsibility, decided to set the card aside for a for-real emergency, freezing it to make it more difficult to access when his attitude reverted to leisure as usual.

Now, he had collected a thick stack of cut-off notices, with the return envelope warning colors—pink for the car insurance, blue for the phone bill, and yellow for electric. The remittance envelopes always came out of the bills a safe white when everything was up to date; but once you fell behind regularly, begging off twangy female customer service voices, it was a splash of pastel PAY NOW OR LOSE YOUR SERVICE! envelopes cluttering up the kitchen table. It'd be about $325 to keep everything on, which the frozen credit card could cover, but what next?

Zane hadn't worked the past two weeks, having gotten booted off his last jobsite for dragging the project along too slowly, making Mondays a regular extension of the weekend, even starting Friday nights early on Thursday afternoon sometimes. There wasn't going to be any more money coming in anytime soon with no billable hours anywhere, and he hadn't tried that hard to line up new work elsewhere. He didn't want to keep siding houses anyways, even though he guessed he had to in order to keep feeding money orders into all these envelopes. He could thaw out the credit card and calm down this crop of pastel past due notices, but when they started blossoming back out of the mailbox in a few short weeks, what then?

Feeling he'd made a proper theatrical attempt for whatever audience might be watching over him while he was alone, Zane whipped the freezer door shut, cool air streaming across his left arm. Zane knew what he was truly building up to here, so he might as well get in the proper mind frame for it all.

The painting that hung on the opposite wall from the kitchen's lone square window wasn't that great a painting. Honestly, Zane didn't much even see the painting itself, it being a gift from a Filipino chick he used to live with from her art school days. At first he kept it out of a polite obligation, long after he and the Filipino chick had exploded into separate directions. It ended up being useful, not for the indistinguishable smears of blood red, puke green, and dripping browns that made up some sort of woodpecker-looking thing, but because of the thick, 3x3 frame the canvas had been staple-gunned into, much thicker than a normal frame.

Pulling the painting off the wall from the bottom, Zane reached behind it on the upper left hand side, pulling out a small cellophane wrapper, twist tied at the top. Used to be Zane would stash his blow at the bottom of the frame, where the bag would sit hiding on its own, back when it was never anything less than cocaine flakes. But eventually, after repeating these motions to the same framed corner with the invisible audience watching, he wasn't sure if it was secure. The downgraded powders he used nowadays to scratch his nose with stiff snorts on slow weekends that meandered into Mondays had helped change his outlook too, causing his mind to wander towards needing new hiding spots within the same framework more often. No accidental bumps against the wall would rattle the painting, causing everything to fall out, exposed to the world, no matter the fact hardly anyone came around except Zane. He'd roll a piece of duct tape backwards against itself to create a sticky tab at the top of the frame's innards. A gentle press of the upper edge of his twisted bag of cheap speed—the bikers called it crank but the wiggers called it meth—against the duct tape, and it'd stay stuck there, ever so slightly, just enough to remain suspended in silence, but easy enough to pull loose when access was necessary.

He tugged out his cellophane of crudely crystallized chemicals, grabbed an empty CD case from off the counter, and sat down at the kitchen table. Pouring a healthy pile on the scuffed face of the light blue jewel case, he chopped at it ritually with a thick paper insurance card. He'd bought a whole long box of the CD cases at the dollar store, tired of his music sliding back and forth inside the pocket of his truck door, loose CDs scratching themselves out of function. The cases came in the same pastel shades as past due envelopes, and tended to snap into two useless pieces easily. Zane dragged the mound of powder into a pair of tight, parallel rows, the second one about half an inch shorter than the first. He pulled a piece of plastic straw from the penny-laden ashtray on his kitchen table, and sucked the long, right rail up his right nostril, shifted the straw quickly, pinched the other side of his face, and up the left nasal passage with the shorter line. Zane leaned back against the creaky chair, and looked out the window at his truck, silent in the yard, clean copper coat shining in the sun, perfect shape broken up by a deep dent in the front quarter panel from a plum tree that got in the way at a Saturday night pig roast party that had almost turned into a Sunday morning.

Motivated by the chemically triggered adrenaline rush, Zane got going. He twisted shut the cellophane, gave it a calculating eyeball to guesstimate how many more lines he could squeeze out of it, and tacked it back behind the painting. He grabbed his truck keys off the counter, a Pepsi out of the fridge, and slammed the kitchen door shut behind him. There was a crack in the wood from a work boot's kick, and the hot water weather coming off the Gulf had swollen the wood. That, combined with foam stripping to keep cool Decembers locked out, and the door no longer fit into its jamb. Without a rough slam, it wouldn't shut all the way.

The two Escambia Counties sat side by side, but in two separate states. Zane lived almost to the eastern county line of the Alabama Escambia, a few miles outside of the almost comically named Dixie, Alabama. Dudes around there took it seriously though, full of a locals-only Southern pride that saw Zane, regardless of the hint of twang in his voice, as an untrustable outsider. He wasn't born from there, and his last name wasn't painted on the mailboxes decorating the ditches up and down these back roads.

Zane turned his truck south onto Highway 29. In four years here, he'd never once driven 29 farther north than the twenty miles or so into Andalusia, always headed south, anchored to the Gulf, having spent all his pre-adult life and about two-thirds of the grown part scattered around the Florida panhandle. Since coming north to just outside Dixie, he'd gone South 29 over a thousand times it seemed.

This first stretch of the highway was his favorite because, before you got to Brewton, it was a normal-paced, two-lane artery through the eastern half of Escambia. The state squeezed as much life out of the asphalt as they could, pavement sun-bleached nearly white, and as cracks would appear, they'd come along with a tar truck and patch the gaps, leaving chaotic black patterns across the road. Zane had ridden that stretch of road many times, studying the scattershot tar patches, looking like alien hieroglyphics, trying to decipher their meaning. Coming home sometimes, as Sunday morning sunrises just cleared the pine trees, with a buzzing grip tingeing his brain, Zane'd imagine something real buried in those patterns. It had a meaning for him, he just hadn't been able to read it right yet.

Once he hit Brewton's four-lane expansion, Florida wasn't far. State lines, like county divides but magnified by twenty, weren't anything tangible you could grab at, except maybe the bright green state sign greeting you after the road humped over the cluster of train lines at the Florida/Alabama border. Zane and his buddy Duane had walked those tracks more than a few times, immersed in strong hallucinogenic mind meanders together, heading whichever way east or west called them stronger, tapping young shoes against dusty railroad ties, wandering through entire evenings until they groggily adjusted their dilated pupils' blurred vision as the sun would crank up on another day of youthful indiscretion.

Those were some great times for Zane and Duane, sharing a sheltered recklessness only kids from successful bloodlines could live. Zane had been sent by his folks to a military school his sophomore year of high school, right after he'd started acting out and getting in trouble. Zane's dad figured it'd whip him back into shape, onto the right track, to fulfill the promise of the last name he was born with. That one year at military school, Duane was the first person he met, another wealthy kid sent off for some shaping up or shipping out, and of course that linked them as best young friends, bonded by a similar mission to survive the rigid structure, sneaking through the militant routines that were supposed to straighten them out, maintaining their hell-bent, recreational drug-fueled attitude, just below the radar of all the crew-cutted instructors and straight-laced older students with pseudo-authoritarian powers. Duane spent three years there, two solo flights through the Florida Air Academy sandwiching his one year spent in solidarity with Zane. Everyone else at the school, if not using their last names, called Zane "Zee," since he and Duane tended to be within ten paces of each other, and rhyming names for best friends at a military school overflowing with budding alpha male teenagers probably was too homosexual. But "Zee" and Duane were tight like a middle and a trigger finger, twisted together to make the sign for good luck.

Afterwards, while Zane had stumbled and staggered his way out of his parents' favor, Duane, perhaps from the extra tours of duty through military school, had mastered the art of parental deception, even well into adulthood, to the extent his folks still supported him, even giving him a potentially functional farm, complete with live-in quarters for farm workers back behind the main house that Duane kept empty of any other people. His farmhouse compound was about thirty miles over the railroad track hump, and after a couple of miles across the blacker, fresher Floridian four-lane surface of Escambia County south, Zane's stomach started churning noisily from adrenaline, Pepsi bottle corn syrup, and amphetamine chemicals.

Zane yanked his truck into a service station, one of those old school joints that had yet to replace the garage bays with the neon shine of sandwich bars and coffee machines and a sprawling buffet of road snacks. The station's bays were locked behind windowed doors, cars still lifted, waiting for Monday morning mechanics to come back tomorrow morning. But the dilapidated little snack center, nothing more than a single soft drink cooler and one metal rack stacked with single-serving potato chip bags and snack cakes, was open, a chubby redneck girl watching a tiny black-and-white TV behind a wall made of cigarette displays.

"You got a bathroom?" Zane asked her.

She looked up. "Yeah, around the side. The key's by the door there."

Zane knew this already, but it helped to act out the scene as if it was your virgin trip into their always-locked, well-stocked bathroom. The actual garage owner, only there during weekdays proper, had been weird about Zane using the bathroom one time coming through this way, since Zane hadn't bought gas or anything. The key itself was zip-tied to a foot-long slab of wood, to discourage loss. The bathroom was kept clean, more likely meant to be an employee perk than a public option. Mint green tiles gave it an institutional feel, with a small, ceramic sink sticking out the wall in front of a fading mirror. Zane sat on the low-slung stool, the chemical orchestra still churning inside. The bathroom's lone wire-reinforced windowpane had a pea-sized fleck missing, spider webbing outwards, ordered yet neglected. Not a mark of graffiti was to be seen, and the metal door automatically locked behind him, with only the one key, so Zane tried to relax.

Duane and his long-time girlfriend were spending the week down at an island beach house his family owned just past Pensacola. He'd told Zane about this last week during one of their frequent three-minute-long phone calls.

Duane's girlfriend didn't think much of Zane, knowing him only as some sketchy dude who lived up in Alabama as opposed to a private school kid who came from a good family like Duane. But Zane and Duane had stayed close, as best as teenage friends geographically split by only an hour's drive could remain a decade later. They'd still get together regularly to run off for weekend indulgences of drugs, drinking, and general indiscretions a couple of times a year, an hour or two in any direction, just to stay young. This, in all likelihood, compounded Duane's girlfriend's disdain of Zane.

Realizing his tossing and turning stomach wasn't going to rest, Zane swallowed it in, settled it as much as a few deep breaths of the tiny bathroom's lemon vinegar air could, splashed water on his face, and got back on the road, picking up another Pepsi from the drink cooler when returning the precious slab-anchored key to the redneck chick inside. He'd be at Duane's in no time.

The driveway to Duane's was long and paved, but about halfway up, there was an iron gate forever propped open by two hefty chunks of white quartz that you could see the front circular drive of the main house from. A newer pickup truck with a long trailer behind it sat there, and Zane saw two guys buzzing around the yard, one standing on a large mower and the other chopping at the edges with a weed-eater. As unseen as possible, Zane did a smooth U-turn onto the flat grass back out the iron gate, down to the main road, away from the house. Over the years, he and Duane had wandered most of this property, so he knew it fairly well, and took his truck up a logging trail just past Duane's driveway that accessed the southern edge of Duane's family's property. Zane pulled off the rutted, red clay truck path at a clearing littered with beer cans. He slid out of the truck, and started pushing through the pines towards the fence line a few hundred feet through the sticky, prickled undergrowth. Deeper into the thickets, he started getting snagged on blackberry bushes, their promising white blooms long turned to dark berries that were either gone from the deer or withered on the vine and left behind as shriveled black balls. Every now and then, a stiff branch of blackberry thorns would fishhook Zane's forearm, and the skin would yank out as spiky thorn and soft flesh struggled to separate. Finally, at the edge, the fence line was thickened with blackberries, and Zane slowly poked his way into the middle, crouching down, putting an eye to the two guys in the yard.

The one on the mower was a stocky pit bull of a man with a shaved head and fu manchu mustache, zipping back and forth in tight circles on grass already flat as a carpet. The other guy was a tall, skinny white kid in last year's hip hop fashions, with a flat-brimmed baseball hat just barely cocked sideways on his head. Zane's left forearm was pockmarked with blackberry bush contusions from pushing through the woods, and it had a dull ache from the natural poisons. He wasn't sure how long he'd have to watch those guys recut the perfect lawn, and he wished he'd brought his Pepsi with him.

The fu manchu guy finally drove his mower back up onto the trailer, and then went up the porch steps to bang on the door a few times while the skinny kid wrapped up, trimming around the front yard boxwoods and two wispy willow trees on either side of the pebble walkway. The door never opened, and fu manchu guy peeked in the small window to the side quickly before heading back to his truck, as the skinny kid strapped the weed-eater to the trailer. Two minutes later, they were gone, leaving the iron gate wide open like always.

Zane straddled over the split rail fence, and walked across the yard. He felt out of place, cellular memory strongly attached to the circular drive and landscaped path up to the front door. Zane hiked across half-an-acre's worth of manicured ryegrass, cut up the front porch without either foot touching the walkway's off-white pebbles. He banged on the door with far more authority than fu manchu did, and surveyed the yard while there was no response. No hundred-year-old hardwood floors creaking from footsteps inside; no sight of Duane's girlfriend's car out front; nothing. Zane knew that no one was home, but still, this was a place he'd visited often, and felt he should go through the standard motions.

He gave the side window a cursory peek, and then walked around the house, back to where the outbuildings were. The first one, an old carriage house, was just Duane's storage zone at this point, though there was a functional bedroom in the back that Zane would lay in if he bothered sleeping during a planned weekend visit.

Beyond the carriage house were two more unkempt buildings, one just a shed, and both wired with electricity that broke off from the main house at its power box, with one meter for the whole compound, which Duane said helped the electric company not notice how much power he used back inside the last building, where he cultivated expensive marijuana plants from expensive mail order marijuana seeds, to supplement his limited access to his parent's wealth. If the shriveled state of the blackberry bushes were any indicator, Zane figured there'd be a healthy stash of dried buds on the workbenches across all four walls of the old building's "kitchen."

There was no porch, just flat slabs of scrap soapstone pressed into the grass from years of foot traffic. The front door was weathered wood speckled green by old paint, with a pineapple-shaped glass doorknob sticking obtrusively out, purpled from long-term solar exposure. Zane gave it a solid twist but it did nothing, as expected. He muled back and gave the door the bottom texture of his work boot as hard as possible, about a foot below the glass knob. The wood rattled, but everything held stiff. Zane repeated the blow, this time with his legs off the ground and his full weight pushed forward through his right foot. The boot struck a second time, and the door's aged oak gave a satisfying crack along the right edge. One final blow and the panel went crooked enough for Zane to heave against the door and gain access. He brushed the hints of a red clay boot print off the door as he entered, lightly, to avoid splinters.

The place reeked of high-caliber weed, and the four kitchen wooden counters wrapping the room had all the signs of a slow, assembly line crop harvest. The first two were camouflaged with dried plants resting across the countertops. The third wall's work bench had white-haired buds sorted into piles on top of a strip of wax paper stretched all the way to the fourth wall, where a cluster of relatively full pint jars and a digital scale sat. Zane knew from experience that the pint jars were going to end up as Duane's personal stash, hiding behind his couch in the main house's high-ceilinged living room. At the end of the last counter were a pair of stacks of heavy plastic orange Tupperware containers, four per stack. Zane popped open the corner of the top one in the front row, unleashing that unmistakable, intoxicating, Pandoran stink. Holding the Tupperware on his fingertips, he figured there to be about a half-pound inside. His thumbs resealed the lid along the edges, and Zane grabbed six of the eight orange containers, leaving the bottom one from each stack, and headed back out the bashed-in front door, past the carriage house, around the main house, and back across the half acre towards the fence line.

The ride home went faster, Zane never having felt comfortable riding around with a few pounds of high-powered weed in his truck, all of it tucked into the tool bin behind the passenger seat. Before he crossed the railroad tracks back into Alabama, he swung into the Piggly Wiggly to grab a twelve-pack, plus a pound of the cheapest coffee. The older guy at the counter held the twelve-pack by the handle and asked Zane if he needed an "Alabama cooler."

"What's that?"

The guy smiled a flat grin missing a few pieces, and said, "I can't believe you never heard of an Alabama cooler." Opening up a brown grocery bag, the older guy packed the box of beer into it sideways, folded down the top of the bag, and handed it back to Zane. "There you go, son…an Alabama cooler."

Back at the truck, Zane tucked the twelve-pack into the pickup's bed, sliced open the bag of coffee with a razor knife from the tool bin, and poured the whole bag inside around the Tupperware containers. Then he shut the lid on the overwhelming coffee smell. The large green sign proclaiming ALABAMA at the hump in Highway 29 was peppered with buckshot.

Back home, having all the weed laid out in front of him, lids off all the tops, Zane realized how much marijuana it actually was. This was high quality reefer, Duane asking nearly three thousand dollars a pound for it. Zane figured even if he sold it dirt cheap to move quickly, he could squeeze a grand out of each container. The only question was whether to weigh it out and bag it up into ounces to maximize the profit factor, or just sell it off as one bargain-priced lump amount. Individually, it had double the money potential, but he'd have to deal with people he either knew a little too well or not well enough, coming and going and interacting and clogging up his evenings with paranoia-laced transactions, sugar-coated with small-talk, dragging the night down with drawling propriety, it being seen as rude to simply show up and outright ask for what you actually wanted around these parts. Plus, Zane would have to ride a wide circle through the upper Escambia County to move this much high-priced weed. Most of the local stoners were bargain shopper varieties, more acclimated to amphetamines, and mostly looking for Mexican dirt weed to help wind down at the end of the night as opposed to the High Times centerfold-quality, nicknamed breeds Duane grew. But Zane knew a guy up towards Auburn that would probably be willing to buy the whole parcel, and sell all of it up there. A good-sized college town tends to have the discriminating tastes and discretionary incomes needed to make the most out of a three-pound score of marijuana like this.

The containers were spread across the kitchen table like hunting spoils, and Zane sipped at his fourth can out of the twelve-pack, still sitting in its "cooler" on the counter. He picked up the cordless phone from its pedestal beside the colored envelopes, and started poking the scroll button on his caller ID, to see if the guy up near Auburn was still in there somewhere, to save the trouble of digging through his phone number drawer—a terribly cluttered collection of paper scraps and shreds of newspaper corners, marked with chicken scratch numbers, most of which lacked any name. It all came from Zane's head, somewhere, and the number scraps were used to trigger recognition more than outright declare. To make it all worse, the cordless had taken more than a few accidental—and even the occasional on-purpose—piledrivers into the linoleum floor, so the screen didn't read out completely, missing a dot matrix piece of an eight here or half a zero there.

While he was scrolling through the broken numbers inside his phone's short memory, it woke up in his hand with a frantic, electronic twang. Even with the busted, distorted screen, Zane immediately recognized Duane's cell phone number.

Zane's mind ramped up like he'd just sniffed down a thick bump of the bathtub crank from behind the painting. "Why the hell would he be calling now?" he fretted. He sucked in a fat breath, stabbed the speak button with his thumb, and spoke, "Hello?"

"Zee, what's goin' on, man. Hey…what do you got going on this week?" Duane's voice was loud, worrisome and bothered, uneasing Zane as to whether this was a stressful coincidence or Duane actually knew something was up. The orchestra in the pit of his stomach started tuning up again.

"Ain't you at the beach, man?"

"Nah, Zee, we left early." There was a long, hanging pause, and Zane heard a door shut on the other end of the phone. Duane's voice came back lower, as whispered as a man could get while still maintaining his rugged bass tones. "The bitch got all crazy on me again, Zee. She's been on me about, I don't know, getting a job, improving myself, whatever. But we got to fighting pretty bad on the way down there, to where she was like, 'I'm outta here.' So we came back home. But when we got here, I saw my grow house door was kicked open, and someone ripped me off for my whole harvest for this year. Well, most of it at least."

"Did what? Say what?" Zane feigned bewildered inquisition, going through the motions again.

"Yeah, somebody ripped me off. So I was freaking out about that, and she just goes off on me even more, how I'm not doing anything, sitting around, selling weed, and then someone comes and robs us at our home, and how she's not gonna live like that, settling for that life like I have, or whatever."

Zane continued with his part. "When did all this happen, man?"

"I guess today. We were arguing last night at the beach after we got down there, and then again all morning and she was over it, so we came home today. But then we got broken into while we were gone, so she's mega-pissed now, and going up to her folks' house."

"Man, Duane, that really sucks."

"Yeah. But honestly, I don't want to be around here either right now, 'cause I'm pretty sure I know who did it, and I don't really want to be around to be tempted to go over to his house until I cool down and figure out how to handle this proper-like. You think I can come up there for a few days?"

"Up here?" Zane wasn't sure if he was getting backed into his own answers, or being out-acted, or what. "Yeah ... I guess. Sure. I don't really have anything going on, just work tomorrow and all. Maybe."

"Awesome, Zee. She said she'd drop me off because she doesn't want me here by myself either. You know how she is. She thinks the dude who ripped us off is crazy and will come back and think we're still not here since her car is gone and then he'll kill me if I'm here."

"Who is this dude?" Zane asked, feeling it out.

"Just some guy I've been dealing with down here. He's not gonna kill nobody, man. He's just a normal dude like us. You know how she is, man." His voice had gone back to normal volume, and Zane could hear Duane's girlfriend's voice pecking through the background. "She's gonna pack up some of her things first, but I'll be that way in a couple hours, man."

"Alright."

"I appreciate it, Zee." And the other line clicked dead. Zane set the cordless on top of the multi-colored envelopes, and stared at six open containers full of the thick-smelling, fat buds of his probable best friend's weed, far too big to fit behind the painting.

He capped the containers back off, and stalked through the house, once overing everything with a frantic glance. It certainly didn't seem like Duane suspected him of snatching the drugs, but he might. If Duane knew he got ripped off, yet someone purposely left two of the Tupperware half-pounds behind, plus the pint jars, he might have figured it was someone who knew him and didn't want to be completely ruthless about it. If Duane thought that, there couldn't be more than a couple of people other than Zane that were crazy enough to rip him off but conscientious enough to leave some behind. "Why didn't I just steal it all?" hind sighted Zane.

He settled on the kitchen to find a good spot to stash everything. The containers were airtight and held the aroma in, but just in case a corner randomly popped open, the smells from the kitchen could help conceal any exposure. The dollar store trash can, old food, plus dishes in the sink from four days ago, there was plenty in here to smell first.

Zane opened the freezer door, looked in on the credit card in its frozen Gatorade bottle purgatory, and realized there was nothing much to hide behind inside there. On the off-chance Duane went looking in the fridge or freezer—or cabinets or closet or anywhere really—Zane would have to keep this stuff far out of place. The freezer's cool air drifted over his left arm, feeling good on the blackberry prickle sores, and on down his leg. He took the steel toes of his work boot and gently poked at the grate in front of the refrigerator's underside. It rattled hollowly. Zane crouched down and peeked through the slats, looking through a heavy collection of dust into a darkness that looked to be five or six inches tall.

The grate had one screw on one side and a clasp on the other, so after Zane backed out the Phillips head, the whole thing popped right off. Zane removed it delicately, trying to keep the dust from shaking off the inside of the grate. He stuck his hand inside and felt nothing but more dust. Reaching back as far as his forearm would let him, he still felt nothing, except for the cool, slightly perspired metal bottom of the refrigerator. He positioned two of the containers along the edge, measuring if he could get them both in long ways. They fit, so he pushed them back first, then two more rows of the weed containers, up under the refrigerator, and then back as far as he could get it all to slide. He went out to his truck, dug a handful of the loose coffee from inside the tool bin behind the passenger seat, and took that back in the kitchen to sprinkle all along the outer edge of the floor under the refrigerator. Finally, he swept the loose grounds underneath, then screwed the grate back into place, peeked in from a few different odd angles, and took a couple deep breaths full of beer.

Zane was sitting at the kitchen table, looking out the window, when he saw Duane's girlfriend's car pull up beside his truck. Duane's girlfriend always drove because Duane had lost his license four years ago for the rest of his life because of too many DWIs. Then, he and Zane totaled his car swerving through back roads just before a Sunday morning sunrise two years ago, and Duane never bothered buying a new one.

Zane got up, yanked open the tight-fitting door and watched Duane, leaned over into the car, saying something to his girlfriend while looking Zane's way. Duane reached in to the floorboard, pulled out a green back pack, slung it over his shoulder, and shut the door of the car. Duane's girlfriend was staring ahead towards Zane, and he waved at her politely. She just rolled her head backwards, shifted the car in to reverse, and the car followed her gaze. Duane's face slipped into a sly grin soon as he heard the gravel crunching under her tires.

"Man, thank God that's over with. What's goin' on, Zee?" He was at the door and they shook hands in the two-stepped casual manner of old friends with a long history of delinquency together, with a thumb-locking tight hand clasp slipping back to interlocked fingers, finally snapping away in a celebratory release.

"Holy shit, man. What is going on?" Zane was genuinely glad to see his friend, alive and in the flesh. "Come on in, dude," he said, stepping aside, allowing full access to his little rented kitchen.

Duane walked in, flopping his backpack down on the counter next to the grocery bag of what was left of the beer. He unzipped the backpack and pulled out a slender glass bong, plus one of the same orange Tupperware containers of weed as was stuffed under the refrigerator.

"Let's burn one, Zee." Duane filled the bong with a splash of water from the croaking faucet, and sat at the table, popping the top off the Tupperware and twisting out a little piece of fleshy plant to stuff into the side of the glass contraption.

Zane slid uneasily into the opposite chair, the refrigerator standing over Duane's left shoulder. Duane's left arm jutted out, offering the bong to Zane. "Here you go, man."

Zane took it with a "Thanks, man." And simple as that, they were at it again, just like old times.

"So yeah, all I've got left is pretty much enough for me this year with maybe a little extra to sell. I've got some still drying out, but those plants were pretty sparse, and not the same as this stuff. This was the shit I was counting on to make the big bank this year."

Zane relit the bud to burn the last of it down to ashes, then handed the glass back to Duane, checking out his old friend's eyes. Zane could see he wasn't suspected in the slightest.

"Man, that sucks. You think you know who did it, though?"

Duane was looking down, refilling the chamber, "Oh yeah. This one guy from down there. He's sniffed around out there before, asking me a bunch of questions and all. Wanting to know a lot more than a dude should want to know, you know?" Duane lit the lighter, and started sucking on the top of the long length of glass. When he stopped, he eased back, ponytail nearly brushing the refrigerator door, a statue for six or seven seconds before turning his head right and exhaling a thick plume of smoke that bounced against the kitchen windowpanes. "But yeah, Zee, it most definitely does suck." He looked back down, mouth quickly back on the glass.

Zane looked past his friend on the other side of the table, freezer door behind his friend's head.

"Know what, Duane? I'm not digging it much lately either, don't like being here right now. I'm sick of this place. Alabama sucks." Duane was repacking the bong again. "Let's go down to Pensacola, get a hotel room, cut loose."

Duane pushed the glass back across the table. "Man, I'd love to, but I don't have much money right now, maybe a hundred dollars. I don't really want to hit my folks up right now either because I'll have to explain to them about why me and the bitch left the beach house early this week, and all that."

Zane tapped his lighter a couple of times against the kitchen table. The bong sat on a corner of the blue phone bill envelope. "I think I've got us covered, Duane. I've got a credit card I ain't ever used in the freezer there. It'll thaw out by the time we get to Pensacola. This is as good a reason to use it as I can think of."

Duane laughed, and said, "Alright, man. I'm down. You can drop me off at home on the way back. And maybe we can go see this dude who ripped me off together, too."

Zane clicked the flame from the lighter in his hand, put it in the right place, and took a deep, intoxicating breath. His stomach was finally starting to quiet down.

A BREATH OF HOT AIR

ALEX KAVA AND PATRICIA A. BREMMER

The pounding came from somewhere outside her nightmare. Maggie O'Dell fought her way to consciousness. Her breathing came in gulps as if she had been running. In her nightmare she had been. But now she sat up in bed and strained to hear over the drumming of her heartbeat as she tried to recognize the moonlit room that surrounded her.

It was the breeze coming through the patio door that jump-started her memory. Hot, moist air tickled free the damp hair on her forehead. She could practically taste the salt of the Gulf waters just outside her room. The Hilton Hotel on Pensacola Beach, she remembered.

A digital clock beside her, with glow-in-the-dark numbers, clicked and flipped to 12:47. She was here on assignment, despite a Category 5 hurricane barreling toward the Florida Panhandle. But forty minutes earlier all had been calm. Not a cloud in sight to block the full moon. Only the waves predicted the coming storm, already rising higher with white caps breaking and crashing against the shore. Maggie liked the sound and had left the patio door open—but only a sliver—keeping the security bar engaged. She had hoped the sound would lull her to sleep. It must have worked, at least for forty minutes. That's if you considered nightmares with fishing coolers stuffed full of body parts anything close to sleep.

She hadn't been able to shut off the adrenaline from her afternoon adventure, hovering two hundred feet above the Gulf of Mexico in a Coast Guard helicopter. It hadn't been the strangest crime scene Maggie had ever visited in her ten years with the FBI. The aircrew had recovered a marine cooler floating in the waters just off Pensacola Beach. But instead of finding some fisherman's discarded catch of the day, the crew was shocked to discover human body parts—a torso, three hands, and a foot—all carefully wrapped in thick plastic.

However, it hadn't been the body parts that had tripped Maggie into what she called her "nightmare cycle," a vicious loop of snapshots from her memory's scrapbook. Some people slipped into REM cycle, Maggie had her nightmare cycle. No, it wasn't the severed body parts. She had seen and dealt with her share of those. It was the helicopter flight and dangling two hundred feet above control. That's really why she had opened the patio doors earlier. She wanted to replace the thundering sound of the rotors.

The pounding started again and she jerked up, only now remembering what had wakened her. Someone on the other side of the door.

"Ms. O'Dell." A man's voice. High pitched. No one she recognized.

Maggie stumbled out of bed, pulled on khaki shorts and a T-shirt over damp, sticky skin. She had shut off the room's A/C when she opened the patio door and the air inside was now as hot and humid as it was outside. Florida in August. What was she thinking shutting off the A/C?

She picked up her holstered revolver on the way to the door. Her fingers slid around the handle, her index finger settling on the trigger, but she kept the gun in its holster.

"Yes, who is it?" she asked, standing back and to the side of the door as she waved her other hand in front of the peephole. An old habit, born of paranoia and self-preservation. If there was a shooter on the other side, he'd be waiting for his target to be pressed against the peephole.

"The night manager. Evans. I mean Robert Evans." The voice sounded young and panicked. "We have a situation. My boss said you're with the FBI. I'm sorry to wake you. It's sort of an emergency."

This time Maggie glanced out the peephole. The fisheye version made Robert Evans look geekier than he probably was—tall and lanky with nervous energy that kept him rocking from one foot to the other. He tugged at his shirt collar, one finger planted inside as though it was the only thing keeping his company-issued tie from strangling him.

"What kind of an emergency?"

She watched his bobble-size head jerk left then right, making sure no one else was in the hallway. Then he leaned closer to the door and tried to keep his voice low, but the panic kicked it into a whispered screech.

"I think I got a dead guy in Room 347."

• • •

Glen Karst sipped his bourbon from a corner stool at the outdoor tiki bar. To his left he had a perfect view of the hotel's back door and to his right was a sight off a postcard—silver-topped waves shimmering in the moonlight, lapping at sugar-white sands. If he ever decided to afford himself a vacation, this would be a great place—that is, if he didn't mind sweating. After midnight and it felt like he had a hot, damp towel that he couldn't knock off draped around his neck.

Didn't help that he was exhausted. It had taken him most of the day to get here. All flights to Pensacola had been canceled because of Hurricane Isaac, which meant the closest Glen could get from Denver was Atlanta. He'd spent the last six hours in a rent-a-car, a compact, the only thing left on such short notice. Not quite his style, nor his body's. But he couldn't blame the Ford Escort for all the tension in the small of his back. A good deal of it had been there before he began this journey, one that he hoped wouldn't be a wild goose chase. As a veteran detective Glen Karst had come to rely on his hunches, his gut instinct, as much as he did his expertise. But coming this far on such short notice and with a hurricane coming, he figured he had maybe twenty-four hours.

A flash of light came from behind him and Glen glanced over his shoulder. A group of college kids mugged for a camera, all holding up bright red drinks in a toast. Hurricane glasses, Glen noticed, shook his head and smiled. Sure didn't look like a hurricane was anywhere near. The beach's restaurants and bars were full of tourists and residents, some spilling out onto the shore and into the parking lots. But he'd also noticed quite a few pickups and moving vans packed and stacked full of belongings, ready to roll. It was Florida. Glen figured the residents knew the drill. But if they were still out eating and drinking then he knew he still had time.

He pulled a brochure from his shirt pocket, laid it on the bar next to his glass and smoothed out the crease. The man in the photo had added a good thirty pounds to his hefty frame. His blond hair had been cut short, dyed dark brown and peppered with gray at the temples. The goatee was new and attempted to hide the beginning of a double chin. At a glimpse, the man looked nothing like Dr. Thomas Gruber, but Glen recognized the eyes, deep-set and ice blue. In his arrogance the good doctor had failed to disguise the one trait that betrayed him most.

"They've canceled," said a young man three barstools over, pointing at Glen's brochure.

"What's that?"

"The conference. It's been canceled because of the hurricane."

"Damn, are you sure?"

"Don't take this the wrong way, but you don't look like a doctor."

"That's good, 'cause I don't like doctors."

The guy stood up, his drink in one hand and nodded at the stool next to Glen, "You mind?"

"I'm not expecting anyone."

Glen sipped his bourbon, not giving the guy much attention. But in the time it took for the man to sidle up next to him, Glen had noted the guy's short cropped hair—military style would have been Glen's first guess except for the Rolex, Sperry deck shoes and Ralph Lauren polo that he left untucked over khaki cargo shorts. Expensive wares for a guy who, according to Glen's estimate, was probably thirty at the most.

"Name's Joe Black." He tipped his glass at Glen instead of offering his hand. The glass was a rocks glass like his own, Scotch or bourbon, neat.

"Glen." From the corner of his eye he could see Joe Black assessing him, too. He was cool, calm, and took only a casual glimpse at the brochure on the bar between them. "So you go to these conferences?"

"You might say I'm a regular."

Glen gave him a sidelong look. "Hell, you don't look like a doctor either."

Joe laughed, but he didn't bother to answer, nor did he look like he was going to. However, his eyes darted to the brochure again before he shifted on the barstool and reached for his glass.

"You know this doctor?" Glen tapped the photo, looking down at it as if he needed to remember the name. "This Dr. Eric Foster?" But in fact, he had memorized every detail about Dr. Foster alias Dr. Gruber. The only thing he couldn't figure out is why Gruber would risk coming back to the states.

Just over a year ago Gruber had fled Colorado after being the main suspect in a triple homicide. Gruber had abandoned his surgical practice, skipped out on a million dollar mortgage and left his wife penniless. He had escaped to South America, somewhere in Brazil, according to Glen's last effort in tracking him. Rumor was that the good doctor might be trafficking body parts, even going as far as buying kidneys from poor struggling schmucks who had nothing else to sell.

Ironically, the conference that had Gruber scheduled as a featured speaker bragged about having human specimens for surgeons to perfect their skills. Nothing illegal. Glen had checked it out. These conferences took place all over the country, though usually at some beachfront resort as an added incentive. Medical device companies planned and arranged them, offering surgeons all-expense paid trips in exchange for them to come try out the company's newest gadgets and hopefully put in several orders before they returned home.

The fact was the triple homicide in Colorado remained open. No other suspects. All evidence pointed to Gruber and the bastard had slipped away during the investigation. Glen was more than anxious to finally nail the guy.

"Yeah, I know Foster. You might say he's my competition." Joe Black finally said without offering anything more. He waved down the bartender and pointed to his glass. "Another Johnnie Walker, Black Label." Then to Glen he said, "How 'bout you? Another Buffalo Trace?"

Glen hid his surprise then simply nodded at the bartender. Joe Black knew what he was drinking. Why the hell had this guy been watching him?

"So what do you want with Dr. Foster?" Joe asked.

"Just want to have a friendly chat."

"You a cop?"

"I don't look like a doctor, but I do look like a cop, huh?"

Joe shrugged and went quiet while the bartender placed fresh drinks in front of them.

"If not a cop, maybe a jealous husband?" This time he looked at Glen, waiting to see his reaction.

Glen fidgeted with his glass but didn't say a word. Sometimes people filled in the silence if you waited long enough. It seemed to work.

Satisfied with Glen's response—or rather his non-response—Joe continued, "I told him it'd catch up with him one of these days. So the blond with all the expensive jewelry? She must be yours?"

This was easier than Glen expected. "Is she with him?"

Joe nodded and tipped back the rest of his Scotch. "Finish your drink," he told Glen. "I'll take you up to his room."

Glen could hardly believe it. He looked the guy over, this time allowing his suspicions to show. "Why would you do me any favors?"

"Maybe because I don't much like the bastard myself."

• • •

As soon as Maggie walked into the room she knew that the big man sprawled on his back in the king-size bed had not died of natural causes. His bloodshot eyes stared at the ceiling. His mouth twisted into a sardonic grin. Trousers lay crumpled in a pile on the floor, a belt half pulled from the loops. Shoes peeked out from under.

"Who found him?" Maggie glanced back at Evans. The night manager had grown pale before they reached the room. Now he stayed in the open doorway, unwilling to move any farther into the room.

"Someone from housekeeping. There was a request for more towels."

Evans couldn't see the body from his post inside the doorwell and Maggie realized he couldn't see her either. Without stepping on or touching anything, she ventured closer. The dead man wore bright blue boxers and a button-down shirt, half unbuttoned. His skin looked like it was on fire—bright red, but not from sunburn.

"He probably had a heart attack, right?" Evans sounded hopeful.

"Was he alone?" Maggie asked, noticing an empty wine bottle with one glass on the nightstand.

"No one else is listed under his registration."

"But he wasn't alone," another voice said from outside in the hallway.

Maggie came around the bed, back into the entrance just in time to see two men standing over the night manager's bony shoulder.

"Are you from the sheriff's department?" she asked.

"I didn't call the sheriff's department," Evans said, bracing his hand on the doorway and making a barrier with his skinny arm.

"911?" Maggie tried again.

"I didn't call anyone," Evans said. Then with wide eyes and an attempted whisper, he leaned toward her and added, "My boss said to get you."

"I'm Detective Glen Karst," the man in the hallway poked his arm over Evans, offering a badge and ID.

Maggie reached out and took the ID but instead of turning on the light in the entrance, she leaned into the bathroom, using its light.

"You're a long way from home, Detective Karst." She handed him back his ID and stood with hands on her hips, waiting for his explanation while Evans kept up his pathetic barrier.

"I have reason to believe the man inside is a suspect in a triple homicide. I just want to ask him a few questions. Mr. Black told me—" Karst stopped, turned, then looked around the hallway as though he'd lost something or someone. The man who had accompanied him was gone.

Maggie glanced at her watch. It was late and she was exhausted. She'd been on the road for half the day and dangling over the Gulf in a helicopter for the other half. Her forty-minute nap had been invaded by nightmares. This dead guy wasn't even her jurisdiction.

"Mr. Evans, I think you should go call the sheriff's department." She put a gentle hand on his shoulder, waiting for him to drop his arm from the doorjamb.

"The sheriff's department?" He said it like it still hadn't even occurred to him to do so.

"Yes." She kept eye contact, hoping to transfer her calm and cool composure over to him. "Detective Karst and I will secure the room until someone from the sheriff's department gets here."

Both Maggie and Karst watched Evans leave, his lanky frame wobbling like a drunk attempting to walk on tiptoes. He missed the turn for the elevators, stopped and backtracked, giving them an embarrassed wave then straightening up like a sleepwalker suddenly coming awake. Maggie waited until she heard the ping of the elevator before she turned back to the room.

"Don't touch anything," she told Detective Karst as she gestured for him to follow her inside.

"Don't worry about me. I didn't catch your name."

"Maggie O'Dell."

"You're not local law enforcement."

It wasn't a question. He said it with such certainty Maggie stopped in the entrance and looked back at him. She wanted to ask how he knew, then decided it wasn't important.

"FBI. I'm down here on another assignment. The night manager thought it would be more convenient to wake me up rather than call the sheriff."

"Son of a bitch, don't tell me Foster's dead?" Karst asked as he came into view of the bed.

"Do you recognize him?"

He didn't need to come any closer. "Yeah, I do. He goes by Eric Foster, but his real name is Thomas Gruber. What's your guess? Suicide?"

"No."

"You sound pretty sure of yourself."

This time she smiled at him. "I do this for a living, Detective Karst."

"I'm not questioning your qualifications, just asking how you reached that conclusion."

Maggie pointed at the dead man's eyes. "Petechial hemorrhages."

Karst leaned closer. "His neck doesn't show any signs of strangulation."

"The ruptures probably occurred during convulsions, maybe seizures. He strangled but from the inside out."

He raised an eyebrow at her, waiting for more.

"I recognize that twist of the mouth and the bright red skin, almost cherry red. I've only seen this sort of skin discoloration once before but it's something I'll never forget. The tissue can't get any oxygen. It happens quickly. Ten to fifteen minutes."

"You think he was poisoned?"

Maggie nodded, impressed. The detective from Colorado was sharp.

Karst noticed her look and it was his turn to smile. "I do this for a living, too."

Then he started looking at the bedding, careful not to touch but bending over and searching the pillows.

"Usually there's vomit," he said and started sniffing the linens, now leaning even closer over the dead man. Then Karst's body stiffened and he stood up straight. "Cyanide."

"Excuse me?"

"I can smell it," he said. "Like bitter almonds."

Maggie came up beside Karst and he stepped back while she bent over the dead man's face. Only forty to fifty percent of people could smell the aftereffects of cyanide. It was a genetic ability. The scent was faint but she could smell it, too.

"I thought it might be something like that," she said. "Cyanide stops cells from using oxygen. He would have felt like he was suffocating—a shortness of breath followed by dizziness. Then comes the confusion and possible seizures, bursting the capillaries in the eyes. Last would be cardiac arrest. All in a matter of minutes."

"Potassium cyanide is a crystal compound." Karst looked around the room and pointed to the wine bottle. "May have slipped it into the wine. Where does someone get cyanide these days?"

Maggie had to stop and think, retrieve the information from her memory bank. The case she had worked on had happened too many years ago—six young men in a cabin in the woods had chosen to obey their leader and take cyanide capsules rather than be taken into custody. She'd lost a friend that day—a fellow FBI agent—so the memory didn't come easily. "Potassium cyanide is still used in several industries. Certain kinds of photography," she finally said. "Some processing of plastics, electroplating and gold plating in jewelry making. If a person buys it on a regular basis for their business it usually doesn't draw any attention."

Now she wanted to dismantle the memory and started looking over the room again. She plucked a tissue from its container on the nightstand and gently pressed her covered fingertip against the dead man's jaw, then his neck. "No rigor."

"So he's been dead less than twelve hours."

"Maybe less than six. Rigor sets in more quickly with cyanide poisoning. You said he wasn't alone?" She turned to see Karst had moved to the desk and was lifting open a folded wallet using the tip of a pen.

"Guy I met at the bar downstairs told me he saw Gruber leave with a blond."

"The guy who took off as soon as he saw your badge?"

He glanced up at Maggie. "Coincidence?"

"I don't believe in coincidences."

"Me either. I'll bet he gave me a bogus name. Hell, he probably lied about the blond, too."

Maggie used the tissue again as she tipped a wastebasket out from under the nightstand. The only thing inside was another tissue, this one crumpled with a blotted stain of bright pink lipstick. She gently lifted it by a corner, pulling it up high enough to show Karst.

"Unless there's something a little freaky about Dr. Foster, I think your friend might have been telling the truth about the blond."

"I'll be damned."

Maggie took a good look at the stain under the light, then gently placed it back where she had found it. Later she'd point it out to the sheriff's investigator.

"What did he do?" she asked.

Karst folded his arms and stared at the dead man. "His nurse was two-timing him with a rich ex-patient. He murdered her plus the patient and his wife. Then Gruber set the nurse's house on fire, hoping to hide all the evidence. He high-tailed it to South America before we could even question him."

"So there were a few others beside you, looking for him."

"Not to mention some new enemies. The guy from the bar mentioned something about Gruber being his competition."

Maggie watched Karst's face. He was still grinding out the case in his mind. She checked her watch again.

"I'd say you no longer have a case, Detective Karst."

There was knock at the door followed by, "Sheriff's department."

• • •

Glen Karst found himself back down at the hotel's tiki bar. This time he and Maggie shared one of the high-top tables. He'd asked to buy her a drink and was surprised when the tough, no nonsense FBI agent ordered a Diet Pepsi. He ordered another Buffalo Trace, glancing around to see if Joe Black was somewhere close by, watching again.

The waves had kicked up and the moon had slid over a bit. A breeze almost made the hot, humid air feel good. The beach restaurants and bars were still full but not quite as crowded and noisy as earlier.

"I can't believe I came all the way down here and the son of a bitch cheated me out of dragging his ass back to Denver. It's hard to let it go."

"Sheriff Clayton will do a good job," Maggie told him. "Anything you can tell him about Gruber will help his investigation."

Glen rubbed at his eyes, only now remembering how exhausted he was. "I suppose the bastard got what was coming to him."

"A wise medical examiner once told me, we die as we live."

"Is that the equivalent of what goes around comes around?"

She smiled and tipped her glass at him, "Touché."

He raised his glass and was about to take a sip when he saw a woman sidle up to the bar. She looked familiar but he couldn't place her. Then he realized: Her hair was shorter. She looked much thinner than when he'd met her over a year ago. But he recognized her walk, the way she handled herself.

"Someone you know," Maggie asked. "Or someone you'd like to know?"

"What? Oh, sorry. No, I think I know her." He sipped his bourbon and continued to watch out of the corner of his eye. She was at the bar, ordering drinks and laughing with her friends, three women at a table near the bar.

"Not a blond," Maggie said as if reading his mind. She sat back and took another look. "Even from this distance I'd say the lipstick's a match."

His eyes met Maggie's. She was thinking exactly what he was thinking.

"No such thing as coincidences, right?" he said.

"It's no longer your case," Maggie reminded him. "She wore a wig, probably stole her wineglass, and the bottle was wiped down. I checked. They'll never pull DNA off that tissue."

"The least I can do is say hello."

The woman's back was to Glen when he walked up and leaned on the bar. He ordered another round of drinks and watched, waiting for her to notice him. The glance was subtle at first, almost flirtatious. Then he saw the realization.

"Hello, Mrs. Gruber."

"Detective." She kept her body turned away from him and looked for the bartender. "I'm sorry I don't remember your name."

But he knew she did remember. He told her anyway, "Glen. Glen Karst. Are you here on vacation?"

"We are. Yes, actually we were until the hurricane."

"No other reason you chose Pensacola?" His eyes waited for hers. She met his stare and didn't flinch. Didn't look away. In a split second he thought he could see her confirmation, her admission that she knew exactly what he was talking about, that she knew he was there and what he had found.

Without a blink she said, "Just having some fun and my friends can vouch for that."

The bartender interrupted with a tray of colorful drinks ready and hovering. Before Mrs. Gruber took them she pulled out a business card from her pocket, hesitated then handed it to Glen.

"I have my own business now," she told him, taking the tray and handing the bartender a fifty dollar bill. "Keep the change, sweetie," she told the young man, and without giving Glen another look she returned to her table and friends.

Glen returned to the high-top with fresh drinks and scooted his chair closer. He placed the business card on the table without looking at it or at Maggie.

"You got lucky. She gave you her number?"

"No, I already have it. What she gave me was a cold shoulder." Glen said. "That's Gruber's ex-wife."

"I think she may have given you more than that," Maggie told him, and he looked up to see her reading the business card. She handed it to him and immediately Glen knew.

Elaine Gruber had her own business all right. Making fine jewelry and specializing in gold-plating.

THE CYPRESS HOUSE

BY MICHAEL KORYTA
AN EXCERPT FROM THE NOVEL

They'd been on the train for five hours before Arlen Wagner saw the first of the dead men.

To that point it had been a hell of a nice ride. Hot, sure, and progressively more humid as they passed out of Alabama and through southern Georgia and into Florida, but nice enough all the same. There were thirty-four on-board the train who were bound for the camps in the Keys, all of them veterans with the exception of the nineteen-year-old who rode at Arlen's side, a boy from Jersey by name of Paul Brickhill.

They'd all made a bit of conversation at the outset, exchanges of names and casual barbs and jabs thrown around in that way men had when they were getting used to one another, all of them figuring they'd be together for several months to come, and then things quieted down. Some men had slept, a few started card games, others just sat and watched the countryside roll by, fields going misty with late-summer twilight and then shapeless and dark as the moon rose like a watchful specter. Arlen, though, Arlen just listened. Wasn't anything else to do, because Paul Brickhill had an outboard motor where his mouth belonged.

As the miles and minutes passed, Brickhill alternated between explaining things to Arlen and asking him questions. Nine times out of ten, he answered his own questions before Arlen could so much as part his lips with a response. Brickhill had been a quiet kid when the two of them first met in Alabama, and back then Arlen took him for shy. What he hadn't counted on was the way the boy took to talk once he felt comfortable with someone. Evidently, he'd grown damn comfortable with Arlen.

As the wheels hammered along the rails of northern Florida, Paul Brickhill was busy telling Arlen all of the reasons this was going to be a hell of a good hitch. Not only was there the bridge waiting to be built, but all that sunshine and blue water and boats that cost more than most homes. Florida was where rich folks went for winter, see, and here Paul and Arlen were doing the same thing, and wasn't that something? They could do some fishing, maybe catch a tarpon. Paul'd seen pictures of tarpon that were near long as the boats that landed them. And there were famous people in the Keys, celebrities of every sort, and who was to say they wouldn't run into a few and…

Around them the men talked and laughed, some scratching out letters to loved ones back home. Wasn't anyone waiting on a letter from Arlen, so he just settled for a few nips on his flask and tried to find some sleep despite the cloaking warmth and the stink of sweating men. It was too damn hot.

Brickhill was still going, this time expounding on the realization that he'd never seen a true palm tree before and in a few more hours they'd be as good as surrounded by them. Arlen heard one of the men behind them let out a chuckle, amused by the kid and, no doubt, by Arlen having to put up with him.

Damned good Samaritan is what I am, Arlen thought, allowing a small grin with his eyes still closed. Always trying to help, and look where it gets me?

Brickhill finally fell silent, as if he'd just noticed that Arlen was sitting with his eyes closed and had stopped responding to the conversation. Arlen let out a sigh, grateful for the respite. Paul was a nice enough kid, but Arlen had never been one for a lot of words where a few would do.

The train clattered on, and though night had settled the heat didn't break. Sweat still trickled along the small of Arlen's back and held his hair to his forehead. He wished he could fall asleep; these hot miles would pass faster then. Maybe another pull on the flask would aid him along.

He opened his eyes, tugged the lids up sleepily, and saw himself staring at a hand of bone.

He blinked and sat up and stared. Nothing changed. The hand held five playing cards and was attached to a man named Wallace O'Connell, a veteran from Georgia who was far and away the loudest man in this company. He had his back turned, engaged in his game, so Arlen couldn't see his face. Just that hand of bone.

No, Arlen thought, no, damn it, not another one.

The sight chilled him, but didn't shock him. It was far from the first time.

He's going to die unless I can find a way to stop it, Arlen thought with the sad, sick resignation of a man experienced with such things. Once we get down to the Keys, old Wallace O'Connell will have a slip and bash his head in on something. Or maybe the poor bastard can't swim, will fall into those waves and sink beneath them and I'll be left with this memory same as I've been left with so many others. I'd warn him if I could, but men don't heed such warnings. They won't let themselves.

It was then that he looked up, away from Wallace under the flickering lights of the train car, and saw skeletons all around him.

They filled the shadows of the car, some laughing, some grinning, some lost to sleep. All with bone where flesh belonged. The few who sat directly under a light still wore their skin, but their eyes were gone, replaced by whirls of gray smoke.

For a moment, Arlen Wagner forgot to breathe. Went cold and dizzy and then sucked in a gasp of air and straightened in the seat.

They were going to have a wreck. It was the only thing that made a bit of sense. This train was going to derail and they were all going to die. Every last one of them. Because Arlen had seen this before, and knew damn well what it meant, and knew that –

Paul Brickhill said, "Arlen?"

Arlen turned to him. The overhead light was full on the boy's face, keeping him in a circle of brightness, the taut, tanned skin of a young man who spent his days under the sun. Arlen looked into his eyes and saw swirling wisps of smoke. The smoke rose in tendrils and fanned out and framed the boy's head while filling Arlen's with terrible memories.

"Arlen, you all right?" Paul Brickhill asked.

He wanted to scream. Wanted to scream and grab the boy's arm but was afraid it would be cold slick bone under his touch.

We're going to die. We're going to come off these rails at full speed and pile into those swamp woods, with hot metal tearing and shattering all around us…

The whistle blew out shrill in the dark night and the train began to slow.

"We got another stop," Paul said. "You look kind of sickly. Maybe you should pour that flask out…"

The boy distrusted liquor. Arlen wet his lips and said, "Maybe," and looked around the car at the skeleton crew and felt the train shudder as it slowed. The force of that big locomotive was dropping fast, and now he could see light glimmering outside the windows, a station just ahead. They were ar-

riving in some backwater stop where the train could take on coal and the
men would have a chance to get out, stretch their legs, and piss. Then they'd
be aboard again and winging south at full speed, death ahead of them.

"Paul," Arlen said, "you got to help me do a bit of convincing here."

"What are you talking about?"

"We aren't getting back on this train. Not a one of us."

They piled out of the cars and onto the station platform, everyone milling
around, stretching or lighting cigarettes. It was getting on toward ten in the
evening and though the sun had long since faded the wet heat lingered. The
boards of the platform were coated with swamp mud dried and trampled into
dust, and out beyond the lights Arlen could see silhouetted fronds lying limp
in the darkness, untouched by a breeze. Backwoods Florida. He didn't know
the town and didn't care; regardless of name, it would be his last stop on this
train.

He hadn't seen so many apparitions of death at one time since the war.
Maybe leaving the train wouldn't be enough. Could be there was some sort
of virus in the air, a plague spreading unseen from man to man the way the
influenza had in `18, claiming lives faster than the reaper himself.

"What's the matter?" Paul Brickhill asked, following as Arlen stepped
away from the crowd of men and tugged his flask from his pocket. Out here
the sight was enough to set Arlen's hands to shaking – men were walking in
and out of the shadows as they moved through the cars and down to the station platform, slipping from flesh to bone and back again in a matter of seconds, all of it a dizzying display that made him want to sit down and close his
eyes and drink long and deep on the whiskey.

"Something's about to go wrong," he said.

"What do you mean?" Paul said, but Arlen didn't respond, staring instead at the men disembarking and realizing something – the moment they stepped off the train their skin slid back across their bones, knitting together as if healed by the wave of some magic wand. The swirls of smoke in their eye sockets vanished into the hazy night air. It was the train. Yes, whatever was going to happen was going to happen to that train.

"Something's about to go wrong," he said. "With our train. Something's going to go bad wrong."

"How do you know?"

"I just do, damn it!"

Paul looked to the flask and his eyes said what his words did not.

"I'm not drunk. Haven't had more than a few swallows."

"What do you mean something's going to go wrong?" Paul asked again.

Arlen held onto the truth, felt the words heavy in his throat but couldn't let them go. It was one thing to see such horrors; it was worse to try and speak of them. Not just because it was a difficult thing to describe, but because no one ever believed. And the moment you gave voice to such a thing was the moment you charted a course for your character that you could never alter. Arlen understood this well, had known it since boyhood.

But Paul Brickhill had sat before him with smoke the color of an early morning storm cloud dancing in his eyes, and Arlen was certain what that meant, had seen it too many times before. He couldn't let him board that train again.

"People are going to die," he said.

Paul Brickhill leaned his head back and stared.

"We get back on that train, people are going to die," Arlen said. "I'm sure of it."

He'd spent many a day trying to imagine this gift away. To fling it from him the way you might a poisonous spider caught crawling up your arm, and long after the chill lingered on your flesh you'd thank the sweet hand of providence that you'd been given the opportunity to knock the venomous beast away. Only he'd never been given the opportunity. No, the stark sight of death had stalked him long, trailed him relentlessly for many a year. He knew it when he saw it, and he knew it was no trick of the light, no twist of bad liquor upon the mind. It was prophecy, the gift of foresight granted to a man who'd never wished for it.

He was reluctant to say so much as a word to any of the other men, knowing the response he'd receive, but this was not the sort of thing that could be ignored.

Speak loud and sharp, he thought, just like you did on the edge of a battle, when you had to get `em to listen, and listen fast.

"Boys," he said, getting at least a little of the old muster into his tone, "listen up now."

The conversations broke off. Two men were standing on the step of the train car, and when they turned, skull faces studied him.

"I think we best wait for the next train through," he said. "There's bad trouble aboard this one. I'm sure of it."

It was Wallace O'Connell who broke the long silence that followed. He was standing under one of the platform lights, which restored his bone hand to rough calloused skin.

"What in the hell you talking about, Wagner?" he said, and immediately there was a chorus of muttered agreement.

"Something's wrong with this train," Arlen said. He stood tall, did his damnedest to hold their eyes.

"You know this for a fact?" O'Connell said.

"I know it."

"How do you know? And what's wrong with it?"

"I can't say what's wrong with it. But something is. I got a…sense for these things."

A slow grin crept across O'Connell's face. "I've known some leg-pullers," he said, "but didn't figure you for one of them. Don't got the look."

"Damn it, man, this ain't no joke."

"You got a sense something's wrong with our train, and you're telling us it ain't no joke?"

"Knew a widow back home was the same way," spoke up another man from the back of the circle. He was a slim, wiry old guy with a nose crooked from many a break. Arlen didn't know his name – hell, he didn't know most of their names, and that was part of the problem. Aside from Paul there wasn't a man in the group who'd known Arlen for any longer than this train ride.

"Yeah?" O'Connell said. "Trains talked to her, too?"

"Naw. She had the sense, just like he's talking about. 'Cept she got her sights from owls and moon reflections and shit like you couldn't even imagine."

This new man was grinning wide, and O'Connell was matching it. He said, "She was right all the time, of course?"

"Of course," the man said, and let out a cackling laugh. "Why, wasn't but nine year ago she predicted the end of days was upon us. Knew it for a fact. Was going to befall us by that winter. I can't imagine she was wrong, I just figured I missed being raptured up and that's how I ended up here with all you sinful sons of bitches."

The crowd was laughing now, and Arlen felt heat creeping into his face, thoughts of his father and the shame that had chased him from his boyhood home threatening his mind now. Behind him Paul Brickhill was standing still and silent, about the only one in the group who wasn't at least chuckling. There was one man near Wallace O'Connell whose smile seemed forced, uneasy, but even he was going along with the rest of them.

"I might ask for a tug on whatever's in that jug of your'n," O'Connell said. "It seems to be a powerful syrup."

"It's not the liquor you're hearing," Arlen said. "It's the truth. Boys, I'm telling you, I seen things in the war just like I am tonight, and every time I did men died."

"Men died every damn day in the war," O'Connell said. The humor had drained from his voice. "And we all seen it – not just you. Some of us didn't crack straight through from what we seen. Others…" he made a pointed nod at Arlen, "had a mite less fortitude. Now save your stories for somebody fool enough to listen to them. Rest of us don't need the aggravation."

The men broke up then, drifted back to their own conversations, casting Arlen sidelong stares, some pitying, some disgusted. Arlen felt a hand on his arm and nearly whirled and threw his fist without looking, shame and fear riding him hard now, leaving him ready to lash out. It was only Paul, though, tugging him away from the group.

"Arlen, you best ease up."

"Be damned if I will. I'm telling you –"

"I understand what you're telling us, but it just doesn't make sense. Could be you got a touch of fever or –"

Arlen reached out and grabbed him by his shirt collar. Paul's eyes went wide but he didn't reach for Arlen's hand, didn't move at all as Arlen spoke to him a low, harsh voice.

"You had smoke in your eyes, boy. I don't give a damn if you couldn't see it or if none of them could, it was there, and it's the sign of your death. You known me for a time now, and you ask yourself, how many times has Arlen Wagner spoken foolish words to me? How many times has he seemed addled? You ask yourself that, and then you ask yourself if you want to die tonight."

He released the boy's collar and stepped back. Paul lifted a hand and wiped it over his mouth, staring at Arlen.

"You trust me, Brickhill?" Arlen said.

"You know I do."

"Then listen to me now. If you don't ever listen to another man again for the rest of your life, listen to me now. Don't get back on that train."

The boy swallowed and looked off into the darkness. "Arlen, I wouldn't disrespect you, but what you're saying…there's no way you could know that."

"I can see it," Arlen said. "Don't know how to explain it, but I can see it."

Paul didn't answer. He looked away from Arlen, back at the others, who were watching the boy with pity and Arlen with disdain.

"Here's one last question for you to ask of yourself," Arlen said. "Can you afford to be wrong?"

Paul stared at him in silence as the train whistle blew and the men stomped out cigarettes and fell into a boarding line. Arlen watched their flesh melt from their bones as they went up the steps.

"Don't let that fool bastard convince you to stay here, boy," Wallace O'Connell bellowed as he stepped up onto the train car, half of his face a skull, half the face of a strong man who believed he was fit to take on all comers. "Ain't nothing here but alligators, and unless you want to be eating them come dinner tomorrow, or them eating you, you best get aboard."

Paul didn't look in his direction. Just kept staring at Arlen. The locomotive was chugging now, steam building, ready to tug its load south, down to the Keys, down to the place the boy wanted to be.

"You're serious," he said.

Arlen nodded.

"And it's happened before?" Paul said. "This isn't the first time?"

"No," Arlen said. "It is not the first time."

THE APALACHICOLA NIGHT

BY MARK RAYMOND FALK

Fifteen minutes outside of Sopchoppy the sun had disappeared completely, and with the way the trees grew over Smith Creek Road, you would have thought the damn thing wasn't ever coming back. So when I tell you it was dark I mean it was *dark*. No streetlights. No headlights. Only the glassy reflections in the eyes of raccoons and the deer as they jumped out in front of my car on a mission for death.

Whether it was theirs or mine, I can't say for sure.

I crawled along under the speed limit, my foot heavy on the brake. Lurching to a stop for threats both real and imagined. My blood and my heart unable to tell the difference.

The AM signal I'd been listening to since Gainesville grew dim, turning the Baptist preacher to static as I drove deeper into the forest. And then it was gone and the radio was turned off and I was left alone with only myself to keep me company.

A poor choice of companion.

It could only get worse.

. . .

I caught her body in the high beams. And like any other son of a bitch with too little sense and too much curiosity, I pulled over to see what the fuck she was doing there.

Dying, I guess you'd call it.

She was wide eyed and shaking, warm from the night air, but growing colder by the second. Even before she said anything to me, we both knew the truth.

"Am I gonna die?"

She held both hands over her stomach. Grimaced.

"What happened? I asked.

"Kenny," she said.

Kenny happened.

"What do you mean?"

"He stuck me." The words came out like hiccups.

"He stuck you?"

"Hunting knife. Just like he said he would."

"He stabbed you?"

Her eyes closed. Her mouth opened.

Nothing but breath.

"Who is Kenny?"

"My boyfriend."

"Where is he now?" I asked. "Where is Kenny?"

She winced and clutched her stomach. "Goin' to Mobile."

"What's Kenny's last name?"

"Don't have one."

I don't know what made me do it, but I put my hand on top of hers and gave a little squeeze. That's when I felt the life she was trying to hold in. It had made her fingers slick.

"Jesus," I said.

"Jesus," she begged.

I reached into my pocket for my cell phone. The battery was almost dead and no matter how I held it—east, west, up towards the moon looking for a satellite—there was no signal to be found.

"I need help."

I nodded. "But tonight there's only me."

And there was only me.

And I was no good for anyone. I looked at my cell phone again but still didn't have service. I looked down the road for headlights, but only saw the high beams of my Chevy.

"Why did Kenny stab you?" I asked.

"Because he's crazy. I love that man. Wanted to be with him forever. But he's so damn crazy."

"That's all?"

"Says I slept with his brother."

"Did you?"

"Does it matter?" I could hear the water in her words. The choke. The soft horn of approaching death.

"Not to me it doesn't." I said.

She shifted slightly, reached with her fingers for my hand, held us both against her leaking stomach.

"What's in Mobile?" I asked.

"His brother."

"Is his brother expecting him?"

"When it comes to Kenny … don't nobody expect anything … it just happens."

Her grip tightened then went loose.

"You think he'll stick his brother?"

The question hung in the humidity of the night air.

• • •

I didn't wait for her pulse to go still. There wasn't anything left but counting minutes. Besides, I figured, if I drove long enough, sooner or later I'd get reception, and I could let the cops know that Kenny had gutted his old lady somewhere deep in the Apalachicola National Forest. If I got a signal fast enough, the cops could wait for Kenny at the end of Smith Creek Road.

So I left her to die on the side of the road and I wound along the dark road with my high beams leading the way, keeping my eyes right down the middle, trying hard not to see anything I didn't want to see. Keeping an eye out for Kenny's taillights.

• • •

I tapped a Winston from the pack and tucked it into the corner of my mouth, hoped I could fool my stomach into thinking it was full. The first drag hit my lungs like sandpaper. The second drag tasted like smoke and blood, and that's when I noticed the tightness on the skin of my fingers—the same metallic taste of years gone by and cuts on the job before Union coffee breaks.

I smoked that Winston and thought about Kenny racing towards the Pensacola Bay Bridge and beyond that, to Mobile.

• • •

The Chrysler was upside down, resting against the slash pines.

I tossed the cigarette out onto the road and pulled my car to a stop on the shoulder. I thought about getting out, but I'm not afraid to admit that it unsettled me the way the car was in the trees, and the nagging feeling that maybe I'd caught up to Kenny. I turned down the radio.

What I hoped then, was that another car, maybe two, maybe a cop would come barreling down Smith Creek, pulling over to see what was to see, but as the minutes passed, grinding like bone, it became clear to me that the only person left on Smith Creek was me, and whoever might have been in the Chrysler.

I opened the door, engine still running. As I was about to get out, my first foot already on the ground, he emerged from the darkness. Long haired. Bleeding. Arms stretched wide.

Christ-like in the glow of the headlights.

He stumbled forward, slow but determined. His mouth moved, but I couldn't make out what he was saying.

"Are you okay?" I yelled over the sound of my idling car. "Do you need an ambulance?"

"I'm hurt."

"What happened?"

"I wrecked. Deer got me."

I studied his face. He was cut up good. *Is this what Kenny would look like? Is this the look of a man who would stab his girlfriend and dump her on the side of the road?* Maybe. But he also did a convincing job of looking like a guy that had tasted his steering wheel at forty miles an hour.

"Where you goin?" I asked.

He took another step closer. His knee shook, then buckled. Collapsed into an awkward pile of limbs and grunts. Stretched out an arm towards me.

"Get me out of here."

"Where you goin'?" I repeated.

"West."

"Where you comin' from?"

No answer.

"Where you comin' from?" I asked again.

"Panacea. The beach. Man, I need a doctor, quit askin' me so many damn questions."

"You got a name?"

He paused, sized me up through squinty eyes. "Rick."

"Anybody with you, *Rick*?"

"What?"

"Anybody in the car with you? Anybody comin' with you from Panacea?"

He pushed himself up to his knees. Rubbed at his jaw. Teeth grit. Squinting into the headlights.

"I'm by myself. Now help me get into your fucking car before I have to do something we'll both regret."

• • •

"You always drive like such a goddamn old lady?" he asked from the passenger seat. "Put you foot on the goddamn gas pedal already."

"Trying not to wreck," I said.

I turned to him, watching his hands, waiting for the knife to come out, to make its way into my chest. With the way the trees grew over the road, and with the closeness of us in the car, I felt even more trapped than before.

Then again, maybe *Rick* wasn't Kenny. Maybe he was just some guy who had driven his car off the road. Such a thing wasn't impossible to imagine. But why hadn't he stopped for the girl?

"I'm trying not to die."

I ignored his plea, kept an even pace with my high beams leading the way. In the quiet I could hear his breathing, labored as it was.

He let his head hang out the window.

"How far west you going?" I yelled. "California?"

When he came back in, he wiped at his eyes with the backs of his hands. "I ain't thought that far ahead. It's been a long day."

"That was a bad wreck."

"That ain't all of it, neither. I found out today that my girl—one I've been meaning to marry—she's been sleepin' with *my brother*. Now can you believe that? Girl I've been givin' everything to and she can't even stop from taking up with my own damn brother."

There was him. There was me. Somewhere in all of it, there was a knife.

"I'm sorry to hear it."

"Not half as sorry as me. First damn time in my life that I think I found one good enough to marry, and what's she gone and done?"

"There's plenty of good ones out there …"

"I thought she'd be forever. Broke my damn heart."

Whether or not she'd really slept with his brother, Kenny was convinced of it, and in the way he told it—it wasn't hard to hear how much it'd hurt him. I actually began to feel sorry for him in the way I could feel sorry for a murderer riding shotgun.

"You know, I ain't gonna lie, I wasn't always faithful to all the girls I've been with. But I never looked at another when I was with her. I've been drunk, I've been high, I've been in jail, I've been everywhere but hell itself, and I ain't so much as cast a sideways glance at another. You understand?"

He clutched his ribs, let out a groan.

"I think, yeah." I looked again for the knife, but only saw his fists clenched, eyes shut tight. "You gonna leave her?"

"Whaddya mean am I gonna leave her?"

"Y'all gonna try and work things out, or are you moving on?"

"Work things out? It's too late for that. Shit … work things out? How the hell am I supposed to do that?"

I shrugged. "Don't know. I guess the way I see it, we all make mistakes. We all need forgiveness. Forgive us our trespasses and all that."

"Some things can't be forgiven." He slumped a little more in his seat. "You go to church?"

"Not lately," I said.

"I'll tell you something—before you showed up, I prayed. I got close with Jesus and his old man, trying to make good."

"And then I showed up?"

"Ain't that the way it's supposed to work? You tell them every bad thing you've done, and then you're saved?"

I tapped the brakes as a raccoon cut across the road. He put his hand on the dashboard to brace himself.

"Son of a bitch."

"Sounds like you ain't completely saved," I said. "What hurts the most?"

"Tired. Dizzy. My head. That's where I got it worst."

"How'd you cut your chest?"

He looked down at his shirt, at all the dried blood. "I don't know. Don't think I did."

"You must be bleedin. All that blood gotta come from somewhere."

"Yeah," he leaned towards the window, "I guess it must."

We drove five minutes in silence, Kenny with his head out the window, me keeping an eye ahead.

"You gotta get me a doctor," he finally said. "I think my ribs are poking into my heart."

"I'm doing the best I can."

The needle hovered a little below thirty.

·   ·   ·

I worried that he was on his way out, twitching back and forth between awake and asleep, on the passenger seat. After he had gone still for a few minutes, I nudged him.

"Rick?"

No response.

"Rick?"

Stillness.

I thought about it then, maybe in his sleep he would give up secrets, would make things known.

"Kenny?"

He rolled his head. Jerked a little. Then went back to sleep.

·   ·   ·

I had a choice to make by the time I got to the end of Smith Creek Road.

"Hey man," I shook his shoulder. "You okay?"

He muttered something. Felt heavier than he should have.

"You want me to go left or right? You want I should head to the clinic in

Hosford or the hospital in Tallahassee?"

I idled under the trees waiting for a response that didn't come, then turned around completely, got back on Smith Creek Road, filled with notions I didn't completely understand, that I couldn't make clean. Every now and then I asked him questions, told him stories about church.

We drove past his car, still on the side of the road, undisturbed. I kept the pedal heavy and the beams bright as I hurried back to her body, afraid that the longer it took the more likely it was for a stranger, some unfamiliar face to get to the scene, the kind of son of a bitch who would have questions and pointy fingers.

When we got there, it wasn't hard to see her if you knew where to look. She was on her back, head on the soft dirt, hands on her chest.

"Is that your girl?" I asked. "She the one?"

"Where are we?" His eyes fluttered, he struggled weakly.

I opened the passenger door and grabbed him by his arms, dragged him out of the car. The heels of his boots scraped along the dirt as I pulled. I rested for a breath, the humidity filled my lungs.

"I need a doctor."

I knew he needed more. They both did.

I let him drop, his head on her arm. He tried sitting up but couldn't. Maybe that was all the energy he had left.

"We are gathered here tonight … Even in death we are reminded of … Kenny was a troubled man …"

Every eulogy I tried to deliver fell flat.

I bent down to lift her head onto Kenny's arm, the two of them looking like stargazing lovers, staring heavenward.

Together.

BURN OFF BY NOON

BY TOM CORCORAN

Spontaneity leaves trails. Opportunity works best.

A close call years ago taught me to take my time. That approach has served me well. At this stage, this time around, the cruises—three of the dreary bastards—were the price to pay. Not a small cost, and not meaning money: talk about cigarette smoke and cattle-call dining. The damned ships are all-you-can-eat chow caverns with bow thrusters and harsh PA systems. You are insulated from the rolling ocean. Unless it's on the schedule, the wind does not blow your hair. There is no scenery beyond foamy wavetops or, closer to land, sticks with red triangles, or with green rectangles. Once a day, unless clouds interfere, you get sunrise and sunset. In the days of film, Kodak loved the profits of sunsets. One thing, certain as hell. After this sailing I will never go back to Ocho Rios.

The hoteliers afloat think highly of their mission, their canned optimism. The hokey departure ritual in Ft. Lauderdale somehow combined a security screening with the issuance of stateroom keys and dinner tickets. The check-in clerks spoke as if the boarding pass—my Glee Ticket—was more important than my passport. Don't we long for the days when our driver's license would get us back and forth to Grand Cayman? Imperative at this stage: I requested the late seating for my evening meals. Sent off like a child in a school hallway, I waved my Glee thing at uniformed smilers and was directed down ramps and chutes. At some point I was no longer on land.

With each offshore trip the passageways became longer, the bulkheads and flooring more dreary. Carpet colored, I supposed, to mask stains of seasickness, though it contrasted oddly with incandescent lobbies, surreal lounges, and Art Deco snack bars. Walking behind a slow-moving couple, I carried my laptop case and camera bag to the aft end of the fourth deck. The couple appeared tormented by the concept that only odd-numbered rooms were accessed in the starboard corridor. I informed them that their even-numbered cabin was to port, thereby doubling their confusion.

A cabin steward in a gray uniform—a man in his mid-thirties—greeted me with a weird smile of despair. Already groveling for his trip's-end tip. He quickly determined that my stateroom was in his area. His buzz-cut head was as round though not as large as a volleyball, his muscular neck a mismatch to his narrow shoulders.

I already knew his name but I glanced at his tag and pretended not to make out the bottom word. "Where are you from, Arso?"

"Bosnia," he lied, with his guttural eastern European accent, "but I left that country twelve years ago. Now, when I am not working on this ship, which I do for seven years, I have a small apartment in Hollywood, Florida."

"Wonderful town," I said. "I've been there a few times."

"My girlfriend from secondary school always told me I was such an actor, I would end up in Hollywood. Wrong one, don't you think?"

"Wrong for the movies," I said, "but a better place to live."

"Many people tell me that."

"And living is better than the alternative, eh?"

Arso smiled. "I have heard that, too, sir."

I barely had time to find a Bushmills miniature in my shaving kit and chug the devil before they called their mandatory lifeboat drill. I followed color-coded arrows to the open deck where lifeboats hung from numbered davits. We hadn't even left the dock. I was amused by the folly of a free-for-all summons to our muster stations—as if an exercise might streamline an emergency evacuation of people too heavy to use stairways.

Arso stood with several other cabin stewards near the starboard entrance to a huge dining room.

"Arso, are there ocean charts in each boat?" I said.

He offered a pensive, puzzled look. "I am not sure," he said. "But a very good idea. I will make a suggestion if this is not so."

Inside, seated at tables among strangers, all of us wearing droopy, uninflated life vests, I noticed a woman thirty feet away scouting the assembly for signs of life. Forty years old, give or take, with a wistful Mona Lisa face but expectant eyes. It was a bad time to make a connection, but I made eye contact, smiled, and promised myself to find her during the cruise. The lifeboat drill—to make lawyers happy—lasted a full half hour. I returned to my cabin, took more time with my next Bushmills miniature, and slept for forty-five minutes. According to the daily guide to events, I missed a Krazy by Karaoke session, a raffle, and a cha cha class.

Here's the short version. In 1995 three young Serbian soldiers in a city called Banja Luka killed two American soldiers in cold blood. The Serbs were arrested by NATO troops, quickly convicted, but let go on a wartime court technicality. They saved my brother from coming home with the war on his shoulders. But they fucking well kept him from coming home. His tags and flag arrived by UPS. I've already taken care of Nikola Bokaj, the barista in Portland, Oregon. It took me five weeks to learn that he was borrowing from a thug moneylender to buy abortions for two different women. I approached the thug, told him Nikola sent me. I tried to beg a loan, told him I needed to buy a special, collectible Corvette. The man told me in venomous words to walk away and forget that I had seen him. Two days later, some vicious maniac whacked the barista, which left two Serbs to be dealt with. After Arso Petrovic, I will visit Petar Djapic, the cab driver in Quebec City.

During the first of my sailings, before my familiarity with the ship had made travel less arduous, I had seen our supper servers use a rear entrance to the dining room. I assumed it led to part of the kitchen, but they never carried anything out or back in. A next-morning investigative walk suggested that they were ducking out to restrooms to sneak smokes—and that the doorway was a fine way for me to avoid the imbecilic line at the maitre d's podium.

I nursed a rum and soda in a piano lounge that afforded two-bit versions of the Rat Pack's best songs and a view of the late-seating supper line. When the caterpillar began to inch forward, I signed my tab and strolled to my special entrance. I chose a table for eight near the door and ordered a bottle from the wine steward before being joined by two couples from central Michigan who met through their bowling league. Three women from Atlanta took the other places, former college friends now raising children and, I would learn, suffering idiot husbands. Not sure what to make of the wine steward, they quibbled about what color wine they might like and compared by-the-glass prices on the menu.

I offered a glass of my Pinot Gris to the woman on my left, the Mona Lisa with searching eyes at the lifeboat drill. I wanted to believe, just then, that she had picked my table and that seat on purpose. She accepted the wine and introduced herself as Margaret, though her chums called her Marge. As dinner progressed, I refilled her glass several times, then ordered another bottle to the amazement of the bowlers. At some point Margaret and I determined that we were Diana Krall and John Prine fans, that sushi would have been better than our prime rib and overcooked veggies, and that I was unmarried and traveling alone.

We were watching the others finish their desserts when Margaret looked down and picked a piece of lint from her low-cut silk blouse. She said softly, "Every once in a while you look at my breasts."

"It's a habit I picked up in junior high. I apologize."

"It's nice for a soccer mom to get noticed," she said. "Should you and I meet in the hot tub?"

"What time?"

She unobtrusively looked at her watch. "It closes at eleven. How about ten forty-five, ninth deck, aft."

"It's directly above my stateroom, three decks up," I said.

She laughed as if I had said something charming, then said, "Take that bottle back to your room. Chill it, and we can finish it under the stars."

I was on an elevator decorated like a disco saloon and smelling of fried food when I had my only doubts. What I needed most at that instant was the swampy smell of twilight in a North Florida slash pine hammock. Was I becoming as evil as the three killers through my orchestrations? I am sure that a Google search would offer hundreds of pertinent quotes about getting even. But in revenge, as with murder motives, each case is different.

I became so lost in thought, I got off on the wrong deck and had to weave my way through a sports bar to find a stairway I recognized. The bar had seven ultra-wide high-definition TV screens on the walls. The patrons had their eyes glued to rebroadcasts of football, basketball, soccer and baseball. Why, I wanted to shout, did you leave your Barcalounger at home?

If it hadn't been a certain route to my sex alibi, I would have bailed on the hot tub. It stank of chemicals with no guarantee that they could fight bacteria. Sitting back in the stew I could see the wake behind the ship, lights of the Upper Keys to the north and I imagined that I could see a glow from the south, from Cuba. The stars, so numerous they were frightening, hung bright and low. There was no one else on the afterdeck, but I heard music from somewhere, a bad version of a fine Elton John song.

Margaret arrived with a "mega-Long Island tea" in a plastic cup. More Pinot Gris for me. A bit tipsy, she climbed the short ladder, crouched, slipped into the water butt first and drifted back toward me. Her free hand, behind her back, found my knee and slid up my thigh for a soft grope.

"Since you were so appreciative," she said, and slipped the straps off her shoulders, "I suppose we can let these …"

"Let me guess," I said, rubbing an erect nipple. "Your husband calls them 'puppies.'"

"That was his high school habit that stayed forever. Can you keep your hand under the water, in case someone walks by? As far under as you'd like."

I slipped my fingers inside her suit, felt shaving nubbies and her matted tuft of pubic hair. She moved her knees apart to assist my probing. I wondered if a more sober woman might be reluctant to expose her genitals to the bath water.

"Look," I said, "this really isn't the romantic moment I'd hoped for. Maybe it's this mystery froth floating here."

Margaret tilted back her drink. "I agree," she said. "It's hard to appreciate the starry night when the chlorine makes your eyes water."

"Shall we go to my stateroom? Show our appreciation to the pillows?"

"I haven't got that much time," she said. "My friends—our husbands all know each other, watch football games together, that kind of stuff. I need to get back to the room before they get ideas. I mean, even friends wag their tongues."

I helped her readjust her shoulder straps. We kissed and made a date to meet ashore the next day in Key West—for a drink and perhaps a few hours in a hotel room. Margaret would call my cell phone at high noon.

I returned to my cabin too energized to sleep. No sign of Arso, though— after the first two cruises—I knew enough about his habits not to expect him at that hour. I put on a pair of Levi's and a sports shirt and went for a walk. I was up for anything except the lizard-packed piano bar. Even the all-night pizzeria. I passed the dregs of a Texas Hold 'Em Tournament, a traffic jam of wheelchairs for the portly at the Midnite Deli—the snack shop that specialized in cappuccinos, milk shakes, giant cookies, chocolate-covered strawberries and eight kinds of cupcakes. I finally gave up on it all and wandered back toward my stateroom.

What I didn't need at this point was a leaper. According to news accounts, our suicidal brethren have forsaken traditional bridge, subway, and tall-building leaps for the cruise ship railings of the Caribbean. What the news fails to mention, of course, is that most jumpers have gone over on homeward legs of the voyages. Does it take a genius to figure out that they're plunging after visiting foreign ports where Zoloft, Paxil, and Prozac are sold over the counter like cough drops? Pills that will be mixed with each other, and with booze, and with the melancholy of hangovers? Fodder for another discussion, I agree. My point is right then, on our first night underway, I didn't need anyone to take the plunge, to throw off the ship's schedule.

I used the do-it-your-damned-self phone codes to order a pre-sunrise wake-up. As I fell asleep I mentally scripted the conversation I would employ to engage Arso in the morning. But it proved unnecessary when I received the glory gift, the visitation—or revenge—of the hot tub three decks above me.

Opportunity works best. Perfection is often an accident.

It woke me at two a.m.—a liquid sound I mistook for the ship's wake. The nightmare of a possible suicide yanked me from a deep sleep. Except for a slight adjustment to avoid a distant fishing craft, there would be no other reason to change course on a straight leg of our journey. Then I heard splashes—never a good sound at sea—and pressed the courtesy light button just above my pillow.

Water was seeping over the elevated bathroom doorsill. That meant that at least three inches of water covered the floor in there. The room carpet darkened as the flow continued, with most of the water draining off toward the passageway. I tossed my camera bag and two pairs of shoes onto the bed and scouted the floor for anything else I owned. A good sign: the water's chemical smell told me that it was not seawater. It also told me that the hot tub, at this late hour, had received a fresh, strong dose of disinfectant.

I phoned Arso and found him already awake. The folks in the cabin next to mine had called to report warm water spurting out of their shower drain. He assured me that a maintenance team was en route and the problem would be fixed immediately. If I wished, I could be moved to another stateroom.

"That's something we can discuss," I said. "I'm not sure I want to move."

I pulled on a pair of shorts. Arso knocked on my door. He winced at the chlorine stench when I opened up, then stood back to survey the damage.

"You don't look like you just got out of bed," I said.

Arso shook his head, dropped his eyelids. "I have been unable to sleep. I received a message after midnight, from Belgrade. My mother is ill and I must call when we reach Key West."

I pointed at my telephone. "Call from right there. Put it on my bill."

"I am not permitted," he said. "They would know it is me. I would lose my job."

"What will you do in Key West?" I said, knowing the answer ahead of time. "Pump quarters into a pay phone?"

"There's a place … I have a way to do this." Arso looked anxious. "Please forget my problems. We must fix your room and … What do you plan to do in Key West? Will you see sights? Do you like to be a tourist?"

"I'll probably rent a bicycle," I said. "See Ernest Hemingway's house and his favorite bar, eat shrimp and take pictures."

What I really wanted to do on the overrun island was to find one small detail of life that no one had ever appreciated. Perhaps on another trip, well into the future.

"You get that bicycle, you watch your streets," said Arso, "and find a free map. One time I did that bike riding without a map, I got so lost, I kept arriving at the cemetery."

"I hate when that happens," I said.

"Yes, yes." He laughed and drew a finger across his Adam's apple. "That made me worry."

"One thing I need to do in port is call Costa Rica and Jamaica," I said, aware of the answer before asking: "Is there a phone bank in Key West where overseas calls are cheap?"

Overacting, Arso drew down the corner of his mouth, put dread in his eyes. "If I told you, they'd kill me."

Do tell.

I reminded myself not to let superstition cloud my thoughts.

A week before my brother transferred out—to the Italian Alps, before going "in theater," as he termed it—he came back to our hometown in North Florida. He rolled into town in a red Mustang Cobra that rumbled like an old Boss 429. He saw a few of his old friends and went through the motions of saying good-bye to our failing father who probably wouldn't remember it the next day. At eleven a.m. the day he left, he and I stood on our dad's porch drinking warm beers.

"Remember those old stories," he said, "about guys who shipped out to Nam and left behind a pristine Corvette? Then they never came back?"

"And their parents kept their bedrooms intact for the next forty years? And the Corvette with only 9,000 miles on its odometer stayed in a garage until some collector paid a fortune for it?"

"I don't want that jinx riding with me," he said. "You're going to drive me to the Hertz office in Gainesville so I can get back to base. And I'm signing over the car's title so you can sell it next week. When I get back from this deployment, I'll spend that money on a Viper because I'm plain over this Ford. If I don't come back, you can piss away the cash however you want, after you pay a titty dancer to do her thing in front of my urn. Got it?"

I slept through sunrise and the ship's entrance into Key West's harbor, but was fully awakened by the rumbling of tugs there to assist our approach to the dock. The bathroom had yet to be swabbed and deodorized; I elected not to shower before strolling to the breakfast buffet. The line for sausage, bacon, eggs and muffins reminded me of dorm cafeterias in my college days. The fresh fruit line was remarkably short, so I opted for health. I saw no sign of Margaret and her friends.

Thirty minutes later I found the hallway and hatch that led to the pier.

The air carried a damp, silvery haze with thin clouds drifting westward. I scanned the sky in search of a promising tropical patch of blue.

"It'll burn off by noon," said a ship's officer at the gangway.

Was I wrong to expect something more original?

I said, "Maybe even clear up by midday?"

He shrugged. It had blown past him.

I left the ship with the first throng of passengers but wandered the pier by the Westin Resort and kept my eye on the ship's crew gangway. For some reason my thoughts went back to Rosa, the lanky "titty dancer" I had hired to perform for my brother's ashes. She was an employee of the venerable Café Olé on I-75 south of Gainesville and a third-year Architectural Design student at the University of Florida. We held the "service" in a ground level room at a Comfort Inn in Alachua where she insisted that I remain fully clothed and pay her fee before she began. She took off everything—there wasn't a hair on her body south of her chin—and danced to a medium-tempo Celine Dion tune. In tears, she kept on dancing for the next five songs on her portable CD player. Before driving away in her Mini Cooper, she gave me her cell number and asked me to call her sometime for a "normal" dinner date. I took her out a few times, even shed my clothes on several memorable occasions. But I never could separate her presence from the image of my brother's urn full of ashes, so we drifted apart. These days, maybe three times a year, she emails me jokes or humorous photographs.

After twenty-five minutes of strolling the pier—shop to shop, from air conditioner to air conditioner—I saw Arso and a male friend descend the crew gangway to the concrete dock. I followed the pair to Front Street and watched them go into the clothing store I suspected was a phony, a dodge for the illegal phone bank. A hokey tourist shop was right across the street—rubber alligators, batch-priced postcards, shell necklaces, authentic Key West ash-trays. The aisles and fellow browsers kept me well occupied and out of sight until I saw Arso and his pal heading up Fitzpatrick toward Captain Tony's. I browsed palm-decorated coffee mugs until I figured the two had ordered their first beer.

My face wouldn't be known in the phone bank, so my attire had to broadcast minimal fashion, maximum need. A dark blue ball cap worn backward, a brown dress shirt buttoned to the top, dark green trousers, a black belt. I walked to the rear of the clothing store and put my most stupid, cold-eyed expression against the door's one-way window. To my relief and amazement, the buzzer sounded. I was in.

Picture a fifteen-foot cube with steel gray walls and green-tinged fluorescent lighting. Add a mix of body odors and Pine-Sol, though the floor looked to have been swabbed with coal tar. Put nine old-fashioned shoe box-sized wall phones a few feet apart, five feet off the floor. Men at six of the phones hid their faces from each other and spoke, I believed, six different languages. Opposite the trip-lock door was a man in a glass-enclosed bullet-proof booth—the type used in all-night gas stations.

I couldn't have guessed the man's nationality. Middle Eastern, Indonesian, Central American. I remembered hearing a Tex-Mex entertainer friend describe the utter panic he once felt on a train in Germany. Four skinheads—who dislike immigrants in general—thought he was Thai and wanted to stomp him. Only when he sang Charley Pride's "Kiss an Angel Good Morning" and "Sundown" by Gordon Lightfoot did the toughs relent. He later joked that it took tunes made famous by a Canadian and an African-American to convince four Europeans that a Texan of Mexican parentage wasn't Asian.

Given the Florida Keys' proximity to Cuba, I opted for Spanish with the man in the booth. With a blatant American accent, I told the man I wanted to call Costa Rica. He asked to see my permit call card.

"I have no card, I'm the guest of Arso. He told me to come here."

He came back with a give-a-shit shrug and shook his head.

"He told you about me," I said.

"Go ahead, speak English."

"He was here fifteen minutes ago. The Serb with the scar on his chin."

He looked aside with disgust. "Show me the number you want to call."

I showed him a slip a paper. It read 2221-4012.

He inhaled deeply, bit his upper lip, then exhaled. "I'll need a thirty-dollar deposit."

I pulled a wad of bills from my pocket and found a fifty. I placed it into the metal cash drawer. The man pulled the drawer away from me, extracted the bill and did not offer change. So far, so good. He had pegged me as a drug dealer wishing to make an anonymous call.

"Dial 0-1-1," the man growled. "The country code is 506." He pointed to a vacant phone on the far wall.

I walked across the floor, picked up, waited for a tone, then dialed 911. I made sure the call connected, then hung up and turned to face the man. "I heard weird noises through this receiver," I said. "I'll take my money back."

His evil smile could've cut right through the cruise ship. Time to go.

I walked out to the warm sunshine, threw away the ball cap, unbuttoned my shirt and went back to the tourist trinket bazaar.

These days no police force in the country ignores a "911-hangup." Too often they're the result of domestic disputes about to go violent. Within ninety seconds two city squad cars and a burgundy Impala were blocking traffic on

Front. For the first minute after that it was Keystone Kops. Then I heard sirens inbound from the south and east.

I wanted to watch the glorious confusion but I couldn't afford to be a witness. I walked to the Pier House and took a one-night "patio" room near the pool. My cell phone rang eight minutes after I had seated myself on my patio.

Margaret had a pleasant shape for a woman in her early forties. I won't bore you with details. I mean, what do people not do in short-term trysts? To quote from the classic rock song, it was over, under, sideways and down. We laughed and, for a few minutes, danced nude without music. We showered, monkeyed around some more, and agreed that we should meet in the future but not pursue the affair while aboard the ship. She put on her clothing, kissed me sweetly and left first.

I walked back down Front Street. What must have been a zoo of activity was now three men in bulky, jet black shirts and trousers on the sidewalk. I stopped into the trinket shop and asked the counter clerk about the hubbub three hours earlier.

"We heard that Homeland discovered a terrorist communication cell," said the woman. "I guess the city never knew the place existed."

I waved my hand at the street. "So where did all the cops go?"

"They got called away an hour ago," she said. "Someone found a man's body in the restroom at Sloppy Joe's."

"What's happening on our little island?" I said.

"Maybe the same as always," she said with an odd smile. "With more people getting caught."

Perfection is often an accident. Sometimes it's plain perfection.

In need of a nap, I showed my passport and Glee Ticket and reboarded the cruise ship. Three men were loitering in the passageway outside my stateroom. After we exchanged introductions, they expressed a desire to speak with me about my room steward, Arso Petrovic. I invited the Key West detective and the Customs and Border Protection agents into my cabin. Even with the residual chlorine stench in my room, their undersized knit shirts stank of cigarettes and gun oil and aftershave.

The Feds let the city guy take the lead. If I had to guess I would say he was two or three years my junior.

"Did you have any conversations with your steward?" he said. "About his plans for being ashore in Key West?"

"Is he in trouble?"

"We're investigating an incident in a local bar."

"He asked what I intended to do in town," I said. "He told me that he needed to call his mother in … Belgrade, I believe. That used to be in, what, Yugoslavia? He said his mother was sick and he couldn't call her from the ship."

"That part of Serbia used to be Yugoslavia," said one of the Feds.

Oh, thank you for your history lesson.

"And what were your plans for Key West?" asked the detective.

"I wanted to rent a bike and wander the back streets with my camera."

"Great idea," he said. "Get many good pictures?"

I shook my head. "I didn't rent the bike, didn't take a single photo."

The larger of the two Feds poked his finger at me. "You've made three sailings on this barge in the past three months. I'm sure there's a good reason, right?"

I nodded. "One reason, three words."

"I'm all ears."

"I chase pussy."

"Gotcha," he said. "No luck on the mainland, back in the hometown?"

I shrugged. "First off, I live in Lake City, Florida. If you've ever gone through there, you can imagine the social life. Second, if you price hotels, rental cars and restaurants, you can figure it out. A six-day cruise is cheaper than four nights in Lauderdale. Plus the ongoing risk of drunk driving. I like my cocktails."

"That's it?" said the city detective.

"Something about the ocean's roll puts spirit in the old cougars."

"Why does this stateroom smell like a swimming pool?"

"The hot tub …" I pointed my thumb upward. "It sprung a leak last night and some of the water came up through my shower drain."

The smaller Fed took his turn: "Can you account for your time ashore today?"

"I took a room at the Pier House."

"While you were already paying for this room, sir?"

"I met someone there," I said. "We spent several hours of … bliss."

"Which hours?" said the other Fed.

"Noon to three, roughly."

"Someone from Key West?" he asked.

"No, a married woman who's on this cruise. She didn't want her two female traveling companions to know that she was being unfaithful to her husband."

"Could you give us her name, please?"

I gave it a dramatic pause. "Can you assure me that her dalliance won't be revealed?"

The city guy said, "Do you imagine that adultery constitutes a scandal in the Keys?"

"How about I just show you my receipt from the hotel?"

The small Fed toughened his voice. "How about that plus the name?"

I told him Margaret's full name and that I had no idea of her cabin number.

The Feds began moving toward the door. I felt a weight lift from my shoulders. The Key West detective hung back as if something was still on his mind. He chewed his upper lip then slowly nodded. "They found your steward murdered in town."

I stared at him, feigned disbelief, and said nothing. Plain perfection.

"Some monster cut his tongue out," he said. "Can you imagine the barbaric mind behind that?"

"No, but it makes me want to skip the evening meal."

The man looked toward the door. The Feds were out in the hallway.

"You're from Lake City," he said. "You have a brother … named Geoff?"

I stared at him again, without words. I felt perfection melt away. After a few seconds I loosened up and gave him a quick nod.

"I was in his National Guard unit. He sure got a rotten deal."

His posture told me another shoe would drop. He looked me in the eye. "I'd bet a bundle that Arso Petrovic fought for the other team."

I was still stuck for words.

"Just to let you know," he said, walking for the door. "We're not total bozos down here. Don't come back."

LILY & MEN

BY JOHN LUTZ

Lily was in her usual back booth in the bar at the Royal Roman Hotel in Miami near South Beach. It was one of the newer, plusher hotels masquerading as twenties renaissance, all pink and blue pastel Art Deco. A hard place to find a sharp angle.

Hard to find a sharp angle on Lily, too. She was a month past her thirty-fifth birthday but looked like a twenty-five-year-old high fashion model that had put on a little too much weight in the right places. In fact, she told her customers who weren't regulars that she was a model. They believed her. They believed whatever they wanted about her. Fantasy was part of the deal. Anyone glancing at Lily wouldn't have guessed. The slender, coolly attractive blonde in the back booth looked more like a travelling conservative business woman than a prostitute. She had her long hair swept back severely and pinned in a bun and was wearing a pale gray pinstriped business suit with tailored slacks and jacket, white blouse with mock bow tie, virtually no makeup. The kind of woman who might own her own company, which in fact she did, though she accepted work contracted out by Willis Gong.

When she'd begun this business ten years ago as a student at the University of Miami, Lily hadn't thought of herself as a prostitute. She'd been simply a college girl in need of cash, making some temporary concessions and rationalizations.

It turned out to be easy money. Even easier than she'd imagined. And nothing like she would have guessed from watching TV or movies. A girlfriend named Doris had introduced her to a bartender at one of the convention hotels who for a small percentage would let her sit in the lounge where men would make contact with her. Lily had a chance to size them up, decide for herself whether she'd trade sex for money, before going upstairs with them to a room the bartender somehow managed to supply even when the hotel was fully booked.

Lily and Doris sometimes worked as a team. Both had been psychology majors; they knew about fantasy. Both were young and unspoiled and attractive, which translated into so much money that both of them dropped out of school to devote more hours to their newfangled occupation. Lily had stayed away from the drugs that were offered free and for sale. Doris hadn't. Now Doris was dead. Lily was bruised.

That was where the years had left them. They hadn't left Lily financially comfortable, but she was close.

Close enough, she thought, to do something she'd been considering since her work had become less fun and more ... well, work. And since Doris had been found strangled to death in a hotel linen closet.

Willis Gong arrived, smiled at Lily, and slid into the booth to sit opposite her. They talked here from time to time. It was dim where the booth was, well beyond the bar in the long, hazy lounge, and far enough away from other customers so that conversation was private.

Lily, no longer an idealist, thought of herself as a prostitute now, but she still didn't think of Willis as a pimp, even though he arranged with employees of half a dozen hotels to allow her and several other prostitutes to operate from their restaurants or lounges. He was an amiable, middle-aged man with thinning white hair and kindly blue eyes, and given to faded Levis and plaid shirts. At first Lily had thought his gentle nature might conceal something ugly, but it turned out that the thoughtful and soft-spoken man who maximized and shared in her profits was exactly as he seemed. Lily couldn't remember Willis ever getting angry or raising his voice, and some of his clients had given him plenty of reason.

He ordered his usual glass of white wine then looked at Lily more closely and frowned. There was a cut near the left corner of her mouth, and bruises around both wrists.

"The fella from Kansas City?" he asked.

"Yeah," Lily said. She decided not to mention the similar bruises around her ankles, or the welts on her thighs and buttocks. When she'd gone to the hotel room she brought her valise of tricks that included her leather restraints; the client had insisted on using ropes. She'd brought her cloth belt; he had a leather belt. Lily felt the pain again from last night. "He turned out to be a son of a bitch."

"Didn't seem the type," said Willis.

"Neither do we."

Willis smiled. "You got a point."

"I'm gonna quit, Willis. It's time."

"You sure?"

"I don't want to find myself with somebody like Kansas City who won't know when to stop. I don't want to end like Doris."

"Understandable." Willis sipped his dry white wine, unperturbed. He'd been here before. "So what'll you do?"

"Go into business for myself. Another kind of business."

"Need money?"

"No, thanks to you. I've got enough for a start somewhere else. In some other city."

"I don't wanna sound like a pessimist, Lily, but most new businesses where the owner doesn't have previous experience fail."

"I'll be working with something experience has taught me a lot about," Lily told him. "Men."

Willis took another sip of wine, then he grinned and squeezed her hand. "Let me know when you go public. I'll wanna buy stock."

• • •

A year later. Another booth, another hotel bar, this time in Sarasota.

Lily was seated alone, coincidentally wearing the same conservative business woman outfit that had been a turn-on for Kansas City. She was sipping a daiquiri and watching a man at the bar. Brad. Lily knew about the Brads of the world. She was waiting until he got halfway through his second drink and would be feeling the effects of his first.

Two days ago in Lily's office, Brad's fiancée, Joan Marin, had smiled nervously at Lily and said, "You have an unusual occupation."

Lily smiled back. "But a useful one."

"That's why I called you," Joan said. "You saved a girlfriend of mine."

Still smiling, Lily shrugged. "I save as many as I can. Here's the deal, Joan. I choose the time and place and make myself available to Brad. I don't exactly come on to him, just make it clear that I could be agreeable to what he might suggest."

"Can you do that?" Joan asked.

"It's a subtle thing, but I've mastered it," Lily said.

"I never could flirt," Joan said, "even though I've worked at it."

Lily looked at her—this attractive enough brunette who'd gone to the right schools and had the wrong hairdo—and thought, not in a thousand years, sweetheart. But she widened her smile and said, "It's my business. If Brad does proposition a stranger a month before your wedding, you've got a right to know about it. And I'll see that you do know."

"Will you …," Joan twittered nervously, "I mean, go all the way?"

"No, no," Lily said tolerantly. "Ours is a business arrangement, and sleeping with your fiancée isn't part of it."

Joan looked down, looked up. There was a glint like a diamond chip in her eye. "But what if I wanted it to be? I mean, there's only one way to have actual proof."

Surprised, Lily nodded. "I understand. I can supply you with a videotape, if it comes to that. But of course my fee will be increased accordingly."

Joan agreed, and didn't find Lily too expensive. But she did ask meekly if she could pay ten percent of the fee up front, the rest after Lily's report. Lily told her that would be okay, thinking how the rich really were different from the rest of us, but very much like each other.

• • •

This Brad, Lily thought, watching him at the bar, was also rich. Joan had told her that, but it wouldn't have been necessary. Lily could figure it out from his obviously expensive blue blazer, Italian loafers, the glitter of his gold watch and diamond ring when he lifted his arm to sip from his glass. A young, good looking guy over six feet tall, with dark eyes and a head of black curls. He was well built enough that he made his tailored jacket look even more expensive.

He glanced over and saw Lily staring at him. Didn't smile, but didn't look away immediately. Lily averted her eyes precisely when he did, so he would know she'd also looked away. Lily knew how to flirt the way an artist knows how to prepare to paint.

When Brad was finished with his second drink, he hadn't come to her, so she went to him, standing close and asking the bartender for a bowl of peanuts.

When she'd returned to her booth and sat down, she saw that Brad had followed her. Big surprise.

"Do I know you?" she asked coolly.

He smiled white and wide, aiming his charm like a gun. "Would you like to?"

Lily waited a couple of beats. "I don't know. Would I?"

Brad sat down opposite her.

He was obviously experienced, and very good. Lily had to admire how adroitly he played her while she was playing him. It took him only about ten minutes to ask if she'd wait while he went to the desk and got a room, then go upstairs with him. Lily dropped the coy act. She told him that wouldn't be necessary, she was staying at the hotel and had her own room.

He was good all the way. No violence or disrespect, only gentleness combined with blatant lust. Lily's style.

Afterward she lay back with her fingers laced behind her neck and smoked a cigarette. Apparently Brad wasn't a smoker himself, but he registered no complaint. Lily watched him watch a bead of perspiration she could feel finding its way around the nipple of her left breast. The expression on his face almost made her want to reach for him, but that would hardly do when she showed Joan Marin the videotape of her fiancée thoroughly enjoying the last half hour with a stranger he'd picked up in a hotel lounge. The camcorder was set up between the wardrobe and desk, concealed in the shadows and focused on the bed, with a piece of tape over its red power light. A small voice-activated recorder was taped to the back of the headboard so it could pick up words uttered even in a whisper.

Brad reached across her for the glass of scotch poured from the bottle he'd brought up from downstairs. Lily gasped and sat straight up as the glass slipped from his hand, spilling ice and diluted scotch over her bare stomach and crotch.

"Damn!" Brad said. "I'm sorry." He leaned down and began to lick her stomach.

Not in the mood, Lily shoved him away. "It's okay," she said, "really." The mattress was wet and cold beneath her. "I'm gonna get up and shower."

"Okay," Brad said. "I'll wait for you. Then I'll buy you a big dinner so you'll forget my awkwardness."

Lily thought, why not? She liked the guy, and Joan wasn't going to marry him after seeing the videotape. Lily had even gotten Brad to say he loved her, always the end of an engagement.

She showered quickly then dried off with one of the hotel's towels from a heated rack, thinking maybe she'd found the right occupation for a woman with her skills and a realistic attitude.

When she wrapped the towel around her and returned to the room to get dressed, she found Brad still nude and seated on the edge of the bed. He was going through her purse. Lily forced herself to be calm, fighting back her anger. She'd had Brad wrong. Now she wondered how wrong.

"Private investigator, huh?" he said, holding up the copy of her license.

The hell with this guy, Lily thought. He was the one with the problem.

"Knowing that will hardly make any difference now." She dropped the towel and stepped into her panties.

He smiled at her, his own coolness disturbing, making her wonder all the more. He should be furious, threatening. "Notice that smell?" he asked her.

For the first time she did, the acrid scent of burned plastic.

"I burned the videotape in the wastebasket while you were showering," he explained. "I figured Joan might hire someone to test my fidelity. It's the thing to do for women in her crowd. So, when I saw you I could hardly believe my luck."

Lily continued dressing, staring at him curiously. He wasn't simply a sneak thief caught rooting through her purse. Something else was going on here.

"I recognized you," Brad said. "You're Lily from Miami. When you came on to me, I knew you were a working girl one way or the other, so I decided to take my chance and hope you were hired by Joan and not still … er, working your other profession."

"I decided on a new, honest profession. A new start in another city."

"You should have chosen a city farther from Miami."

"I like Florida and don't want to leave. But I won't miss Miami. Are you a former client of mine?"

"No, I only recall you from someone telling me about you at the convention in South Beach. I admired you enough to remember your face."

"Then you don't really love me?" she asked wryly, using humor to stall for time while she finished dressing, trying to figure out what this was about, how she would deal with it.

"I meant it when I said it. And I'm glad you turned out to be you, because it makes what I'm going to ask a lot easier."

Lily felt better. He wanted something from her he couldn't simply take.

Something he had to ask for. She bent forward to display her cleavage while she fastened her bra, looking at him to let him know she was waiting.

"You see, Lily, I have a prison record, and I'd rather not have Joan find out about it. What I'm asking is for you to give her a clean report on me."

"She only has my word anyway, now that you destroyed the tape."

"But I want you to go beyond saying I didn't betray her. I want you to tell her you checked out my past and it's unblemished. That way she won't hire someone else to check it. Rich women are suspicious."

Lily couldn't resist grinning at him. "You don't think they have good reason?"

He gave her a sheepish look and nodded. Lily didn't buy into it.

"There's something more, isn't there?" she said.

He gave her a level stare that went right to her core, surprising her with its effect. Joan would be crazy not to marry this guy even if he murdered his last five wives. He said, "You're no fool, Lily, which is why I think you'll go for what I'm going to propose."

"You already proposed to Joan," she pointed out.

"I'm being sincere now, and not about marriage. I'm marrying Joan for her money."

"Shocking," Lily said, zipping her skirt. "I would have guessed you had money of your own."

"I did, and now I don't. But I will again. Joan's."

"Unless she finds out about your past," Lily said. She knew how to play the Brads of this world.

"That's true. Especially my recent past."

Here is comes, Lily thought. "How recent?"

"As long ago as the New York Diamond District robbery."

Lily sat down in a chair near the bed, not bothering to button her blouse. She remembered the multimillion dollar jewel heist from when it was all over the news about six months ago. Four men had held up separate shops in New York's diamond district simultaneously, then somehow faded into the throngs of pedestrians on the sidewalks. Later the police theorized they'd worn the dark clothes of Hasidic Jewish diamond couriers beneath their coats, then placed hats or yarmulkes on their heads and passed for diamond merchants themselves. Lily recalled thinking the robbers might just as easily have dressed as cops, but the cops would never advance that theory unless they had no choice.

"You were one of the robbers?" she asked.

He nodded. Didn't seem to be kidding.

"Then you should be rich. None of you were ever caught."

"All of us got away," Brad said, "but when the four of us split up, only three of us had diamonds."

"Your partners robbed you of the robbed diamonds?"

"Yes. I was stupid enough to give them the chance. That leaves me just about broke. Which is why I need Joan." He fixed her with that dreamy stare again. She felt it. "I'm being honest with you, Lily."

"That doesn't seem to be your pattern."

"It is when my back's to the wall, like it is now."

She finished buttoning her blouse, then bent over and reached her shoes and slipped them onto her feet.

"You didn't say no, Lily."

"Since we're being honest with each other, " she said, "I'm wondering, if I report to Joan that she's about to marry a saint, what's in it for me?"

"You get half."

"Of what?"

"Millions. Joan's not very careful with her financial records. Her first husband died five years ago and left her over four million dollars. It's grown since then."

"If you get half after the divorce, that's a million for me. All that just for giving Joan a favorable report about you?"

"Well, there's more. I want you to befriend Joan, keep building me up, make sure she doesn't do any more checking into my background. Right up to the marriage and beyond."

Lily was thinking ahead. "I guess part of my job would be to talk her out of a prenuptial agreement."

"Not necessarily," Brad said.

"Then what makes you think you'll walk away from the marriage with a couple of million dollars that you'll then split with me?"

"More like six million," he said, watching Lily closely now. Knowing it was the kind of money that shortened her breath.

"How six million?" she asked, thinking this is just the sort of stupid but simple plan that might work, only there has to be a catch because there always is.

He gave her his handsome smile. "The inheritance …"

"Uh-huh …"

"Plus the life insurance."

"Oh Jesus!" Lily said.

• • •

The wedding was a small one, with only a few family members and friends. Joan's old college friends were a snooty lot, but they seemed to accept Lily easily enough. It helped that Joan introduced her as "my very dearest friend."

The reception was at one of the best hotels near the marina and down-town Sarasota, less than half an hour's drive from Joan's luxurious home on Longboat Key. A portable dance floor had been set up, and there was a four-piece band playing softly enough that there could be conversation.

When Lily and Brad were dancing, Lily found herself feeling good in his arms. She resisted the temptation to press herself against his lean body in front of everyone. Instead she moved just close enough so she could whisper to him. "Mr. and Mrs. Brad Masters," she said. "Is that even your real name?"

"Real enough. Want some punch?"

"I want you," she said. "And as soon as possible after the honeymoon is over."

• • •

During the next two weeks, Lily tried not to think about Brad and Joan in Hawaii.

The distance from Brad gave her time to do some reconsidering, and she drove to Miami and met with Willis in the bar at the Royal Roman Hotel. Like old times. It didn't feel good.

"I'm glad you're doing okay," Willis told her, leaning across the table and patting her wrist. He was wearing Levi's and a long-sleeved plaid shirt despite the eighty degree temperature outside. "You said on the phone you needed a favor. If I can help you, I will."

"I need to know about a guy who calls himself Brad Masters. Whatever you can find out about him."

"That his real name?"

"I doubt it."

"I thought your new business was finding out things like that."

"This one's over my head, but maybe not yours." She paused, but she knew Willis would keep her secrets. He had in the past. "He was involved in that big New York diamond theft last year."

Willis's expression changed to one Lily had never seen before. It gave away nothing. "I've got lines to it," he told her. "I might be able to learn something for you. But it would help if I knew his real name. Or at least what he looked like."

"Here's his photo," Lily said, handing him a copy of a snapshot taken by Joan. A smiling Brad at the wheel of her vintage Jaguar convertible.

"Nice looking guy," Willis said. He looked closely at her. "You involved in a romantic way?"

"'Fraid so."

Willis smiled and wagged a finger. "You of all people should know what they say about mixing business with pleasure."

"He's not in the detective business."

"I didn't mean the detective business. You're supposed to be smart about men, Lily."

"That's why I want to learn more about this one."

"This is a favor I'm glad to do," Willis said. "It might save you some heartache."

"To tell you the truth, I'm surprised I still have a heart."

He patted her wrist again. "I'm not."

● ● ●

The day before Brad and Joan were due back from Hawaii, Willis phoned.

"Your Brad is Bradford Colter from Buffalo, New York," he said. "He's got a police record, but nothing violent if you don't count blowing the doors off safes. He's an expert at it. That's what he and the others did in New York, used plastique explosive to blow open safes so they could get at where the real value was in those shops. Did it in broad daylight when the sidewalks were crowded. The sounds of outside heavy construction in that block masked the noise of explosions."

"Clever."

"The word is, if you're involved with this Brad guy, you can trust him. We're talking honor among thieves here, though not necessarily honor in romance."

"Honor among thieves will do, Willis. Thanks."

"Trust is relative, Lily."

Lily told him she knew that. And she did. That's why she'd kept in her safety deposit box the audio tape that matched the video Brad had destroyed that night in the hotel room. Though she was reassured about Brad, she decided to hold onto the tape.

After all, he was deceiving Joan.

• • •

Lily met Brad and Joan at the airport the next day, kissed them both on the cheek, and welcomed them home.

The three of them went out to dinner that night at Sharkey's down the coast in Venice, and a glowing Joan hung all over Brad and couldn't stop talking about their time in Hawaii. Lily kept smiling and playing along, her leg resting against Brad's beneath the table.

They didn't have a chance to be alone together, to make love, until almost a week later at the house on Longboat Key, in Joan and Brad's bedroom.

Brad made love to Lily in the controlled violent way she'd learned to enjoy. He was the only man she trusted, the only man she'd let out all the stops for in years. The intent way he looked at her while he drove himself into her again and again, when he released in her. And afterward, even as he rolled off her onto the other side of the bed. She'd seen enough of fantasy to know this was real. He wasn't like the other men. In his way, he loved her. His way was enough for her.

Exhausted, she lay back perspiring on Joan's pillow, listening to her own ragged breathing in counterpoint to Brad's.

She wasn't surprised when he chose this as the time to tell her how Joan was going to die.

"I'm an explosives expert," he began. "It's my specialty and you're going to have to trust me on that."

She lay quiet, staring at the ceiling and pretending this was news to her.

Brad continued: "I'm going to place in the gas tank of Joan's Jaguar a small detonating device that can be activated by a plastic timer beneath the seat. I've substituted some old wiring near the tank with the insulation worn off, so that it will look like electricity arced and ignited fumes from the tank. This is most likely to happen just before or during a thunderstorm. It will be assumed that lightning struck nearby, momentarily spiking the voltage and causing the arc."

The first question Lily asked was a practical one. "What happens to the timer?"

"It will melt and be unrecognizable. Likewise the detonator itself. I know explosives, Lily, and I know cars. Trust me, this will look like an accident."

She rolled onto her side and looked into his eyes. "Are you really that good at your specialty, Brad?"

"Let me show you," he said, and pulled her to him.

●　●　●

It was the time of year for storms in southwest Florida. They struck all around Sarasota, but not there. While the city lay dry in heat beneath low dark clouds, a tornado destroyed three houses in nearby Punta Gorda. Lily sat in the evenings with Joan and Brad in the veranda behind Joan's house and watched distant chain lightning illuminating the sky and sipped Margaritas and prayed for rain.

She was surprised one morning after spending the night at Brad and Joan's, as she often did, when Brad gave her a wicked look and a nod. Lily glanced outside. The sun was shining.

Joan came downstairs already dressed and carrying a small overnight case. "I'm driving over to North Palm Beach to visit an old college friend who just moved there. Moira Brent. Remember her from the wedding?"

"I think so," Lily lied. She'd already prepared some coffee and buttered toast, just about the extent of her cooking skills. Aren't you going to eat breakfast?" she asked, seeing Joan kiss Brad good-bye.

"Gonna skip it," Joan said. "I want to get on the road and beat the morning traffic. Got a long way to go."

Neither Brad nor Lily said anything as they watched her gulp down half a cup of coffee, then start for the door.

With a backward glance at Lily, Brad followed her outside.

Lily watched from the window as Brad opened the Jaguar's door for Joan, then bent down as if he'd dropped something, his body blocking Joan's view as he leaned into the car. Lily's heart accelerated as she realized he was setting the timer that would activate the detonator. She watched as he kissed Joan good-bye again, more passionately. Then he smiled and waved as she drove away. His head was bowed as he trudged back toward the house.

"Done," he said, when he was inside.

"It isn't raining," Lily pointed out.

"It is in south central Florida," Brad said. "The weather channel even has tornado warnings out. Joan's taking Highway 72 east and will be driving right through the center of the storm activity. I don't think we'll see my wife and your best friend again."

Lily walked overt to stand directly in from of him, close to him. Her heart felt as if it were trying to escape from her chest. "How do you feel about that?"

"Elated," he said. "What are you feeling right now?"

"Turned on," she told him.

"It'd be better if you and I were in two different places an hour from now. That's another reason I chose this morning. I've got a job interview in forty-five minutes."

"A job interview," she said. "That's wonderful."

He kissed her, she judged even more passionately than he'd kissed Joan good-bye.

"What will you be doing while I'm gone?" he asked when they'd separated. She smiled up at him. "Watching the clock."

• • •

At 10:06 AM, two minutes before Joan's scheduled departure from the world, Lily was seated at the kitchen table sipping her fourth cup of coffee. All that coffee had been a mistake. She was nervous enough to scream.

She calmed herself by envisioning Joan in her Jaguar speeding along desolate Highway 72, probably with the radio on high volume. By now she'd be in the rain, would have the car's top up and the wipers scything across the windshield. But in less than a minute …

The jangling phone propelled Lily up out of her chair and almost did make her scream.

She lifted the receiver and said hello, trying to keep her voice level.

"Lily, it's me, Joan."

Lily almost dropped the phone. She kept her composure. "Are you in Palm Beach already?"

"No, I'm calling from my cell phone in the car."

Lily considered this. They'd be talking when the gas tank exploded, when Joan died. Despite herself, Lily felt a warm, tight knot in her stomach. The heat spread to her groin. It was terrible of her, she knew, but she was actually going to enjoy this. How many people had this kind of opportunity?

"I have something to confess, Lily. I hope you won't think too poorly of me when I do."

Not that it matters, Lily thought. "Why, go ahead, Joan. You can trust me not to turn on you."

"I'm a terrible person, always have been. I have what some people call a checkered past. Evil lives in me, Lily, and I have the police record of a confidence woman to prove it. There's enough money in the bank to pay rent for the house till the end of the month, then nothing. I fooled Brad into thinking I was wealthy so he'd marry me."

Lily sat back down, feeling light-headed now. Cold despite the warming morning.

"I hope you won't think too poorly of Brad, either. He's no more what he seems than I am, Lily. I've known from the beginning he was part of a gang of robbers who stole millions of dollars worth of diamonds in New York last year. He never told me he was rich, but because of the diamonds I assumed he had hidden assets. I only married him for his money, Lily."

Lily sat stunned, not knowing what to say. "Joan … Ah, Joan …"

"I hate to tell you this because you've been so sweet, but I haven't re-formed, Lily. There's only one way to turn my marriage into money now, and that's to hand Brad over to the police for the reward. A consortium of dia-mond merchants has offered over a million dollars to anyone who can furnish information leading to the arrest of any of the thieves. Brad is in Sarasota now, three blocks away at a job interview. I can send the police directly to him. I know Brad will hate me. I hope you won't, Lily."

"Joan, don't call the police! Please!"

"I'm not going to, Lily. I didn't drive toward Palm Beach. I just drove around getting up my nerve to do this. I'm parked on Ringling Boulevard in Sarasota, right in front of Police Headquarters. When I hang up I'm going to walk inside and—"

"Joan!"

The receiver emitted what sounded like a loud animal growl, then the static of a disconnected line.

An instant after she slammed the receiver back in its cradle, Lily knew the questions that would be asked: Why had a car, parked with the engine off and miles from any electrical storm, suddenly exploded in front of Police Headquarters? What was actually known of its dead driver, Joan Marin-Mas-ters? Of her new husband Brad?

Of their good friend Lily?

The eventual answer to all those questions would be murder.

On numbed legs, Lily staggered outside to sit in the fresh air on the ve-randa. Her mind was whirling in tighter and tighter spirals, as if boring deep into a black future.

She'd figured right—she knew men. It was a woman who'd fooled her.

She couldn't catch her breath. In the direction of the mainland, she could see a dark plume of smoke in the clear blue sky over downtown Sarasota.

The breeze seemed to be carrying it her way.

WILD CARD

BY LISA UNGER

"I don't want you to go." Emma's voice was always light and sweet, like the tinkling of bells—even when she was whining.

"I know, baby. I don't want to go either. But I have to."

"But I just don't *want* you to go."

"You'll have fun," Maura said. She kept her voice crisp and light. If she showed any weakness, she was dead.

"No," Emma said. "I *won't*."

No, she wouldn't. Not really. Maura was not sure anyone had *ever* had fun with her mother Lizzie. Lizzie was not a *fun* person. But she could be counted on to keep routine, and that was the important thing. Maura could always count on Lizzie to cook a good meal—maybe roast chicken and potatoes, some kind of green. She would make sure Emma ate her vegetables. After dinner, she would give Emma her bath. And Maura knew that Grandma would *certainly* get to that gunk that collected behind the ears. Then a story, and lights out. No nonsense. One look from Lizzie—former high school principal, current head of senior neighborhood watch—and nonsense withered into a heap of ash on the floor.

Maura stepped from the cool interior of the Prius that Lizzie had bought for them last year, and into the heat. She walked around to the back and helped Emma from her car seat. The new car smell made her feel guilty, reminded Maura to be grateful for her mother, whatever her faults. Nobody was perfect, and Maura should know that better than anyone.

The sun was drifting low, the sky a sleeping tiger—orange fingers against an encroaching black. It was October and the heat was still with them, a blanket of humidity raising sweat on the back of Maura's neck as they walked across the blacktop that still radiated the day's blistering memory.

Her mother's condo building rose, a hideous blue tower against the darkening sky. White balconies boasted plastic deck furniture; some people already had their Halloween decorations out. A plug-in jack o' lantern grinned on a glass table. A cardboard skeleton cocked its head on a glass sliding door.

As Maura pushed through the double glass doors, Emma's hand still in hers, she could hear the boat halyards in the marina behind the building. A warm wind was picking up. There was something comforting about the slow rhythm of that clanging, and about the waters of the Intracoastal slapping against the seawall. Florida born and raised, Maura had been listening to this music all her life—the sound of wind sighing through palms, of waves lapping against the shore. They were good sounds, the sounds of things right with the world.

Emma wasn't crying *yet*. But she had started a pre-meltdown sulk, purposely pushing down the corners of her mouth in a pantomime of sadness. Secretly, Maura was glad for it. She wouldn't want her daughter to be *too* happy to stay the night with Grandma. She loved her mother but they were just different, that's all. The chemistry wasn't always there. Lizzie was good to them. She had been a good mother, in all the important ways, and she was a good grandmother. But there were things about Lizzie that Maura didn't like and didn't respect—and visa versa; she couldn't bear to see Emma prefer the other camp. The "no nonsense" camp.

Maura had always thought of her mother as a person without color, someone forever in khaki and gray. So it had surprised her when, after retirement, Lizzie took a class at the community college, bought a florist shop that was going out of business on the mostly residential island where she lived, and started arranging flowers as her second career. On the days she helped out in the shop, Maura watched in wonder as Lizzie smiled among pink stargazers, waxy red roses, lush purple hyacinth, humming as she artfully placed hydrangeas and freesia, then happily drove arrangements around in her truck.

"*Blooms away!*" Lizzie called as she sped off. It simultaneously annoyed and fascinated Maura. She had come to like Lizzie best when her mother was working in the shop, cheerful and artistic. But Maura wondered where *that* woman had been when she'd been growing up under lock and key, withering under with stern glances, bracing for hard words. She tried not to resent it.

Entering the building with her key, Maura was slightly depressed by the Florida cliché of it all, the white tile floors, the bad art—palm trees, boats in a marina, frolicking dolphins—the bank of faux wood-paneled elevators. It was one of those buildings that must have looked just nifty when it was built a million years ago. But now, to Maura it looked like a place where hopes had faded and dreams had passed by without stopping.

Maura and Emma shared the ride up to her mother's condo with an elderly lady pushing a walker. She smelled of honeysuckle, and something else, something medicinal.

"Look at that red hair," the woman said. She gazed at Emma with watery green eyes. Her voice was soft and youthful. "What a pretty girl!"

"Thank you," Emma said. Pout forgotten, she offered her brightest smile, preening under the attention. The older woman let out a girlish giggle, and Emma followed suit.

"Good-bye," Emma said when the woman exited before them. "Have a nice night!"

"Oh, what an angel!"

When the door closed, Emma went back to sulking. She was four years old and she already knew the power of her sweetness and beauty. Maura wasn't entirely sure this was a good thing. But she supposed she was to blame, adoring her daughter as she did. Emma was her only love-at-first-sight, her only ever head-over-heels.

They walked down the hallway, passing a row of blue doors until they reached number 333 and pushed inside, the door left unlocked for them.

"Hi, Mom!" Maura called.

"Hello, girls," her mother answered.

They followed her voice to the kitchen, where Lizzie stood at the counter, preparing a salad. In the five years since Maura's father died, her mother had put on an unhealthy amount of weight, though she never seemed to eat very much. And it looked to Maura like she was having trouble getting around, leaning heavily on things to get up, reaching out for support when she moved about the apartment. Lizzie's legs were a road map of spider and varicose veins, which didn't stop her from wearing gigantic shorts she bought at Target. Maura wanted to say something, but didn't know how. She didn't know how to offer her mother help; Lizzie had always been so strong, so in-charge. There was no script written with Maura doing the care giving, so she found months passing, still saying nothing.

"Hungry?" Lizzie asked. Emma was settled in front of the television, momentarily distracted from her misery by *The Wonder Pets*. "Want to eat before work?"

Maura felt her mother's eyes on her body, taking in the tight jeans and clinging black top. Not slutty, not *cheap*—which is what Lizzie would say if she dared—but suggestive enough. She needed tips; wearing baggy clothes to her bartending job at a bar on the beach was not the way to get them. Like Emma, she too knew the power of her sweetness and beauty.

"No, thanks," Maura said. She hated the way she felt self-conscious and tense around her mother, always preparing for some criticism. "I'll get something there."

"Nothing good," Lizzie said. She wiped her hands on her apron and turned down the volume on the small television on the counter. "What will you eat there? Chicken wings at ten?"

Maura smiled, walked over and grabbed a baby carrot from the cutting board. She leaned in and gave her mother a kiss on the cheek and was surprised when her mother grabbed onto her and pulled her into a tight embrace.

Lizzie was not normally an affectionate woman. Maura could count the number of kisses and bear hugs, the times her mother had told her she loved her, on the fingers of one hand. But Maura gave her mother a squeeze back, liked the comfort of Lizzie's soft body. Her mother still felt strong, solid. She was glad for it.

"I'll have a little something with Emma," Maura said when her mother released her.

"Good girl," Lizzie said.

It was just five minutes over the causeway from her mother's condo to the Rockin' Iguana, the bar on the beach where Maura worked, a proximity that made her happy. She liked being that close to Emma, knowing she could be back in a heartbeat if she was needed. When her shift was over at two AM, she'd go back to her mother's where the pull-out couch would be waiting, made up for her.

She'd be there when the munchkin woke up, and then take her to school. After that she'd go back to bed at home for a while. Around eleven, she'd get up again, do the laundry, grocery shopping, cleaning—whatever needed doing—then go back and get Emma at school. She'd have the next two days off from the restaurant, so she'd put in some time at her mother's flower shop.

She thought about this as she walked in the near darkness through the lot and into the bar. She didn't have time to think about what kind of life it was or how she was going to change it, do something better. She wouldn't think about those things until she was lying in bed trying to sleep. Instead, she said her hellos and took over for Kate, the afternoon bartender.

"How was it today?" Maura asked. She tied the green, Iguana-shaped apron around her waist. The other girl, a willowy blonde with washed denim eyes, was young, maybe twenty, paying her way through community college. Kate had aspirations to be a physical therapist, work with stroke victims. Maura always thought *she* should do something like that, too. Something that had meaning. But she hadn't. She didn't know if she ever would.

You've just thrown your whole life away, Lizzie had said the afternoon Maura told her she was pregnant. She'd since apologized, claimed she hadn't meant it and had been speaking out of fear for Maura's future. But she'd been right. Maura got pregnant in her junior year of college and hadn't finished her degree. She'd been planning to write; was studying journalism. But all of it just got washed away in a tide of sleepless nights and milk-soaked days. For the first two years of Emma's life, her mother nagged and nagged for her to go back to school. *You've been dealt a wild card, kid. It changed your hand but you don't have to fold. Go back to school. I'll help you.*

Maura promised she would go back. But she didn't, and eventually Lizzie stopped saying anything. Maura almost wished she'd start nagging again. Otherwise, what would keep her from working in a dump like the Rockin' Iguana for the rest of her life?

"Busy today," said Kate. "But lousy tips. Recession doesn't keep people from drinking, but they're definitely holding on to their spare change."

"I know it."

When the real estate market was booming and everyone's house was worth a fortune, people were feeling flush, tipping generously. Now, even her mother's island—once the jewel of the area with its big waterfront homes—was studded with foreclosure properties, overgrown lawns, tipping mailboxes, and algae-filled pools.

"Damn fools," Lizzie would complain. "Don't people know what they can afford? Since when is it up to the bank to tell you what you can pay?"

Maura thought it was a bit more complicated than all that, but social issues were just one of the many topics she avoided discussing with her mother.

"And watch out for Bill," said Kate. She rolled her eyes as she threw her apron in the hamper under the sink. "He is in a foul, foul, ugly mood."

"Great."

The Rockin' Iguana *was* a dump. It pretended not to be with a big laminated menu featuring things like "Spring Rolls with Fancy Asian Dipping Sauce!" and "Bourbon Marinated Shrimp!" But the food was all frozen crap, the well liquor was just north of nail polish remover. As if that wasn't bad enough, Bill encouraged them to pass off the cheap stuff as top shelf and see if they could get away with it—which they usually did.

"I'm outta here," said Kate, shouldering her backpack. And something about the way she said it made Maura feel so sad for a flash, so oddly desperate, that she had to blink back a sudden rush of tears.

It was a Friday night, so when the clock passed nine, the place got packed. And Maura was glad she'd eaten at her mother's place, because she didn't have even a minute to get someone to cover so she could run to the bathroom. It was the usual crowd—vacationers who couldn't afford any place better, locals tying one on, some loud-mouthed college boys. She just served the drinks, smiled, laughed at any stupid joke that was tossed her way, and occasionally pulled down the neckline on her shirt ever so slightly. The hours flew by; the tips piled up.

It was past midnight when she saw him come in. Something about the way he entered and didn't look around, just came straight to the bar and took a seat near the end made her look at him twice. He had a body that was built for the jeans he was wearing—tall, strong thighs, lean waist. He wore a distressed black tee shirt with some kind of faded white design, boots in spite of the heat. He had a leather jacket with him, a large canvas duffle bag. He had the look of someone who'd just arrived from somewhere else and who wouldn't be staying long. A sheen of sweat on his brow told her that he wasn't from Florida. The humidity was getting to him, even though the air was on.

When you see trouble coming, cross the street. Advice from her mother that had never quite taken hold.

"Patrón," he said to her. "Anjeo." Tequila. The good stuff.

"Salt and a lime?"

He shook his head. He wasn't partying. He was medicating. She poured him a shot from the Patrón bottle that actually contained Cuervo, thinking as she did that he might notice the difference. He tossed it back, and then gave her a look.

"I'm not paying for that," he said. He rubbed the sweat from his brow with the back of his arm. He had close-cropped dark hair, receding a touch, just a whisper of widow's peaks. A good face, strong jaw, full lips. Dark, dark eyes. Trouble. At least she knew it when she saw it these days. That was an improvement, wasn't it?

"Sorry about that," she said. "My mistake."

She returned with the real deal. He drank that down, too.

"That's better," he said.

"On the house."

He lifted the glass again, placed a twenty on the bar. She brought the squat, thick bottle over. As she poured, she saw that the knuckles on his right hand were split.

"I'm looking for Bill," he said.

Maura realized she hadn't seen her boss all night, which was rare. He was usually hovering over her, trying to tell her how to do her job, striving to graze her ass or breasts, as he pretended to reach for this or that. He was a pig —a nasty, sweaty, functioning alcoholic. God help you if you did anything wrong. He'd ream you in front of everyone—staff, customers, anyone in ear shot. Her mother actually knew him; he'd attended the high school where she'd been principal. *Bill Lowenstein? That kid was a loser from the day he was born,* Lizzie said when Maura mentioned him. *Always in trouble. Barely a C student. If he had half a brain in his head, he'd be dangerous.*

"I haven't seen him," she said. "But I can call up to his office."

She pointed to the stairway that led to the hot windowless space, which Bill called the Lion's Den and everyone else called the Rat's Nest. The stranger turned around and looked in the direction she was pointing.

"What's your name?" she asked. "I'll see if I can get him for you."

"Jake."

Filling a tray with Coronas for one of the servers, mixing two margaritas for a couple at the bar, she tried the intercom to Bill's office, then left a message on his cell.

"I left word for him," she said, returning to Jake.

"Okay," he said. But he barely seemed to hear her. He looked past her, past the bar into the darkness outside. During the day, you could see the white sand beaches and jewel green water. But now it was just black. She wondered what he was looking at; she was about to ask him, just because of the look on his face—something wistful, something far away. But then he said, "Can I get a Corona with a lime?"

"Sure thing."

When she finally made her way back to him, he was gone. She left the beer by the money he'd put on the bar, figuring he'd headed to the restroom. But an hour later, he had not returned. She watched the bottle sweat, moisture collecting in the coaster, lime sinking to the bottom. Finally, she dumped it in the metal sink. She pocketed the change, not without a twinge of disappointment. What did she think? She hadn't had a date since Emma was born. She'd had plenty of offers—an occupational hazard.

But Maura had an impulse control problem, a problem with the moment—it washed her over, swept her away. She could get caught up in a fantasy, make foolish mistakes that wound up costing her everything. It was best to avoid any temptation, better to just walk the line for Emma. Her mom was paying for Emma's fancy private preschool. And even though they didn't have much right now, they had everything they needed. That was enough. Maybe if she saved more, or could bring herself to talk to her mother, she'd go back to school so that they'd have a brighter future. She definitely didn't need a man to mix things up. Emma's on-again, off-again father was bad enough, confusing and upsetting for her little girl. She didn't need some other dog sniffing around.

By 2:15, the place had cleared out. She was wiping the counter, rinsing the sink, closing out the till, and counting her tips. The waitresses were gone; the cleaning crew hadn't arrived yet. The evening had passed without an encounter with Bill. She stared at the narrow staircase leading up to his office. He could be up there, passed out. It had happened before. She needed to ask him for next Thursday off so that she could go to Parent's Night at Emma's school. But, oh, she dreaded how he'd make her sweat for it. He was the kind of man who loved being in the position of deciding whether or not to grant favors; it was the closest he ever came to respect.

She could always call, or drop him an email. She'd already asked Kate if they could trade shifts but Kate couldn't; she had an exam the following day. Maura really needed that evening off; she didn't want to be the kind of parent that missed events at the school. She decided she'd suck it up, though she was dead on her feet, ready for bed. At least she could see if he was up there. And if he said no? Well, she'd call in sick. And if he fired her? Well, maybe that would force her to make some decisions.

She finished the till, took the paperwork and the lock box, slung her bag over her shoulder and headed upstairs. At the landing, she knocked on the door and it drifted ajar. She knocked again.

"Bill?"

When she pushed the door open, the scene revealed itself to her in snap-shots. There was a spray of blood on the wall behind Bill's desk. His fleshy form tilted to the side, his head lolling back, eyes bulging in a paper white landscape of skin, a wide red gash across his throat. The office was trashed, file cabinet overturned, papers littering the floor. The safe was wide open, emptied of all its contents, whatever that had been. A cheap beige sofa, pat-terned with palm trees, was slashed, its cushions tossed every which way.

She started to back away, a scream delayed in her throat. A voice in her head, whispering, *Don't make a sound. Get out. Get out. Get out.* She started backing away, for a second unable to avert her eyes. Then she turned to run, but as she did, he was there — the man from the bar, just a dark form in the dark stairway.

"Let me ask you something," he said. He began moving slowly toward her. His voice had a gravelly quality she hadn't noticed in the din of the bar. Every nerve ending in her body tingled.

"I have a little girl," she said. She could feel the dry suck of fear at the back of her throat, but she managed to keep her tone level. She had only one goal, to get back to Emma. She didn't give a shit about Bill, or who might have killed him.

"I didn't see anything," she said, hearing only the sound of blood rush-ing in her ears. "I don't remember your face or your name."

"That's good," he said. He gave her a quick, pragmatic nod. "You're smart. But you didn't let me ask my question."

She stood very still as he reached the top of the stairs. He was still hold-ing his jacket and his canvas bag. He had no blood on him anywhere that she could see. He didn't really look like *that* bad a guy; there was no menace to him, nothing nasty or mean about the eyes or the mouth. Then again, she'd never been the best judge of character. She found herself thinking that her only advantages were the heavy metal box in her hands and the fact that his back was to the staircase. She would hit him in the head with the box as hard as she could, and then push with all her strength. He'd fall and she'd scream her head off, run for her car. Except she didn't. With her heart a thrumming engine in her chest, her breathing ragged in her throat, she stood paralyzed.

"What's your question?" she said.

"What would a hundred grand mean to you?"

Downstairs the phone started ringing. She wondered if it was her mother, calling to see when she'd be home.

"A hundred thousand dollars?" she asked.

"That's right."

She issued a nervous laugh, deciding to play along and buy herself some time. "I don't know. It depends what I had to do for it."

He dropped his duffle to the floor, keeping his eyes on her, and pulled open the zipper. It was full of cash—a huge stash of hundred dollar bills.

"All you'd have to do is what you've already done. Forget what you've seen and forget my face."

But no, that wasn't all, of course. She could see it in the half smile on his lips.

"And?"

"And—run a quick errand with me. Not even an hour of your time. Risk-free. And then you go home to your girl, and none of this ever happened. Except, for once in your life, you have money in the bank. Pay off those credit cards."

As if he knew her. As if he knew anything about her. But there *was* debt, of course—a credit card with eight thousand and change. How had it ever gotten so high? A trip to Disney, clothes for Emma. The washing machine broke. *What would a hundred grand mean to you?* She could pay off that stupid card, work part time at the flower shop, finish her degree. Was she really thinking that? With a man dead, murdered—someone she knew—just a few feet away?

As adrenaline deserted her, it was replaced with a kind of numbness. Maybe it was shock, or just fear. She found in that moment that she only cared about how to save herself for her daughter. What did she need to be to do that? Whatever it was, that's what she'd be.

She opened her mouth to speak, but he raised his hand.

"Before you answer me, I'm going to tell you two things. First, I didn't kill Bill. I didn't *like* him." He lifted his palms. "Come on. No one did. But I didn't kill him. That's one. And two, I can't let you leave unless you help me."

So what was he saying? He didn't kill Bill but he'd kill her if she didn't do what he wanted? She decided not to ask for clarification. She listed a little to the side, her shoulder touching the wall.

"What kind of an errand?" She was just buying time, of course. Thinking of a way out. But did she feel a little jolt, a little shock of excitement beneath her fear? No. She wasn't that.

"Okay," he said. "Good."

Just by moving closer to her, he pushed her back into the office. He closed the door behind them. She didn't dare turn around and look at Bill. If she did, she knew she'd vomit or become hysterical. She couldn't even watch someone throw up without throwing up herself. She sank onto the slashed-up sofa and stared at her feet.

"What do you want me to do?" she said, looking up at him.

He had those eyes trained on her; and that's when she saw the hard glint to him. The edge. She also saw the gun tucked into his waist and her heart started hammering again. This was real.

She remembered how afraid she'd been when she realized that she was pregnant, that stone cold drop in her belly, the denial, the well of tears. But then there was Emma, the little peanut. Now, Maura couldn't imagine herself without her daughter. Everything she was before seemed so silly, so frivolous. So maybe something good would come from this, too. Maybe there was redemption in this ugly, horrifyingly real moment.

Jake's eyes drifted behind her to Bill, and she was surprised to see Jake lift a hand to his temples and rub hard with thumb and middle finger.

"You're looking at a dead man," he said.

He wasn't whiny about it, just matter of fact, easy with it. She watched him. He had a tattoo on his arm, playing cards, the faces faded and blurry with age. She could only make out the joker. She still had that box clutched in her hand, thought again about rushing him, smashing the sharp metal corner into the temple he was rubbing now.

"Two," he corrected himself. "Two dead men."

He gave a little laugh. Maybe he was trying to put her at ease, being funny in this sick way. She found herself getting angry.

"Are you going to tell me what I have to do, or what?" This time her voice betrayed her with a quaver, and then the tears welled up from some deep, terrified place. She couldn't stop them. "Just tell me what I need to do to get back to my little girl."

She thought she saw a flash of empathy, something real and sincere. Then it iced over and he looked away from her.

"The men who did this to Bill were looking for something. I was supposed to deliver it to him yesterday. I'm late. So Bill's dead. If they don't get it soon, I'll be dead, too."

"So give it to them."

He gave her that look he'd given her when she'd slipped him the cheap tequila.

"Oh, okay," she said.

An errand. He wanted her to help him deliver whatever it was.

"Fine," she said. She stood quickly, and saw him jump a little. "Let's just get this over with."

• • •

The moon was a wide, high platter, opalescent and strange, painting the black sky silvery gray. The water slapped against the floating dock and they walked down a long row of boats—yachts, skiffs, bow riders, fishing boats, pontoons—at a marina not far from the bar.

He wasn't easy with it; didn't have his sea legs, walking like a drunk as the dock shifted, raised, and dropped with the water movement. There was a fairly strong wind from the north; it was dancing palm fronds on the shore across the Intracoastal. There was a sizeable chop to the water.

"That's it over there," he said from behind her. She didn't see where he pointed. Up ahead was a Boston Whaler, small and light. On a night like this, something bigger would have been better.

"The Whaler?" *Hey, Maura, want a ride on my whaler?* Bill used to say behind the bar, thrusting his hips forward and laughing like a fool. God, she had really hated him.

"Whatever," he said, getting edgy. "The white one."

"They're all white." *You idiot.*

"The Wild Card. That's what it's called."

"Like your tattoo."

"Yeah," he said, annoyed. "I had my tattoo first. Bill didn't have an original thought in his head."

Something about the way he said it reminded Maura of her mother. *If he had half a brain, he'd be dangerous.* She hoped her mother wasn't waiting up. She'd be worried. Or judging, maybe thinking Maura had hooked up or was staying late with some of the servers drinking—even though she hadn't done anything like that since Emma was born. Lizzie would be all attitude in the morning.

Jake—if that was even his name—moved in front of her and tossed the duffle and leather jacket on the boat.

"It's the money, isn't it?" she said. She squared her shoulders and looked at him. On the ride over here, she'd been thinking. You have the thing, whatever it is—the drugs, guns, stolen goods—or you have the money. He had a duffle full of cash, and little else.

He turned to study her, seemed to size her up. Whatever he saw caused him to put his hand to the gun at his waist.

"I mean," she went on anyway, "there's no hundred grand, right? You're going to turn this money over." She nodded over to the duffle. "You owe it to someone, or you're buying something illegal. But that money is going away."

"Just get on the boat, Maura."

Did she tell him her name? She must have, but she didn't remember.

"You don't really need me," she said. She said it easily; they could have been talking about anything. "And I don't care about your money. I swear to god I'll never say a word to anyone about you or about what I've seen tonight."

He didn't answer her, kept those dark eyes on her.

"Tomorrow, someone's going to find Bill's body. It's not going to be hard for them to figure out that I was the last one in the restaurant. When they find me and start asking questions, I'm just going to tell them that I went right home, never saw Bill all night, never saw you. They'll believe me. There's no reason not to."

He was staring at her. She couldn't read his expression.

"Let me go home."

For a second, a blissful split second, she thought he was going to do it. But then he rolled his eyes and released an exasperated sigh.

"Get in the boat, please."

Back at the bar, he'd taken the box from her before they left and removed the till money, stuffing it into his jacket. It seemed like the actions of a petty thief, not someone who had a hundred grand lying around to pay out. When he'd taken the box from her hand, she thought: *I should have pushed him down the stairs and run, called the police.* As he'd put his hand on her arm and they walked out through the deserted parking lot to her car, she'd felt a flash flood of regret. Another terrible mistake in a long line of mistakes—sleeping with the wrong man, getting pregnant, dropping out of school and never going back. All of that had led her to *this* place.

Now, he took the gun from his waist when she didn't answer and didn't obey; she took a step back from him.

"You have no reason to trust me," he said. "But I'm going to ask you to do that. If you just do what I say, you'll be home with your girl in an hour. I promise."

He was lying; she could feel the lie in her bones. He had a gun. She couldn't outrun him. He'd kill her before she reached the end of the dock.

Slowly, she climbed on the boat to buy herself a little more time, panic constricting her throat, causing her whole body to quiver.

As she sat on the captain's bench where he pointed for her to go, her fate was crystal clear. She was here because she'd seen Bill's body, because she'd seen Jake. Why he hadn't just killed her in Bill's office, or even here on the dock, she didn't know. Maybe he thought it would be too loud, make too much of a mess. Maybe he'd been afraid he wouldn't be able to make his exit from the restaurant. She thought that he must have been waiting for her to leave for the night, maybe to get the money from the till. But she hadn't left right away. She'd gone up to ask Bill for next Thursday off. If she'd just left the box and the paperwork by the register and gone home for the night, she wouldn't be here right now.

He untied the lines, started the boat and pulled slowly from the dock. He flipped on the GPS and fish finder equipment, and the screens glowed an eerie green. She sat paralyzed, her mind racing through scenarios and options. One thing was obvious: When he was done with whatever he was going to do, or maybe before, he'd kill her and dump her body in the Gulf. Her breath started to come more ragged.

The worst part about it was that she'd actually been *attracted* to him. If he'd been nice to her at the bar, asked for her number, she'd have given it to him—even though she hadn't given out her number in years. She'd been that drawn to him. What did that say about her? That she had no instincts for survival; she didn't know enough to step out of the way of an oncoming train. Maybe Emma would be better off without her. The thought gave her a physical pain in her chest.

They made their way through the no wake zone and once they'd passed the causeway, he sped up the boat and they headed for the dark expanse of the open water. The low homes and tall condo buildings glittered on the shoreline, growing smaller and smaller as the little boat headed into the black. When the shoreline was just a glimmering strand of Christmas lights in the distance, Jake killed the engine, and they floated in the chop.

What if she jumped and swam right now? Could she make it to shore? If he shot into the water, how likely would it be that he'd hit her? Would he come looking for her later?

"I know you're scared," he said after a minute. "But this is going to be over soon."

She didn't say anything, just looked out into the distance for the red and green navigation lights of another boat. Emma's father was a fishing boat charter captain. He'd told her about scenarios like this one—boats meeting in the night for drugs and arms deals. They picked a GPS coordinate and met there, did their business on the water and sped away from each other. The coast guard couldn't watch every inch of shoreline all the time. Private boats were the way to get contraband into the US, Emma's father had told her, hinting that maybe he knew something about it. There was no one back at the marinas checking who came in with what, no one to check the thousands of private docks.

Jake walked unsteadily to the bow of the boat, gripping the rails nervously. Then he stood, scanning the waters around them. The boat was rocking with some vigor. It was not a calm night at sea, probably a two- or three-foot chop. The sea air was cool and damp, the humidity cut by the steady breeze.

Then she saw them, at first not certain if it was just a trick of the moonlight on the water. But as the vessel grew closer, she saw the red and green lights in the distance. It was still too far to hear the engine. Jake was looking in the wrong direction, didn't see the boat coming. She knew with clarity that if she did nothing, she was in the last minutes of her life.

The moment swelled and expanded, and then she was nothing but pure action. While his back was still to her, she moved quietly, quickly to Jake. She remembered he hadn't been steady on the dock, that he didn't seem comfortable on the water. She'd seen people who were afraid of the water before, people who couldn't swim well. She suspected he was one of them. She hit him just right, just hard enough with her shoulder to his middle back that with the way he was standing he tipped right into the water, issuing a winded grunt. She stood a moment, and watched him surface and start to flail, reaching for the boat.

Then she raced back to the captain's bench and started the engine. She heard him yelling, "I can't swim! Maura! I'm going to drown. Don't do this! You're making a mistake."

She blocked him out completely, though she could hear his horrible thrashing and gurgling, the panic in his voice as he begged her not to leave him, and brought the boat around toward the shore. She killed the navigation lights so the other boat wouldn't see her.

Then she leaned on the throttle, and was racing back to land, unable to hear anything but the engine and the wake behind her. She didn't look back, didn't even think about how she'd left a man to drown in the Gulf of Mexico. She didn't feel the slightest shade of regret. Inside, she was stone cold.

Obeying all the rules of the water on the way in, she easily docked the boat in its slip, tied it off with the lines still hanging from the hull, thinking he hadn't even known enough to bring them in to the boat.

As she shouldered the heavy bag with effort and made her way back to the Prius, the dock rocking beneath her, there was still not a thought in her head. At her car, she dumped the bag in the trunk and climbed into the driver's seat. Then, in the quiet, it all hit her. Before she closed the door, she vomited onto the black top. Once she was done, quaking at her core and safely locked in her vehicle, she sobbed. Great wracking coughs shook her body and the car itself. She sat there until she felt steady enough to drive, and then made her way home, not speeding, not driving too slowly. All she would need was a DUI stop, and she'd lose it completely.

She parked in the grocery store parking lot across the street from her mother's condo building and sat for a minute. There were a few other cars in the lot, left overnight for whatever reason—all the shops and the supermarket, even the small smoky bar frequented by island residents, were long closed. When she got out and shut the door, the sound echoed in the quiet.

She decided to leave the money in the trunk. On the island, the likelihood of her car being randomly stolen or broken into was low. But what if someone had followed her home from the marina? Or what if Jake had survived and knew where she would go that night? He *had* known her name and she really didn't remember giving it to him. If someone was watching her now, they'd see her leave the money in the car—maybe they'd just take it and leave her and her family alone. Or if someone came looking, they'd easily see the car parked under the light in a nearly empty lot. She was banking on the assumption that whoever came looking cared only about the money; they'd take it and get lost fast. She'd watch the car from the condo.

Before going upstairs, she opened the trunk and looked at the bag, then slowly opened the zipper. It was filled with cash. Somehow she thought it might be a trick, some real bills on top, the rest just newspaper or something. She had no idea how much was there. She'd never seen so much money in her life. But she did know one thing. This was her wild card.

Lizzie was waiting up, the television on. It was four thirty AM. Maura entered the room and sat in the chair across from where her mother lay on the couch made up for Maura. She felt utterly drained, as though all her limbs were filled with sand.

"You're late," said Lizzie.

"Sorry, Mom. Something came up. A girl at work had an emergency. I had to help her." An easy lie; it rang true even to her.

"It's not like you not to call. I was real worried, Maura. Your cell was off."

"Battery died." Not a lie. It had died before her shift. She forgot to charge it.

"Well," said Lizzie. She lifted herself heavily from the chair. She must have been tired, too; there was no trace of anger or judgment. Just worry, like she'd said. "Next time give an old woman a call so she can get some sleep."

"I will. I promise." Then, "I'm going to check on Emma."

Lizzie smiled. "She missed you tonight. She wanted her mama. She woke up after midnight, called out for you."

"I missed her, too." She helped her mom off the couch and walked her to her bedroom. "A lot."

She sat for a minute after her mother left and looked around the room. Pictures of her and Emma sat on every surface. She picked up the photo sitting on the end table beside her. Maura must have been four in the shot. She was sleeping on her father's shoulder; he was wearing khakis and a white undershirt, his hair was a mess. He had his head back on the chair, was giving the camera a peaceful, happy smile. She missed her father. She wished he were here now, that she could talk to him and tell him what had happened to her. He'd know what to do.

At her mother's door, she said, "You know, Mom, I think I'm going to quit that job, look for something else."

Her mother looked surprised, face brightening. "I need someone at the shop."

That wasn't exactly what she had in mind. But Lizzie looked so happy and hopeful, that Maura just smiled.

"Okay," she said. "Can we talk about things tomorrow?"

"Sure. Of course." Another tight hug from Lizzie, two in one day. They had a *lot* to talk about tomorrow if the money were still there. But even if it wasn't, she was going to do better with her life, make better choices for herself and for Emma. Instead of going to the couch, she crawled into the twin bed where Emma slept.

"Mommy," Emma breathed. She tucked herself into Maura's body, and Maura wrapped her arms around her child, felt her grow heavy as she instantly felt back asleep. She knew at some point, someone was going to discover Bill's body. The cleaning crew never went into his office, as per his direction. So it wouldn't be in the early morning, probably. Since Bill would be the one to count the money and go over her paperwork, no one would notice that the cash drawer wasn't back or that they money had been stolen until about eleven when the next shift came on to start setting up for lunch. Whenever it happened, the police were going to come looking for Maura. She was just going to say she did what she should have done—left the till by the bar and gone home. She didn't know for sure, but she thought Lizzie would cover for her, if it came down to that. If not for Maura, then for Emma.

And if there were cameras she didn't know about? In the bar, in the parking lot? Well, she didn't know. It would be too late then. Maybe she'd tell them that she'd been kidnapped, which she had. But that she'd gotten away from him, which was also true. That she'd been in shock, too terrified to call the police. She thought she had to keep quiet to survive. All of this was somewhat true. She didn't have to say that she should have tried harder to get away right in the beginning. Or that she'd stolen his money. She was convincing when she had to be. She thought she might be able to pull it off.

From where she lay, she could see the little car in the empty lot under the yellow glow of the lamplight. With a hundred thoughts turning in her mind, she watched it until the rising sun lightened the sky, then she drifted off to sleep.

The sun was streaming in hot through the gauzy drapes. Maura was sweating, the sheets damp with it. Her mother never kept the air cool enough.

Emma was gone from the bed. Maura heard the television. With a rush it all came back; she sat up quickly and looked out the window. The car was still there, not visibly tampered with—windows intact, trunk closed. She breathed through a wave of relief, a little tingle of excitement.

She left the room and headed toward the living room. "Good morning," she called.

"Maura? Can you come here, please?" There was something odd about Lizzie's voice, something taut and unfamiliar, lacking its usual authority.

The first thing she saw was Emma sitting on the floor, happily eating Froot Loops from the box inches from the television. There was some type of crazy cartoon blaring on the screen, the type of thing Emma was never allowed to watch. Other things Lizzie would never allow: a bowl of sugary cereal. And there was no eating in front of the television—ever. But there was Lizzie sitting stiffly on the couch. For a moment, Maura wondered if she was ill. Maybe she was having a stroke or something.

"What's going on?" she asked.

"Mommy," said Emma, not taking her eyes from the set. "Your friend's here."

That's when she saw him. He sat easily in the chair in the far corner of the room by the window.

He was wearing the same clothes he had been when she pushed him into the water. And she could smell the salt water on him; the briny scent filled the room. He looked unwell—pale, with dark circles under his eyes. His hand rested inside his jacket. Lizzie stared at him with unmasked malice. Maura's mouth felt like it was full of gauze; she could hardly breathe through it.

"I thought you couldn't swim." It came out sounding petulant and incredulous.

"Why can't he swim?" Emma asked. "Swimming is so easy."

"Because some people just aren't that smart, kiddo," he said. His tone was light and easy, an old friend making a joke. But Emma wasn't fooled. Maura watched her brow crease with worry.

"How did you find me?"

"Your file in Bill's office," he said. She remembered then that she'd been living with Lizzie when she got her job at the Rockin' Iguana. "You're new at this, aren't you?"

He was all sharp edges now—mean eyes, a sneering mouth. She saw him, who he really was, and it made her stomach clench.

"Where is it?" he said.

Maura felt Lizzie's eyes on her, but she didn't dare look at her mother.

"It's in the car. I'll give you my keys. You can have that, too. Just get out of here." Her voice sounded so cool and level; she felt like someone else was talking. All she could hear was the manic soundtrack of the cartoons on the television.

"What's wrong, Mommy?" Emma asked. Her voice had taken on a pitch of worry.

"I have a better idea," he said. "You go get it and bring it back. I'll stay here with Emma and your mom. And don't dilly-dally."

She could smell it then, his desperation. There was sweat on his brow, his breathing thicker than it should have been. She walked over to the window and saw a black Eldorado parked downstairs, close to the exit of the lot. It had dark tinted windows and flashy rims.

"Mom, take Emma into the other room."

"You're not giving orders—," he started. He moved to stop them then fell back, let out a moan of pain.

"Mom!" she yelled. "Do it."

Lizzie got up more quickly than Maura would have thought she was able. She grabbed Emma, who started crying.

"Mommymommymommymommy," she wailed as Lizzie carried her down the hall.

Jake hadn't moved again from where he sat, hadn't drawn the weapon she thought he had under his jacket.

"Are you hurt?" she asked.

He let out an agonized groan. "Just go get the fucking bag, Maura. Christ."

"When you give them that money, they're going to kill you. They're going to kill all of us."

"News flash genius, they're going to kill us all anyway. If I don't go back down there soon, they're going to come up here and tear this dump apart looking. The only reason you're alive at all is I told them I could get the money from you, that you didn't know anything about them."

"Why would you do that?" she asked. "I left you to drown in the Gulf of Mexico."

He looked up at the ceiling and then back at her. "I can't really blame you for that. Look, just give me the keys. I'll go."

Something passed between them, a kind of recognition of each other. He was in way over his head. "Really?" she said.

"Really."

She was about to toss him the keys, kiss the money good-bye and just pray they all made it out of here alive, when she heard Lizzie behind her.

"You're not going anywhere, son." She had a gun in her hand. Maura recognized it as her dad's old revolver, something Lizzie always hated having in the house. "The police are coming."

As she said it, Jake started drawing the gun from his coat. And as everything blurred and warped, Maura moved to stop him, to put herself between him and her mother. Two clear shots rang out, filling the apartment, Maura's head with a deafening concussion. She saw Jake double over and fall to the floor, his gun landing beside him. He looked like a doll stuffed with rags, the way he fell, arms flailing. She watched him there, for a moment disbelieving it all. Then she turned to look at Lizzie who was frozen, the gun still in her hand. Over the terrible ringing, she heard Emma screaming in the bedroom and ran to her, the floor feeling like quicksand beneath her feet. She felt it, rather than heard that screaming because the whole world was absolutely silent, and then she was holding her little girl in her arms, feeling her hot body. And Emma's wail was a song that brought her back to reality. Then it mingled with the keen of sirens as the police cars approached.

Maura lifted her daughter and ran to the front room, where Lizzie still stood stunned, the gun in her hand by her side.

"Mom," said Maura. "We have to get out of here."

But then she looked out the window and saw an old man walking across the circular drive. He looked off into the distance, then he turned back around to look at the building. There was someone pounding the door. But Maura just watched as the old man continued walking, then climbed into the black El Dorado and drove off. There were no thugs waiting downstairs to kill them and take the money. There never had been. That moment of connection she sensed between them, where she thought Jake was trying to spare harm to her and her family, was a lie. She almost laughed. Jake was a really good liar. So good, he didn't have to say a word.

Emma was clinging to her like a spider monkey, whimpering into her hair. Maura looked at Jake's lifeless body on the floor. He was already going pale. It was her second corpse in twenty-four hours. Still, she felt nothing. Not fear, not revulsion. It all had the cast of unreality, a foggy sequence of events that were so far out of her frame of reference that she almost couldn't get her head around it. *You're new at this, aren't you?* She *was* new at it. But she had a feeling she was going to learn the game pretty quickly.

The pounding at the door was frantic now. She could hear someone calling her mother's name. But she found she couldn't move. Once she opened that door, it was all real.

"Who was he?" Lizzie asked. She put the gun on the table beside the chair and sank heavily down.

"I don't know," Maura said. It was the truth. Now the knocking on the door was a heavy pounding.

"What did he want?"

She felt her mother's eyes on her as she started moving toward the door.

"Is he dead?" Emma asked in a whisper.

"Yes, baby. He is."

And then she did it. She turned the knob and let the world in.

• • •

"Is he dead?"

"He's dead, honey. He can't hurt us."

"Are you sure?"

"Positive."

"Can he see us like Grandpa? Grandma said that even though Grandpa is gone and I never met him, he can see me. He's with God and he can see me. That's what she said."

"It's not like that with the bad man. Bad people don't get to see us."

"But why not?"

"Those are just the rules." Lame answer, sure. But Maura was at a complete loss. A week had passed. In the daytime, they were all okay. But when the sun went down, things were hard, especially for Emma. Maura wished she had something to say to her daughter to allay all her fears. But she didn't.

The truth is a funny thing. It moves like a river though the path created for it; it changes with each perspective. And Maura did tell the truth. Or most of it. She'd read somewhere that someone who is lying, or not telling the whole truth, tends to say too much. They offer too many details, explain things that don't need explaining, answer questions that weren't asked.

So she simplified her story. She finished her shift and needed to talk to Bill, so she went to his office. Jake cornered her with a gun and told her he couldn't let her leave but if he helped her, he'd let her go. She had no choice; she went with him. But she'd noticed he wasn't comfortable around the water and when she had her chance, she pushed him and took the boat back to shore.

At first they asked a lot of questions, like why didn't she call the police after she got away, and why did she think he came looking for her, how did he survive, how did he know where she lived and how did he get into the condo building? She told the detectives that she had been terrified, maybe even in shock. She probably would have called the police when she came to her senses. And she didn't know why he came looking for her, probably to kill her. He told her he'd found her address at the bar. He said something about wanting money. She could hardly remember it, she'd been so afraid for her daughter and mother. She'd told Jake (if that was his name) that he could have her car, that he'd find some money in there, which was a lie; she didn't keep money in her car. (She purposely used the word *some*, instead of *the*, just in case Lizzie said something about Jake looking for money.) She told him he could have that too if he would just leave them alone. That's all she knew. And how could she know how he survived or got into the building? How could she possibly know?

It was all true. But not quite true. And, of course, there was one big omission. Still, the words came out smoothly, she never hesitated or changed a thing, even though the older detective asked her all the same questions a couple of different ways, trying to catch her in a lie. But she wasn't lying. And she cried a lot. That was real, too. She was shaken to her center and every so often she just broke down. The police handled her gently. And the money sat in her trunk, undiscovered. Unclaimed.

Emma was back in school now. Lizzie was over it, she said. She said she was only sorry that she couldn't have killed the bastard twice. Maura had heard her say that sentence a dozen times over the phone, and to her customers in the shop, to her friends. But on the few nights they'd spent at Lizzie's, Maura had heard her mother cry out in her sleep a couple times. Lizzie never said a word about the money. If she heard or remembered the exchange between Maura and Jake, she never brought it up.

Maybe it was because Maura had quit the Rockin' Iguana and reenrolled in classes starting next semester to finish up the twenty credits she needed for her degree. Or maybe it was because Maura was working in the flower shop every afternoon, with Emma playing happily with her toys or watching television in the back, or helping out … pretend sweeping, handing customers their change and saying, "Thank you! Come again." Maybe Lizzie was just happy that they were all together and not fighting, that things were exactly the way she wanted them to be, at least for now.

There was exactly $82,000 in that bag—not hundreds of thousands, like she thought. And Maura hadn't touched a cent, just had it sitting on the highest shelf in her closet.

The truth was she was afraid. What if the money was marked (even though she wasn't completely sure what that meant)? Or what if someone was still looking for it? She was going to let it sit for a while. Just knowing it was there, for Emma, for emergencies, relieved some kind of pressure she didn't even know was bearing down on her. Plus, keeping it was one kind of wrong. Spending it was another. People were dead. She'd hid that money from the police. It had to do some good, or she was a bad person. So she'd hold onto it for a while.

Lizzie had offered to pay for school and to pay off her credit card, and Maura accepted with a promise to pay her back by working in the shop. She was still looking for another bartending job, but she'd work afternoons for her mother. Lizzie declined Maura's offer to pay her back with hours in the shop. "You'll get the money when I'm dead. Might as well have it when you need it." Maura had a new gratitude for her mother, a new level of respect. She was starting to see something in her mother that she'd missed—a formidable mettle, a hardcore strength.

Sometimes Maura dreamed about that night. Sometimes, lying in bed, she thought about Jake and how he died, wondering who he was, and what he would have done if her mother hadn't shot him. There was a lot she didn't know. Bill's murder was still unsolved. She'd never found out anything more about Jake or who he was, what he was involved in. She supposed she could call the detective working on the case, but she didn't want to push her luck.

Maura and Lizzie didn't talk about that night at all. The carpet and some of the furniture in the living room had to be replaced. And once it was all gone, they both knew they shouldn't bring it up unless Emma needed to. She was having bad dreams, wouldn't let Maura out of her sight except to go to preschool. She kept telling Emma that everything was going to be all right, that a bad thing had happened, and now everything was okay. And she hoped that it was true. She really did.

Sometimes, like tonight, when she tucked Emma into bed and kissed her hair, she thought of the fading tattoo on the dead man's arm, the wild card. And Maura wanted to believe that this time, when it came her way, she'd played her hand well.

QUIET

BY JONATHON KING

It was his love of silence that made him kill them, and why that sweet cone of quiet, that wondrous calm feeling of a total enveloping quiet, was such a driving need, he did not know.

It might be construed as a strange miasma for someone whose beloved grandfather was a demolition expert and who'd taken his favorite grandson out onto Alligator Alley during that highway's construction to let him watch the blasts that turned ancient limestone into rubble and made a bombing range out of an incomparable meadow of grassland beauty. He could still recall being a nine-year-old kid standing in the heat of a Florida summer next to his towering grandfather and hearing the patriarch of his family call out in his booming voice: "Fire in the hole!"

The explosion that followed that order seemed to begin as a rumble, a vibration that would start in one's heels and travel up the ankle and leg bones and somehow settle in a young boy's chest, tickling his small heart. He would cover his ears, knowing from experience the rip of noise that would then assault them. His grandfather, like all the other men on the job, would simply shade his eyes and look out to the blast site to witness the WHOOMP and the following dirt cloud that signified success. He and the others would smile. But no one would speak. They would instead all go quiet, remarking nothing, until the moment had passed. And it was that moment, that silence after such an insult to the air, that the boy coveted. God he loved that quiet.

Then his own father followed in the patriarch's footsteps, also becoming an explosives man. But his father blew up suburbs instead of highways. He could recall those times too, accompanying his old man out to the tracts of land west of Fort Lauderdale on Saturdays when the blasting was underway. His father liked to say he was creating lakes, but even a teenager knew better. What his father did was blow the limestone crust of the Everglades to bits, which allowed the giant backhoes to roll in and scoop out the busted rock and vegetation that was once an untouched habitat and then deposit it in piles along a newly created shore. By digging a big hole in the earth, the surrounding water would flow in and thus lower the area water table. The big earth graders would then move in to level out the piles of limestone and sawgrass and black muck and voila! Dry land on which to build more houses!

And just like when he was out with his grandfather, the silence that followed each of his father's eruptions was like some internal blessing to him. Maybe the shaking that followed the dynamite explosions caused every nearby person to stop for a second — stop talking or walking or clanking the dishes at the sink. Nearby homeowners would certainly stop to stare at the lengthening cracks in their own plaster walls as the earth shook. Whomever you were, whatever your reaction, all seemed to go quiet. And it was that blessed lack of noise that the boy, even as he grew to adulthood, would savor like a glorious taste on one's tongue.

He loved silence. So why marry a woman who would not shut up?

He first saw her at a new employee induction meeting in the auditorium of the South Florida Investments Corporation. Across the room, she was the young woman with a smile that reached across ten yards of bobbing heads and flashing faces and through an air thick with apprehension and not a little anxiety. And it struck him, she was the one smiling, comfortable in the crowd. Yes, she was yakking, but also smiling that easy, fresh, beaming smile. It was a look that drew him. Charles Noland III, CPA had not become a dynamite man like his father and grandfather before him. He was an accountant. He liked numbers. They were quiet. He liked to sit with them in an office, even a pod office, because he could work with them, follow them, align them with the immutable rules of mathematics. And no, it was not lost on him that he might be strange. Yes, he had dated a few women, but he believed his silence scared them. He believed they thought his refusal to enter into mindless conversation and rattle over the newest sitcom or what Betty the receptionist was wearing on her nails or even last night's fabulous score of the fabulous game indicated that he was inept, intellectually stunted, or somehow retarded.

None of that bothered Susan. She just talked right through it. If he had nothing to say on the matter, fine. There was all the more open air for her to fill. Now okay, that's perhaps unfair. He did know, even after the first few dates, that she was a nurturer. He gave her credit for being the kind of person who wanted—no, had—to help others. She would save him from his shyness. She would introduce him to the social world we all must enter in order to function. She saw his weaknesses, and would make them right. Right?

On their wedding night they made love for the first time. Susan's mouth seemed to have been going nonstop for days—oh, the planning, oh, the decisions, oh, the reception, oh, the humanity. But that night, the sex, the first true sex he'd ever had, was incredible. Susan was a screamer. He hadn't known that from earlier, more muted explorations. But the noise and the sensation was to him not unlike the explosions he had witnessed as a boy with his grandfather, and forever more when the two of them reached orgasm he would think of his grandfather's shouted orders, "Fire in the hole," but would of course never repeat them. And when they were done, exhausted and spent, oh beauty of all beauties, Susan would fall immediately into a deep and completely silent sleep. He would stay awake in the quiet, listening for, but hearing nothing, his wife next to him, not uttering a word, for hours.

So it worked. For a couple of years anyway. Put up with the yak when you had to: when she got home from work, when she had to vent, when she was on the phone in the car, when she was watching television, when the family visited, when she was in the theater, and even when she was listening to music (once he had even played an old 1960 cut of Frankie Ford singing Joe Jones's "You Talk Too Much," but it went right over her head).

But marriage is all about concessions, right? He tried to remember that. After all, she did let him frequent that fishing camp five miles out in the empty Everglades and not once did she question the fact that he never fished. She didn't argue once when he purchased the airboat that was essential to getting out to that remote spot that was perpetually and naturally in one to three feet of water in the middle of Marjory Stoneman Douglas's "River of Grass." Heck, the one time she'd accompanied him, she loved the roar of the airboat's airplane engine, the rush of air through her hair as they sat high over the sawgrass blasting over the open acreage. He knew that she didn't appreciate that envelope of silence that would surround one's head after the engine was shut down and you were miles away from anything that could be defined as noisy.

Concessions. He was good with it.

Then came Maria and Lance. And it was all too much. And he was sorry, but they all had to die.

Yes, Susan's constant need to talk was bothersome, unrelenting, exasperating, but he never considered homicide until the Conners moved in next door.

Maria and Lance. Lance and Maria. The were young, artistic (by their standards), ambitious (or so they said), garrulous, and possessed of an almost demonic ability to talk simultaneously for immeasurable lengths of time. They read *People* magazine. They debated the meaning of life through the episodic lens of *Desperate Housewives*.

And his wife loved them.

Their first night in the neighborhood, Marie and Lance came over to introduce themselves—afraid, it seemed to him later, to be alone. Within ten minutes he knew he was in terrible trouble. Introductions were quick: Lance was from L.A., a self-described "film guy" come to settle in with The Love of His Life and "probably write screenplays." Florida was the new hotspot for films. Lance winked when he said this and all Charles could think of was Mr. McGuire stage whispering "Plastics" to Dustin Hoffman in *The Graduate*.

Maria was Cuban, her Spanglish so rapid and bereft of punctuation as to remind one of a bilingual auctioneer trying to sell a bin lot of Spanish handbags to a crowd from Dubuque. During his lifetime in Florida, Charles had met Cubans from the old 1980 Mariel Boatlift days who refused to learn English because they planned to go back to the island after Castro died of lung cancer or was overthrown. But Maria, he was to learn later—about fifteen minutes later—was third generation and had never set foot in the nation she claimed for her heritage and had for thirteen years gone to school in Miami-Dade public schools and should know English like a native. These thoughts remained his alone.

He only nodded and smiled. At least he thought he was smiling. After an hour and a half his wife and her two new best friends had broached forty-three subject areas from the death of the iconic Michael Jackson ("That was the big one for me. It was the the disaster *por la vida a me*") to the professional death of Ricky Martin (the segue no doubt was motivated by Maria's use of the phrase *la vida,* which was the way this so-called conversation was obtusely carrying itself out; one participant would seemingly pick up a single word or phrase uttered by one of the others and then simply and loudly introduce a brand new line of discourse all their own).

In time, beer and the new Maria's requested drink, a Rob Roy, were introduced by his wife, and Charles sat back sipping his Bud and daydreaming while simultaneously keeping a running tab on the topics contained within the three-person babble. Eighty-seven in two hours. No commercials. No public service announcements. All Talk, All The Time.

"So Charlie, seen any good movies lately?"

Charles realized the question was being directed to him. He had made his introduction as Charles Norland III. Now, after two hours of rambling and drinking his booze, he was a neighborhood friend, Charlie.

"Well, I did see *Unforgiven* recently on a late-night cable channel. It was about—"

"Yes! Clint Eastwood. Excellent director," Lance cut him off. "Too old to still be acting though. I would have casted a Sean Penn, you know? Someone the whores would have fallen for, like, you know, to add the romantic interest in there."

"Right, but that really wasn't the point," the new Charlie tried again. "In my humble opinion, I thought—"

"So Clint Eastwood, the *gringo,* eh?" Maria jumped in. "Making the Hispanics look all the time *pobre* and *estupido* in those pasta westerns."

"Spaghetti westerns, honey," Lance corrected the love of his life.

"*Sí pero …*"

The new Charlie was out of it by then. Conversation moved on. Eighty-eight, eighty-nine, ninety.

But Susan was enthralled. These would be new people to talk with after her daytime job of talking to people. Oh joy. The Connors for dinner. The Connors for weekend barbecues. The Conners for double-dating at the movies where all three of them would whisper constantly during the show despite the shushes from the folks seated around them that made Charles III hunch his shoulders and duck like an embarrassed turtle.

But he endured. He made concessions. He tried until he reached the point where he would have to shoot them all or shoot himself.

Then, he had a better idea.

Ten in the morning and the noise was, well, deafening. Even with those little yellow marshmallow-type ear plugs, the sound of the engine was an assault. He pushed the airboat throttle higher, the pitch went up, the wind in their faces increased, whipping hair and distorting cheek flesh and causing all of them to squint. But he could still hear them.

"Whooooooeeee. Yeah baby. That's what I'm talkin' about!"

Lance.

"Wooooooo." In that high-pitched, female cry that every schoolgirl somehow learns. "*Dios Mio!*"

Maria.

"So I was telling Gracie about Tom and his new girlfriend …" Her attempts at gossip conversation were not to be deterred by some thirty-mile-an-hour rip across the western Palm Beach County Everglades. She'd just yell as loud as possible.

His wife, Susan.

When he had suggested that the Connors come out with them on the airboat, Susan had looked at him in that way she did whenever he took a chance and stepped slightly out of character and did something crazy like wear a blue button-down oxford shirt to work instead of a white one.

"Really?" she said. "Out to your secret place?"

It wasn't really a secret. The fishing camp had been in his family for three generations. It was out in a secluded meadow of sawgrass. Nothing around. An unbroken landscape from horizon to horizon with the exception of two green hammocks farther to the west, but you had to have good eyes to see them. It was a place where you could sit of an evening on the wooden deck at sunset and swear you could hear when that glowing orange globe touched the earth at sunset and hissed—sssssssss.

No, he was not taking them there, even though that is what he told his wife. That in fact is the last place on earth he would take them. The contamination would be too much. After the one time Susan had accompanied him, her constant chatter nearly spoiled it for him. She never asked to go again. And he had not offered. So on this day when voices were going to be silenced, it wasn't going to be at a place he would ever remember, nor a place he would be able to recall, or ever find again. No, he was not heading toward the camp, but was swinging them in essentially a big circle, all according to plan.

"Charlie! Look! There!" yelled Lance while pointing out in front of the racing boat at what appeared to be a grey log floating in the open water of that path they were racing down. "Is that a gator?"

Charles III just nodded, kept his speed, and watched as the log grew eyes and then, just before being run over by the slanted nose of the flat-bottomed airboat, flicked its tail and dove under for cover.

Yes, wildlife was here: Alligators and the turtles they ate. Herons and the fish they ate. Fish and the water spiders they ate. Kites and the snails they ate. Well, you get the picture. The Glades was nature. And that's the way it is. You kill what you have to kill to survive.

Charles had explained all this to the Connors, when he could get a word in edgewise, while he instructed them where to sit on the airboat. He had in recent weeks had a welder install the two extra seats on the raised carriage that kept pilot and passengers high above the boat's platform, and thus above the top of the sawgrass. From that vantage point one could see everything. And you were also up in the air, the self-made breeze keeping you cool in the stark sunshine. But even from on high, you had to be familiar with the area in order to know where you were. The landmarks were subtle. To the uninitiated, everything that you could see looked all the same. Charles knew this well and he had counted on it.

Finally, at the designated spot, he eased off the throttle, let the boat slide across the water and run up into a thick marsh, tamping down the grass in front of them and creating at unnatural mat just off the bow.

He choked out the engine and there it was. That silence. That feeling around the head like when you pull the car up into the driveway after too long a ride on the interstate and the sudden lack of noise feels like a balm. It only lasted a second.

"Whoa, dude," Lance yelled, his voice not adjusting to the new quiet. "That was awesome. That's an airplane engine, right? Man, the vibration, dude. This thing kicks out the jams!"

Charles only nodded. Indeed it does. Kick jams out, that is.

"This is like being out in the cane fields in Cuba," Maria stated authoritatively as she stood, shading her eyes with one hand like some kind of explorer, and surveyed. "*Me recuerdo esta* scene in *The Bridges of Madison County* when they are staring out on the fields of wheat. It is the same, no?"

No, thought Charles. This grass grows up out of two feet of water. And you have never been to Cuba, or Iowa.

"Ha! That's Eastwood again," said Susan, pointing a finger at Maria as if she had just made a joke. "But I loved Meryl Streep in that one. You know she had her neck done."

"But of course, there is no way a woman her age could look so well, and another thing …"

Charles tuned them out. He would not be deterred. He took extra pains to change his face to one of concern as he climbed out of the pilot's seat and began to trace a cable from the throttle back to the engine's carburetor. He stood at the stern of the boat platform, wrinkled his brow, bent into a kneeling position and stared at the machinery.

The others kept talking. Susan about what a wonderful view this would be for a good restaurant. Maria about how the view on Varadero beach in Cuba was much better. Lance about how difficult it would be to get a film crew out here to shoot a feature. Their overlapping chatterings didn't seem to bother them and despite his facial antics, they paid no attention to Charles until he said in an overly loud voice for him: "There's a problem."

The others were not used to someone disagreeing with their visions. Everyone usually just nodded an assent to their various statements and then charged in with their own. A phrase of disagreement seemed to startle them.

"Charles?" Susan said.

"The, uh, fuel line," he said without looking up. "There's a problem with the fuel line." He bent and fiddled some more, pretending to do something, but actually just checking the explosive that he had so carefully placed next to the gas tanks the night before.

"Can I be of any assistance?" Lance said, but did not approach, knowing of course that his total lack of knowledge in all things mechanical would be of no assistance at all.

"No. I'm afraid not," Charles said and then stood staring for effect. He then climbed back up into the pilot's seat and with some physical grace stood up on the seat and looked out into the distance.

His wife shaded her eyes with one hand and looked in the same direction, seeing nothing. Maria followed suit. Lance held his ground.

"I'll have to go for help," Charles said and then climbed down.

"I have my cell," Lance said, reaching into the pocket of his safari shorts, purchased just for this occasion.

"No," Charles said, again with an authority that was uncharacteristic for him. "There aren't any towers out here. No reception."

While Lance, then Maria, then Susan all grabbed up their cells and checked their bars, Charles reached into a cooler and removed one bottle of water.

"It's only a mile," he said, tucking the water into a high vest pocket. "Won't take me long. There's plenty of water for you, and Susan knows how to drape the rain tarp over the seats to give you some shade."

Susan looked at her husband. With such authority in his voice, she was sure that she must know how to put up the tarp. Charles rarely spoke with such command. She simply nodded in agreement. It's an old maxim that Charles had seen himself a million times and thus took it as truth: If you say something with enough authority and assuredness in your voice, ninety percent of the people will believe you even if you don't know what the hell you're talking about. Businessmen, marketers, advertising spokespersons and P.T. Barnum have been doing it forever. He zipped up his multi-pocketed fishing vest and suddenly, at least suddenly in the eyes of the others, jumped overboard.

He landed crotch-deep in the water and a spume of mud-colored water bubbled up around his shorts. All three others adopted the same look on their faces, as if they'd suddenly tasted something gone bad in their mouths, their noses wrinkled, their eyes squinted.

"Better you than me," Lance stage whispered.

"Only take me an hour or so," Charles said. "You can find something to do for an hour, right honey?" he said, and Susan again turned her look from soured to perplexed. Charles never called her honey.

"Oh yes. Sure," she finally said. Speechlessness did not become her. "It's kind of an adventure."

"We could work out a script," Lance said with a tone that was actually more than half serious. "*An Afternoon with a View*. There we are. Once you have the title you're half done."

Charles winked and turned to move off to the east, taking large, awkward strides. Lance responded to the wink with a quizzical look of his own. He'd never seen Charlie wink before.

Within twenty minutes, Charles could no longer see them. The airboat was out of sight. But he swore he could still hear them chattering, something about being contestants on a thing called *Survivor: Samoa*.

He kept moving, with some difficulty, he admitted. With each step he was both pulling one foot out of the muck, and then stretching to plunge it back into the swamp. But at this point he wasn't considering the effort.

This ain't Samoa, it's the Everglades folks, he thought. And there will only be one survivor on this day. When he figured he'd made at least thirty yards, he looked to find purchase on a thick mat of built-up vegetation and silt in the eddy of a flow of water. He got one foot on top and then stood up on it, gaining maybe two feet in elevation. He checked what there was of the horizon to see; the unbroken blue sky and the green-brown tops of the saw-grass. Nothing more, or less, than nature itself. He reached into a chest-high pocket of his vest and withdrew an old television remote that had cluttered a drawer in his kitchen for years. It had not been much of a task for the son and grandson of blasting experts to rig it as an electronic igniter to the package of black powder he'd attached to the gas tanks of the airboat. Hell, his dad had shown him how to do it with the garage door opener years ago. It was a matter of setting the right frequency. Punch a button. Create a spark.

He raised the remote as high in the air as possible to give it a clear signal. He did not waver. Did not hesitate. "Fire in the hole," he whispered. And then he mashed the MUTE button.

The explosion shivered the air. Charles did not feel the same rumble of the ground and vibration in his legs that he had always felt when his dad and granddad blew holes in the limestone. But the air quivered and the sound, the BALLLLOOOM and the rush of unnatural wind whumped against him in a most satisfying way. He closed his eyes then and breathed deeply. As the echo of the blast faded, the silence rushed in. The quiet was total, earth stopping, ear molding, and to him, nearly orgasmic.

"Oh," he whispered and nothing more. He let the lack of sound wash over him, cleanse him, anoint him. It was bliss. Not the death of his wife. Not the death of her friends. But the quiet. The aftermath of the explosion had muted everything; the buzz of insects, movement of birds, disturbance of the water, even the wind seemed to have stopped as the concussion created some kind of vacuum.

He did not know how long he kept his eyes closed. A minute? Ten? Finally he let his lids part and then let his eyes focus on the horizon. A funnel of black smoke rose in the distance; a curled, fat finger pointing up into the sky. That would surely be spotted by someone, he thought. There were other people out here; fishermen, birders, other airboaters, even several private planes above that used the open space and lack of air traffic to practice low-level flying and stunts. Someone would see the plume and investigate. Still he stood for some minutes, reveling, not in what he had done, but in what he had created. But even his quiet euphoria could not levitate him. He soon became aware that he was sinking, his weight finally overpowering the loose purchase of sawgrass and detritus. The soak of the water moved up to his knees. He watched the smoke plume begin to dissipate and knew he needed to go, needed to move fast to the berm that he'd carefully calculated to be a mile away.

He could make a mile. Hell, he walked more than that every day to and from his Tri-Rail commuter train stop to the office. No, he'd never actually walked the Glades, but who did? It wasn't necessary. Even the native Seminole Indians used their dugout canoes to travel the watery landscape. But a mile was just a mile. Five thousand two hundred eighty feet. He'd best get moving. He was now the only survivor of a tragic airboat accident in which the heat of an overused engine had somehow ignited some dry stalks that got caught up in the blade cage of the engine and then in turn ignited the fuel tanks. A terrible explosion had occurred and he had been blown some distance and had miraculously escaped the full impact and had then made his way to civilization. He'd rehearsed the story. He stepped down into the water. It was the temperature of a warm bath. Soothing really. He took out the compass from his pocket, got an eastward bearing and started moving, step by step, foot pulled up and then replunged. Foot pulled up and replunged.

Within the first half hour he'd begun counting backwards. It was a goal, he told himself, a concentration exercise, it would occupy his mind, keep him focused. Four thousand eight hundred and seventy-four. Damn it was hot. He'd considered ahead of time that the moisture and the shade of the tall sawgrass and being down low would mean a natural shade and relative coolness. But he had been wrong. At the count of four thousand eight hundred he stopped to take a drink from the water bottle he'd taken from the boat. He recalled that stupid look on his wife's face. Be back in an hour. He now shook his head, a bead of sweat flew. When had he learned to be such a liar? He took another swing of the water. Half the bottle left. He checked the compass and started east again.

The sounds of birds came back. The flutter of wings through air, but he was too far down in the grass to see anything in flight. In between steps he would hesitate and picked up the buzz of insects. It had started innocuously, but had risen to a steady hum. He was also beginning to notice the sound of the ripple from his own wake as he sloshed along. Three thousand seven hundred and forty-eight. He thought he heard a crackle of grass, the sound coming from behind him. Gator? Doubtful. Alligators are not stalkers. They wait, unmoving, for their prey to cross within snapping distance. They're opportunistic creatures, not outwardly aggressive until they strike. Surprise is their thing. He wiped the sweat from his face with a sleeve and peered back. Green-brown walls, murky and dark water, blue channel of sky above. His slogging through the grass had left a distinctive path. That was good for his story, he thought. But good for following too. A cloud of mosquitoes suddenly fogged around his head and he waved them away. Best if he kept moving.

Two thousand six hundred and forty. That's halfway. Right? He was an accountant. Of course it was right. Numbers were his thing. He went for the water bottle again, forgetting that he'd already emptied it one hundred steps ago, had tossed it high and to the right, over the stalks, well off the path.

Throw them off if they were following. Following? Where had he gotten that idea? Don't lose focus, Charles, he thought. Don't let the heat get to you. He kept moving but stopped twenty steps farther. He thought he'd heard something; a dull, rhythmic sound. Was someone talking behind him? Someone's deep voice? A male voice? Lance? And why would he stop talking whenever Charles stopped? He went to wipe his face again, but his forehead and cheeks were dry. What was that rule about sweat? It was a sign of dehydration. Or was the lack of it the sign? Damn it was hot, and close, and now that whumping and the crackling and the buzzing were starting to get to him. "Fucking noise," he whispered, and the words sounded foreign to him, the voice not even his. He hardly ever swore.

Shit. If only he could get up into the air. It was suffocating down here. It was a steam bath sucking the energy and the moisture out of his body and clear focus out of his head. He had a vision of fat men sitting in towels. He thought at one point he saw steam rising off the dark water. Again, something rustled behind him. He snapped his head around. Was that Susan's new safari shirt? It was teal, wasn't it? He crouched lower, his chin actually touching the water. It was cooler, right? Isn't that what they tell you to do in a fire, go low to the ground because the smoke will rise? He peered again past the last few stalks of sawgrass that he had trampled. Was Susan stalking him?

Fuck. How did she survive that blast? "No way. Yes way," he whispered, or tried, the words coming dry and strange to his mouth.

It was an old teenage comeback. No way! Yes way! He opened his mouth and let the Glades water spill ever so slightly over his bottom lip down into his throat. God he was thirsty. The water was brackish, the odor of mold and wet, rotting straw. He threw up, the yellowish spume spreading out before him. Another path to dehydration he was beyond recognizing. He needed to stand but could not gather the strength. He was bent at the waist, arms submerged in the water, heels of his hands on his knees. He was fighting the pull of gravity, straining simply to keep from pitching forward. Again the wump, wump, wump. He turned his head back to the path. Was Susan coming? He hoped she was coming. His head hung now, forehead dipped in water, gravity winning. But before he pitched forward and let the water wash into his lungs, he uttered four last desperate words: "Susan. Talk to me."

Western Palm Beach County—*Four people airboating in the Everglades west of Atlantic Park Road on Tuesday were found dead after an apparent explosion, said a county sheriff's spokesman.*

Investigating the report of a fire about a mile from the L-16 canal berm, a sheriff's helicopter at about 2 PM flew over the site of a charred airboat that had been destroyed by fire. A county airboat operated by the sheriff's office was also dispatched and officers arrived at the scene to find three badly burned bodies within the twisted and blackened wreckage.

"It appears that a privately operated airboat somehow caught fire and ignited the fuel tanks," said Palm Beach County Sheriff's spokesman Ron Torre. "The resulting explosion nearly incinerated all three victims."

Torre said that investigators also noted a newly beaten path leading away from the fire sight and when they tracked the path a fourth body was found.

"The fourth victim appeared to have survived the fire and was going for help," Torre said. "But the Glades are extremely difficult to traverse in high water and in the direct sun, the heat, and humidity, the grasses can often reach over one hundred and twenty degrees."

Torre said the fourth victim had apparently been overwhelmed by heat stroke and exhaustion. Identification of all four victims was being withheld pending notification of kin.

According to an eyewitness who was among several people at the dock when officers brought the bodies ashore, all three of the burn victims had their mouths open and appeared to be frozen in the act of speaking.

Asked to verify that report, spokesman Torre said: "I certainly can't speak to that. No comment."

ULTIMA FORSAN

BY MICHAEL LISTER

She never takes off her watch—not even when we make love.

She'll be completely naked—no earrings, makeup, or pubic hair—but she'll have that damn watch on. It's one of the things I like about her. One of many.

It has a small brownish leather strap and an oval face that glints in the dashboard lights as she leans up from the passenger seat to search for a better song.

We're on a dark, rural road in North Florida, so there's not a lot of stations to choose from—one rock, two country, two top forty, one religious, an NPR playing classical at the moment, and a ninety-eight-point-something with an irritating DJ who doles out sappy sentimental bullshit between a truly awful selection of soft pop love songs.

She looks at her watch, though the light to do so comes from the greenish glow of the car clock.

She has narrow wrists and large, long-fingered hands that I love to watch—even when all she's doing is checking the time.

Her delicate wrist and thin watchband both bear a slight dusting of dune sand from where we made love on the warm beach beneath a single star to the rhythmic returns of the tides, the infinite green Gulf a nearly unseen mass of undulating blackness.

The lovemaking in the sand fortress of the dunes had been our second dessert of the evening. The first, a white chocolate key lime tart, followed a Greek-style open-hearth charbroiled red snapper that we shared with a bottle of Mantazas Creek chardonnay.

We were celebrating—still are.

Depending on who you ask, it's either our tenth anniversary or close to it. I mark it from the moment I saw her—that magical fall afternoon in the old creaky wooden-floor bookstore. She marks it from the first time we made love. Either way, we've been each other's for a decade—or nearly a decade.

The night is dark and hot. We're driving home on a straight, flat, empty rural highway that stretches out in seemingly endless lonely miles in either direction, framed by rows and rows of silent planted pines.

She passes on a love song that's too soft, too elevatory, and a rock song that's too hard, too head-bangy, and is about to zip on by the religious station, but stops when she recognizes the poem or passage that's being read.

—To everything there is a season, and a time to every purpose under the heaven, the hoarse, preachery voice intones.

—I love this, she says.

—A time to be born, and a time to die; a time to plant, and a time to pluck up that which is planted. A time to kill, and a time to heal; a time to break down, and a time to build up.

—You don't really think there's a time to kill, do you? I ask.

—Just listen. It's beautiful.

—A time to weep, and a time to laugh; a time to mourn, and a time to dance, the radio preacher continues.

—Isn't it nice? she asks.

That's my Ansley. Poetic. Literate. Lyrical.

Her watch, the one she never takes off—even when we make love—is not just any watch, but one she searched extensively for. She'd seen plenty of clocks with the phrase *ultima forsan* on them, but never a watch. And so her search began.

I have no idea where she found it, but I never doubted she would.

And I never asked her what it meant. I looked it up myself.

Ultima forsan is a Latin phrase that means *perhaps the last*. It's a reminder that it's later than we think, that any moment may be our last. Death is always at hand. Unseen. Unbidden. Unalterable.

And that's the way she lives—full bore, squeezing every drop out of every last moment—and did long before she found the watch.

—A time to embrace, and a time to refrain from embracing.

—I hope we never have a time of not embracing, I say.

—We won't, she says with such certainty that I believe her.

—A time to rend, and a time to sew; a time to keep silent, and a time to speak. A time to love, and a time to hate; a time of war, and a time of peace.

—It's always the time for love and peace, I say. And never the time for hate and war.

—I don't know, she says, changing the station as the preacher begins to expound idiotically on the sublime words he's obviously not understood.

I look over at her.

—There may be those times.

I think about it. That's what she makes me do—think. It's another thing I love about her. She's never obvious, never predictable, this lovely, peace-loving, war-protesting, gentlest of gentle souls says there may be those times for hate and war.

—When? I ask.

—Huh?

—When would those times be?

—I'm just say—

She stops as the next press of the Scan button brings our song—Eric Clapton's "Wonderful Tonight."

She turns and looks at me, her eyes wide, her expression communicating what I know she's thinking—that nothing short of the universe is conspiring to make it a magical evening.

—It's official, she says. Best anniversary ever.

She leans in over the console toward me. I put my arm around her, and hold onto her like I've been doing since the moment I met her, and we listen to the unmistakable guitar and the simple, sweet lyrics.

When the song ends, she reaches up and turns off the radio and we sit in silence for a few moments.

Eventually, the first few intermittent raindrops begin to dot the windshield.

—Only one thing could make this evening more perfecter, she says.

I nod.

I don't have to ask. I know what she means.

—I'll see if I can find an open store.

She wants a half gallon of vanilla ice cream, two packs of Reese's, two Kit Kats, and a bag of Oreos, and our only hope is a small convenience store in the middle of nowhere a couple of miles up the road.

If the store is open, and the items are in stock, she'll dump out half of the ice cream and stir in the Kit Kats, all four Reece's, and a third of the bag of Oreos, and eat something, as far as I know, only she does.

—They'll be open, she says, and I believe her.

We ride in silence, following the short, narrow lead of the night and fog-diffused headlights down the dark road, Ansley snuggled beneath my arm.

By the rhythm and sound of her breathing, I can tell she's getting sleepy. And it's no wonder. Not only is it past her normal bedtime, but our anniversary celebration had included an entire bottle of wine and our lovemaking on the beach had been particularly vigorous.

—Sure you're not too tired for ice cream and—

—Positive. 'Sides I need it to rebuild my strength for the second helping of anniversary sex I'm gonna give you when we get home.

Sweet, lovely, generous girl. I'm the luckiest, happiest, most grateful man in the world.

The small store is a neon and halogen-lit burst of brightness surrounded by a sea of dark—a single star in a black hole.

Beyond a faded green canopy that hovers over the gas pumps, the crowded porch of the storefront hosts a large ice cooler, a locked mesh cage of propane tanks, newspaper boxes, trash cans, and two booth-style tables littered with Styrofoam coffee cups and overflowing ashtrays, their built-in seats cigarette-burn speckled.

The panel of plate glass windows above them running the width of the building are filled with neon Florida Lottery and beer signs—pink and green and gold—ATM and Open signs, posters for smokeless tobacco products, and various official looking stickers and notices.

An old pickup and a battered Accord are at the side, but the front lot is empty, and I pull up and park near the double glass doors.

—I'll get it, Ansley says, sitting up.

—You save your energy, I say.

She smiles up at me as I get out, a sweet, sleepy, slightly wanton smile that elicits a variety of reactions in me. Love. Gratitude. Desire.

She lays her head back on the seat, continuing to gaze at me and smile in her dewy drowsiness as I close the door, and I'm fairly certain I'll return with her ice cream and goodies to find her sound asleep.

The store is cold and smells of dust and deli—the thick, pungent odor of old grease hanging in the atmosphere.

The large, grimy man behind the counter is a mouth-breather with a camouflage baseball cap and a solid green T that doesn't quite cover his enormous belly.

He is working on the register when I walk in, studying it as if for the first time, and doesn't look up, just nods and grunts.

As I scour the aisles for the items to satiate one of Ansley's appetites, the clerk continues to punch buttons with his fat fingers and continues to receive electronic rebukes and rebuffs in the form of shrill beeps, each time responding with a litany of whispered angry profanities.

The air conditioner, mammoth cooler along the back wall, and box fans on each end of the building give the aural illusion of a wind tunnel, and make the small, overly lit store seem even more arctic than it is.

After finding what I can, I toss everything on the counter, and the man looks from the register over to it.

—Can't make change, he says. Can't get in the damn till.

—I may have it, I say. How much?

He eyes the items, squints, touches each one with his enormous mitts, then shrugs.

—Ten bucks? he says, returning his attention to the register.

I pull a ten from my wallet, drop it on the counter, gather up my things, and head toward the door.

—Thanks, I say. Have a good night.

—Flip that sign around for me, he says, looking up long enough to nod at the Open/Closed sign hanging on the door.

I do.

The moment I'm outside, lights start going off—over the pumps, then the porch.

I look at my watch. Quarter til twelve.

It's raining harder now, but it's still nothing more than a late summer shower.

Easing open the door, I try to keep from waking Ansley, but she stirs and sits up.

I climb in and begin passing over the rain-speckled stash.

—No bag?

—Service, I say. Not so much. Got everything but Kit Kat.

—Why?

—They were out.

—What about Nestle's Crunch?

—What about it?

—It's the substitute for Kit Kat in this recipe.

—I didn't know that, I say and smile at her.

—I'll be right back, she says, sliding over and opening her door.

—He just closed.

—Does he know it's our anniversary?

—We didn't get to that.

She closes the door and I watch through the rain-streaked windshield as she runs onto the porch, pauses a moment to straighten her hair, and continues inside, her water-muted figure blurred and wet textured.

For a moment, I just sit, taking in a deep breath and letting it out, feeling . . . what? Just so damn happy.

Ten years.

Ten years.

We're still youngish, but we're approaching a transition. Will we have something more traditional? Will we have kids? God, is that where we are? It is, isn't it? We're young but not young enough to live like kids, to live so carelessly, to fritter away our finite moments so frivolously.

There were moments through our decade together where I honestly didn't think we'd make it—and certainly didn't think I could ever feel this way again, this thoroughly and completely and utterly—well, happy. Downright giddy.

I reach up and twist the stem that turns on the windshield wipers and watch as the water rolls off in a wave, removing the opacity, restoring my view, the bright lights from within the store rushing in—and with them something that stops my heart.

Maybe I had been too distracted to notice before, or maybe the canopy and porch lights had created a reflective barrier. Whatever the cause, I had somehow missed it.

How could I have—it doesn't matter now.

What am I gonna do?

First thing—I've got to get Ansley out of there. Now.

The wipers remove the buildup of water again, and I look to make sure I saw what I thought I did.

I did.

Blood.

Body.

Murder.

Robbery.

In the large security mirror hanging in the back corner of the building,

I can see the distorted reflection of another mirror, and in it a dead, blood-covered body lying in a pool of blood behind the deli counter.

Jumping out of the car, I rush through the rain onto the porch and into the store.

Ansley is standing at the counter, two Crunch bars in front of her.

—I forgot to bring money, she says turning to me. Do you have—

—Yeah, sure, I say pulling out my wallet.

I toss three dollars onto the counter.

—Come on, I say. We've got to go.

—What is it?

The man looks up from where he's still punching buttons on the register, and studies me.

—Work, I say, looking at him. Just got called in.

—*Work?* Ansley says.

—Yeah.

—He tell you it's our anniversary? she says to the man.

He doesn't respond.

—Come on, I say. We've got to go.

—I can help you with that, she says, nodding toward the register. Worked in one of these during college. Here.

She begins to walk to the end of the counter.

I can tell she intends to go behind it to help the man, which would cause her to see the blood if not the body.

—We don't have time, I say, reaching for her arm.

—Ouch. Okay.

—Take the time, the man says, reaching beneath the counter and coming up with a large revolver.

—What? she says, confused, starting to laugh, but then realizing it's not a joke.

—Open this goddam thing for me. You, he says to me. Let me see your hands.

I raise my hands.

Ansley begins to head toward the back of the counter, but I grab her arm again.

—Do it from here, I say. Just lean over the—

Thunder cracks outside and Ansley and I both jump.

When we've recovered, she slowly steps toward the register. Her self-conscious, stilted actions make it appear that any sudden movement will trigger an explosion.

Reaching over the counter with trembling fingers, she leans in so she can see, careful to stay as far away from the big man as she can, and begins to press a series of keys.

Her hands shake so violently, her first attempts result in as many protests from the machine as the robber's had.

After a few seconds, the beeps stop. A moment later, the drawer springs open.

—Thanks, the man says in a fat-thick, airy, mouth-breather voice.

He then shoots her in the head. No big dramatic gesture. Just squeezes the trigger nonchalantly.

The explosion is as jarring as it is deafening.

I'm stunned.

Shocked.

Disoriented.

As she falls back, I reach for her, finding her wrist, her watch, which comes off in my hand as she continues to fall.

I turn to the man, holding her small watch up in one of my outstretched hands that form the ultimate question for the random, chaotic, suddenly violent universe, and see that he now has the gun leveled at me.

I spin around and dive toward Ansley—not out of fear, not out of some misguided attempt at avoiding the bullet with my name on it, but because I want to be with her, to be touching her, want us to be together when *ultima forsan* becomes *ultima Thule.*

THE CYPRESS DREAM

BY CAROLYN HAINES

The silver surface of Lake Eloise ripped and tore in the wake of the huge speedboat powered by three Johnson outboard motors. Kit McCallum gripped the ski rope, blinked the wind-driven tears from her eyes, and took a deep breath as she waited for the signal. The vivid colors of the botanical garden—reds and yellows, greens and purples—bled past like melting stained glass as she climbed onto Amy Guiseppi's and Carla Bainer's shoulders and completed the third tier of the human ski pyramid.

Along the shore, the crowd jumped to its feet and applauded. The announcer's voice was a blur of long vowels as Kit held the wooden handle of the ski line with one hand and raised her right arm in victory.

The boat turned closer to the shore and pulled the formation past tourists dressed in plaid shorts, white shirts, sundresses, and sandals. Kit didn't associate with the spectators but she knew them—solid middle-class people who brought their kids to Cypress Gardens for good, clean fun and a bit of education on the natural beauty of the Florida chain of lakes. They modeled themselves from photos in *Life Magazine*. Perhaps in their world, father did know best, but that was something Kit would never know. She'd once dreamed of such a family, but that was when she was still a kid.

She gave the spectators the signature wave she'd rehearsed all spring. The ski team, which was the biggest attraction at the gardens, had worked hard to perfect the pyramid routine. Cypress Gardens had been the first to add the third tier. It was a coup, and Kit was proud to crown the top. She reveled in the attention.

Without warning, Amy's shoulder fell away. For a long moment, Kit wavered, trying to rebalance, but it was useless. Amy was falling. Thinking how she'd kill Amy as soon as possible, Kit threw her ski line forward and flipped backwards. To fall in front of the pyramid—sixteen bodies, sixteen ski lines, and nine pairs of potentially deadly skis—was suicidal. Kit had seen enough accidents to heed the dangers. If she had to fall, she wanted to be behind the other skiers.

Her body cut the water in a clean dive, and she took satisfaction in the applause of the spectators. Even though the pyramid had collapsed, she'd given the crowd a bit of flash and dazzle. Kenny, their coach, might be mad at the skiers for screwing up the show, but he'd praise her for her innovation and skill. Yet again, she'd come out smelling like one of the exotic blooms in the plantation rose gardens.

As her mother, the bitch, would say, Kit had a talent for looking good. It was one of the many things that Laura McCallum hated about her daughter. Lord, the woman had a list a mile long.

The dive took Kit deep into the crystal water, and she caught sight of a form that wavered in the dark depths. For one fantastic moment, she thought she'd found a mermaid, but the burning need for oxygen drove her to the surface before she could investigate.

She erupted into the air and a wail of noise. Water distorted her vision. The faces of the spectators were pulled into Os of dismay, and she spun in the water in the direction they were looking. The speedboat circled some of the skiers and finally came to a stop. Chuck, the driver, knifed his body over the side toward someone floating in the water.

One of the skiers was hurt.

Kit struck out across the lake for the huddle of skiers. She was the strongest swimmer in the group, though she was only four-eleven and a scant eighty-five pounds. Chuck called her Minnow, a name that both pleased and annoyed her.

She kicked strong, and when tendrils of grass caught around her ankle, she fluttered both feet. Instead of breaking free, her foot tangled more. Taking a breath, she dove.

She met the corpse face to face, the eyeless sockets huge and dark. Clumps of flesh clung to the skull, floating like pale cod fillets. Long hair wafted around the corpse's head, undulating on the water, strands of it wrapped tight around Kit's left ankle. She kicked. To her horror, the dead girl jerked violently but refused to release Kit's foot. The corpse held her.

She screamed. Water rushed into her lungs, and she churned for the surface. As she burst into the air, she coughed and panicked, flailing in the water.

"Help! Help!" Her voice was too weak to carry, but the spectators heard and pointed in her direction. A small boat headed her way just as the tangle of hair and the weight of the body began to pull her down.

• • •

She shucked off the cold and clammy swimsuit and stepped under the hot spray of the shower. The red straps of the Catalina one-piece tangled around her feet and she kicked it against the shower wall with a wet splat. Outside the showers, locker doors slammed. The other girls spoke in hushed whispers, and twice she heard someone tiptoe to the stall where she hid.

"Kit, we're ready to go," Amy said. "Chuck said he'd take us to the hospital to check on Mel."

"Go on. I'll come later." She wanted to be alone. The transport of Mel to the hospital in a neck brace, the recovery of the dead girl's body, the clamor of the media—it had all been too much.

"Are you sure?" Amy sounded scared.

"Leave me the fuck alone." Kit knew how to be hard.

Amy's footsteps retreated on the tile floor.

Water trickled down Kit's body, and it didn't bother her until it sluiced down her calf, and the feel of it was like the tendrils of hair, floating like some cold, fine seaweed.

Had she not fallen during the ski show, Jess Livingston's body might never have been found. Jess, formerly the best skier at the gardens, had left at the end of February, just as the ski team had begun to practice routines in Lake Eloise.

The water was cold and the work exhausting in February, but Jess had been Cypress Garden's star for the past four years. She had her own publicity photos, and last year a talent scout from MGM had been to see her show more than eight times. There was talk that Jess had the potential of being another Ester Williams.

When Jess didn't show up for practice one morning, Chuck and Kenny went to her place to check on her. They'd found a note that said she was heading to Tampa to work with dolphins. She'd had enough of skiing.

And that had been that.

Until today.

Jess Livingston had not left the show. At least not voluntarily. Whatever the coroner ruled as cause of death, Kit had seen the cement block tied to Jess's feet. Heavy, but not heavy enough to keep her in one of the blue holes where she'd likely been dropped.

Leaning against the aqua tile wall of the shower, Kit swallowed her tears. Hell, why was she crying? She was fine. Mel had a serious injury, but he would recover. Jess Livingston had been no friend of hers. In fact, they'd been bitter rivals. It was Jess's sudden departure that had given Kit the opening she needed to be top skier. Kit had wished the petite brunette dead on more than one occasion.

She turned the shower off.

There was no need for tears. She was fine. Totally fine. She grabbed a towel from the hook outside the shower, aware of the silence in the locker room beyond. Everyone had left, just as she'd dictated.

She dried, dressed, and walked out of the lady's locker room. A man in gray slacks, white shirt, tie, and fedora rose from the bench outside the bathroom door. The locker room was hot, and his shirt stuck to him in places. He didn't make a sound, and he spooked her, the way he stared.

"No one is allowed in here." She spoke with authority. She'd learned the hard way that tentative conduct around men resulted in difficulty. Her diminutive size drew bullies to her like flies to a turd, as her mother often pointed out. Her mother, who had shoulders the size of an ox, took it as a personal insult that Kit had been born tiny and had never "filled out."

"I was waiting for you, Miss McCallum."

Something in the way he spoke made her uneasy. "Yeah, well keep waitin', 'cause I don't know who you are and I don't want to know." She brushed past him, but he caught her elbow, not harshly, but firm enough to stop her.

"I'm Pete Paladin, with the *St. Pete Times*."

"Good for you, Pete from St. Pete." But she didn't leave. The St. Pete paper was big. A story there could lead to something national. It was possible he wanted to interview her. After all, she'd found the body.

"Could I buy you dinner, maybe ask a few questions, for a story for the paper?" He picked up his jacket from the bench and removed a narrow notepad. "Tomorrow, the newspaper is sending a photographer if they like the story I do. If that's okay with you."

She lifted her wet hair off her neck. "I need to fix up. Before dinner."

He nodded. "I'll pick you up at seven. What about Korbet's Restaurant? I've heard that's a good place to eat."

She nodded. Korbet's was nice. Expensive. "I'll be ready."

He stepped back to let her pass and followed her into the fading sunlight of the May evening. The perfume of gardenias floated to her from the gardens. The scent of twilight, they always smelled strongest just before the end of the day.

• • •

Kit applied a fresh coat of fingernail polish as she sat under the dryer. It would be better if the photographer would take her picture now instead of tomorrow. But they'd probably want an action shot. Her at the top of the pyramid. That would work. She held her right hand up by the hair dryer to hurry the process.

When her fingers and hair were dry, she removed the curlers and brushed out her auburn hair. She slipped into the red polka-dot dress and her strappy sandals. She'd just applied her lipstick when the doorbell buzzed. Her phone, too, began to ring.

"Just a minute," she called to the door as she hurried to the small table in the hallway to pick up the phone. "Hello."

The only sound on the other end was labored breathing.

"Hello." Her grip tightened on the phone. "Who is this? Who's calling?" She waited, hearing only the raspy sound of someone inhaling and exhaling. "Pervert!" She slammed the phone in the cradle.

"Hey, you okay?" Pete Paladin called from the other side of the door.

She opened it and let him in. "Some heavy breather on the phone." She tried not to act rattled.

"Do you get those calls often?" Pete asked.

She thought about how that would look in a newspaper story. She'd come across as cheap. Someone that men felt they could toy with. "No. It must be because of … the body and all. My name was on the radio. Amy called and told me."

Pete glanced around her apartment, taking a good look at her door. "You need a deadbolt and a chain. Never hurts to be safe."

"Are you trying to scare me?" She didn't like it when someone tried to make her feel unsafe. Her mother had ruled her life with fear for seventeen years, until she'd finished high school and took off.

"We have reservations at seven thirty." He offered his arm.

She picked up her purse, taking care to lock the door behind her before they left the apartment building. "You didn't answer my question," she said as they walked to his Chevrolet.

"I don't try to scare women," Pete said. "Not even ones who might need to be a little afraid."

"Why should I be afraid?" she asked.

"Because," Pete said as he assisted her into the passenger seat, "Jess Livingston was murdered, and whoever did it had gotten away with it until you found her body. Doesn't it make you wonder who killed her?"

"That doesn't have anything to do with me," Kit said.

"Maybe it didn't when they offed her, but after today it surely does."

• • •

The grilled pompano was delicious, and Kit was surprised when Pete asked her to dance. The four-piece combo kept the music lively, and Kit enjoyed the way Pete looked at her. There was none of the boyish adoration. Pete was a man, and he made her feel like a woman.

"What kind of name is Paladin?" she asked him when he seated her at the table. "It's made up, isn't it? Like on that TV show with the gunman."

"No, it's Spanish. It means knight." He poured her another glass of wine. "My father always told me that our family descended from the Medieval court of Charlemagne. Knights of the court."

She was intrigued despite herself. "Did he have any proof of that?"

"You'd make a good reporter," Pete said. "My father would be insulted, but it's exactly the right question to ask."

"Men make up things all the time to tell women. It shouldn't insult your father that I refuse to be a fool."

Pete laughed out loud, and she felt the burn of a blush touch her cheeks. "Walk a mile in my shoes if you think that's so damn funny."

"Hey." He touched her arm. "Take it easy. I was laughing because I enjoy you."

She didn't believe him. He was educated and smart and had a job writing. She knew the kind of men who pursued the girls at the Gardens. Most of them were married, and the rest were up to no good. Jess Livingston had let it be known that she had caught the eye of a politician, a man with power. Gossip was that he'd helped her move on to Tampa and bigger exposure.

"Ask your questions, I need to get home early. We'll have a hard rehearsal 'cause we have to figure out what to do with Mel injured." She pushed her plate back and shook her head when the waiter offered dessert. Without asking, Pete ordered coffee for them both.

"So tell me about Jess Livingston," Pete said. He pulled out his pen and notebook.

Kit told him how she'd originally been hired as Jess's understudy. "The girl on the top of the pyramid has to be small. Think of this. My weight is on the shoulders of Amy and Carla, and then all of that is on top of the men below us. The whole thing is pulled through the water."

"It's impressive," Pete agreed. "What kind of girl was Jess?"

Kit hesitated. Anything that made one Garden girl look bad reflected on all of them. "She was okay."

"Did she date?"

"Why does that matter?" She braced her palms on the edge of the table, ready to get up.

"Look, she was a pretty girl. Like you. Someone killed her. Either she was in the wrong place at the wrong time and got whacked accidentally, or she was killed because she saw or heard something she shouldn't have." He leaned forward. "I'm putting my money on the latter. And I want to know what information cost her her life."

Kit studied his hazel eyes. He didn't flinch. "She was dating a politician. She said he was very powerful." She looked down. "Probably married, or else she would have said his name."

"What did she say?"

"You're going to put this in a story?" Kit thought it might not be smart.

"Not yet. Not until I get the goods on him. And I won't use your name."

"What about my story? The photographer is coming tomorrow …" His expression was a dead giveaway. She'd been had. At least she'd gotten a good dinner out of it, and she hadn't said much at all. She pushed back her chair. "I don't appreciate being played. Now I'd like to go home."

"Sure thing." Pete pulled a fat money clip from his pocket and dropped several bills on the table.

• • •

Kit floated in the crystal green of Lake Eloise. In her dream the water was smooth, like the top of a jewel. Indian stories told of an alternate world that could be seen beneath the surface on still days. Kit had never seen such things—had never looked—but she loved the way the water supported her without effort, cooled her from the oppressive heat. She drifted beneath the shade of a moss-covered limb that dipped almost to the water. On the shore, a cluster of brightly hued belles in the swinging skirts of antebellum days rocked past the beds of bearded irises, lantana, salvias, daisies, foxglove, and snapdragons. The colors were so vivid, Kit closed her eyes.

In the distance a phone rang. She struggled to place the sound in her dream, and when she finally awoke, she could still hear the ringing. She got up and went to the narrow hall and picked up the receiver.

"Hello."

A long rasp of breath slithered down the line.

"Hello." The last grip of sleep loosened, and she found her heart pounding. "Who is this?"

The breath came again. She'd never imagined that someone breathing could sound so intimidating.

"What do you want?"

There was no answer. Only the long, ragged breath.

She smashed the receiver down and stood with her hand holding it in the cradle as if it might fly up to her ear. When she felt she could walk without falling, she went into the kitchen. It was three thirty. Outside the open kitchen window, the frogs sang a low lullaby. The night was soft and quiet.

Her apartment had a small screened porch, and she went there and scrunched into an old wicker chair with faded floral cushions. No cars passed on the two-lane highway fifty yards from her door. The windows of her neighbor's were dark. She'd chosen the apartment that had been cut from a large, older home because of the porch. Hugging her knees, she listened to the night.

Movement caught her attention. On the far side of the highway walked a man in a long coat and a narrow-brimmed hat. He stopped when he was directly opposite her and turned to stare. He couldn't see her. She was safe in the darkness, but she didn't feel safe. His gaze seemed to bore into her, drilling into the bone and nerves of her spine and leaving her body numb and unresponsive. He turned away and kept walking.

When he was gone, Kit rushed back into the apartment and locked the door. It was a flimsy latch that even a kid could push through. Pete was right. She'd call the landlord when it was daylight.

She closed the kitchen window. Instead of going back to bed, she went to the hallway and sat beside the phone, not touching it, but afraid to look away.

• • •

Pete was waiting for her in his car when she went outside. "How about some breakfast?" he asked.

"I don't eat breakfast." But her heart wasn't in the disclaimer. She was glad to see him. Glad to know that someone bothered to check on her.

"I do. It's a bad habit I started when I wanted to grow tall enough to be a ball player."

She opened the door and got in, not waiting for his assistance. "Well, it worked. Maybe I should have eaten more."

He laughed, and she liked the way he did so without holding back. "That's a thought, Minnow. With more nutrition you might have been Bream."

She was both pleased and annoyed. "Who've you been talking to?"

"Mostly Amy. Chuck, too. They both seem fond of you, and they're both worried about you."

"I'm worried, too," she said almost under her breath.

"Something happen?" he asked.

She told him about the phone call and the man walking. "No one walks along the highway there. It's suicidal."

"You think he was watching you?"

"Yes." The iron taste of blood touched her tongue. Her teeth had pierced her lip, a bad habit she thought she'd broken. When she was little and her mother had beaten her with a hairbrush, she'd bitten her lip to keep from crying. The end result was that her mother only beat her harder and she had tiny lumps of scar tissue on the inside of her mouth.

"You want to go to the police station and make a report?" he asked.

She shook her head. "They don't take these things seriously. Some of the other girls ..." Each year there was at least one guy whose infatuation with a Garden girl turned ugly. The police acted like the girls brought it on themselves.

They pulled into Jolene's Diner, and Kit settled into a booth. When Pete ordered an omelet for her, she didn't say anything, just sipped the hot, strong coffee that the waitress produced.

"I'm glad you're not mad at me anymore," Pete said.

She shrugged. She wasn't sure if she was mad or not, only that she was relieved not to be alone.

"Will you talk to me about Jess?"

"Okay." What did she have to lose? He'd played her about the news story, but wasn't that his job?

She told him about the expensive flowers, the telephoned instructions of places to meet, the excitement of the secrecy, and Jess's belief that her honey man had set up the deal with the MGM scout. "I was so envious," Kit concluded. "She had everything I wanted. Attention. Potential. Things were happening for her."

"All benefits of a powerful lover. Did you want that, too?" Pete asked.

Her laugh was rueful. "No. I didn't envy that. Jess believed she'd always control him. That he couldn't do without her. I told her she had six weeks, max. Probably less. Girls, for a man like him, are a dime a dozen. That's why, when she disappeared, I thought she'd gone off to Hollywood. That she knew, like I did, that she had to take what he offered then. Otherwise it would all be a mirage."

"You sound like you two were close."

"Jess wasn't close to anyone really. I guess you could say she talked to me more than anyone else, but we weren't best friends."

The waitress cleared the breakfast dishes and refreshed their coffee. Pete sat back in the booth. Even though she'd given him what he wanted, he didn't seem to be in a hurry to leave.

"She never said his name?" Pete asked.

"No. She was careful."

Pete flipped his notebook closed.

"She said things to confuse the issue. Like he was in Washington, and then he would be in Tallahassee, like we were too stupid to figure if he was state or national. I graduated high school, and I got an A in civics. When she said he helped the president build up Eglin Air Force Base, I knew he was a US congressman."

"Did she hint at who it might be? Maybe we could put it together."

She found her lip between her teeth again and released it. "I don't want to know who she was seeing. You figure it out. I need to get to the Gardens. Kenny will drill us this morning. We've got to come up with a plan without Mel. He was the strongest guy in the pyramid."

"I checked at the hospital. The doc said he only bruised his neck. He'll be good as new in a week."

"That's a relief." Kit discreetly opened her compact beneath the table and checked her lipstick.

"Kit, would you have dinner with me tonight?" Pete asked.

"I've told you everything I know. No point spending more money on food for me."

"Not for a story. Just for … pleasure." When he really smiled he had crow's feet at the corners of his eyes. He was older than she'd first thought. Maybe thirty-five. Closer to her mother's age than her own. Where her mother was old, though, Pete was mature.

"Okay," she said.

"How about Pelican Point?"

She frowned. "That's a long way to drive for dinner."

"I might get a story out of it. You know, colorful local joint, out of the way. Newspaper readers eat that kind of stuff up so they can pretend to be in the know about all the righteous places." He lifted his chin a fraction. "I hear some movie stars hang out there after visiting that spiritual place, Cassadaga. Say, now, that would be a story. You could have your fortune told, and I could do a story about that. I've got a camera in the car. Take a picture having your palm read or whatever they do. I feel bad that I led you on about the other story. This one I could do legitimately. You're a pretty girl, no telling who might see the story."

Kit thought about what Kenny would say if she ditched drill practice. He'd be furious, but there would never be a better chance than now. She'd discovered a dead body. If she acted a little strange, folks would expect nothing less. Kenny would get over being mad. "Okay. But I'd better not go in to work at all or I won't be able to get away."

"So we'll have the whole day?"

"Yeah." She pulled her coffee cup toward her and stared into the black depths. Her own distorted reflection stared back.

• • •

Pete was patient while she changed into her favorite short set and her white sandals. They had two-inch heels and made her legs look longer. She wasn't certain how she felt about having her photograph made for the newspaper with a fortune-teller. Her mother would have a conniption. The bitch was always so worried about what the neighbors would think, and consorting with fortune-tellers was considered by some of her mother's Catholic friends as having truck with Satan. Still, she got in the car with Pete and they headed northeast to the small village.

"What will you do when you get tired of being the top of the pyramid at Cypress Gardens?" Pete asked her.

"I don't know." The plastic seat cover on the car was making the backs of her legs sweat. She wished she'd thought to bring a towel.

"A girl like you, I figured you'd have a plan."

"A girl like me can't afford big plans." She kept her gaze out the window. "I guess maybe I'll marry and settle down. Maybe work in a dress shop or cosmetic counter. I'd be good at that."

"You would." He watched the road but glanced her way occasionally. "You want children?"

She shrugged. "Sometimes. Mostly not. I don't want to wake up and find I've turned into my mother."

"That bad, huh?"

"Let's just say Annie had a better time at the orphanage than I did growing up with her. She beat the hell out of me every chance she got, and when she wasn't whaling on me, she was drunk."

He didn't speak or look her way. She regretted telling him so much. The past was over and done. Now she'd let the stink of it catch up to her. "What about you?" she asked. "Smart guy like you must've had parents who were proud."

"Things were okay for me."

"Listen, maybe we could skip the fortune-telling thing. My mom will have a fit about it. Let's just have something to eat, okay?" She was worried she'd piss him off.

"If that's what you'd like. I didn't have the impression, though, that you saw much of your mom."

She laughed, and the harsh sound of it made him turn to her. "I haven't heard from her in eight months. But sure as I got in the newspaper, she'd find a reason to be upset about it."

"Well, today's your day." He drove for a while before he spoke again. "There's a ghost town in the Ocala State Park. Kerr City. Want to grab a picnic lunch somewhere and take a ride through the park?"

"That would be fun."

"There's bound to be a diner before long. We'll get something and get them to pack it up for us."

"Do you mind if I play the radio?" she asked.

"Don't know if there's a station we can pick up, but give it your best shot."

The staticky strains of a Hank Williams song filtered out of the radio and Kit sat back. She was too self-conscious to sing along, like she would have done if she'd been alone. But it was good, sharing the road with Pete Paladin. Maybe they wouldn't go back to Cypress Gardens. Maybe her life had taken a turn.

Pete stopped at a diner and got fried chicken and cathead biscuits for the picnic, then hit a liquor store and got a bottle of wine. When they drove into the state park, Kit felt as if the real world fell away. Pete turned down a sandy road that took them deep into the heart of the park. When they were off the main road, he stopped long enough to open the wine and pour them both paper cups full.

The sun filtered through the dense pines, and Kit felt a lethargy settle into her limbs. "Not a lot of traffic here. Maybe we should look for the picnic tables," she said. She wasn't nervous, just aware of the isolation. When she looked at Pete, her stomach tightened pleasantly. He hadn't made a single advance toward her, but why else would he be driving her to such a secluded place? She hadn't planned on screwing him, but once the idea took root in her imagination, she could think of little else.

"The town is right ahead," he said. When he went around the next curve, she saw the empty buildings.

"What happened here?"

"Folks settled here to grow citrus. Freeze hit about 1894 or '95. Killed the trees. Everyone left."

She looked at the empty buildings as they drove past. "It's sad, isn't it?"

"How so?"

"That people lived here. Planned on homesteading and having a life. Then they all just left." Maybe it was the wine that had brought on the melancholy. Or the emptiness of the buildings. The windows were sightless, and it made her feel that something had passed her by, too.

Pete drove through the town and kept going. They passed a sign directing a right hand turn to the campsites, but Pete turned left, down a narrower trail. Kit's stomach growled, and the wine was making her a little nauseous. The afternoon sun made the slow moving car an oven. On the highway, a breeze had cooled her.

At last they came to a lake. To her relief, Pete pulled over and stopped.

"This looks like the perfect place for a picnic," he said.

Cypress knees ringed the lake, and moss draped the branches of the trees. It was beautiful in a wild and dangerous way. "Think there are snakes?" she asked.

"Maybe. Could be gators, too."

"Thanks," she said as she got out, glad to stretch her legs and get free of the plastic seat cover. Her thighs were sweaty and hot. She walked to the edge of the lake. While the surface was perfectly still, the water wasn't crystal and blue like Lake Eloise. This was darker, untamed.

"Want to take a swim?" Pete asked.

"Not on your life." She wasn't a baby, but stepping out into the dark water held no appeal for her.

"I gotta pee," Pete said. "I'll be right back."

She watched him walk into the trees, his body disappearing in the gray haze of the trunks. She went to the car and got the food and wine from the back seat. The grass looked stubbly and harsh, so she returned to the trunk to look for a blanket. Pete was the kind of man who had such things covered. If he intended to seduce her, he would have thought to bring something to lay on.

The trunk wasn't locked, so she opened it. A plaid blanket was tucked into one corner, and she pulled it out. It was wool, an unpleasant scratch to its texture. As she started to close the trunk she saw the two cement blocks and the rope. Her hand faltered on the trunk lid, and the air left her lungs in a whoosh. She turned to run, but Pete was right behind her. She slammed into his chest, and his hand caught her hair.

"Easy there," he said, holding her hair so tightly she couldn't get away.

"Who are you?" she asked.

"It doesn't matter, Kit."

She made no effort to fight the tears. "Why?"

"Girls talk. My boss can't afford rumors."

"I don't know anything. I don't care about any of it."

He shook his head. "Can't risk it. The senator has a family he has to protect. Jess thought she could blackmail him."

Kit tried to think but fear paralyzed her brain. "I don't want anything. I don't know anything to tell anyone."

"You're a smart girl. You might have decided to poke around. I'm already in trouble since you found Jess's body. The senator was very disappointed in me."

A large splash made her jerk toward the water, but Pete's grip in her hair kept her from seeing.

"I won't make the same mistake twice," Pete said. "The gators won't leave anything of you to identify." As he spoke he hauled her toward the water. "If you hadn't gone poking around in the trunk, you could have had a nice picnic and I would've put something in your wine to knock you out. As it is, I've heard drowning is an easy way to go. My partner wanted to shoot you, but I told him that was too messy. This is much better for all of us."

"They'll hunt for me. They'll know I wouldn't just leave." Her words broke through the surface of her sobs.

"That's why you'll write a note. They'll find that in your apartment when they hunt for you. Like Jess. You'll say that finding the body was too much. That you've gone on to some place else. Maybe Nashville. You're an ambitious girl, Kit. Folks will believe it." He grabbed the rope and dragged her toward the lake. "Come on, little Minnow. It's time for your last swim."

JOHN BOND

John Bond is a shanachie—the Gaelic term for storyteller—living in Dania Beach, Florida. A licensed pilot and boat captain, he has been a lawyer, Realtor, adjunct professor of journalism and creative writing, tour group leader, SCUBA instructor, columnist, newspaper editor, political campaign manager, lobbyist, developer and more. John's day job is to love his wife, Jeannie Deininger, who is too good for him. Instead of children they have Shih-tzus.

JAMES O. BORN

James O. Born is the author of five police thrillers from Putnam. *Escape Clause*, was the winner of the inaugural Florida Book award for best novel in popular fiction. His first series featured state cop Bill Tasker. His second series features ATF agent Alex Duarte. In 2009 the first of several science fiction novels, *The Human Disguise*, was released under the pseudonym James O'Neal. In 2010 *The Double Human* was released. Born is a career law enforcement officer who has worked in all areas of investigation.

PATRICIA A. BREMMER

Patricia A. Bremmer is the author of eight titles in the Elusive Clue Series. Her series is being considered for movies with Red Feather Productions. A standalone book, *Guided Destiny*, has already been optioned for a major motion picture. Patricia has also penned the Westie Whispers Collection of picture books for children and is currently writing mysteries for middle grade. Patricia traveled the nation with a stable of thoroughbred racehorses including

Miami, Florida where she lived for a short time. She currently resides in western Nebraska. And, to add to the excitement of her appearances, she frequently includes her real life detective who has become the sleuth in her novels. Together they charm and entertain the crowds. She is a member of Sisters in Crime and the International Thriller Writers. www.patriciabremmer.com

TOM CORCORAN

Tom Corcoran moved to Florida in 1970. His six-novel Alex Rutledge Series is set in the Florida Keys. *Hawk Channel Chase*, released in March 2009, went to trade paperback in April 2010. *Jimmy Buffett - the Key West Years* is in its third printing—Tom's photographs appeared on seven Jimmy Buffett album covers. Over 160 of his photos were collected in 2007's *Key West in Black and White*, with an introduction by Randy Wayne White. Tom co-wrote the Buffett hits "Cuban Crime of Passion" and "Fins." In recent years he has returned to songwriting, collaborating on seven songs for John Frinzi's recent "Shoreline" CD. Tom's author portraits have appeared on book jackets for Thomas McGuane's *An Outside Chance*, Winston Groom's *Forrest Gump*, Les Standiford's *Black Mountain* and *Last Train to Paradise*, and James W. Hall's *Hot Damn*.

JOHN DUFRESNE

John Dufresne is the author of two story collections, four novels, most recently *Requiem, Mass.*, and two books on writing fiction. His stories have ben selected for *Best American Mystery Stories* in 2007 and 2010. He teaches writing in the MFA program at Florida International University in Miami.

MARY ANNA EVANS

Mary Anna Evans is the award-winning author of the Faye Longchamp archaeological mysteries. The sixth book in this series, *Strangers*, will be released in October 2010. Her novels have received recognitions including the Benjamin Franklin Award, the Florida Literature Award, and a Florida Book

Awards Bronze Medal. Her short fiction has been published in collections including *North Florida Noir*, *A Merry Band of Murderers*, *A Kudzu Christmas*, and *Plots with Guns*. A licensed engineer, her interests in math, science, and fiction have converged in a non-fiction book for teachers called *Mathematical Literacy in the Middle and Lower Grades*, to be published in June 2011. For more information on her work, visit her website, http://www.maryannaevans.com, and her blog, http://www.maryannaevans.blogspot.com, for those curious about book publishing called, "It's Like Making Sausage: Sometimes you really don't want to know how books are made..."

MARK RAYMOND FALK

Mark Raymond Falk attended the University of Texas—El Paso where he majored in English before the real world interrupted and he went to work on a cattle ranch. The cattle ranch, generations ago, was part owned by his grandfather. He currently lives in McCamey, TX with his wife Victoria and their German Shepherd, Bowie. In his free time he writes and thinks about Maximillian's Treasure, allegedly buried within seven miles of his house in Castle Gap. He is currently at work on his first novel. His fiction has appeared in *Plots with Guns*, *Powder Burn Flash*, and *Flash Fiction Offensive*.

CAROLINA GARCIA-AGUILERA

Cuban born Carolina Garcia-Aguilera is the author of eight books, but she is perhaps best known for her first six, which feature the Cuban-American private investigator, Lupe Solano. Carolina has written for assorted publications, and has contributed short stories to several anthologies, the most recent being *Miami Noir*, *Havana Noir* and *Hit List: The Best of Latino Mysteries*. Carolina, who has been a private investigator for the past twenty-one years, has been the recipient of many awards, including the Shamus for *Havana Heat* (Best Private Eye novel of 2000), and the Flamingo for *A Miracle in Paradise* (Best Florida Mystery of 1999). She has lived on South Beach for the past fifteen years with her three daughters and assorted pets.

CAROLYN HAINES

Carolyn Haines is the 2010 recipient of the Harper Lee Award for Distinguished Writing and the 2009 Richard Wright Award for Literary Excellent. She is the author of the Sarah Booth Delaney Mississippi Delta mystery series, the most current of which is *Bone Appetit*. She also edited a collection of short fiction, *Delta Blues*, which features some of the finest writers working today.

JAMES W. HALL

Winner of the Edgar Award and Shamus, Hall is the author of sixteen novels, a collection of stories, four books of poetry, a book of essays, and a forthcoming non-fiction work on the biggest bestsellers of the twentieth-century. He and his wife, Evelyn, divide their time between Miami and the mountains of North Carolina.

ALICE JACKSON

Alice Jackson is a veteran journalist who has reported on crime, politics and public corruption for newspapers, television and magazines, including *Time*, *People* and the *New York Times*. During the 1990s, her investigative reporting of questionable land deals and government bond issues led to the indictment and prosecution of a prominent Mississippi politician and resulted in the return of millions of dollars from off-shore bank accounts to taxpayer coffers. Her first published fiction, "Cuttin' Heads," appeared in the short story collection *Delta Blues* from Tyrus Books in 2010. She resided on the shores of the Mississippi Sound until Hurricane Katrina destroyed her home in 2005. She now lives in Mobile, Ala., where she is studying for a master's degree in creative writing from the University of South Alabama.

ALEX KAVA

Alex Kava is the *New York Times* bestselling author of the critically acclaimed Maggie O'Dell series. Her stand-alone novel, *One False Move*, was chosen for the 2006 One Book One Nebraska and her political thriller, *Whitewash*, made

January Magazine's best thriller of the year list for 2007. Published in twenty-four countries, Kava's novels have made the bestseller lists in the UK, Australia, Germany, Italy and Poland. She is also one of the featured authors in the anthology *Thriller: Stories to Keep You Up All Night*, edited by James Patterson and the upcoming anthology, *First Thrills*, edited by Lee Child. In 2007 she was the recipient of the Mari Sandoz Award presented by the Nebraska Library Association. Kava divides her time between Omaha, Nebraska and Pensacola, Florida. She is a member of the Mystery Writers of America and the International Thriller Writers. Find out how Maggie O'Dell survives Hurricane Isaac while tracking another killer by reading *Damaged* (Doubleday, July 2010). www.alexkava.com

JONATHON KING

Edgar-award winning author Jonathon King is the creator of the Max Freeman crime series set in the Everglades and on the hard urban streets of South Florida. His newest book, *The Styx*, is a Florida Book Award-winning novel that probes the deadly fire that drove the working class off Palm Beach Island at the turn of the 20th Century. King was a journalist for 24 years and lives in Boca Raton.

MICHAEL KORYTA

Michael Koryta is the author of five novels, including *Envy the Night,* which won the 2008 *Los Angeles Times* Book Prize for best mystery/thriller, and four entries in the Lincoln Perry series, which has earned nominations for the Edgar, Shamus, and Quill awards and won the Great Lakes Book Award. His work has been translated into more than fifteen languages. Michael's first novel, *Tonight I Said Goodbye,* an Edgar finalist, was published when he was just 21 and an undergraduate at Indiana University. A former private investigator and award-winning newspaper reporter, Michael now divides his time between Bloomington, Indiana, where he teaches at the Indiana University School of Journalism, and St. Petersburg, Florida

MICHAEL LISTER

Michael Lister is an award-winning novelist, essayist, screenwriter, and playwright who lives in North Florida. A former prison chaplain, Michael is the author of the "Blood" series featuring prison chaplain/detective John Jordan (*Blood of the Lamb, The Body and the Blood,* etc.). His second series features Jimmy "Soldier" Riley, a PI in Panama City during World War II (www.FloridaNoir.com). Michael's recent literary thrillers include *Double Exposure, Thunder Beach, Burnt Offerings,* and *Separation Anxiety.* In addition to fiction, Michael writes a weekly column on art and meaning titled Of Font and Film (www.OfFontandFilm.com), which includes reviews of film and fiction. When Michael isn't writing, he teaches college and operates a charity an community theater. His website is www.MichaelLister.com

JOHN LUTZ

John Lutz's work includes political suspense, private eye novels, thrillers, regional suspense, urban suspense, humor, occult, crime caper, police procedural, espionage, historical, futuristic, amateur detective … virtually every mystery sub-genre. He is the author of more than forty novels and 250 short stories and articles. His awards include the Edgar and the Shamus and the Short Mystery Fiction Society's Golden Derringer Award. His novels and short fiction have been translated into almost every language and adapted for almost every medium. He is a past president of both Mystery Writers of America and Private Eye Writers of America. His latest book is the suspense novel *Urge to Kill.* His novel *SWF Seeks Same* was made into the hit movie *Single White Female,* starring Bridget Fonda and Jennifer Jason Leigh, and his novel *The Ex* was made into the HBO original movie of the same title, for which he co-authored the screenplay.

RAVEN McMILLIAN

Raven McMillian was born and bred from the neglected nether regions of southside Virginia, where he learned the old stubborn and reckless ways of shooting yourself in the foot, surviving, and spinning a long tale out of the whole process. After various meanders around the United States, he has ended up in that same nether region, raising a family and assorted animals, as well as taking in wayward teenagers to teach them to balance their inherent self-destruction with creative expression. He has been involved in various forms of self-publishing for over twenty years, but nowadays mostly Dremels haiku into back roads guard rails.

JIM PASCOE

Jim Pascoe believes that noir is larger than a historical period or a genre; it's an ethic. His crime fiction street cred comes from running the cult publishing house UglyTown for almost a decade. Recently he finished his dark fantasy series UNDERTOWN, the first volume of which was serialized in newspapers worldwide. And as a multiple-award-winning creative director he has worked on the packaging/advertising for such blockbusters as *Mad Men*, *Coraline*, and *Avatar*.

LISA UNGER

Lisa Unger is an award-winning *New York Times*, *USA Today* and international bestselling author. Her novels have been published in over 26 countries around the world. She was born in New Haven, Connecticut in 1970 but grew up in the Netherlands, England and New Jersey. A graduate of the New School for Social Research, Lisa spent many years living and working in New York City. She then left a career in publicity to pursue her dream of becoming a full-time author. She now lives in Florida with her husband and daughter. Her writing has been hailed as "masterful" (*St. Petersburg Times*), "sensational" (*Publishers Weekly*) and "sophisticated" (*New York Daily News*) with "gripping narrative and evocative, muscular prose" (*Associated Press*).

Photo by Jordan Marking

MICHAEL LISTER is an award-winning novelist, essayist, screenwriter, and playwright who lives in North Florida. A former prison chaplain, Michael is the author of the "Blood" series featuring prison chaplain/detective John Jordan (*Blood of the Lamb*, *The Body and the Blood*, etc.). His second series features Jimmy "Soldier" Riley, a PI in Panama City during World War II (www.FloridaNoir.com). Michael's recent literary thrillers include *Double Exposure*, *Thunder Beach*, *Burnt Offerings*, and *Separation Anxiety*. In addition to fiction, Michael writes a weekly column on art and meaning titled Of Font and Film (www.OfFontandFilm.com), which includes reviews of film and fiction. When Michael isn't writing, he teaches college and operates a charity an community theater. His website is www.MichaelLister.com